'Looking for love while co
unlikely heroine feminist:
Delightful, relevant, and fu
delivers the feminist angst of
with dark humour.'

Amanda Coreishy, author of *Reputation*, Editor of *Trouble at Taboo Junction*

'A mind-blowing page-turner novel. It's sleek, flirty, fun and terrifying. I read it in one sitting!'

Ozge Gozturk, author of *Lupu*, shortlisted for David Oluwale Prize

'Oh wow! Even if you don't approve of Lily's methods...well, we all have *that* ex. Plenty of twists and turns along the way, and a clever cliffhanger to boot.'

Yvonne Vincent, best selling author of *Frock in Hell*

ALSO BY O.M FAURE

THE LILY BLACKWELL SERIES

Before the Fall

Forty Dates and Forty Nights

Before The Fall, the date-packed prequel is yours for FREE. Simply visit www.omfaure.com to claim your FREE NOVELLA today!

THE CASSANDRA PROGRAMME SERIES

The Disappearance

Chosen

Torn

United

FORTY DATES AND FORTY NIGHTS

A SADLY TRUE AND TRULY SAD MODERN DESERT CROSSING.

O.M. FAURE

Copyright © O.M. Faure, 2023
All rights reserved.

The right of O.M. Faure to be identified as the author of this work has been asserted by her in accordance with the Copyright, Designs and Patents Act 1988.

ISBN: 978-1-9164370-8-1

Published by Forward Motion Publishing, Ltd.

Cover design by Rejenne Pavon | cover images © AdobeStock

This is a work of fiction. Names, characters, places and incidents are either the product of the author's imagination or are used fictitiously and any resemblance to actual persons, living or dead, or to actual events or locales is entirely coincidental.

I wrote this book between October 2019 and March 2020. All the incidents in the novel precede the tragic events that shook the city of London in 2021.

It is very sad to me that reality comes sometimes so close to fiction and that in this day and age, we still have to fight for women's rights and live through such traumatic events in our own lives and in the news cycle. I have tried my best to channel my anger into art and I hope this fantasy on the page will provide some catharsis to others as well.

Trigger warning: this book contains references to sex, murder, drug use and sexual violence. Please use self-care when reading it. If you need support, this is a good place to start: https://rapecrisis.org.uk

For Bénédicte, Delphine, Dorothée and Juliette. Thirty years passed in the blink of an eye. Here's to the next thirty and more.

It's hard not to be a fighter when you're constantly under siege.

Cassandra Duffy

FORTY DATES AND FORTY NIGHTS

1

AND THEY LIVED HAPPILY EVER AFTER. THE END

I clutch the wet stems. Sweat tingles along my palms as the bouquet rustles, exhaling a fragrant sigh.

'Do you Jonathan Richard Stone, take this woman to be your lawfully wedded wife?'

How many times did I practise signing his name, secretly binding him to me with the whorling scrawls, as I whispered:

Lily Stone

Lily Stone

Lily Stone

Like an incantation and a wish held together with a prayer.

Maybe a hole will punch through my ribcage and my heart will flop out, gasping and thrashing like a fish at the priest's feet.

Jonathan's eyes crinkle with love and I remember dreaming about this moment and planning it with him, while we lay in bed, our naked legs jumbled together, our fingers entwined, reaching playfully towards the ceiling as the Sunday morning light poured in through billowing curtains.

Everything looks perfect today, just like we planned.

'To have and to hold, from this day forward, for better or worse for richer, for poorer, in sickness and in health, to love and cherish until death do you part?'

Jonathan's gorgeous lips stretch into a smile and I long to kiss him.

'I do,' Jonathan's smile widens.

I roll the bouquet in my hands and flinch as a pin pricks my finger. Blood wells like a red tear on my finger.

Everyone's eyes are on us, the weight of their stares like a beam of light on a lonely stage. I suck on the blood and close my eyes to keep the tears captive, behind my eyelids. Not now, Lily, not now.

'And do you, Vivian Margaret Appleby, take Jonathan—'

'I do,' she says. Too early. Too keen.

'— to be your lawfully wedded husband?'

The priest makes a joke I cannot hear.

Our friends and family laugh.

Jonathan's eyes dart past Vivian and meet with mine.

I raise my chin and smile.

His eyes flicker to Vivian again, as he takes her hand. They exchange the rings, they kiss. Vivian's long pale neck bends gracefully as his hand grazes the lacquered smoothness of her blond bun.

'—husband and wife.'

Everyone cheers.

As I hand the bouquet back to her, my fingers strangely reluctant to let go, I'm the only one to notice a red stain marring the white ribbon.

They rush out and emerge, radiant, into the summer morning. Everyone is already there, waiting to shower them with rose petals and confetti. Laughter rings in the bright morning sunlight.

Hanging behind, in the church's darkness, I gather the order of service booklets, weaving through the pews, as the hem of my long purple dress trails behind me.

'Lily! Where are you?' Mum's hat is askew. She's doing a good impression of the Queen in a head-to-toe bubble gum pink suit. Minus the gravitas.

'Stop moping, your sister will think you're not happy for her, duckling.'

'Half-sister,' I mutter, throwing an armful of booklets in the rubbish with a small twinge of satisfaction.

She stares at me, puffing from the exertion of running back in, full of effervescence and social glee. Her hand reaches for my brown curls out of habit and tries to fix them, in vain. She gives up with an exasperated sigh.

'Coming.' I press on the bleeding cut, relishing the jolt of reality and pain.

Outside the sun blinds me as Mum's hand pushes me forward. *Don't even think of slinking back into the shadows*, it says. *What will people think if they suspect you were his before she was?* it says. *Why can't you be a source of pride, like your sister?* it says. A strained smile is painted on her face, as she manoeuvres me into the family photo. The unwanted daughter. The spinster. The one with the dark exotic origins.

'There's my beautiful daughter!' Mum trills... embracing Vivian.

Jonathan's hand brushes against my naked arm and goose bumps erupt as I feel his gaze burning the side of my face, seeking a connection, but I walk past him and hug Vivian instead.

'You look perfect,' I whisper, bending to arrange the folds of her dress.

Her arm loops possessively around Jonathan's arm, 'Thank you.'

What for? I wonder, as something jagged and painful lodges itself in my throat. I don't trust myself to speak. We all turn to face the photographer, smiles frozen.

'Say cheese!' my mother screeches.

'Cheese!' everybody responds.

I lift up my head and face forward as the shot is taken.

2

BEST-LAID PLANS

Of course Bridget gets Mark Darcy. Of course she does. What about the other one? The competent, non-ridiculous one? The one who's succeeded professionally and can string a sentence together. What does she get?

Sitting cross-legged on my sofa in flannel pyjamas, eating chocolate, I sympathise with the other girl and cry. Why not watch *The Sound of Music* and root for the Baroness while I'm at it? God, I'm so cliché I could scream.

I turn off the TV and darkness descends on my flat like a shroud. Sunday stretches before me, empty and final. Jonathan is gone.

I'm going to die alone.

Worse than that.

I'm going to live alone.

I grab my phone and browse through my contacts, pondering whom to call. No one springs to mind. They all have families, children. None of them have time for my puerile drama. They've all grown up and long left behind the heart breaks, the hook-ups and the agony over whether their crush likes them or not, I'm the only one who's permanently stuck in a teenage time loop of romantic entanglements, first kisses and dashed hopes. Most have been married for ten, fifteen, twenty years. They're tired of hearing about my failures.

There's a plant dying in a corner of my flat. I should get up and water it. It's the plant I decided would signal my readiness for a pet. If I could keep it alive, I vowed, then I would get a cat. Then an upgrade to children perhaps. But that's no longer on the cards. Not that I was ever sure I wanted any.

I get up and walk to the kitchen past the drooping ficus, its head hanging sorrowfully above a carpet of yellow leaves. *Die, why don't you? See if I care.*

On the cupboard shelves, precarious piles of translucent porcelain wink at me, hopeful trinkets of a hostess life I never managed to live, for lack of friends and dearth of opportunities. The bone china parades in a hopeful march; dots of gold adorn night-blue flowery sugar bowls, curlicues of pink unfurl elegantly around cups' elbows. The crystal glasses tinkle inquiringly, asking 'today? Do we get to come out today?'

A fleeting glimpse of what my life was supposed to be flutters in front of me. The kitchen fills with life and laughter; Jonathan smiles over his shoulder as he gets a champagne bottle from the fridge. I lift his arm, place it around my shoulder and snuggle close as I breathe in the light and warmth of him. Our friends call behind us, hooting 'Come on you lovebirds! We're waiting for you.' I smile and send him out to refill their glasses, as I get a cake out of the oven, its heat spilling out, golden and sweet while I arrange the delicate cups and saucers on a tray.

The vision dissolves and a sepulchral silence descends

on my kitchen. Outside, the drab foggy day broods and humidity sneaks in through an unseen open window. I should do something about that. Instead I just grab more biscuits, and flee the scene of my dead dreams.

I don't even live in the right sort of place. I wanted a house with a small but well tended garden, a messy fridge with children's drawings held together by ludicrous souvenir magnets. I wanted to have neighbours who stop by, I wanted to live in Kensington or maybe at a push Fulham. Instead I'm on the wrong side of the ~~tracks~~ river, in a soulless steel and glass tower, in Nine Elms.

Everything here is under construction. I look out of my floor-to-ceiling window at the river and, as often, feel that instead of having a view on the outside world, I live in a shop window where the entire world stares at me and there is nowhere to hide. Nibbling on a biscuit, I lean my forehead against the cold glass and stare out at the grey river as the soggy day's dull light bounces off the scaffolding.

When will the building works ever end? I bought off plan, with the ridiculous amounts of money I make in my high-flying job at the bank. It seemed like a sound investment at the time and really what else did I have in my life, to spend the money on? Might as well spend it on that.

I'm one of only a handful of new residents in a building thirty storeys high. The corridors' rough cement floors are lined with plastic tarpaulins, the walls in the common areas are still bare plaster, light bulbs dangle out of the ceiling like eyes out of sockets. The whole place smells of damp and chemicals. I should have waited before I moved in. But surely, soon, it will be finished. Surely. Soon.

Vivian and Jonathan moved out to Surrey practically as soon as he proposed to her. Their life is a picture perfect *Country Life* string of shopping at garden centres in muddy

Barbour jackets, hunts for silverware at antique shops and sips of Chardonnay at tastefully updated country pubs. I wonder what they're doing this morning. Probably fucking like rabbits. I wonder if he takes her like he used to take me, I wonder what sound she makes when he...

I shake my head. *No Lily, no. You have your own life to live. That's over.* If ever there was closure, surely this has to be it. He's married now. To your bloody sister.

Life could still be good, if only I could find The One. I had a plan. It should have worked: meet man of my dreams by age twenty-six, fall madly in love, date two years, get married, adopt dog, buy terraced Victorian, convert loft and add kitchen extension, pop out two kids by age thirty, live happily ever after.

Crying my eyes out and eating Jammy Dodgers to soothe my broken heart was not what I was expecting to still be doing at age thirty-nine. But here I am. Single. Still looking for a man to spend my life with.

I stare at the biscuit's gooey, bloody heart, leaking red filling and think *Huh, appropriate*, as the tears flow and the Thames passes by, indifferent.

But amid the haze of snot, ugly crying and sugar overload, an idea surfaces.

I've had my fill of silence and regret.

I'll be forty soon. Only half of my life left to live.

I need a plan B.

Yes, that's it. It's just like any problem at work, if I deal with it rationally, I can find a solution. It's just a probabilities game, isn't it?

Yes, that sounds right. I... I'll go on forty dates before age forty.

That should do the trick: a dating battle campaign.

I *will* find The One before the big four-O.

So help me God.

Oh wow, OTT much Lily? I might as well be channelling *Gone with the Wind* here as I raise my fist to the heavens yelling "as God is my witness, I will never know loneliness again!"

Actually yes. That's perfect.

3

THE GOOD PARTY: PLANE CRASH

Emma is dishevelled. Her hair is hanging like cobwebs from her bun. She's speed walking on weirdly shaped soles that are supposed to add muscle to parts of our anatomy best left to their own devices, IMHO. I'm doing my best to catch-up with her bent form, as she folds herself at the waist in an effort to walk faster, pushing the pram forward. Her backpack dangles from one arm as she drags her reluctant five year old while opening a crisp bag with her teeth.

Ladies and gentlemen, behold the eight-armed goddess: the modern urban mother.

'It's time Lily. You have to get over him. It's been how long since your last... erm... meaningful relationship?'

'Two years.' I pant, trying to catch up.

'So, not since Jonathan,' she winces, clearly regretting saying the name out loud.

We were together for three years, he was at all the Christmases, the birthdays, we lived together, everybody thought... I thought... and then Vivian happened. She's ten years younger. She's blonde and slim. She's easier, more compliant, prettier.

'You were so well suited for each other, you should have held on tighter, you'll never find a better one now. It's a pity that… you'd have made a… Oh well, it is what it is,' Emma sighs.

I don't know how much tighter I could have held on. My knuckles were white from all the clinging. My cheeks were hurting from all the cheerful smiling. I didn't let go. I compromised, I dieted, I kept my roots dyed and my wardrobe up to date. I let him win arguments, I praised his achievements and let mine go unnoticed. I did the cooking and cleaning and I planned the holidays, I counted myself lucky that he wasn't the type to go to the pub, that he wasn't a womaniser, that he was so handsome. I bought his underwear and I didn't nag when he chose weekend activities that didn't involve me. Turns out the so-called activities involved my sister and hotels in Brighton but that's besides the point. The point is: I don't know what more I could have done.

Why does everybody always imply that it's my fault he left? So what if it took me two years to remember who I was before him?

'I did hold on.'

'Oh I'm sorry, you know I don't mean it like that,' Emma says.

I let it pass as she recovers.

'Anyway, I've just decided to start dating again,' I laugh uncomfortably, thinking how this will sound to her. Childish, ridiculous.

'Ooooh that's fantastic. Finally!' she gushes, 'so what can I do to help?'

'Do you know any single men?'

'Well, yes, there's one I've been meaning to introduce

you to but you know how it is with Charles and the children... and then... well you know what it's like.'

'No, not really.' I'm always available. I'm always the one who reaches out to her but I don't mind. These little snippets of friendship after Mass every week, are just enough to keep the relationship alive, so I drink them in, as I try to keep up with her speed walking and count my blessings that she didn't eject me from her life the minute her eldest was born.

She scrolls through her phone, pushing the pram with her elbow as we speed walk through Sloane Square. My hands itch to fasten the strands of her unintentional mullet back in her bun. I tell my hands to be quiet.

'That's my friend, the one I told you about. He's in his mid-fifties. I've always thought you should be with someone much older than you.'

She shoves the packet of rice crisps in her kid's hands and shows me a picture of a balding man who looks like a beehive landed on his head and then proceeded to sting every inch of his face. He's wearing an Arsenal scarf against a football stadium background.

'Mmh. He might be a bit too old.'

'Well. He's really very kind,' she enthuses, out of breath.

'I'm sure he is.' Hope leaks out of me like sand from an hourglass.

'Oh but wait! I know who will be exactly right.' Her eyes brighten and she starts to flick through her phone feverishly. 'He's really smart and handsome.'

'Really?' I brighten up. 'What does he do?' I catch her gaping backpack and carry it for her.

'He's. Literally. A. Brain. Surgeon.' A sheer veil of perspiration blossoms on her plump cheeks as she spits out pieces of aluminium packaging.

'A doctor?' That's encouraging. 'And he's really single? How come?'

'No reason.' Her eyes perform an evasive manoeuvre to the left, as muffled alarm bells ring in remote corridors of my mind.

We reach her glittering suburban tank and I collapse the pram and stuff it in the boot while she straps her toddler son in and continues with her sales pitch, peering at me through the tangle of child seat contraptions, cadavers of past snacks and assorted child paraphernalia. Her daughter is humming to herself, her mouth stained with ~~dried blood~~ beetroot rice cakes crumbs as she grimaces at the ceiling, oblivious to her mother's devotion.

When we're both in the car, Emma scrolls again and with a small triumphal grunt, shows me the photo. She needn't have bothered. She had me at brain surgeon. But he's nice looking, blond curls, easy smile, broad shoulders, posing on a sailing boat of some sort. *Wow, this could be Him* I think with a tiny palpitation as hope lights up the world around me. I haven't even fantasised about anyone for years. It's odd to have someone to cut and paste into my dreams again. A face, a smile to superimpose on the happy picnic scene, the first time at the opera scene, the mini-break in Cornwall scene.

'Go on then, give him my number,' I laugh, hating that I sound so keen.

We are now approaching No-Man-By-Age-Forty, please fasten your seatbelts and put your seat in the upright position for crash landing. Your lady parts will stop working as soon as the social pressure sign starts blinking. Place your oxygen mask over your face and breathe in deeply. Brace, brace!

I'd give anything to have Emma's life. She's always

glowing with happiness, surrounded by people she loves. Her house is the perfect Edwardian in a fantastic catchment area complete with a conservatory, a kitchen with an island and a fireplace with original features. The two-up two-down is full of boisterous life, children's toys, laughter and love. Her husband never comes to our drinks, so I know him from afar with the false familiarity of twenty years of hello-long-time-no-see-how-is-work-we-should-do-this-more-often.
But I know all I need to know about him through Emma's gushing: he's tall, handsome, successful, a good father and a devoted husband.

I should be so lucky.

~

DATE 1

AND HERE WE ARE: the dreaded Blind Date.

I push through the throngs of people who have descended on Charing Cross; irritable office workers hurrying to catch their trains, tourists searching for a pre-show sandwich, homeless people and their dogs watching the human flood pass by. Friday night rush hour is pounding the beer-slick pavement as I swim against the current, towards the forlorn beer garden and the man who doesn't get up to greet me.

'Hi, you must be Hugh.'

'Yes. You're Lily. You don't look like your photos.' He sneaks a glance at my arse.

I sit down as quickly as I can. I should try to make a positive impression before he realises how truly humongous my bum is. Pushing myself through the plastic arms, I sit gingerly on the wet grimy chair. My forearms stick to the gluey table, so I roll down my sleeves and try smiling.

All around us, colleagues are unwinding, friends are welcoming the weekend, inebriated couples are groping each other, while our conversation blunders on and we try to ignore the fact that this isn't a fortuitous meeting, that we have no particular interest in each other (yet?), that we'd probably never be friends. It feels rigged. The lovely, delicate spontaneity of a chance encounter is absent, replaced by graceless, prosaic checklist ticking. Because, at the end of the day, we're really on a cringey job interview to determine whether we want to swap bodily fluids.

Oooooooh right, we could have sex! Perhaps even tonight. My stomach ignites with fireflies as I detail his straight jawline, his thick curly blond hair and his nice blue eyes. Yes, he's not bad looking at all. This is very promising indeed. *Smile Lily, smile.*

'Nice bag. Did you wear it to impress me?' he says, as he comes back with my diet Coke and another beer for him.

'No, no.' I smile brightly, 'I wear it every day.'

I glance at the black Prada Galleria and bite the inside of my cheek. I should probably have downplayed exactly how financially well off I am. *Damn it Lily, you knew this.* All the dating self-help books said clearly that you should appear less successful and confident than you actually are.

'I don't get why women spend so much on bags.' He takes a swig from his pint, 'do you know how much a bag like that costs?' he shakes his head in disbelief, wiping his frothy lip on his sleeve. 'You could have bought a computer for that amount.'

Well yes, I do know how much a bag like that costs, seeing as I bought this one with my first bonus, after years of lusting and saving up for it.

I catch myself before the snark spills out. I shouldn't be too hard on him. He couldn't possibly know that. Men don't understand handbags and that's ok. Mars and Venus and all that. Jonathan never got it either and yet we loved each other madly. Well I did... *Don't think about Jonathan now, Lily, FFS.*

Hugh continues, not really expecting an answer, 'and what is the point of all women buying the exact same bag? I mean, where is the originality?'

I nod and press my lips together. Brain surgeon. Normal looking. Good party. Keep calm and carry on.

'So you're a doctor?' I ask, casting around for topics he'll feel comfortable talking about. I need this to go well. Men like women they can talk to, don't they? *Just let him speak, nod and look impressed. And breathe.*

He doesn't disappoint. He launches into a play-by-play description of his day at the hospital, complete with graphic, gory details, God-complex and petty rivalries. I listen to the whole ~~half-hour of pontificating ego-fest~~ fascinating account, careful to look rapturous.

'Oh wow, that's so impressive.'

'I know.'

He's somehow forgotten to ask me any question whatsoever. I haven't said much beyond 'I see,' 'Interesting,' and 'Wow' for the last hour. But that's ok, I mean my job at the bank is pretty boring compared to saving people's lives on a daily basis.

We move on from the beer garden to a nearby greasy spoon.

Emma told me that she sent him a lot of contenders before tonight and they never make it past the evaluation drink. So, it looks like I've passed some kind of test. Woohoo! This is going well.

We sit in a dark booth on the pub's first floor.

'So, why are you still single?'

God how I hate that question. It's inevitably asked by older aunts who mean well or by men who aren't too sure about asking you out on a second date. When men ask, what they mean is 'What's wrong with you, really? If you were normal you'd have found a bloke by now, *so why are you still single*?' They just cut out the first part of the question.

Being incorrigibly eager to please, I usually proceed to trip over my own feet, as I rush to find a flaw in myself that would explain why no man has picked me up yet even though I'm in the final discount aisle.

Usually, I say the first thing that comes to mind and immediately regret it: *I guess I'm too keen to get married so I send men running for the hills, ha ha ha.* But no, tonight I stick to the self-help books' advice: 'I just haven't found the right person yet.' Add smile. Let it sit there.

The slender twenty-year old waitress comes to take our order, looking harried and tired but still somehow fresher than me.

'Ah, I love a woman who knows that her place is in the kitchen,' he jokes, grabbing her wrist and complimenting her on her figure. She lets out a forced laugh and glances at me, blushing. Abruptly, we've become a triangle and she's the one with all the power. Her long glossy hair swishes from side to side as she giggles. At length, he stops caressing her palm and lets her go. She scuttles out of there, fast.

Come on Lily, stay positive. There's nothing here that can't be fixed. He's a good man who's dedicated his life to saving people's lives, so what if he's a bit...

'You ordered the wrong thing.'

'I'm sorry?'

'Keto.' He stuffs a chip in his face.

'Erm... I haven't tried keto but I've done everything else, the cabbage soup diet, Slimfast, protein powders, intermittent fasting, Atkins, Herbalife...' I look down embarrassed, hating myself. For being who I am. For looking the way I do. For my ingratiating apologies.

'Well, you're clearly not doing it right if you're incapable of sticking to the diet.'

'I... well no, it's just... I do reach my target weight,' I chuckle with embarrassment, 'but the pounds always comes back.'

He holds his middle finger up 'Nowadays, fat is a sign of either of two things: 'poverty or' his index finger rises too (not much better) 'lack of self-control. Given your expensive bag here, you must be weak-willed.'

My mouth opens and closes again. The waitress comes back, with her tiny bum, her long thin legs and her delicate neck. I feel like a mastodon next to her. Oblivious, she serves him the pint and his gaze lingers on her retreating silhouette as she flits away, light-footed and lovely.

'So like I was saying, you must do Keto. Eat only proteins and fats. No carbs, no fruit, none of this salad nonsense' he points at my plate, 'it isn't going to achieve the three-stone weight-loss you need.'

I know I need to lose a stone or so. I'm not fat exactly, just unfortunately padded around the hips. But he's a doctor so he must be right. Something hard and lumpy has lodged itself in my throat. I'm a tub of lard. Why did I think this was even a possibility? He looks perfectly normal and thin.

'You see, in ketosis, your body converts your fat into energy and your liver produces ketones which improves your brain function. So you become thinner and smarter...' he continues in that vein for a while, as I squirm in my seat, feeling ashamed. People as fat as me shouldn't eat in public.

For some reason, he still hasn't removed his red plastic jacket and pungent smells waft from its folds every time he moves. While he scoffs his chips, I notice that the lapels are grubby with dirt, the Velcro riddled with undetermined fluff.

Grimy, overlong finger nails.
Barbecue wings sucked into his mouth.
Moist drooly lips.
Barbecue sauce smear on his left cheek.
Oily sticky fingers.

I watch, mesmerised as his right hand climbs up, unable to avert my eyes from this slow motion plane crash. His spittle flies sluggishly and lands on my cheek while his words wash over me, meaningless, muffled and distorted and still, his right hand lifts up inexorably, covered in barbecue sauce. My forkful of salad suspended midway to my mouth, I gasp as his fingers rake into his blond curls.

Then he sucks his fingers one by one and pulls a hair out of his mouth, still prattling on about everything that's wrong with me.

My eyes flop into my salad.

For some reason, my fingers test my knife's sharpness. The blade's point pleasantly pushes into the ball of my finger. Jarred by the jolt of pain, I let go and smile vacuously at him as he drones on.

BEER ON HIS BREATH, beer foam on his lip, beer sloshing from his pint onto his trousers. The music blares and he yammers on. He talks about a plane crash that's all over the news. I think, *how apt*. He moves on to all the plane crashes that have happened lately, body count and possible reasons for the accidents. I think, *why are we talking about death*?

More flirting with the wide-eyed waitress.

She looks at me. I shrug.

More beer for him.

Wiping greasy hands on trousers.

More drunk boasting and a wobbly exit from the pub.

Bear hug.

A burp in my face. I feel it move the curls against my forehead in a lukewarm shockwave.

As I escape into a black cab, I glance back and see him puke his guts out, his forearm against the yellow brick wall. It splatters on the pavement as passers-by give him the wide berth Londoners usually reserve for homeless people.

Oh dear.

As far as dates go, I'd say that wasn't very good. Or maybe I'm just too negative. And too picky.

It's started raining. London's drab streets blur together through the cab window, drenched in misery against the shadowy backdrop. An old woman walks a small dog. A couple embraces happily and kiss. A group of drunk girls stumbles out of a bar. Raindrops splatter against my window.

40% of people meet their other half through their friends but I've been trying that for years and look where it got me.

It's time for a change.

Online dating's the new way to meet people, I hear all the cool kids are doing it. Maybe I should give it a try?

4

THE UNBEARABLE WEIGHTINESS OF BEING

Wilkommen, bienvenue, welcome!
Welcome to Ze circus of Tinder, Match.com, OKCupid, eHarmony, Uniformdating.com, Elite singles, Mysinglefriend.com et al.

Let's start with a few standard questions.

<u>Height</u>: 172

Oh dear, I'm taller than fifty percent of the blokes in here; this isn't going to be a walk in the park, is it?

<u>Weight</u>: Argh. Nymph-like Catherine who's bordering on anorexic at the best of times can hardly believe it. Yes, you're supposed to proclaim your weight to the whole wide world.

As in, 'Step on this table, yes right this way, love. Careful with the china and the glasses, thaaaaat's it. Can everybody hear her? Can everybody see her? Good! Go ahead, darling shout out your weight so that every single man in this pub can hear it.'

Right, just what I thought. You wouldn't particularly like that either, huh? I guess the dating site designers must be men.

Anyhoo, we've already covered the fact that I'm padded around the hips (translation: fat-arsed) and pretty standard everywhere else. I click on "Curvy". Apparently it's more self-confident than selecting "A few kilos too many". But men know how to translate that into "fat" no matter which one you choose.

It's like estate ads, you just get it after a while; "Charming" means a flat so tiny that a sofa won't fit in. "Curvy" is code for "I'm fat, get over it, you're no Apollo yourself, you know".

'You could always leave it blank. Your weight, I mean,' says well-intentioned Catherine who's been single for even longer than me. She's wearing all black and she's perched on the sofa's edge like a crow about to take flight.

'Nah' I shake my head distractedly swiping through profiles. 'Apparently if you don't fill it in, men will just assume you're morbidly obese.' So hey ho, in goes my weight.

Seeing me flounder at the first obstacle, Scarlett takes matters into her own hands while I disappear into the kitchen to fight with the corkscrew and a bottle of red. Well into her thirties, Scarlett has been prowling these sites for over a decade. She's a dating warrior and she's not taking any prisoners.

<u>Style</u>: Classic, professional.

<u>Age</u>: end of shelf life coming soon.

Arms laden with supplies, I head back into my living room to find Scarlett cross-legged and hunched over the screen, her face the picture of concentration. Her extensions are pulled together into a high ponytail, emphasising her wrinkle-free botoxed forehead.

<u>Pets</u>: None.

<u>Kids</u>: None and doesn't want any.

'Lily doesn't want kids?' Catherine whispers, 'are you sure Scarlet? Maybe we should ask her—'

'Irrelevant.' Scarlet interrupts her, 'men our age don't want any, she stands a better chance that way. She can negotiate that later.'

'Isn't it too late anyway?' Catherine says, fiddling with the gold cross around her neck.

'Hey, I'm right here!'

Scarlett snorts and waves Catherine's comment away, 'nowadays? Nonsense. Janet Jackson had one at fifty. If Lily meets a rich bloke, it's a fantastic way to lock him in or at the very least get some alimony out of it and never work again.'

Catherine looks scandalised 'But Scarlett, how can you...'

'Just put down *Doesn't want children*' I say, rolling my eyes.

Scarlett and I have been inseparable since childhood. We lived on the same terrace, growing up, so we went to nursery together, then school, then Uni. We've shared everything since the beginning: from first ice-creams to first kisses, from first boy-band crush to first pay check, from first heartbreak to first night-club outing. She's sharp and hard but she's also fiercely loyal and protective.

She also loves to rile up our resident novice/aspiring nun/super religious/celibate friend but clearly Catherine didn't mean to hurt my feelings.

'Don't pay Scarlett any mind sweetie, I haven't got a maternal bone in my body anyway,' I sit on the carpet and pop open my Diet Coke.

'Yeah let's focus on getting another kind of bone into your body,' Scarlett chortles as she grabs some crisps and then continues tapping away on my computer.

'Really Scarlett.' Catherine shakes her head.

<u>Smoking</u>: Never smoked.
<u>Drinking</u>: Never drinks.
<u>Drugs</u>: Nope. Never. Ever.

'God you're boring,' Scarlett says, 'how come I never realised that before?'

'You did and you stayed anyway. Isn't it marvellous?'

<u>Education level</u>: Masters of Law.

<u>Income</u>: Men don't like it when you make more than them, right? Jonathan always made little passive aggressive comments about it. Lie or leave that empty? Leave it empty.

Scarlett takes a long gulp of wine and pushes back the computer, angling it so I can see the screen. 'Here you go, you're all set for your Sex Blitz to begin.'

'Dating campaign to find love,' I say.

'Whatever. Potato-pot-ah-to. You should reach out to these ones there.'

We're on *the* supposedly up-and-coming website and suddenly I can see how that's going to help me rationalise the whole process.

'You can pick and choose them based on education, income and whether they want a committed relationship?' I whistle. 'That's amazing! It's going to be so much easier to sift through and select than just randomly meeting strangers.'

'Yeah, don't get your hopes up, most of them lie,' Scarlett says.

'Should I write a blurb or something?' I ask.

'Don't bother. They only look at the photos anyway.' I wonder where she found the photo of me where I looked semi-sexy. Won't they be disappointed when they see me IRL? Maybe I should upload a more realistic one. I'll just change the picture later.

Catherine grabs the mouse and starts to scroll. Forbidden fruit. Sparkling eyes. She pauses on one profile and sucks her lower lip pensively.

She smells of goat cheese. Outside, it's raining.

'Oh that one's nice! How about that one?' she says.

I have a look. 'Not bad.' He's her type: clean cut, tall, gaunt-faced and pale.

'This is so exciting! So many choices!' she titters.

'Don't bother writing long messages,' Scarlett tempers. 'At a push you can "like" them but that's it. Half of them quit the site years ago. Either that or they don't bother answering. So don't waste too much time on any one profile.' Her long red nails look blood stained in the darkening evening light.

'You need to date as much as possible before you turn forty,' Scarlett says with an air of authority about her. 'You become invisible after forty. Men's search criteria exclude you. Trust me. Date before you go over to the other side.'

She sounds like I'll be dead.

'Oh don't listen to her, Lily. You're such a catch,' Catherine says encouragingly, as Scarlett magics a few dozen photos of semi-decent blokes for me to poke or nudge or whatever. 'You're smart, you're successful, well off, you've got your own flat, you're pretty, you'll bag yourself a good man, in no time!'

'Maybe, but the more I achieve elsewhere, the less I seem to be able to convince men that I'm sweet and lovable.'

'But you *are* sweet and lovable!' Catherine squeaks.

'Thank you but you're biased darling.'

'Oh look! You're getting likes already!' Catherine grins 'See? What did I tell you?'

'Fresh meat,' Scarlett says, sipping from her wineglass

with a tight red-clawed grip. 'Take advantage while they're circling the waters. It won't last.'

'Jeez, you make them sound like sharks,' I say.

She shrugs. 'You'll see.'

5

INTERLUDE: LOVE IN THE TIME OF (CHOLERA) SOCIAL MEDIA

Friday night eight-ish.

Him: 'Hi cutie, are you free tonight?'

Me: Sitting in a train, on my way to visit my Mum. 'Oh sorry no, I'm going away for the weekend. But I could meet up next week!'

Him: 'You want me to wait two days? What is this? 1852? Go fuck yourself.'

~

Scrolling, scrolling, scrolling.

Him: 'I'm looking for a girl who's honest, loyal and truthful.'

Is he looking for a dog?

~

Me at home, in my PJs, scrolling on Happn the app that matches you with people you cross paths with on the street. It's currently geolocating me and offering me the profiles of completely unsuitable men just because they're in a few miles radius: there's the eighteen-year-old Goth, the seventy-year-old widower, a guy with waist-long dreadlocks, sitting on a throne, wearing a fur cape. Mmmmh.

Him (he looks normal, age appropriate, yay!): 'Hi Lily.'

Me: 'Hi,' I text, semi-hopeful.

Him: 'I'm downstairs, fancy a coffee?'

I turn off all the lights in my flat and part the curtain. A man's leaning against the lamppost looking up at my windows. Fuckety fuck, fuck, fuck.

Me, locking the front door: Block.

∼

Him: 'Hi'

Me: 'Hi'

Him: 'Have you read my profile?'

Me: unsure, scrolls through it in a panic. There are a few tasteful black and white shots of him, handsome, right age, posh haircut and... uh-oh. A whip.

Him: 'I'm looking for a naughty girl, so I can show her the ropes.'

Show her the ...

Block.

∼

My friends: 'You're too picky. There have to be good men out there. You know my friend Charlotte met her husband on an dating app.'

Me:

6

SATAN'S SPAWN= 1, SISTERHOOD OF WANDERING PANTS= 0

I'm staring at a penis.

Not that I ever wanted to see this one. In fact, I once wanted to see as few as possible in my lifetime.

Alexander78 (DATE 4) didn't like his chances of getting a second date with me so as a parting shot, he sent me five pictures of his beigey frankfurter.

Obviously, I recoil and squeal with laughter.

'What? What?' Scarlett whispers.

'In the name of the Father, the Son and the Holy Ghost,' the priest intones and we bend our heads. Catherine glares at us over her shoulder then turns back to the altar, hands clasped tightly together.

'Amen.' I tilt the phone towards my friend, feeling guilty. I should be focusing on the sermon. I only spend one hour a week on my soul and I managed to sully this moment. I'll need to confess later. Jesus deserves better.

'Eeeeeew! No no no!' Scarlett grabs it from my hands and zooms in on the photo.

"Shhh,' Catherine hisses from the row in front of us.

Scarlett tips the screen towards her.

'Oh my God!' She signs herself and swings forward looking outraged, as her shiny curtain of black hair slides back into place.

'What's going on?' Emma's sitting on the same pew as Scarlett and me. Her picture-perfect family is on the other side of the aisle, all dressed in their Sunday best. The kids look like they've been teleported directly from the fifties with their miniature duffel coats and their shiny patent leather shoes.

Emma sneaks a glance and starts mouthing insults at me.

Laughter, fits of giggles, disgusted faces. The priest throws us a pointed glance and I blush crimson. Mea culpa, mea maxima culpa.

'The Mass ends,' says the priest.

'Thanks be to God,' I say with feeling.

We emerge into the morning sun still giggling. There's a marquee in the priory's rose garden, instant coffee in Styrofoam cups, children chasing each other, gossip, birdsong and chocolate bourbons: our usual Sunday routine.

Emma, Scarlett and I shared a dorm room twenty years ago. God, was Uni so long ago already? The three of us used to sneak out of the all-girl dorm to go to nightclubs, get blind drunk and hold each other's hair back as we puked our guts out.

Then at the break of dawn, we'd load up on Berocca on the way back to Uni and barge into class, looking fabulous, in our party clothes and sunglasses at eight am. We were the rebellious ones, the cool ones, the free ones. The boys in our year liked to pass around caricatures of what they supposed we looked like naked. Our mousy female classmates shied away from us and we were oblivious to it all, absorbed in our first sexual awakenings with unsuitable boys, listening to Lenny Kravitz in the dorm's attic while we ate strawberry laces and Allsorts and smoked cigarettes without inhaling, one foot in childhood and one in adulthood.

That's when Emma wasn't yet a respectable mother and wife that is. She met slightly shy, blue-blooded Charles while we were still reading law and consequently never had the privilege of registering on a dating site. Lucky cow.

He leads the kids away to give us time to chat. He's nice and thoughtful that way. She watches her family walk across the lawn, a small smile playing on her lips.

'I'll go get us teas,' she chirps and goes after them, probably to go sneak a kiss from Charles or arrange the ribbon in her daughter's hair or something.

We were all raised in pretty conservative families and used to go to church as children. So when Emma said she needed to go to Mass every week in order to get her kids into the only Ofsted-outstanding school in her catchment area, Scarlett and I decided to join her, so we could see each other regularly. It's worked a treat and more often than not, we end up brunching somewhere afterwards. So here we all are, on a normal Sunday morning.

Well maybe it's not a completely normal today. The one-eyed monster hangs in the air between us, intruding on the morning's wholesome simplicity.

'That's the most intimate part of him, you were only supposed to see it after weeks, months of careful conversation, courtship and trust.' Catherine shakes her head despondently. Perhaps she's mourning more than just this image she will never be able to unsee; perhaps the end of a golden age of romance and decency or perhaps the end of the illusion that such an era ever existed.

Catherine came later to our little group. We met her at Mass a couple of years ago and she seemed lonely, having just moved to London from Australia, so we included her in our little band.

'He must be a pervert,' she concludes. 'Do you think he may be dangerous? Maybe we should call the police.'

Scarlett snorts.

I suppose Catherine's got a point. I've mostly seen the funny aspect of this but really, what's the difference between a guy like Alexander78 and one of the creeps who roam the streets, wearing a trench and nothing else, flashing passers-by? The only difference is one of means and reach, I suppose. Not much else.

'Mmh,' Scarlett throws Catherine an amused glance, 'or maybe he just thought his mini-me would convince Lily to go on a second date with him. A lot of guys do it, you know.'

Catherine looks distressed at the thought.

My fingers part on the smudged screen, enlarging the member. It's not even good looking or particularly exceptional in any way, average sized, weird textured skin. I zoom in and see that he's just come. A bit of jizz is sticking forlornly to his hairy thigh. Maybe I should wash my hands, disinfect the screen or something.

Sighing, I look up 'I mean, seriously, if you think this is going to lead to hanky-panky, at least you could invest some thought into framing, lighting, angle.'

'I guess he wasn't thinking with his brain,' Emma giggles, coming back with four Styrofoam cups with their content half spilled.

'I've read that men think we *like* dick picks,' Emma ventures. 'As in: they'd love to see ours, so they can only imagine that we'd want to see theirs.'

'But... but... just no.' Catherine can't really form words anymore, she's just shaking her head at this point.

'Let me see the bald-headed yogurt slinger again.' Scarlett bites the cup's soft lip, holding it precariously, as she slides through the photos.

She's wearing a sequin dress with a giant Lichtenstein drawing down her front. The blonde's pulpy pout and crying eyes ripple mesmerizingly in the morning sunshine. Scarlett curses as the heels of her bright coral pumps dunk into the grass, then pulls them out, still engrossed in the genitalia perusal, looking effortlessly OTT and fabulous.

'So we all know how Lily's hunt's going, how's yours?' Emma asks Scarlett.

'Only one date this week. Slim pickings.'

'Mmmh, something's up'. She usually goes on three dates per week at least. I don't know how she's been maintaining that rhythm for years, it's like a second full-time job. I'm exhausted just to think about it. 'Found a good one then?' I ask.

'Well I wouldn't go quite that far,' she hesitates, 'François's back.'

Catherine groans with a martyred look on her face 'Oh here we go again.'

'Noooooo! Way to flog a dead horse, Scarlett. Come on,' Emma says while I start humming *Let it go, let it go.*

Scarlett lifts her gaze from the smeared screen and glares at us through her false eyelashes. 'What?'

'Nothing,' I laugh. 'I didn't say anything. Earworm, that's all.'

François is the heir to a French luxury empire, he's flash, he's a brat, he's so rich that he can get away with being ever so slightly stupid. They collided into each other a year ago, had a steamy, tempestuous affair and she walked away when he failed to propose. They've been on again, off again ever since.

'So, is it still as...earth-shattering as before?' I ask.

'He's leaning a bit to the left these days, but otherwise yeah.' She doesn't mean politically.

'That's disgraceful and you're both disgusting.' Catherine smoothes her black skirt, hunting for imaginary lint and adjusts the cuffs of her white buttoned-up shirt, with metronomic gracefulness.

The rest of us go to Mass out of habit more than anything else but Catherine, the newest addition to our Sisterhood of Wandering Pants is a tad more serious about the whole thing. She once dragged me to an Opus Dei meeting and tried to sign me up. I had to admit to her afterwards that I'm not *that* kind of Catholic. I mean, I don't want my daily life to be a path to sanctity and holiness, there's more to life than that. Still, she tries to steer us onto the straight and narrow, whenever she can.

'That just confirms it, you know.' Catherine puckers her lips as she gestures to my screen, 'what I've been saying all along.'

'Here we go again.' Scarlett rolls her eyes.

'Men. Spawn of Satan. All of them.' Catherine removes the phone from us, like a stern schoolmistress confiscating a toy.

'Maybe #NotAllMen?' Emma ventures.

Scarlett bursts into raucous laughter and sprays milky coffee all over herself.

Catherine looks blankly at the three of us while our giggles slowly become chuckles.

'I don't get it, what's so funny?'

She doesn't do social media, it's not good for her inner peace. Wiping tears from my eyes, I glance at her hands, surprised to see something gold glinting there.

'New?'

'Oh yes, it's Dior,' Catherine lights up. The pretty gold

branches loop around her finger, each cradling a small diamond. 'I wanted something that would look like the Crown of Thorns. To remind me of our Lord's sacrifice.'

'Oh for the love of God,' Scarlett sighs, 'you know they won't let you keep any of your jewellery don't you?'

'Maybe if it's religious they might.'

'That's not the point, Catherine, you can't seriously be considering becoming a nun, can you? I mean look at you,' Scarlett waves vaguely at Catherine's ex-ballerina silhouette and her lovely face.

'Wouldn't you rather find a good man? Love and be loved?' Emma asks kindly.

Alexander78 chooses just that moment to have a little aftershock. Catherine turns the vibrating phone up and white shows around her eyes. She just lobs it at me and stalks away.

On my screen, there is a stock photo of a bloke giving head to a naked woman. I notice fleetingly that her thighs are perfect and fat-free. The caption reads "Breakfast, the meal of champions."

Alexander78 has added (in case I didn't get it): 'Wanna have breakfast? [blushing smiley]'

Jesus.

A post-cum dribble text and it's not even eleven am yet.

7

HATS ARE SO EASILY LOST. A REUNION

I get ready, straightening my shoulder-length hair into a semi-professional look. It's hard, my curls resist being tamed, but I'm pitiless. It's a school reunion so I should try to prove that I've become an adult, shouldn't I? The straightening iron hisses and splutters like a torture device. Ouch! I suck on my finger and look critically at myself.

The wince has revealed wrinkles at the corner of my eyelids. Eye shadows no longer glide smoothly on, now they pool and hide in creases. My lips also sometimes tighten, primly commenting on my life without my knowledge.

I don't really want to go but I have to. Do I have to? My palms are sweaty and eels of anxiety are roiling somewhere near the bottom of my self-esteem.

I PUT the pink gloss on and pull the mass of curls carefully out of my face, so they don't get trapped on the sticky surface of my plump lips. My hair sways against the small of my back.

'Yes, I'm coming, I'm coming!' I laugh, calling down to my friends. My parents are away for the weekend and the coolest girl in our year is throwing a party. Everyone is going.

I put my coat and my brand new bell-shaped hat on and throw a last glance at the mirror, smiling brightly in anticipation. Party!

STANDING OUTSIDE THE HOTEL, I shuffle from side to side in the uncomfortable heels. This is a mistake. I start to walk away but someone calls my name with mock delight and I turn to find a woman striding towards me, a cigarette trapped between her fingers. I've been spotted. Too late to escape now.

She looks effortlessly serious, I so often fail to do that. She's wearing a stewardess bun and a taupe dress with expensive stilettos. With a pang, I recognise Pippa's face and yet also not: there are harder lines in it than before.

THE THREE OF us arrive at the party and make our rowdy entrance, alternating between fits of giggles and feeling more grownup and fabulous than we actually are. Tonight Pippa's parents are away, and the whole school is here. My friends scatter into the crowd and, not knowing what to do, I shed my coat and hat onto the parents' bed and make my way to the kitchen, pulling down on my short-ish dress. Every horizontal surface is covered with alcohol. Wow there are even boys from other schools! Maybe someone will notice me tonight.

THE HOTEL'S quite grand and the high-ceilinged room is packed with people whose names I've forgotten but whose faces look familiar. There's a band playing nineties hits and a half-hearted attempt by a couple of women to make the dance floor happen. I'm parked by the buffet table, my back to the wall, keeping a longing eye on the door as I check my work emails, out of boredom more than zeal.

'Drink?'

I flinch and focus on the sweaty little runt who's slithered next to me, holding a bottle of gin. As he starts to pour me a glass, I cover the rim of my tonic water and hunch my shoulders.

'No, no, thank you. I don't drink.'

'That's new,' he guffaws and pours himself a tall one, then plonks the bottle on the table and corners me. He's too close.

'Soooooo, what have you been up to these last twenty years?' He takes a gulp of the clear liquid and leers. 'I hear you're still single.' His eyes slide downward and he continues the conversation with my breasts. 'How many boyfriends have you got these days?' he counts on his fingers '1, 2, 3, 4?' My breasts don't answer anything meaningful, so I pitch in. 'No boyfriend, George. That's usually what single means.'

Meanwhile, I look over the top of his balding head at his wife Amelia who's put on five stones since I last saw her. She's stuffing a canapé in her mouth.

I remember when they first got together during our class trip to Bath. Hormones were flying high, parental supervision had been lifted and our teachers were much too young to put a stop to our shenanigans. A lot of my friends popped their cherries that week. I didn't. George and Amelia must have stayed together since then. The Spice Girls were still at the top of the charts. It's been a while.

. . .

I can't remember exactly how many drinks I've had. A helpful boy I've never met before takes me to the garden, so I can clear my head. The taste of the whisky and Coke is thick on my tongue. Maybe I'll get kissed tonight. Drunk butterflies careen in my stomach as the helpful boy dry humps me in the garden, hiking my skirt up. I push him away and stagger back to the kitchen. It's bright and loud and my girlfriends are nowhere to be seen. Pippa cackles 'you're drunk' and taps the sofa. I slump down next to her and accept the glass she's holding out, while trying not to stare at her blond moustache. Where are my friends?

George and Amelia are slobbering over each other's faces in a corner. She's mounted atop of him and he's massaging her perky bum. The drink burns a path down my throat as I giggle vaguely and the room starts to spin.

PIPPA ADJUSTS her bun and taps the sofa next to her. I sit holding my tonic water, back held upright. She did well to pluck, no one ever had the heart to tell her that dying her upper lip blond didn't make the hair invisible. She launches into a long-winded explanation of her very-important-job. There are flaky crumbs on her tailored mousy dress. I toy with the idea of explaining what I do for a living. The two hundred employees. The six figure income. The posh flat in the glittering building. But my lips stay shut.

JAEGERMEISTER.
Drunk inexpert flirting.
Music blaring somewhere.
Neighbours knocking at the door.
I go pee. Open a door. Wrong door. Mel looks up, naked,

sweating and red-faced, an impish grin on her face, as the muscles in JC's back, ripple beneath his pallid skin. He ploughs on, oblivious.

I stumble out, the stark light triangle on the carpet becomes a narrow slit and then obscurity engulfs them as I close the door. I flatten against the corridor wall, eyes wide. I thought she was saving her virginity until marriage, isn't she a devout Catholic? A surge of lust electrocutes me. It'd be nice to maybe kiss a boy tonight.

'There you are. I heard you were here tonight!' Mel says. Her hair is short and grey now, the ash, lead and steel layers stacked in elegant hues through her expensive cut.

'It's been twenty years since the last time we saw you!' JC is bigger, barrel-chested now, red beard, puffy eyes. Golden bands glint on their ring fingers. One Ring to rule them all and in the darkness bind them. The joined-at-the-hip gushing continues.

'So where did you disappear to? All of us have seen each other every year but we never quite seemed to know what had become of you,' she says lightly.

I should have stayed off Facebook and stayed away for the next twenty years. Too late now.

'I suppose I've been busy with work,' I take a sip of the bitter bubbles.

'Oh really? What do you do?' she asks.

'I'm on the board of a bank.' I don't say which one, that would be bragging.

'You didn't marry I see,' she glances at my bare fingers.

She says it like I never will. Like that's done and dusted.

'No.'

'Too busy, I suppose,' she smirks. 'You must lead a very glamorous life, a single girl in London, at what forty?' There's a note of something sour in her voice. 'Oh Gosh, I could never do it! I wouldn't have the stamina.' She sounds like a hyena when she laughs.

JC actually flinches then comes to my rescue. 'Well better that than being one of those bitter old spinsters who have nothing better to do than look for causes and make a fuss over "climate change", I bet you anything that half the nutters in the Oxford Circus protests last week were sad embittered women.'

Mel looks me right in the eye and adds with a smile, 'Present company excepted of course.'

'Well, actually, I voted for the Greens at the last election and I think protests are a brilliant way to bring the public's attention to climate action. It's long overdue, don't you think?' There's a silence at that. Looks like I'm a spinster with a cause after all. Awkward.

'What about you? What do you do?' I ask.

'I'm a home maker,' she says. The next ten minutes are spent extolling the virtues of stay-at-home mums and wholesome lives '... and that requires love, patience, understanding. It's not a selfish life.'

JC weaves his fingers through hers and they smile Siamese smiles.

'Right,' I stare at the bottom of the crystal tumbler as the silver bubbles fight their way to the surface, pushing the lemon this way and that. 'That sounds wonderful Mel, I'm so happy for you.' I press my lips together.

A tall man sporting a square jaw, an artful stubble and a well-cut suit, smiles at me with commiseration from across the room.

. . .

A GANGLY BOY is trying to kiss me on the neck. 'You're so different when you're drunk. I like you so much better like this, you're more fun.' His lips are too wet.

Wiping my neck dry, I duck under his leaning arm and escape into the living room. Yells of glee jolt me out of my drunken fog. A group of kids are raiding the parents' bar. Someone thrusts a glass in my hand.

Colours.
Lights.
I think I might puke.
Someone pushes another drink in my hand.
I need to go home.

'You look like you need this,' the handsome man offers me a plate of canapés. The Mel-JC unit has moved on to their next target, fingers still woven together.

I smile and take one. Our fingers brush lightly against each other and a shiver shimmies up my spine. There's gold on his fingers, *damned*. Oh but it's just a signet ring. All systems go. I look up and take in his perfect smile. The posh Eton drawl. The handsome features. The aura of power floating around him.

'So, come here often?' he says, relaxed, confident.

'Yes, every twenty years or so,' I bat back.

He laughs. Maybe more than the joke warrants. He's the up-and-coming judge that Amelia mentioned. *A minor celebrity in our midst, haven't you heard?* she was all aflutter.

He must be connected to someone here, I suppose, because he didn't go to my school.

'You don't look old enough to be at this reunion,' he says.

I smile and tuck my hair behind my ear. Let the games begin.

. . .

It's dark in Pippa's parents' bedroom. I rummage through the mountain of coats and scarves, trying to find mine. I want to go home now. The room is swirling around me, the ceiling looks like a merry-go-round. I sit-fall on the floor. Where are my friends? Maybe they left without me. The nightstand's handle digs between my shoulder blades as I pull through the tangle of coats and fight with my jacket. My arms are made of overcooked spaghetti, my knees are refusing to carry me. Finally the coat's on. Now buttons.

A group of boys comes in. 'There she is!' One of them kneels next to me and helps me remove my coat. 'No, no, no,' I giggle. 'I'm trying to put it on, not remove it!'

I SLIPPED OUT during a lull in the reunion. This is all a bit much and I'm not entirely sure I should have come. On a hunch, I took the stairs to the top floor and found myself on the hotel's rooftop with London at my feet. Wrapping my arms around myself, I breathe in the summer air, relieved to have a few moments to collect my thoughts. It's funny how seeing people you once knew as a teen makes you revert to who you were then. I'm no longer the shy, introverted pushover I once was. Not overtly anyway. Maybe my presence here says I still am but I've built a better carapace around my core frailty than when I was seventeen.

I get as close as I dare to the edge and throw a glance at the street, five storeys below. This roof terrace clearly isn't meant to be used; the railing is only knee high and there's no seating anywhere. I'd better get back downstairs.

'Ah, there you are. I thought I saw you take the stairs.'

Startled, I turn around and see the handsome man

walking towards me, a slight swagger in his step. He's holding two champagne glasses and my heart does a little flop in my chest as I realise quite how handsome he is; rectilinear, classic features, dark brown hair with a pleasing tousled look, impeccably-cut suit and dazzling smile.

'I just came here for a breath of fresh air,' I say apologetically, as he hands me the champagne.

'Believe me, I understand. I'm not sure what I'm doing at this reunion either.' I hold the champagne glass but I don't drink and he doesn't notice. Night has fallen and it's dark and quiet up here. A welcome respite. The moon's quiet glow gives everything a magical hue and the city's lights wink at us.

'I wonder what that building is,' I muse, looking at the skyline.

'Well, I'm glad you asked.' He slides smoothly behind me and hunches over my shoulder to point at something in the distance. He whispers the building's name and some random trivia about the architecture while I absorb myself in the feeling of his presence. He's nearly touching me but not quite. Warmth radiates off him and makes my back tingle with anticipation as his breath caresses my neck from behind.

THERE'S something wrong with my eyes. Or is it my neck? I can't seem to lift my gaze up to see his face. I sense more than I see him shoo his friends out as he locks the door behind them. They make hooting noises and bang on the door, catcalling and laughing. I don't feel very well. The room swims in and out, stroboscopic scenes flashing in and out of darkness, as they brand themselves on my soul.

Darkness.
Where are my friends?
Darkness.
He's pulling my jeans off. I didn't say that I wanted this.
Darkness.
Is there anything I can do to stop this?
Darkness.
He's inside me.
Darkness.
It hurts.
Darkness.
I don't know what to do to make it stop. I need to vomit.
Darkness.
His smell is inside my nostrils. His cock is ramming into me, burning a path of pain and self-loathing. I don't want this. I don't want this. I don't want this.
Darkness.

HE TURNS ME AROUND, like a slow-motion silent dance and now I'm in his arms somehow. My lips part and I look up at his face. His lips are no longer smiling his Colgate smile. In the semi-darkness of our privacy, his intense brown eyes detail my face and come to rest on my lips. Both his hands land gently on my shoulders, slowly backhanding my hair out of the way. Then his fingers trails down my naked arm and goose bumps pop up along the invisible path he traces to my wrist. He leans in, towards the inevitable consumption, towards the inevitable possession.

THE NEXT MORNING, I wake up. There is something moving inside my vagina. His fingers are in me, painfully digging in against my raw flesh. My head is pounding. I squirm away and open my eyes, the lashes are sealed together with dried tears. I feel so dirty. I need a shower. Right now. I slide from under him, avoiding his eyes. What must I look like? I'm naked. My brain is frozen. I can't think of anything: only escape. I hold my clothes against my body, not looking back, not looking at him.

Hand on the key, as I unlock the door, I pause. 'What's your name?' I ask.

'Cameron,' he says.

I run out to vomit in the bathroom and from there, make my way back home before anyone else sees me.

He never even asked my name.

HIS HAND GRIPS around my ponytail, pulling my head back and he kisses me voraciously, his stubble rough against my skin. His smell hits my nostrils and a wave of nausea swells up, engulfing me. I reach up for air.

'What's your name?' I ask.

'I thought you knew.' He chuckles.

Could he be who I think he really is?

He gives me the fake smile, 'I'm Cameron.'

The smell of him is inside my lungs, coating me with shame, self-disgust and regret. I need to get out of here. Oh my God. It's him. I'd forgotten his face. But his smell. My soul remembers his smell.

I start to go but he wrenches me back into his arms.

'Where do you think you're going, you cock-teasing bitch—'

It's him, I have to get away. My breath. Comes. In. Short. Bursts. My heart is bouncing inside my ribcage, like a panicked bird.

'Sorry I should go… I'm so sorry, I didn't realise…'

His fingers wrap around my forearm, painfully digging in. I panic, shoving him back, as I try to escape his grip.

His fingers clasp empty air.

He expected to pull me towards him but I've stepped back.

He's destabilised.

He flails, his face the picture of surprise.

And then he tumbles over the railing and disappears into the night's dark blue air.

Crouching in my shower, I make a very small ball and let the scalding water pelt me as I rock back and forth, crying silently. Then finally, I unfurl, taking in the ugly bruises on my breasts, the burn and the blood between my legs.

I don't understand why I feel so sad. This was my first time. Maybe it's painful because I'm inexperienced? A long time later, I wrap myself in a towel and pick my clothes off the floor. The movement makes the smell of him waft up. Head in the toilet bowl, I retch until there's nothing left to bring up.

Oh, I lost my pretty cloche hat.

He's sprawled on the pavement. Legs at an odd angle. The back of his head split open on contact with the asphalt. Dark, black blood is spilling out of the wound sluggishly, like melted chocolate out of a lava cake.

His dead eyes are trained on me, shock painted on his features.

It's late, there's no one in the back alley where he fell. But I hear a woman scream.

Vertigo.

I back away from the edge, knees shaking.

The night sky is swirling dangerously above me as cold sweat clings to my skin.

Time to go.

8

INTERLUDE: #ME TOO

Last year it was #MeToo, now it's #WhyIDidntReport. I feel like a voyeur as I read. Life after life, laid bare, the pain so raw.

#WhyIDidntReport: I had drunk too much.

#WhyIDidntReport: I thought it was my fault.

#WhyIDidntReport: He didn't hold a knife to my throat and attack me in a dark alley, so I didn't think it was rape until today.

#WhyIDidntReport: I was nearly passed out, so I'm not sure who did it.

#WhyIDidntReport: Was it still rape if I didn't say the word no?

#WhyIDidntReport: I was ashamed.

#WhyIDidntReport: I wanted to be kissed that night. Maybe I wanted more.

#WhyIDidntReport: I behaved like a slut. I brought it on myself.

#WhyIDidntReport: Surely it wasn't rape? Or maybe it was. I don't really know.

#WhyIWontShareOnTwitter: I don't think admitting

that I was once a victim will make me feel better.

I don't think it will make society fairer or safer.

I think the only thing it will achieve is to change how people perceive me. Downgrading me to victim status. Possibly painting a target on my back. After all, people who were once vulnerable make easier prey.

Women are just exposing themselves for no discernable benefit, or maybe they're doing it for the faint glimmer of hope that, one day, their candour will result in change.

I don't believe it. Society isn't changing. Men aren't changing.

More likely the victims will find each other and create support groups. And we'll all talk and talk and talk some more and wrap ourselves in pretzels trying to understand why it happened and commending each other for being "brave" for sharing and we'll seek closure and blah blah fucking blah.

Then everything will be forgotten when the next hashtag comes along. *#vaginacandle* or *#hornyyyyyyasf* or *#MySexLifeInMovieTitles* and all the outrage will be washed away in a tsunami of words that mean nothing and change nothing.

Predators in positions of power will continue to exist. Women will continue to suffer.

If only we could pass on everything we'd learnt, wholesale, at birth to our daughters. Instead, even as I scroll down the posts, the next babes in the woods are being born in their droves. And men pass on the mantle of power and entitlement to their sons.

And on and on it goes.

#WhyIWillNeverReport: because I killed him last night.

9

DERAILMENTS

Cameron's surprised face flashes before my eyes, leaking blood on the pavement of the hotel's back alley. Shuddering, I flick feverishly through the news and take a minute step forward to stop feeling the commuter's groin moulding against my bum in the crowded Tube carriage.

It's been a few days. The press is running on empty and resorting to speculation now. Cameron was an up-and-coming judge. A powerful man. I'm going to get caught. I'll spend the rest of my life in prison.

Oh God.

I was still clutching my champagne glass when I ran away, in a panicked daze, what did I do with it afterwards? Did I let the roof door slam shut on my way out? Did I leave fingerprints on the handrail? I've no idea. Probably.

I didn't know what to do, so I went back to the party pretending I'd returned from the loo, with wet hands and reapplied lipstick. Found a couple of "friends" to chat with until I was reasonably sure that someone would remember me being there the whole time.

'Do you want to meet The One and keep him?' An ad starts on my phone and I struggle to stop it, as the Tube doors shriek open and the crowd buffets me this way and that while I cling to the pole. On my screen, a man with curly brown hair and a Ross-from-Friends vibe is beaming up at me, as he drawls with an American accent. 'Don't you think you deserve to be loved?'

My finger hovers, as I try to close the ad but something holds me back. It all seems so pointless now: the dating campaign, my search for romance, my naïve hopes. It's all so mundane compared to what happened on the roof. The call of the Twitter feed is like a train wreck, it's nearly impossible to look away from the stories of pain and abuse but for some reason my finger doesn't come down on the small X and the ad stays open. The dating guru cups his oversized ear, as the shrill miniature crowd yells its assent on my screen. 'Tell me the truth now, do you want to have everything you've ever dreamt of? Do you?'

I do. I really do. For a moment I imagine being sorted, at last, and having all the trappings of a normal life. Being able to attend functions, weddings, reunions, my fingers laced in His. Finally knowing what it's like to fit in, to be accepted, to be complete. I've only got one shot left. One shot before I turn forty. Then the life I want will slip away forever. I don't have time to get side-tracked by my past and the sordid incident with Cameron. I'm on a mission. I still have thirty-two dates to go.

The Tube grinds to a halt and we're all jostled, rearranged and pressed against one another. By the time the doors blare open, I've made my decision: I should continue to live my life as if nothing had happened. It won't do to attract attention to myself. Yes. That's what I'll do: I'll just continue with my dating campaign, act normal and hope no one saw me on the roof.

Pushing through Waterloo's rush hour throngs, I head for Southbank, feeling marginally better.

Catherine is already at the conference venue and Scarlett arrives a moment later, full of righteous rage about being passed up for promotion. Again.

Then the conference starts: it's some sort of feminist talk about gender pay gap and glass ceilings. In the vast wooden auditorium, there are only women and girls as far as the eye can see. Feeling fragile and a bit flustered, I soak in the feeling of safety and camaraderie and let the words wash over me.

When it's over, we head to a nearby Italian restaurant and we're not the only ones; the place is filled with chattering, perfumed and made-up women. It's lovely and bright and my spirits lift up a bit.

The waiter doesn't know quite what to make of our table. One of us is ordering wine and cursing like a trucker, one of us looks slightly distracted because she feels guilty about murdering a bloke (*wait he can't possibly know that*) and the other one is clasping her hands, head bowed in prayer. He puts bread and olives in front of us and retreats, looking vaguely alarmed.

A few glasses of wine later (Diet Coke for me), we're trading horror stories, as one does when the subject veers onto dating.

'Truth or dare?' Catherine asks.

'Really?' I say, holding back a snort.

'Why do you never drink, Lily?'

'Actually that's a really great question,' Scarlett intervenes. 'You won't believe this, but our teetotal Lily here used to be the life of the party. We were by far the coolest chicks in school and the first year of Uni was a blast.' She grins, 'you remember when you got so drunk that you ended up singing on a street corner until you gathered enough money to get us into that posh nightclub we were all dying to get into but couldn't afford.'

'That was a good night.' I smile, remembering how free, how unselfconscious I felt then. 'You guys did the chorus girls behind me.'

'Yeah, those were good years,' Scarlett beams fondly at me.

'They were,' my smile falters. It was a few days before... I've never told anyone about the night I lost my hat. I've kept it close to my heart, buried deep, like a tumour. It defines me but it also shames me. How stupid I was to drink so much. How easily preyed on. How I lacked the courage, the strength to defend myself. How maybe, just maybe I caused it.

I never let it see the light of day, this wound in my past and the even more blood-stained one in my present.

The shock on Cameron's face as he fell backwards.

The ripping pain inside me as he ploughed on, oblivious to my tears.

His flailing hand as he fell, grasping for me.

The smell of him as I vomited the next morning.

Shame falls on my shoulders, submerging me. It's easier to just lie.

'So why did you stop drinking?' Catherine frowns.

'Oh, I just realised that I don't like the taste of alcohol. Might as well save myself the calories,' I say automatically as I take refuge in the gnocchi's comforting texture, their doughy, plump little shape dissolving into mashy flavoursome pops on my tongue.

Eager to move on, I ask Catherine quickly: 'Truth or dare?'

'Truth,' Catherine says.

'Why are you even considering the orders? Don't you want to be with someone?' I ask.

'Well, actually, I... I have news I've been meaning to... I've gotten back together with my ex.'

Scarlett and I stare at her, agog.

'What? Who?'

'When? How?'

She squirms in her chair. 'Well, we were together for years in Melbourne and it ended when I moved here. He found... he just arrived in London and I suppose we're back on.'

'But what about the orders? Why would you... are you still planning to become a nun then?'

She hesitates, 'well I suppose that's off, now that Brett's back.'

'You dark horse! Well done!' Scarlett actually claps.

~~Our nun in training~~ Catherine blushes twisting her crown of thorns around her finger, while Scarlett gushes and asks to see a photo. I hate myself for the jealousy and sadness that pass fleetingly across my mind like clouds against the sun. Then I rally and congratulate her too.

While we look at the photos of the handsome bloke with a posh haircut, intellectual glasses and a smart blazer, I watch Catherine's face, she looks... I don't know. She's biting her lip.

'How come you haven't once told us about him in the two years we've known you?' I ask.

'Oh you know, he... I... I wasn't the same person back then, I was too proud, we... we had a few disagreements.'

She rubs her wrist absentmindedly. The one she once told me she broke.

'How cool that he moved to London too! It's so romantic that he did that for you,' Scarlett says, appreciating the photos more than is seemly.

Catherine lowers her head. 'Yeah, yeah, really cool.' She turns to attract the waiter's attention. Her pashmina slips off her shoulders and before she has time to tighten it around her, I notice dark purple marks on her upper arm.

'I'll have the torta Caprese please.' Catherine smiles like she's doing something naughty.

'You can totally afford to have pudding with your figure,' I say, thinking of the enormous behind I'm sitting on. No pudding for me.

'No it's not that. It's just that Brett can't have any nuts. He's severely allergic to them. So I have them when he's not here.'

'How about you Lily?' Scarlett asks.

I shake my head.

'Oh come on! You haven't had pudding for years, for God's sake.'

'Blasphemy,' Catherine mutters.

'Lactose intolerance,' I shrug, looking longingly at the menu with its panna cottas, its tiramisus and its gelatos.

Scarlett rolls her eyes. 'Come on Lily, live a little. No booze, no sugar, no sex. You gotta have *something*.'

Murder? Does murder count as something?

'It's not like it's making any difference anyway.' Catherine's eyes go round and she slaps her cupped hand over her mouth as if to take the words back. But they're already out, floating in the air between us.

She's right, all this 'being careful' and 'watching my diet' and 'no thank yous' has accomplished fuck all. The older I get, the more effort I exert to just stay in place, the scale stuck stubbornly on the same enormous number for years. Who knows what would happen if I just accepted myself as I am? Just embraced that I'm curvy and enjoyed myself a little more?

Maybe the world would implode and the sky would fall. Or maybe I'd just tip into obesity and waddle everywhere, a pained look on my face, clutching my chest when I ran to catch the lift. Maybe I would become entirely invisible to men. I'm already semi-transparent but if I let go... their eyes would skim over me like I'm not even in the room, their appreciative gazes directed at the thinner women while I became little more than a piece of furniture. I look around the restaurant, as I often do, assessing my fatness against other women's.

'What will it be ladies?' The gorgeous Italian waiter asks.

'Tiramisu' Scarlett closes the menu with a definitive thunk.

'Nothing for me,' I smile.

'Torta Caprese, please.' Catherine, the rebel.

Scarlett twists in her chair to glance at the waiter as he weaves through the tables, away from us. 'He's delicious isn't he, Lily?'

'He's too young,' I retort admiring his tight posterior.

'Nonsense, he's what twenty? That's legal.'

'I'm *literally* old enough to be his mother.'

There's another life encapsulated in that sentence. Another life that never happened.

Maybe Cameron broke something in me that night, twenty years ago, even though I didn't realise it at the time.

Maybe, even though I didn't fully understand what happened, it opened a fault line in my life that no professional achievement ever quite repaired.

Maybe the long string of loser boyfriends afraid of commitment were just another way for me to avoid ever feeling trapped and powerless again.

Suddenly my whole life takes on a darker hue. Maybe I didn't just fail on my own, maybe I was derailed. Maybe I was meant to have another life and Cameron stole it from me.

His hands grab desperately for me as he falls backwards, clutching empty air.

The puddings arrive and I tear my gaze away from their plates thinking of the path not taken. I could have had love, a husband, and a twenty-year old son by now.

It's surreal to think about.

It's also a waste of time.

10

THE MAKEOVER (EPISODE I – A NEW HOPE)

'How's it going in there?' Emma's waiting *outside* of the cabin (small mercies).

My wardrobe is mostly populated by work outfits. I usually wear tasteful tweed pencil skirts with bourgeois roll-up cashmere sweaters and a side of pearl earrings circa middle-aged frumpy.

So Emma's doing an intervention. We're in the slutty corner of a global-mass-produced-by-child-slave-labour fashion shop. Oh yeah, it's cheap. It's youthful. It's disposable.

So this is the point in every rom-com where the main character (me) is transformed from an ugly duckling into a graceful swan.

Don't look away! Here comes the fairy tale!

I come out of the cabin in a too short leopard miniskirt looking like a prostitute.

'Oooh nice!' her eyes skim over my enormous glutes in full view in this outfit.

'You're sure?' I tug on the skirt and shuffle this way and that to get a look at myself in the mirror. Not great.

'Yes, definitely sure.'

'Mmmh,' I say.

'Try the next one!'

She must know better than me, I mean look at her life:

Handsome husband: check.

Beautiful kids, one of each: check.

Semi-detached with a rose garden: check.

What have I got to lose? *I'll just follow her advice,* I think, as I pull the décolleté up and fidget in the pink tube dress she's picked for me. I look like freaking breakfast pork sausage but when I come out, Emma ~~squeaks batting her hands spastically like a seal.~~

Note to self: *No. No, no, no. That won't do.* I must watch out for how mean I am to her. Even if they're only thoughts. Emma's been nothing but kind to me, all the years we've known each other and I repay her by having uncharitable thoughts about her weight all the time.

I'm not exactly a wisp of a girl myself... I suppose that's why I'm so cruel to her: I hate in her what I hate in myself. The flab, the wobble, the slight ridiculousness of fatness. As I jump up and down to try and fit my thighs into a too-tight pair of jeans, I realise that what really gets me is that even though she's fatter than me, she still managed to get the life I want, when all the magazines say that you can only get love if you're thin. So Emma's whole existence is an indictment of my failure to find a man despite being thinner than her. Something doesn't add up here. It's almost as if magazines have been lying to us all this time. Shock, horror.

Ok, new resolution: I will stop having mean thoughts about Emma's love handles and focus on getting a man of my own. Even though, damn it, ~~I look better than her, I should have found one way before she did.~~ *Stop it Lily*!

This whole competition thing has got to stop too. I'm not

even competing for the same man, there's no need to compare myself to her or anyone else for that matter. Huh. Maybe that's why we're all so mean and judgemental to each other. The system pitches us against each other. Well whatdoyouknow, turns out my mean thoughts weren't really my own. Even in the privacy of my own skull, I was in thrall to the patriarchy and I didn't even realise it.

That's it. No more mean thoughts about Emma. Or fat. Or other women.

Girl power!

Well, right after I'm done selecting a tarty outfit in order to achieve the ultimate goal of patriarchy: to tie myself to a man and (possibly) procreate (or have fun trying). Yes, girl power right after that.

AT LENGTH, all shopped out, we select:

1. An insanely tight, much too short dress, which I'll wear exactly once (regretted it).
2. A black leather skirt for adding Instantaneous Concentrated Tartiness ™ to any outfit.
3. Fishnet stockings. Because of course.
4. Polyester tops with plunging necklines that make my armpits stink.
5. A pair of black jeans so tight they might as well be leggings.

BACK AT MY PLACE, a feverish wardrobe upheaval starts.

A mountain of clothes grows on my bed.

Emma is sitting on top of the covers, legs extended in

front of her, texting her husband in between my outfit changes.

'He won't babysit for much longer, I'm going to have to get back.'

'It's not babysitting if they're his own kids,' I yell from the bathroom as I wiggle into shape-controlling tights and have to stop breathing for a minute. 'It's called parenting for God's sake.'

She doesn't answer. I come out and strike a pose in front of her, wearing a tastefully cut midi dress I just got last week.

'No. Nope. Out of the question.'

'Why?' I wail.

'You look like you're going to present in front of a boardroom full of executives. That's why.'

'Well, to be fair, that's what I do for a living. At least, he'll get a realistic view of how I dress and who I am. No?'

'No. Off, off, off. Show me the slutty outfits we got you today.'

Grumbling, I go back to my bathroom and come out wearing a Sandy-from-Grease outfit. Sandy-after of course. The only thing that's missing from this costume is the *you-can-fuck-me-anywhere-you-want-bad-boy* expression, the cigarette dangling from the lip and the eighties perm. Instead, I'm sporting a *do-I-really-have-to* look on my face, I'm brushing my teeth and my hair is straightened within an inch of its life.

'Aaaah. That's perfect.'

'I look fat and ridiculous.' I mumble, spraying toothpaste.

'Try the miniskirt on then. You know, men like curves. Look at the [insert name of latest trashy reality TV minor celebrity here]. She shows off her rump and men lap it up.'

'Urgh.' Well, what did you expect? A Cinderella moment where I'd shave my legs, slather on some makeup and somehow morph into a sex symbol and proceed to turn heads at the school prom?

Oh get real.

Make-over scenes are a ploy to keep women obsessing over their appearances and believing that a magic wand can somehow fix everything we hate about ourselves and make men see us as we want to be seen: with loving eyes.

I particularly hate it when they remove the glasses in those films. Do men really feel so threatened by women who are smarter than them that it's practically mandatory to have the symbolic dumbing-down, eyeglass-removal scene in all teenage rom-coms?

Emma shoos me out of my own flat and says a flustered goodbye, wishing me luck on the date as she hurries back home before her gorgeous husband has a chance to miss her.

Watching her go, I feel an odd mixture of gratitude and resentment. In a vaguely sickening way, what she did today reminds me of pre-sex, pre-nuptial rituals of old, when large groups of women ~~trussed~~ pimped-up the ~~turkey~~ bride, plucking her ~~feathers~~ hair in preparation for ~~Christmas~~ sex. There's something atavistic about the ritual and so we warm to it and recognise it in our millennia-old bones. But don't you wish sometimes that the guy grew to like the girl just as she is? That you could just rock up to a date wearing your usual and feel valued for your authenticity?

Ha.

So off I go, looking like a two-bit whore and guess what? My date likes it.

11

INTERLUDE: FROGS. SO MANY FROGS

DATE 11

He takes me to a salsa class for singles and then dances with anyone but me. But hey hoe, when in Rome…

Moist hands clutching mine too hard.

Inexpert feet traipsing over my toes.

Foul breaths against my face.

Happy days.

I approach an ok looking guy and ask him to dance. He looks me up and down thoroughly and then says: 'no.'

'Wow, gallantry is still alive and kicking.' I mutter.

'Hey, you wanted equality, so now you gotta live with the consequences.'

He's got a point. But still. Arsehole.

DATE 13

SHISH KEBAB GUY chats me up on the phone for two solid hours the night before, to convince me to come on a date with him. He's an estate agent and I have to admit, his sales technique worked, but while he looked quite adventurous, posing with an ice-axe against an Artic landscape, he turns up to the date looking like a shell of a human being, dark bags under his eyes, bad teeth, scrawny.

He takes me to a pool hall for teenagers and then we drift to a shish kebab joint under the pouring rain. I really don't mean to be demanding but I'm no longer sixteen.

Sensing that we'll probably never see each other again, we walk to the Tube platform and wait for the train to arrive. It's Saturday night, so of course everything down here smells of vomit as drunk people make a spectacle of themselves up and down the platform, cackling like idiots.

As the foul air starts to swell, lifting my hair, stirring the noxious smells and toxic fumes and rustling through my skirt, he lunges, grabs my neck (*don't grab my neck*) and rams his tongue down my throat. Perhaps he wanted to take something before he leaves. Something I would not have given him willingly.

Mind the gap between fairy tales and real life.

When I get home, there's a lovely text on my phone:

'Good night to you and your tongue.'

Ew.

Ew, ew, ew.

12

WHAT DO JUSTICE AND MY DATE HAVE IN COMMON?

DATE 15

I've just locked my front door when the sound of a throat being cleared makes me jump out of my skin.

'Lily? Lily Blackwell?'

They never look like their photos. But man, this one's a good surprise! Hubba hubba.

'I... yes. Oh, I didn't realise we'd meet here...' I stammer, reaching up on tiptoes to give him a kiss on the cheek. His stubble lightly scratches my lips as his hand loops around my waist. I breathe in the warm, musky scent of him.

Mmmh, nice.

Flustered, I detach from him and start towards the stairs. Who knows, this blind date could turn out ok. Scarlett didn't send me a dud. Hurray!

'May I come in?' His voice is deep and sexy.

'Well,' I laugh, looking at him over my shoulder as I walk towards the lifts, 'that's a bit forward. We'd better go have a drink first, don't you think?'

He frowns but doesn't move an inch. A beat later, his

face relaxes as he gets his wallet out of his pocket and lifts it up.

Oh crap.

Crap. Crap. Crap.

'Detective....Uh... Mulligan? I... oops sorry.' I laugh but it comes out sounding frantic. 'I thought you were my date.'

'Yes, I figured as much.' He clasps his hands behind him and just stands there, feet apart, looking delicious and terrifying.

I fumble with my keys and despite trembling hands and slight hyperventilation finally get my door open. Then, trying to sound breezy, I show him to the living room, noticing all the things I should have tidied up.

'May I offer you a tea or a coffee?' I say, picking up a discarded jumper from the sofa.

'Tea please.'

'Milk? Sugar? I call out from the open kitchen as he checks out the photos of my family and friends who are smiling up at him from their frames. 'Oh sorry, I only have almond milk, is that ok?'

'That's fine.'

I flinch. He's so much closer than expected. Distractingly, his voice sounds deep and dark, like melting chocolate.

'May I ask why you're here?'

He doesn't answer right away and as the silence stretches, it occurs to me that until a week ago, having a handsome policeman in my kitchen would have been a source of unmitigated, innocent delight, on par with hunky firemen coming to sell me a calendar. I hate this; I want to go back to being good and feeling blameless, but something tells me, that will never be possible again.

I feel his gaze detailing me as I put on the kettle. He's

leaning against the kitchen bar, completely relaxed. His conscience is probably at peace. Lucky bastard.

'There's been a death. We're interviewing anyone who might have witnessed the events.'

A shudder slithers up my spine. I make sure there's a surprised expression on my face before I turn around, holding the box of teabags against my chest.

'Who died? Anyone I know?'

'Cameron Stanley,' he says observing me.

'Oh my God. That's terrible. I just met him the other day.' I let my eyebrows rise up.

He flips through a notepad, 'at a school reunion, is that correct?'

The kettle starts to whine as my heart tries very hard to knock itself out against my chest wall.

'Yes.' I plop two teabags in the mugs, hands shaking. 'Yes, that's right. What happened? Did he have an accident? He seemed fine a few days ago.'

'We can't divulge any details of the investigation. Did you notice anything odd or suspicious, anyone who shouldn't have been there?'

'Oh it's hard to say, I hadn't seen these people in twenty years, I couldn't possibly say who half of them were.'

He makes a note, 'And I was told you left the event for a significant amount of time?'

Fuckety, fuck, fuck, fuck.

My back is to him. The hot water splashes on my fingers as I pour, trembling, but I bite the inside of my cheek and turn around with the tray in my hands and a smile on my face.

'I have no idea what you mean. If I went anywhere it was to the loo.'

'For how long?'

I chuckle, 'well the usual, ten maybe fifteen minutes. You know how the lines can get on the ladies' side.'

'At what time did you get home?'

'Mmmh, I don't know.' Why is he asking me all these questions? Does he suspect something? 'Why?'

'Oh, it's just so I can confirm the ME's estimate for the time of death.'

Gosh, they're doing an autopsy. *Shit. Shit. Shit.* Is the Met treating this as a murder?

'Erm... I think I got home at about 11:00pm'. Which I know is a good hour after he died. But I don't know if I just included myself in the pool of suspects or exonerated myself. Hopefully the latter. Maybe there won't be any suspects at all if they rule it an accident.

'Nice place you've got here,' he says as he sits on the sofa.

'Thank you.'

'Do you live alone?'

Now what kind of question is that?

He sees me hesitate and clarifies, 'is there anyone who could attest to your whereabouts last Friday night? Anyone who could confirm at what time you came home?'

'No, I'm single. I mean, there is no one who can confirm it.'

'Right. Well it would help a lot if you could find someone to vouch for you that night.'

'Oh, I know! I took a cab. I'm pretty sure I still have the receipt,' I grab my purse, glad not to have to look him in the eye for a while. A few moments later, I find the piece of paper and hand it to him. 'But I don't understand, didn't you say it was an accident?'

There's the tiniest beat of silence. 'This is just procedure,' he smiles.

I wish he weren't so utterly irresistible. It's hard to focus on pure terror through the haze of blooming pheromones.

'Maybe the porter will be able to help. Shall I take you to see him?'

'No, that's fine I can manage.' He probably wants to question him about me. *Oh this is not good. Not good at all.*

He drains his cup and gets up. Tall, very close.

'Right, I'd better let you get back to your evening.' His eyes glide over my too-short black dress, the sparkly threads shining darkly through the fabric, as it hugs my curves in all the right places.

I lower my burning face and tuck my hair behind my ear as I walk him back to the door, pulling on my coat to hide my exposed thighs.

'I don't usually dress like this...'

'You look lovely.'

His voice feels like the first sunshine on my skin after a long winter. For some reason I feel an urge to talk to this man, to explain myself to him.

'Oh, erm... thank you... you see I've decided I've had enough of being alone and I want to be happy. So I'm going on forty dates this year, before... well, in order to find love.'

'I see...' he says it kindly, I search his face for sarcasm or pity and find none.

The lift is on the fritz again, nothing works in this building quite yet. So we walk back downstairs together, our footsteps echoing in the empty staircase, the chill of the unadorned, unfinished walls lending a strangely expectant quality to our time together.

'I figure that, you know, it's a numbers' game: forty-four percent of people in London are single. That's a little under four million people, of which two million are men, skim off the minors and the seniors and you should still be left with a few hundred thousand to choose from.' What on earth am I doing? *Just stop talking Lily for Pete's sake.* 'If I approach it rationally, there's no reason I can't find someone to settle down with. It's just maths, isn't it?'

'Happiness is not an ideal of reason but of imagination,' he says pensively as he holds the door open for me at the bottom of the staircase. Wow. I can't even remember the last time a man opened a door for me.

'Sorry? I didn't get that.'

'Happiness. Kant didn't think you could achieve it through rationality. I just mentioned it… erm… in case it helped.'

'Oh, I see' but I don't see at all. 'Kant?' that seems like an odd source for a policeman to quote.

'Philosophy. A hobby of mine. Never mind.'

I look up and it's his turn to blush slightly. I'm not sure why.

We look for the porter but there's no sign of him, as usual. The entrance area is little more than a building site, with its semi-damp plaster, scaffolding and tarps, so we give up and he says he'll try calling again another day. I'm all at once happy and apprehensive about that.

As we step outside, in the fragrant summer night, we stop, facing each other. It's like the slow motion rewind of a good night kiss scene.

He hesitates and sort of sways a bit, as if I were a magnetic gravity field, but he pulls back. I don't want him to look at me too closely, he'll see my guilt somehow.

'Sorry I couldn't be more help,' I say, wanting him to kiss me. Absurdly.

He says nothing. He knows. He already knows what I did.

'Hey, you're Scarlett's friend, right?'

The hunky policeman and I turn to see a man approaching with a big smile. My blind date. Scarlett didn't lie, he's not bad looking. Big ears, toothy grin, goofy. I turn around to the handsomer, more intense detective.

'I won't keep you,' he says, 'contact me if you think of anything that would help the investigation.'

'I will.'

I won't. I can't.

He leaves and I'm equal parts relieved and heartbroken to see him go. I stare much too long at his back until Scarlett's friend closes the distance, plants himself in front of me and gives me an awkward half hug, half air kiss.

'Matt, right?' I sigh.

Why are they all called Matt?

MATT HASN'T BOTHERED to plan where to take me, so I end up suggesting a place and, as it's Friday night, of course it's crowded and noisy. Perched on a bar stool that's meant to make the drinks trendier or something, I try to find my balance while also battling with the hem of my skirt and straining to hear him.

The policeman is onto me. I can feel it. He made it sound like an innocuous routine inquiry but why would they investigate an accidental fall?

'Red or white?'

Why question *me*? How does he know that I'm involved? Was there a witness?

'Would you like something to drink?'

He knows. I should turn myself in before it goes any further. Say that it was in self-defence. But it wasn't, was it? Cameron wasn't trying anything. Not this time anyway.

'Hello?' Matt sounds like a petulant child.

'Pardon?'

'Wine?' he asks.

'Oh sorry, I'm doing dry May, you know, raising some money for charity.' I'm not. I'm doing dry-all-year-long. But the excuse usually does it although he looks disappointed. It's usually easier to kiss a girl who's drunk, I suppose.

'What was your name again?'

'Lily.'

'I'm dyslexic so names don't mean anything to me. I can never remember them. It's not personal.'

I really can't imagine anything much more personal than bothering to remember my name before a date.

'What do you mean it has no meaning?'

'Well, a table means table.' He points.

'Yes, I know what a table is.' *Dial down the sarcasm Lily.*

'But what was it again…?'

'Lily.' *For fuck's sake.*

'Lily doesn't have a meaning, so I forget it.

'That's ok, Pete, I don't mind.'

'My name is Matt actually.'

Gee really? Apparently he has no sense of humour either.

'Oh sorry.' *Not sorry.*

13

INTERLUDE: RIP BUNNY

I object to porn. *I really dislike the whole tawdry, repulsive, exploitative industry,* I think, as I come with a sigh/moan, while watching porn.

What can I say; it's been two years. I'm not made of stone. And the book of erotic short stories I used to read fell to pieces. *I'll just have a peek online*, I thought a couple of years ago. And then I fell down the rabbit hole.

I scroll through the site looking for a video. Ah there, maybe this one. No. Really no. Half way through the two-minute clip I have to stop. The girl looks like she's in pain and she's throwing scared glances at the cameraman. I'm worried she's being exploited. I wonder if there's anything I can do. Probably not much. Definitely not come.

This happens to me all the time; instead of focusing on the action, I find myself scrutinising the girl's face. Who is she? Why does she do this? Has she been tricked by her boyfriend? *He doesn't love you sweetie, don't do it for him.* Does she think this is the path to film stardom? *Oh honey, no. You'll never make it that way.* Where are her parents?

My mind wanders, guilt lacing the pleasure, as I question my feminism, my ethics, my basic human decency. Am I not perpetuating the exploitation of my fellow sisters by financing an industry that thrives on consuming and spitting out its victims? Of course I am and I despise myself for it. But mostly I despise this industry.

I mean it's not difficult to hate it. A scroll through the main page (the main page!) of a standard site (not even kinky or anything) unearths gems like: "Sweet tiny teen used by Daddy for anal" Ew. *Child services please, I'd like to report a crime. Who watches this shit?* Or "Japanese girl faints and all her colleagues take advantage." Ew. Ew. Ew. *What the fuck is wrong with men?*

The videos on page one usually start out with abusive spanking, then it veers into strangling on page two and somehow suddenly slips right into gang rape on page three. The level of violence and normalised abuse against women just takes my breath away. Not in a good way. They zoom in on the abuse. They like it. It's like the boys are taking revenge on the small abdications and failures of their daily lives. Their bruised egos get a little makeover in this dark corner of the net.

I'm not invited. I snuck in here unannounced and I definitely know that I'm not welcome. These male POV videos they're not meant for me and they tell an interesting tale about how men really see us: we're just anuses, vaginas and assorted holes, pieces of meat to stick their dicks into.

And don't even get me started on the cookie-cutter-iness of it all.

<u>Step one</u> *(it's always step one because we all know who comes first, don't we?):* man gets blowjob – that part usually takes seventy-five percent of the video. Hey maybe the dating coach was onto something after all. Men do seem to like a BJ, complete with gagging sounds and white

showing around her eyes when the oxygen makes itself scarce.

I *hate* it when the man holds the poor woman's head further down his shaft even as she starts to gurgle unappetisingly. *That's coercion. Get your hands off her.*

Step two: perfunctory fanny exploration. Porn actors clearly have no fucking clue about giving head to a woman. Their tongues slobber all over like overeager puppies eating their dinner, their fingers pathetically nudge the beast, as if a forefinger's girth could compete with a penis. *That's not the point of fingers you numpty.* Fingers bend. Aaaaaaah, now the penny drops. Clearly they haven't had any briefing about the G spot and aren't even looking for it. And I have to admit the women aren't helping as they start yelping with fake orgasms as soon as the guy's tongue vaguely comes into the vicinity of their hoo-hahs.

Step three: penetration: usually in a position (a) as uncomfortable as possible for all parties involved and (b) as visibility-enhancing as possible for the camera. Cue woman sitting on a man, her back to him, so the cameraman can sit below the jiggling scrotal sack and give the viewer a good ogle. I won't even mention the acne on the actresses' bum cheeks from all the plucking and the unsanitary back to front stuff. Ew. Frankly, if anyone ever came in that position, I'll eat my hat.

Step four: some sort of ode to spunk. Pearl necklaces, creampies, whitish globs dripping from overheated holes. Pretty much every video always ends with a bloke essentially saying "Look what I did! Aren't I powerful and mighty? Look at the sheer volume of jizz I got out of my wand!" *Yes, well done boy wizard.* Women routinely get four kilos of miniature humans out of their vaginas. But nice drip of yogurt you got there.

My trusty pink rabbit hiccups. I got it at Emma's hen do, nigh on fifteen years ago. My exes were always a bit intimidated by the sheer size of the bubble gum pink contraption but if I'm honest, the dildo side of things leaves me indifferent. The vibrator on the other hand… Men always think it's about the penis. Penis size, penis girth, penis shape and penis bend. But it's really all about the clit, guys.

I'm nearly there, nearly there…nearly…

And then my pink rabbit dies.

Not out-of-batteries-dies. Really dies.

Oh no.

Ludicrously, the first thought that crosses my mind is how will I dispose of my pet bunny's body? Should I put it in recycling? Or general waste? First world problems.

What am I going to do now? Finish by hand I suppose. And then I should probably find myself a real-life boyfriend. I've been in this dark recess of cyberspace for far too long.

14

THE ONE WITH THE OTHER WOMAN

'Lily?' Someone's banging on my door.

What the hell, it's ten pm on a Wednesday.

'Lily! Are you there?' It's Emma.

'Just a minute!'

Flushed, I yank my pyjama bottoms on, wash my hands and hurry to my front door. Emma's on my welcome matt, looking bedraggled and drenched and as soon as the door opens she pushes past me and into the living room.

'Where is he? Where is he?' she yells.

'What? Who?'

'Don't pretend! I know he's here. I heard the two of you together.'

Blushing crimson, I stammer 'I... no...'

She's crying as she barges into my bedroom, finds the messy bed sheets, slams the ensuite door open yelling 'Charles! Charles!'

'Erm... look, Emma, there's no one here.'

She turns around, eyes wild, her hair like fumes around her red face.

'I... erm... what you heard. I was, you know... having a moment... on my own.' I add unhelpfully.

It takes a full minute for the information to process. Then she seems to deflate.

'Why don't you go sit, I'll be right back.'

I root around until I find a bottle of Amaretto I once bought to make tiramisu. It's a couple of years old but maybe it will do the trick. Grabbing the biscuit tin, I go meet her on the winter balcony. She's collapsed on one of the armchairs and is staring blankly at the river. Today the Thames is dark liquid pewter against the inky sky and London's ochre lights glow like embers against the night.

'He's gone.'

I know better than to ask who. Charles. But why? They're so in love. They're so perfect together. The life-goals couple.

'What happened?' I ask, offering her the biscuits.

'Nothing! We were just having a normal day. Everything was fine. Then he gets up from the breakfast table and says it's over. He's leaving me.'

Her eyes are haunted as she stares at me. 'He said he couldn't bear to live with me anymore and he left.' Her face is the picture of astonishment. 'He just up and left.'

She struggles with the bottle's square cap and takes a long swig, choking a bit.

'But why on earth would you think he was here?'

'You... He... for the last fifteen years he's been saying that he wished I'd be more like you. That I'd let myself go. That I wasn't as smart as you, that I was a parasite while you properly succeeded. I mean look at you,' she waves vaguely at me 'look at this bloody flat. Of course I thought he left me for you.'

'But sweetie, I would never do this to you.'

She deflates a little at that, 'where is he then?'

I stay silent for a few minutes, working through my own incredulity.

The story comes in dribs and drabs, interspersed with sobs, and swigs of Amaretto. 'It's all my fault, Lily. You remember, at the start, I had to give him in an ultimatum after seven years together. He said that ever since, he felt coerced and resented me for everything in our marriage from childcare to in-law visits.'

Little by little a different picture emerges, a far cry from the picture-perfect image I'd fabricated in my mind. He used Emma's guilt to great effect to do next to nothing and extricate himself to go to the pub with his mates several times a week, coming back drunk at 2 am. There was not a whole lot of sex from what I gather. A few half-hearted couple therapy sessions.

'Maybe it's just mid-life crisis... he'll come back. I mean, it's Charles, he's head over heels for you and —'

She starts to quietly sob, 'I found receipts, Lily. He's been leading a double life for years. He bought her a car and—'

'— I'm certain it's a misunder... *What?*'

'— jewellery. All the weekends where he had to work... he was on mini-breaks with...' She looks at me askance. '... with her.'

I'm stunned. All these years... I yearned to have Emma's life and now that the veil lifts, I'm starting to see that maybe my idea of couple life might be naive.

'I'm so sorr—'

'That's not even...' her sobs become hiccups and she has to stop, nearly choking on her grief. 'I found invoices... he... he paid for her fertility treatments.'

'Oh wow.'

There's not much to say after that. We both sit, staring

out the window. I think about all the times Charles praised her. All the times he seemed to be a devoted husband, a kind father. All the times, I wistfully watched them on the dance floor thinking *why can she have a man like that and not me? She's even fatter than I am.* All the times I prayed to God to send me my very own Charles. All the times I resented her for having an easy life. Meeting him in Uni. Marrying so young. Not needing to work much. All the times I wished he'd chosen me, back when we were all teenagers.

On the other side of the mirror, Emma was looking at me and wondering if he'd have preferred a more successful wife. A slimmer wife.

I dart a glance at her. My friend. A splinter had wedged itself progressively between us and neither of us said anything. All because of a man. Having one, keeping one, competing for one.

I put my arm around her shoulder and we silently watch the river wash away the day.

15

SMELLS LIKE TEEN SPIRIT BUT ALAS, NO NIRVANA

DATE 25

School was awkward. Nerdy. There was a lot of talking in circles about philosophy and discovering Existentialism. And boys.

Unsurprisingly, few fifteen-year old boys wanted to discuss Sartre, Kafka and Nietzsche.

Well there was one.

Lennox.

Victoria station unfolds its ballet of harried travellers and décor of cheap food stalls, its chorus of pigeons and symphony of announcements, as a smile plays on my face. Two teenagers peck at each other lips. She's a brunette with curly hair down to her waist. He's ebony with sharp cheekbones and an easy smile.

Like an echo of Lennox and me, an eternity ago.

He'll be here in a few minutes surely. He's not that late yet.

Lennox was my boyfriend for a while in secondary school. We had no idea what we were doing and failed miserably to achieve what looked so easy on the silver screen. Flawless bodies arched gracefully. Camera pans left to billowing curtains as you *take my breath away. Pom-pom. Pom-pom pom-pom. Pom-pom-pom.*

Our prides wounded, still virgins, we each retreated into our own lives and regularly crash into each other, the memory of our affection, like a siren song attracting us over and over to rocks we know will sink us. Until next time.

Finally, he's here. Looking more mature, infinitely better dressed than in the nineties, his gorgeous dark brown lips parted sensually. He rubs his thumb against them and smiles.

'Aww, there you are, my Butterfly.'

I reach up on tiptoes and kiss his cheek, perching my hand on his shoulder, taking in the shaved hair, the scarf, artfully thrown around his neck, the expensive suit. He made an effort.

He smells like first fumbling kisses and inexpert bra removals. Like fevered groping and too-long goodnight kisses in the darkness outside my parents' house. He should be a small forgotten corner of my life that has faded away into distant memory, but here, in his arms, my nose remembers. My lips remember. My skin remembers, as his arm loops around me easily, as his large hand presses the small of my back, pulling me close in a long, sigh-full embrace.

'How have you been?' It's been ten years. For all I know he could be married by now. He could have five children.

He peels himself away from our full-body hug and considers me, his groin still tantalisingly pressed against mine, his arms around my shoulders. I'm fifteen again. Or as close as I'll ever be.

'Oh very well.' I tinkle happily, soaking in his attention.

'So where are we going? This is your city.'

He lives a world away. In town only until tomorrow.

The little razor cut above my ankle stings as the small wound opens again. Heavy-duty landscaping has happened for his visit.

He wraps his arm around mine and we walk to Harrods where an afternoon tea awaits. I didn't want to seem too eager. It's an appropriately London thing to do. There's alcohol involved only if one wants it to be. It can end politely with a see you next time. Or it can end late into the night. The perfect compromise.

A harpist tickles a few chords somewhere off-screen as Lennox regales me with the latest news on his awesomeness. He had potential. He imagined himself to be an exceptional life-coach but he informs me that (un)fortunately, he doesn't have clients anymore.

'So you don't offer counselling anymore?'

'No. I just trust in the universe to bring me the people I need to help. I just follow where I'm sent. Look, on the way over here, I had a really interesting session with a cabbie. I think I've changed the course of his life.'

My lips do that thing where they press together of their own volition. The array of hot pink and purple macaroons calls to me. Better than sending a barb on the improbability of a life-changed-cabbie and ruining the mood. I stuff a pop of colour in my mouth and taste its purpleness dissolve on my tongue. The diet can wait. I'm always on the bloody diet. Today's my cheat day. There.

'You don't want to eat?' I ask, worried, eying a cluster of redcurrant that's reclining languidly on a bed of lime green fluffy mousse. He hasn't touched anything.

'No, I'm fine,' he says, looking smug. 'It's too much food.' A half a cucumber sandwich is wilting on his plate, the corners of the crust-free toast looking pale and Britishly flavour-free.

I'm an ogre. I'm so fat. Why can't I stop eating? I definitely shouldn't be having this much sugar. But he did agree to have afternoon tea, didn't he? What did he expect? A paleo salad?

What is it with people and food? Can't they just enjoy it and fucking be done with it? Why does it always have to be such a statement of moral superiority?

He sips his Lapsang Souchong, surveying my distress over the rim of the porcelain cup like a cat.

'Did you get your letters?' I ask, biting self-consciously into a scone lathered with clotted cream and jam.

'Oh yes, thank you.'

After his father got a promotion, his family moved to the US so we sent each other letters, ten pages long, written by hand, every week for over three years. There are easily a hundred a fifty of them, dripping with hormones and wide-eyed puppy love. For a while, he was my diary and I was his.

Because of this mirroring emotional growth, he likes to pretend that we're one person with two bodies, one gender each. *You know, you're the woman I'd have been, if I'd been born female*, he used to write. He doesn't say that anymore.

'You're the man I'd have been, if I'd been born male,' I say.

I used to think that. I don't think it anymore. *Why do I keep saying it?* He looks at me and smiles. A faint tinge of pity on his stretched lips.

I smile back, wondering if we'll fuck tonight.

Over a thousand pages worth of teenage angst and idiocies were stacked in a shoebox in my flat. He wanted them photocopied. I spent a long evening at work, copying them for him but he complained about the quality of the copies. So I just sent his letters back to him, wholesale.

'I love re-reading the letters I wrote to you,' he says.

'Frankly, I cannot fathom why.'

'They're such a great insight into who I am.'

I suspect Lennox might be a bit narcissistic.

'Could you send me mine back please?'

It's not the first time I ask. Maybe it's the tenth. I've read enough Jane Austen novels to know that letters should always be returned. It's the gentlemanly thing to do.

'I can't. I finally figured out where they are. My ex's mother has them.'

'Which ex?' Lennox once boasted he was in the high three-hundreds.

'They're in an attic in Violet's parents house.'

Oh FFS. She was the poor girl he mentally tortured twenty years ago. He used to conduct mind experiments on her. He'd say to her 'Tomorrow, when we see each other, you will cry.' And then, he'd say to me, all proud. 'And the next day, since I'd programmed her to cry, she did!'

~~There's no way he'd try that shit on me.~~ Scratch that. He probably ~~did~~ is still doing it, as we speak. But he wouldn't tell one of his guinea pigs that they're the subjects of an experiment. That would screw up the results. Not scientifically sound.

'So why can't Violet's mother send me my letters?'

'I've lost track of where these people are.' He shrugs. I wouldn't be surprised if he actually had the lot and read his letters and my answers regularly. Like nostalgic intellectual masturbation.

There's something hollow about him, as if behind the

puppeteer's threads was really just an empty husk, behind the manipulator's bluster nothing but empty air. I can never get him to talk about anything other than women. His conquests, our long defunct relationship, the woman he hypothetically will meet one day. Although we both know she's an unlikely chimaera.

So we talk about love or what passes for love in his life. Not his job or friends or what truly matters to him or anything authentic and real. He's a stranger who used to be my (evil?) twin.

I wanted to see him today because of a promise we made to each other long ago. A pact. If neither of us is married by the age of forty and so on and so forth. Back then, forty seemed impossibly old.

If I'm honest, I'm not even sure I want him anymore, but I'm so broken and damaged with everything that's happened that I don't know who else might want me. At least he knew me before. Before I lost my hat, before I lost Jonathan, before I became a killer. Maybe if he honours the pact, we could build our relationship up again. Maybe if anyone can still love me and see something worthy and good in me, it is the man who has known me the longest and explored the depths of my soul and come back for more time and again.

'So how's you're your love life?' I tuck a strand of my glossy, straightened hair behind my ear. My heart does a little sidestep and then goes back in line, beating a tad faster. That's the question I've come here to ask. *Breathe, Lily, breathe.* I went to the hairdresser's, had the eyebrows plucked, bought a new outfit, skipped a class I normally take on Wednesdays.

'Great!' He looks up from his phone, as he finishes texting someone and puts it back on the table (face up), then changes his mind and turns the screen to show me. A twenty-year old girl is posing naked except for a red boa wrapped strategically around her limbs.

'Erm, yes?'

'She could be The One,' he says.

My heart stops for a second. Then it decides it's ok and starts beating again. Well then. No point in mentioning the pact I suppose.

'What does she do?' I say out loud. *Seventies porn star?* I think silently.

'You know, funny you should ask, I have no idea.' He bursts out laughing.

'What is she like?'

'She's really fun and easy and sweet. So young.' He smiles to himself. He really means easier to manipulate.

'How about you?' he asks.

'Oh. No one.'

He gives me a once over. 'I'd still do you.'

AND THEN HE DOES.

We walk to his hotel in the gathering dark, my cunt on fire with expectation and desire. I haven't had sex for two years by this point and my virginity has probably grown back. I wonder if it'll hurt. We're silent. All our banter exhausted by the profound lack of interest we feel for each other.

I abstain from the unbearable awkwardness at the hotel reception and simply wait for him by the lift as he gets his key.

In the dismal hotel room, the business furniture is worlds away from the teenage bedroom that witnessed our first fumbles. He undresses me perfunctorily, knowing already what my clothes hide. Knowing already what I taste like. It's like getting the same Christmas present over and over every ten years. Except it's been used. And every time there is less joy in opening it.

We get on the bed and he compliments me on my technique. Jokes that I've learnt a lot. Maybe it's an insult.

His breasts have puckered into sour little promontories and his once gorgeous ebony skin is dry and grey. He looks tired and ready to get it over with.

He kisses me, his lips engulfing mine, slobber gets all over from my chin to my nose. Then the automated gestures start. Push this, pull that, suck here and flip me over like that. I slow him down, trying to find a connection. An emotion. Something worth doing this for. Finding none, I cling to the memory of his scent. Like a madeleine, transporting me back to a time when I cared for him.

'You haven't changed,' I smile, searching for warmth in his eyes, finding none.

He says nothing.

I let him finish, taking what little pleasure there is to be had. This time feels particularly hollow. There are no feelings between us anymore. Just ghosts of a love that barely existed once. Our sex is like a haunted house. Noisy and empty.

I don't know why I keep doing this to myself.

As I get dressed while he checks his phone, spread-eagled on the devastated bed, it dawns on me that I actually do know why I'm here: I'm clinging to my youth, my naïve notion that I'd get married, maybe even with a boy I loved once. I'm still clinging to this Hallmark movie dream despite all the signs pointing to the boy becoming a cruel man that I'd want nothing to do with as the rational adult woman ~~I've become~~ I'm becoming.

Maybe this is good, maybe this is what becoming an

adult means: letting go of dreams that need an update. Maybe love isn't the answer to everything like I once thought it was.

I put my shoes on and go without a word. What would I say? See you in ten years? And probably, not even then.

16

GOING ONCE, GOING TWICE, GONE

The machine counts the moments like a heartbeat in the stretching silence. The hospital called me in the middle of the night. I didn't know I was Catherine's ICE. I'm oddly touched by that. I also find it heart breaking.

I push a strand of hair off her face and even unconscious, she shudders. Her face is smashed like a pumpkin thrown from a first floor window. It seems to have burst into red bits and pieces, the skin barely holding everything in.

The nurse said the police think she was mugged. She let me into Catherine's room, she didn't have to but she did.

The ICU is calm, it's three am. I sense the room-full of other beds behind our blue curtain, the rhythm of other breaths taken in agony, the shadow of other small shapes huddled under thin blankets.

Catherine is so broken that it's hard to imagine she'll ever be whole again. She has permanent damage to one eye, bruises all over her torso, a broken rib and they can only guess at the state of her internal organs. Her Crown of Thorns ring is still on her intact hand, glinting in the darkness. The machine's red light bounces off it at intervals, looking like blood on the sharp little thorns.

I MUST HAVE FALLEN asleep because I'm woken by a hand on my shoulder, softly shaking me. I wake up with a start, grabbing the wooden chair's handles and blinking to take in the new day. It's early morning. The nurses are bringing the patients' trays and a very handsome man leans over me, his face only a few inches away from mine.

'You must be Lily.' His Australian accent is just audible under the words' surface. 'I'm Brett, sorry to meet in such circumstances. Cathy has told me so much about you.'

'Oh, um, hi,' I manage, rubbing my eyes.

He smiles, his perfect teeth aligned in a neat Ken-like row. His perfect face is the picture of gratitude and concern, his perfect jaw is strong and forceful, his perfect features are elegant but sexy. His perfect hair is thick and glossy and as he stands back up, he runs a hand through it.

His hand is not perfect.

The skin over his right knuckles is torn and angry red.

He sees my glance and chuckles. 'Serves me right for trying to fight them off, eh?'

I swallow and straighten my clothes, sitting up. 'I hear the police are looking for the muggers.'

'Thank God I was there. Imagine what they'd have done to her otherwise.'

'She's so lucky,' I feel a tremor of unease as I say it and wonder why. Given the state of her, I suppose I mean lucky to have a man to defend her. A man who looks like Brett. Yet the unease burrows deeper in my gut and I can't chase it away.

He goes in search of a chair and while he's gone Catherine stirs.

'Hey there, sweetie.' I whisper as I hover, unsure what to do. I don't know where to touch her. No part of her seems intact. So I alight on her uninjured hand. 'I'm here, I'm here,' I say, over and over.

The machine must have sounded an alarm somewhere because the nurse comes back to check in on her. 'Ah, there you are, love. Welcome back to the land of the living,' she says.

Catherine tries to talk but instead, she winces and whimpers.

'Don't move, don't try to talk,' the nurse soothes, holding her down gently. 'You're going to make a full recovery.' checking her pupils and jotting something down on her chart. 'Look your friend is here. Everything's going to be alright, love.'

One of Catherine's eyes is bandaged but the other one is opened just a sliver, the lid swollen and already turning deep purple. Her eye follows me, as I adjust her blanket and she makes a soft sound, somewhere between a moan and a thanks. The nurse throws us both a glance and a smile as she leaves.

'Just lie down.' I whisper, fighting tears. 'Rest. You're safe. I'm here. I won't let anything happen to you.'

The curtain rattles as Brett comes back. Absorbed with his chair, he doesn't notice that Catherine's awake, doesn't see the expression on her face when he comes in, but I do. Her eye widens and I feel her tense under my palm, as the heart rate monitor emits little pings of panic.

Nobody else notices, in the bustle of the morning activities. Nurses are pushing trolleys of breakfast trays, curtains are pulled with a racket of metal rings, hellos are exchanged. No one notices. But I do.

No one notices as he turns around, having put down the chair and leans over her, whispering, 'Darling, finally, you're awake. I told the police about the muggers who attacked you yesterday.'

She recoils as he kisses her forehead.

'You're just fortunate they didn't have acid or knives.'

Her hand clenches under my palm.

'You best tell the police about the three young black men I chased away.'

Then remembering that I'm here, he turns to me and smiles his perfect smile, taking his seat.

The nurse arrives with Catherine's tray and she reminds us sternly that only one person can be at her side. I say my goodbyes but as I leave Catherine's small hand clutches mine and I have to open her fingers one by one, whispering that she'll be ok, that I must go to work.

'Brett, do you have a moment?' I say, as I put my coat on.

He hesitates.

'Just a coffee, then you can come back here in no time.' I smile, making sure to pitch my voice high and needy.

'Of course,' he smiles widely.

We walk out of the hospital, making small talk until we find a busy Starbucks. I order us two lattes and he goes in search of a table. While the barista is busy making our drinks, I check my texts and bring Scarlett up to speed, then gather the two coffees and join him. Pulling the extra chair towards me, I perch my handbag on top our two trench coats and turn towards him.

'So, Lily, what did you want to talk about?' He takes a big swig of his double shot large latte and observes me over the plastic rim.

'It's so nice to finally meet you, Brett,' I say, involuntarily flicking my hair. Yes, he's *that* handsome.

'I've heard so much about you and... Scarlett and Emma, right?'

'Oh yes!' I smile. I don't mention that Catherine never spoke about him to us at all. In fact, this suddenly strikes me as odd. If I had a boyfriend like Brett, I'd shout it from the rooftops. I'd be posting shots of his gorgeous face on Insta every five minutes. The unease squirms in my stomach again.

Why am I being so ditzy? Oh gawd, I'm being that girl, aren't I? *Get a bloody grip Lily, he's pretty yes. But you need some answers.*

'Listen Brett, I asked you here because there are a few things I can't work out. Why was Catherine alone on the street, at this time of night? Where were you?'

'I was parking the car, she shouldn't have been alone that long. I just couldn't find a parking space.'

That seems reasonable. But the worm of doubt continues to burrow. 'But why did they attack her and leave her gold ring? That makes no sense.'

'Maybe I got there just in time,' he shrugs, wrapping his injured hand around the hot drink and taking another long gulp.

My wood stirrer falls off the table and as I bend down to pick it up, I notice blood on the toe of his shoe. He must have gotten that when he strained to pick Catherine up, right?

Back up top, I study his handsome face as he finishes his coffee and I can't help but blurt out 'What did you mean when you said it was lucky they didn't have knives?'

He smiles but the perfection of it is marred by an unpleasant edge now. 'Just what I said.' He checks his watch. 'Look I have to go back to Catherine. What is this about?'

'Oh sorry, it's nothing,' I chuckle with embarrassment. I can't put my finger on it. Why am I so uneasy?

'I understand that you're on your own, Lily. So you must know what can happen to a woman alone at night. London's a dangerous city.'

Is that...? Did he just...?

I'm trying and failing to reconcile his perfect face with his words when his expression changes from smugness to doubt.

He breaks eye contact and reaches for his jacket but it's under the pile of my stuff.

'Allergy' he rasps.

'What?'

'EpiPen.' He's fumbling now, trying to pull out his jacket, looking panicked.

'Oh gosh, come I'll help you inject it.' I take our coats and my bag and hurry downstairs, searching through his pockets while he wheezes and loosens his tie.

There's no one downstairs, it's a dusty basement full of cardboard boxes and sacks of coffee grounds. I guide him to the disabled loos and he collapses on the bathroom floor, hands clasped around his throat.

My stomach gives a flop and a painful churn. This doesn't feel like fear though. It's... *Oh no.* My stomach's contorting in pain from my lactose intolerance. I drank his coffee. I gave him my almond milk latte by mistake.

Oh my God, oh my God, oh my God.

What have I done?

Hands shaking, I search his jacket and extract the EpiPen from the inside pocket as he tries to unbutton his shirt but his hands are too weak by now.

Wait.

A thought pushes its way to the surface of my panicked mind. Maybe I could use this to get some answers. What is it about this guy that makes me so uneasy? Catherine's smashed face flashes in front of my eyes, the ruined eye, the blood, the bruises.

Yes, I should get some answers.

Standing above him, clutching the EpiPen against my chest as he writhes on the floor, I fight the urge to help him and say 'Tell me the truth, what happened to Catherine?' I was hoping to sound calm and firm but really I sound like a petulant child.

'She...' he rasps, '... it's none of your fucking business what happens between a man and his woman. Just open the... EpiPen.' He tries to reach for it but misses.

And with a flash it all becomes clear. He's the one who hurt Catherine. There were no muggers. His angry red knuckles are the ones who disfigured her delicate face. His expensive shoe has blood on it because he kicked her until her ribs broke.

Watching him struggle with his breath, lying on the grimy floor, I realise that I have a unique opportunity here: I must use it as a warning.

'Promise you'll leave Catherine alone, go back to Australia and never bother her again.' I squeak.

'You... did this on purpose?... I'll fucking kill you, bitch.' his expression morphs and his perfect features distort into something so intense that I recoil. *Uh-oh.* What do I do if he doesn't promise to leave Catherine alone? Kill him? Ha, ridiculous, I just don't have it in me.

Or do I?

It was just an accident on the roof. It was.

He's making gurgling sounds now as the air squeezes

through his constricting throat. *Oh my God. He's really dying, what am I doing?* This goes against everything I've ever been taught. I'm a good Catholic, a kind person.

'Come on, come on, come on,' I mumble as I drop his jacket and kneel next to him, on the floor strewn with loo roll and unidentified stains. After a few awkward attempts, I finally manage to break the device open, startled by the mechanism, the syringe, the popping cap but just as I raise the EpiPen to jab him in the thigh, I see his eyes. His hateful, evil eyes staring at me. Silently describing what he'll do to me now that I know who he truly is. He'll never stop hurting Catherine. He nearly killed her already this time.

'Mmh.' I hesitate, lips pressed together, head cocked, hand poised to strike.

He's reaching for my hand, his nails scratching weakly against my skin, as he wheezes.

I press my eyes closed, shutting him out.

I just need a minute. Just a few seconds to think.

And as I kneel there, hands clasped around the EpiPen as if in prayer, it dawns on me that the sounds have stopped, the trashing has stopped and when my eyes fly open, I realise that the decision is no longer mine to make.

My breath has stopped as well. I've forgotten how to breathe and remember with a gasp.

'No, no, no, no, no, no, no, no, no...' on my hands and knees, I try to revive him with awkward learned-on-TV-CPR, unsure whether I'm applying my hands in the right place. But nothing happens. His eyes are empty of evil now and his face looks beautiful. The slate wiped clean.

I don't know how long I pump his chest, saying 'No, no, no, no, no' in an endless loop. But at last, I have to admit it to myself. He's dead.

The finality of it is like a punch in the gut.

Did I mean to kill him? I can't have. I'm a good person, aren't I?

Yes, it was an accident, I was just about to inject him but I ran out of time. That's all that happened here.

Look, the syringe is right there on the floor, I was going to do it.

For a long time, I just kneel there, next to him, my mind blank as the minutes plop by to the rhythm of the leaky faucet.

Then a sort of cold calm takes over. I slip my leather gloves on my shaking hands, grab a loo roll and start wiping down surfaces. The EpiPen gets a thorough clean then I drop it back on the floor next to his hand. I wipe the handles, the sink, his cufflinks. Anything I can think of.

Then I get up, very slowly and flinch when I see a woman in the mirror, staring at me. I don't know who she is. She says nothing, she just looks at me, identical in every way but somehow different.

I push the door just a little and peek out. There's no one there. Above us, the morning's hubbub mingles with bland music but here in the darkness there's only silence and the smell of disinfectant and urine floating in the basement storeroom. I slip out, get a coin from my purse and turn the lock, so that Brett is locked in.

Then, composing my face and adjusting my clothes, I climb the stairs and emerge into the main coffee shop.

Everyone knows. They can see it branded on my face as I walk calmly to the table where we sat. People are going to prevent my escape. Or at least yell for someone to stop me. Or something.

But no. Nothing happens, no one hears my stomach churn with painful cramps as their headphones blast music into their eardrums. Nobody looks up from their screens as I grab the coffee cup I drank from. No one talks to me as I exit the shop, rummaging in my handbag, so my face is hidden from CCTV cameras.

I want to run down the street, away from my crime. But I force myself to walk normally and dive into the Tube station's bowels.

No one will remember Brett and me together.

I hope.

17

INTERLUDE: FIXED IT

"NRL player Rowan Baxter's estranged wife Hannah Clarke and their three children Aaliyah, six, Laianah, four, and Trey, three, died after their car was set on fire during the school run." (Mirror 24 Feb 2020)

What the car spontaneously combusted? Ah no. It appears the sports star committed suicide after murdering his family. See, not so hard to add this word to the headline: Mu-r-de-r.

"BRITISH SUSPECT DEVASTATED by fiancee's betrayal." (Telegraph, 28 Feb 2020)

Oh poor lamb. Wait. Then he decapitated her and put her body in a suitcase. So maybe the headline should say, oh I don't know... murder?

"BESOTTED... but when he was spurned he stabbed her 49 times." (Daily Mail, 13 April 2019)

Oh wait, then she totally deserved it. I mean how dare she leave such a "perfect", "devoted" boyfriend. A good party too, he was a maths graduate. And look at the lovely photos of him with his arm draped "protectively" around her. "Unhinged man murders his ex, stabbing her 49 times." There. Fixed it for you.

"Teenager Accused of Rape Deserves Leniency Because He's From a 'Good Family,' Judge Says.

The family court judge also said the victim should have been told that pressing charges would destroy the accused's life. He's clearly a candidate for not just college but for a good college. His scores for college entry were very high." (The New York Times, 2 July 2019)

Well, then, clearly it's all her fault. How dare the little strumpet ruin this boy's future by enticing him to rape her? I mean clearly she was a siren of temptation and he doesn't deserve to have his life ruined by her.

Funny how no one asks or cares about her future. Maybe it's because in this blooming dystopia we live in, her future mattered less than his even before *he raped her. Her value to the economy was always going to be lower than his, wasn't it? And her value to patriarchy is even lower now that she's damaged goods. So of course the judge says: save the boy. Save the better economic asset. Save the system. Sacrifice the disposable asset.*

"Man who assaulted woman worried conviction will affect yacht membership." (The West Australian, 9 Feb 2020)

Well he bloody well should... oh wait

"Assault Conviction sunk without a trace (Courier Mail, 10 Feb 2020) A man who assaulted a woman, causing her bodily harm, has had the recording of the conviction set aside- partly because of his Royal Queensland Yacht Squadron membership."

Lord, give me strength.

"Machete attack leaves woman dead in Scarborough." (The Star 11, Sept 2019)

Apparently an inert object came to life.

"Roman Polanski pulls out of César awards fearing 'lynching'. The director, whose film *An Officer and a Spy* has 12 nominations in the French 'Oscars', will miss Paris ceremony after alleging threats by activists." (The Guardian, 27 Feb 2020)

Actually No. Just no. The headline isn't that this despicable coward fears a few protesters outside the event venue. The headline is that in March 1977, Roman Polanski, 43, was charged with drugging and raping 13-year-old Samantha Jane Gailey, he pleaded guilty but escaped the US to avoid being jailed.

Fast forward to March 2020, the French equivalent of the Oscars awards him best picture. French feminists are understandably enraged. The man continues to live "on the run" from US justice, which involves jet-setting around the world, working with the best actors and winning awards.

"Girl, 17, kills herself after giving rape evidence." (The Telegraph 19 July 2002)

As described by the mother of the victim. [She was] "torn to shreds by [the rapist's] defence lawyer after spending all day on the stand. They basically called her a tart who deserved to be raped."

. . .

"Woman 'drank six Jagerbombs in ten minutes on the night she was raped and murdered'." (The Sun 20 July 2016)

How dare she drink? She was clearly asking to be murdered.

"Woman dies following alleged assault at her Cumbrian home." (The News & Star 27 Sept 2019)

Wait, what? Did this simply happen to her? Like a freak weather event? She dropped dead of her own accord? Ah no. There's a man involved. Really, what a shocker. He's in remand for grievous bodily harm with intent. How about "A man murders woman at her own home." Yeah? Enough with the passive voice already.

"Details of comic Jeff Ross' alleged relationship with underage woman publicized." (Page Six, August 5, 2020)

Underage woman. What does that even mean? A fourteen-year old is a child. Repeat after me: a child. I was still writing everything with a pink pen at that age. I hadn't had my first period yet. I can't, I just can't. Reading the press makes me perpetually furious. Oh and by the way there's no such thing as "underage sex" either. That's statutory rape.

"Number of female homicide victims rises 10% in a year. The number of women killed by a current or former partner has surged by nearly a third, fresh figures have revealed, as overall numbers of female victims of homicide hit a 14-year-high." (Guardian 13 Feb 2020).

. . .

"It is estimated that 35 % of women worldwide have experienced either physical and/or sexual intimate partner violence or sexual violence by a non-partner (not including sexual harassment) at some point in their lives." (UN report, November 2019).

That's one in three. Look to your left, look to your right. One of you has been harassed, molested or raped. Maybe it was you.

Enough is enough.

Women, if you want to stay safe, stay at home. Except that you are more likely to be killed at home by someone who claims they love you, so don't stay at home. Make sure you don't have a boyfriend because he's the most likely person to kill you, but don't go out without your boyfriend because you need someone to protect you. Don't show too much skin or laugh too loud or dance too much but come on love give us a smile. Carry your keys and your phone at all times and make sure you run far enough to burn off all those calories but don't do it in public and for God's sake don't run in shorts, that's just asking for trouble. Public transport is dangerous, but so are taxis and walking and driving on your own […] so don't do any of those things.

Men, just carry on as you were, this is not your problem ok?

Jane Gilmore (author of *Fixed It*)

18

WHAT LILY REALLY MEANS IS

The board members' eyes are trained on me like lamps in an interrogation. '...so in conclusion,' I say with all the gravitas I can muster, 'we propose to go live and we're confident that the end customer will be minimally affected by this change.'

The sharks were circling and now they jump into the fray as I sit down next to Ethan.

'This is crap,' one of them starts, 'these results should be at least ten percent higher by now, Ethan.'

Sorry but what the hell. I'm the one who just made the presentation. Can you fucking address your questions to me and not to my closest male supervisor?

'Well, actually Mark,' I say, 'you'll find that our results are perfectly in line with the projections I presented last quarter and—'

At the head of the table, the CEO holds up his right hand, his meaning clear. *Shut up, woman, leave the floor to your betters.* He doesn't even look at me but I'm so thrown by this that I stop talking for a second. It's only a hesitation, only for a second, but the damage is already done.

The amount of testosterone and tension crackling in the room is staggering. Actually come to think of it, I'm the only woman in here. There's a lot at stake today and they're all at each other's throats.

Ethan's jaw clenches. He always does that rather than say something rash. Raking his hand through his blond hair, he whips out his usual charm and jokes with the regional heads, trying to keep them at bay. The strands of his hair rearrange themselves in golden layers that fall over his eye while he tries not to antagonise the managers so much that they'll stop following his lead. *Stop mooning over your boss and get back to the task at hand, Lily.* I've had a crush on Ethan pretty much since the day I walked in to this building for my first interview eight years ago. I was so young back then and he was older, charismatic, charming. I glance at him, taking in his familiar profile: he looks older now, mid-forties, lines have appeared at the corner of his eyes but he still makes my heart lurch like a drunk.

I give an explanation on the impact for users and look at the faces around the table, they're all closed or hostile.

Darren, jumps in, 'What Lily really means is that the latest stage in the project will be completely transparent to the end user and...'

For fuck's sake. He's just repeating what I said with different words, but now everyone's nodding.

Screaming inwardly, I re-explain the mitigation plan in slow measured tones, careful not to let my voice become high-pitched. Men stop listening when you get too ~~shrill~~ passionate.

Pitch or no pitch, the men completely ignore me as Darren holds his hands out and with a joke, brings everyone to a halt. 'Lily would you mind scrolling back to the slide?' He doesn't even spare me a glance.

Fuming, I glare at him but what can I do? I comply, reluctantly relegating myself to the position of assistant. He's my blooming employee. Who even invited him to the meeting? He's not supposed to be in this room. I'm the department head for God's sake.

The room is getting more and more aggressive; years of power plays culminating in this move for Ethan's job. I'm just the pretext for the mutiny. Finally, tired of being sacrificed, I turn to Ethan, '... and we're confident that this will be the correct way forward,' I say.

Ethan and I have prepared for this meeting for over a week. Staying late in his office, heads close, as we argued over the project's feasibility while eating a hastily grabbed sandwich for dinner. We plotted how to gain the other board members' buy-in and how to present it so it became a win for the CEO until one am last night.

Ethan knows my slide deck inside and out; there isn't a single word of this presentation that we haven't pored over together and that he hasn't approved. I smile confidently at them, waiting for Ethan's confirmation. There's a beat of silence.

'Actually, Lily,' he doesn't look at me, 'this is very poor and I'm surprised you would come to this meeting so ill-prepared and waste everybody's time with this. Clearly this needs more work and you should have sought my approval on the proposal before coming to the board. Let's take this offline.'

He still doesn't look at me. 'Next item on the agenda.' The rest of the board's work is confidential, so I get up to leave and it's only when I'm out of the room, closing the door that I realise Darren has stayed inside.

. . .

FIGHTING TEARS, I make it back to my desk and suddenly all of it is just too much for me to bear. Here I am, on the one hand trying to convince a bunch of irrelevant men to do what I want them to do and I'm not even succeeding at that, while on the other hand I'm playing God and take it upon myself to end the lives of other men.

I'm ridiculous.

Who gave me the right to be judge, jury and executioner? I'm not fit to make these decisions. Only God can decide whether they should live or die. How on earth did I ever think that I could shoulder that responsibility? The weight of it...the weight of it. It's too much.

'Hey Lily, are you alright?'

Tamsin, my lovely team member is looking straight at me and she sees me. She really sees me. The others don't look up, most of them have earbuds anyway.

I wish I could tell her. I wish I could warn her not to waste her life here, so close to success that she'll feel like she's in, like she's made it. Until the day comes, when the charade is revealed in all its ugly truth. *They'll never let you in Tamsin*.

Her mauve coloured hair sways from side to side as she gestures for us to go talk somewhere private. Sometimes, I feel like her Gen-Z-ness make it impossible for us to understand each other. Then a moment like this happens and the years that separate us dissipate and I realise that we're closer than I'll ever be to my peers, who all remained in the boardroom.

She's the changing of the guard, isn't she? When I leave, she'll take over the battle. I'll be sixty and she'll be forty and she'll be where I'm now. Close and yet never in. What's the point really? What's the point of any of it?

I shake myself with a smile 'Thank you Tamsin, you're a

good person. I'll be ok. Carry on. I'm just going to take the rest of the day off, ok?'

Her eyebrows rise but she says nothing. I never take days off. I never take sick leave. I never shirk off responsibility. This is highly irregular.

Grabbing my bag, I get up and leave the irrelevance of it all, behind me.

I MARCH through the reception area, dimly registering the receptionist's urgent hand gestures through the blur of nascent tears.

'Hello Miss Blackwell,' the policeman stands up, unfurling his considerable size in my path and I nearly jump out of my skin.

Shit. At my workplace now? That's not a good development. This day just keeps getting better and better, doesn't it.

'Oh hello, mmmh... officer...'

'Detective. DS Tom Mulligan.'

'Ah. Yes.'

The receptionist's eyes go wide and her long teal-coloured nails start sending the gossip through IM with insect-like clicking. Sighing, I guide him to the meeting room floor, while my brain goes into full panic mode. Was there a CCTV camera inside the coffee shop? Did they figure out my connection to Catherine? Oh God. He's come to arrest me, hasn't he?

'Is everything alright?' he says, his gaze firmly locked into mine.

'I've had better days,' I say and then curse myself. *Jeez could I be anymore obvious?* 'It's nothing, just office politics. I shouldn't let it affect me.'

'The life of money-making is one undertaken under compulsion.'

Well that was...odd.

The man is so irritating. Always appearing when you least expect him and spouting nonsensical philosophy quotes.

'I'm sure you're more than equal to the task, whatever it may be,' he smiles. Aaaaand now I'm melting again. God really has a sense of humour doesn't he? Sending me this gorgeous, gorgeous man to be my nemesis. Ha. I'd forgotten how he makes me feel and how I can't seem to keep my mouth shut around the guy. I feel the absurd rise of words in my chest, oh wow, I *want* to tell him everything and he hasn't even asked me a single question yet.

Biting the inside of my cheek to avoid spilling my guts out, I show him to a small interview room with floor to ceiling windows on both sides and we sit down, as he takes in the luxurious surroundings, the sweeping Canary Wharf skyline, the muted elegance of the chrome furniture.

'What can I do for you Detective?'

'There was an accident. Someone died.'

'Yes the young magistrate, what was his name...'

'No, I'm afraid it's *another* accident,' he says pointedly.

I suck at this. Why did I need to remind him about the other death? *Shut up Lily.* 'Another one?' my hand lifts itself to my chest of its own accord. Blanche Dubois lives.

'Yes, your friend Catherine—'

'Oh my God is she ok? I saw her in hospital yesterday morning, did something happen to her since then?' *Oh no! Did she die in the night?*

'No, no, you misunderstand me.' He sits back and cocks his head, studying my reactions. 'Your friend is fine.

However her fiancé,' he flips his notebook to the right page, 'Brett Kelly is dead.'

'Oh how awful! Catherine must be devastated. I was going to go back to visit her today. Thank you for letting me know, I'll go see her now.' I get up but he doesn't move, so I hesitate and then sit back down.

He just observes me and says 'she was quite badly hurt.'

'Yes, she was mugged, did you find her attackers?' I mustn't trip over my own feet in my eagerness to please and answer everything.

'Did you ever meet her fiancé?'

This is a dance, isn't it? It feels like date-banter, a battle of wits and charm, a tango of smiles and words. He's trying to size up ~~his opponent, I mean date~~, erm... suspect. I ask if he found the muggers and he answers fiancé. Does that mean he knows that there were never any muggers?

'Did you ever meet Brett Kelly?' he repeats, crossing his legs and sitting back in the leather chair.

'Very briefly when I visited yesterday.' I think for a second and try to guess what he would know. 'Are you sure he's dead? He seemed fine when I left, what happened?'

'It was very sudden, allergic reaction to nuts apparently.' His eyes scan my face as he jots down something in his notebook.

'Oh no. Poor Catherine, first she gets attacked and now to lose her fiancé so soon after,' I try to imagine how I'd feel if someone decent had died instead of that scumbag.

'Wait, so why are you here?' I ask 'Are the police investigating allergies now?'

He details my face as a silence stretches and his gaze lingers on my lips. He sighs. 'Did you notice anything as you were leaving the hospital?'

'I don't think so.'

'Ah,' he jots something down in his booklet. 'You see, Lily, we know you left together, there's footage.'

Shit. 'Ah yes, you're right, it had been a long night in the hospital, so I needed a coffee and he came along to get one too. We didn't say much on the way and I had to leave right after I picked up mine.' Is that too much detail? Gosh. I need to do some research on how to successfully build an alibi and talk to the police without incriminating oneself. Also, note to self: get a lawyer.

'How long did you remain in the coffee shop?'

'Baristas, morning rush, checking my emails, you know how it is. I'm not sure,' I shrug 'anywhere between five and fifteen minutes. I was pretty out of it, didn't get much sleep. Why? Does it matter?'

He doesn't answer and some instinct tells me I just dodged a bullet.

'Where was he during that time?'

'He said he had to use the loo. I didn't pay much attention to what he did, I was in a hurry, so I just grabbed my coffee and left.'

'I see. And where did you go after that?'

'Back to my place to shower and go to work.'

'Can anybody attest to that?'

'I didn't get a live-in boyfriend since the last time we spoke, if that's what you're asking.'

He lowers his head and absorbs himself in his notes but I could swear a little smile twitches on his lips.

'Ah yes, the life of man is solitary, poor, nasty, brutish, and short.'

'Sorry? Who? Brett?'

'No, Hobbes.'

'Oh. Will that be all? I'd really like to go visit Catherine.

A couple of friends and I have been on a rota to stay with her at all times in hospital. It's my turn tonight.'

'She's not a suspect. You can visit, of course.'

'Have you told her yet?'

'Yes, an hour ago. You should go, she was very upset.'

She was? Oh gosh, what if I got the wrong man?

'Thank you Detective, I'm sorry I couldn't be more help.'

He says nothing and just observes me, as I get up and guide him back to the lifts. We take one together.

The man unnerves me. I'm sure he knows what I did.

Why else would he come to interrogate me after what looks like an accidental fall and an allergic reaction? It makes no sense.

I leave him in the grand entrance hall, feeling uneasy. He doesn't look back at me, as he steps out on the street.

I stay rooted to the spot, staring at the revolving doors as they twirl round and round, reflecting sunshine into my eyes, while he lifts his collar up and walks away.

19

COME JESUS COME

A frisson of excitement ripples through the congregation, a je-ne-sais quoi of anticipation and hope, as we bow our heads, kneel, stand up, sit, kneel some more.

The eye-candy priest is distracting me. I mean why choose a life of celibacy when your face pretty much guarantees you'd have gotten laid from-here-to-Sunday your entire life? Just looking at him makes me wet for God's sake. How's a girl supposed to concentrate on her spiritual salvation that way?

'The body of Christ.' He holds the enormous wafer up in the air like he's Charlton Heston coming down the mountain with the Ten Commandments. His head is thrown back, his eyes semi-closed in adoration. The server who holds the bell gets a tad too excited and we're treated to a symphony of tinkles as the moment stretches three beats too long. The painfully handsome priest's face is so steeped in adoration that now there's something quite off-putting about him. That level of transcendence usually comes with a healthy dose of dogmatism and craziness.

Catherine's face is healing slowly. It's been ten days already since Brett's... since the accident. She's at the green and yellow stage now and it looks like her eye will recover after all. She was lucky. Maybe it wasn't exactly luck... *you get my meaning.*

Jesus stares at me accusingly, pinned like a butterfly on his cross, dangling a few metres above our heads. It looks like his gruesome wounds will drip on our heads and his face is gaunt and lugubrious. I'm damned. I have killed a lamb of God's flock. I'm going straight to hell.

But it was an accident. *I didn't mean to switch his latte with mine* I plead with ghastly Jesus. *You have to believe me, I just took too long to help him. I tried to give him CPR but it was too late.*

Is that really what happened though? Or did I subconsciously want him to die? I should have injected him earlier. I should have tried harder to save him. Oh God. What have I done?

I'm full of tears today and it's like the merest prick will empty me. Maybe it's being here in church. When I'm out there in the world, my anger is raw and all-consuming but when I'm here it's quietly, gradually replaced with guilt and shame until I'm no longer angry at anyone but myself.

We all kneel.

'Lord I am not worthy...' I whisper, meaning every syllable.

'That you should enter under my roof...' Scarlett waggles her eyebrows, pointing at the priest with her chin.

'...but only say the word and my soul shall be healed,' Catherine enunciates, her scabbed forehead resting against her intertwined fingers, eyes tightly shut.

When I embarked on my dating campaign, I thought only of my fortieth birthday but now it occurs to me, as I release an incense-laced sigh that I'm inadvertently mimicking Jesus's desert crossing for forty ~~days~~ dates and forty nights. Except he passed with flying colours while I fell prey to the demons.

Is the devil in the temptation of the flesh or in blood and vengeance, I wonder? Not sure at all. In any case, I failed miserably at both.

I can't even face confession anymore. I'd surely be excommunicated. It's a wonder God doesn't strike me down for daring to enter His House. I stifle a sob and clasp my hands together tighter, begging for forgiveness.

'Did you hear?' our pew neighbour asks.

'Yes, of course, that's why we came tonight,' Scarlett whispers, breathless with glee.

We don't usually come to Saturday evening mass but Scarlett insisted. Said it would do us all good to cheer up. The church is nearly full because our pastel coloured newsletter, printed on the ancient machine at the back of the church announced it last week: Singles event after Mass tonight!

Maybe this is the solution: finding a good man who will save me from the slippery slope into sin. I can make up for the two ~~murders~~ accidents by being loving, charitable and pious every day for the rest of my life. That's what repentance and redemption are all about, right? Isn't my God merciful?

I let my eyes roam discreetly over the congregation, trying to guess who will come to the singles event. I don't know anyone here, we're Sunday morning gals. There are nice looking men though, clean-cut, handsome, full-heads of hair. My heart soars. Yes, that's clearly what Jesus is telling me to do. My contrition will be so complete, it will be positively Biblical.

How thoughtful of the priests to organise a dating event for their singles community. We all heard the story of the elderly couple who met at Mass, each one sliding closer and closer on the pew each Sunday, until finally they started chatting and then eventually got married. I look down the length of the polished oak bench in case the love of my life is sitting there. Only old biddies. Figures.

'They do these events at the Brompton Oratory too. My friend Isla met her husband that way,' Scarlett says.

My heart quivers in my chest, as my palms begin to tingle. Dressing up for this evening was quite a conundrum. How to appear sexy while at the same time remaining modest enough for church? Dilemma dilemma. I settled on a black wrap dress that reaches below the knee but has a not-insignificant décolleté.

The interminable mass finally consents to end and we file out while the choir sings something about Jesus not abhorring the Virgin's womb. Ha.

There are quite a lot of women here tonight, excitedly chatting, waving at each other at a distance with nervous little smiles. The loos, usually commandeered by an army of nappy-changers looks like a nightclub's nose-powdering room tonight, as lipsticks get touched-up and hair gets tamed into submission. Little spurts of laughter burst through the decorum, as we all look at each other with anticipation. Nobody wants to be the first desperate soul to go in, so we all pour into the event room as a group, filling it with perfume, babble and hopeful smiles.

The rotund canon sits on a small stage, deep in conversation with the pretty priest. Next to them is a large whiteboard and the chairs are arranged in neat rows, to face them. There are no canapés. This is a conference. *Erm... ok.*

We all take our seats and I swivel in my uncomfortable folding chair to take a look at the room. Where are all the single men? There are at least forty women here tonight but only two men: an eighty-year old geezer sat in the last row who looks like he wishes he'd brought his oxygen tank along and... Kevin, the organist who's staring at us, as always, brow furrowed, his thinning hair mussed into dark foamy curls. Somehow his moustache seems askew. He sends a tentative smile my way and I look down, rediscovering my shoes.

The canon and the priest gesture for silence and kick us off.

In the teeth.

'We are here today to discuss singlehood. As you know, marriage is one of the Church's holy sacraments and procreating is a divine obligation.' Midi dresses in interesting patterns rustle uneasily.

'So I'd like to start us off today with a quiet minute of reflection on why you've all failed to perform this most sacred duty, squandering the gifts given to you by God.'

The women stare at each other and it's like they've opened a crack in our dam.

'Where are the men?' one shouts at the back.

'We were told this was a singles mixer.' A dignified older lady interjects, pursing her lips.

'Ladies, ladies, this is an event for the singles of this parish, yes. But we are here to discuss what personal flaws have led you to this dead-end. It's a brainstorming session about the single person's life in Christ and—'

'Why are the women always the ones who are blamed for being single?' Scarlett interrupts.

'Why don't you ask the men for once?' another woman yells from the back. 'For every single woman in this room, there is a corresponding man of our generation who's out there, not being asked why he's still single.'

Murmurs of assent ripple across the assembled women.

'She's right you know,' I whisper to Scarlett. 'This generation has Peter Pan syndrome. They play video games, wear ridiculous clothes and act like teenagers. They date us and fuck us with no strings attached and when they're ready to settle down, they pick younger women and leave us to rot.'

'Now, now, Lily, watch the bitterness and cynicism, it's not sexy.' Scarlett says, oozing irony.

The delicious priest licks his lips, looking for salvation in the crowd and his eyes alight on potential allies. 'We have men here tonight,' he says brightly. 'Why don't we ask them?'

The eighty-year old stands up. It takes a while. His hand shakes on the cane's handle and his knees wobble until finally, he's up and clearing his throat, looking apologetically around.

'My wife just passed, I... I just came here to understand how to be single now that she's gone. I don't know how.'

'Yeah, more likely he came to pick up his next piece of ass,' Scarlett whispers.

Catherine sucks her breath in, looking scandalised. 'Shhh.'

There's some aawwing and aaahing but soon in the lull created by this potentially heart-warming moment, a lone hand goes up and the Sunday choir leader's high-pitched voice brings everybody back on topic. Tonight's crowd is like a dog with a bone, we won't be distracted, no matter how fashionable senior romances might seem.

She straightens her red hair and asks her question, fiddling with the cross around her neck. 'Yes, so ok... I get that we're an inconvenience because we don't fill all the boxes and all that. But what are we supposed to do to find men?'

'Yes,' a few women mutter, 'what does the Church propose we do?'

'The church... erm... doesn't really...' the young priest starts.

The canon comes to his rescue. 'That's up to you ladies, but whatever you do to secure a mate, the Church certainly does not condone having pre-marital sex.'

Snorts of disbelief can distinctly be heard in the back of the room.

'How else are we supposed to convince a bloke to date us and marry us?'

'The right man, the faithful man will do the right thing.'

'Yeah, good luck finding a man who'll stick around for zero sex and doesn't run for the hills at the mere mention of marriage,' someone stage whispers in the row behind me.

'Why isn't this a singles event? Why can't the Church help us meet suitable Catholic men?' Scarlett asks, perhaps a tad more forcefully than necessary.

The seventy-year-old canon's enormous paunch quivers under the onslaught as the crowd's angry invectives fuse.

'Well, ladies,' he chuckles uncomfortably, 'it's not our job to find you mates. For most of you it's too late anyway.'

'What do you mean?' says a woman in her fifties, who's looking fabulous with her Chanel flap, Louboutins and LBD. I've had fashion envy ever since I set eyes on her at the start of mass.

'Well, the purpose of marriage is to have children and most of you are much too old to have them, so what's the point, really? You're better off considering a life of celibacy and prayer. Speaking of which, I've brought leaflets tonight about our sister institution The Magdalena convent, should any of you be interested.'

Catherine perches on the edge of her chair playing with the golden crown of thorns on her ring finger. The expression on her damaged face is so heart-breaking I could cry.

'This is ridiculous. In other words, our purpose in this life is either fertility or redundancy,' I whisper to Scarlett.

She shrugs, absorbed in her phone. 'François is busy tonight. I'm still going to pretend that this shindig is hopping with hot single men. Will do him good to be a bit jealous,' she whispers, tapping at the speed of light. From time to time, she likes to throw him off. I glance over at her screen and see steamy banter being exchanged, aubergine emojis and lots of peaches. I'm guessing he's going to wrap up his business meetings pronto tonight and head to her place to mark his territory, just in case.

'As you know, couples are too busy to participate in the Church's activities, as they are fulfilling their duties to raise the future flock of God. We've found over the years, that single women have a lot more time to dedicate to the parish's many duties. For example, the church needs cleaning—'

'Cleaning! Is this a joke?' The anger that had subsided comes back with a vengeance. A few of the women walk out, wrapping their coats around hope-bedecked dresses as they leave in a cloud of perfume and outrage.

Eye-candy priest holds his hands up, a bit of white showing around his eyes. 'There's solace and dignity in the meditative act of cleaning.'

'Why don't they do it themselves, then?' Scarlett mutters.

Catherine already has her hand up to volunteer for the cleaning rota. I pull her arm down.

The canon's eyes slide towards the exit but he rallies and says tentatively 'We also need some volunteers for flowers?'

'Flowers? Flowers? We thought you wanted to help us find love!'

'But we do, we want to help you find the love of Christ—'

'Why are we listening to this bullshit? We could be in a bar picking up dates right now.' Scarlett looks at us for reinforcement but Catherine is having one of her bouts of intense praying and inexplicably, I've started to cry.

And now that the tears have started flowing, there seems to be no way to ever stop them. Even in this place, where I expected to be unconditionally loved and accepted, I'm judged, diminished and exploited. And why? Am I less of a person than my married friends? Am I less intelligent, resourceful or capable? No the only thing "wrong" about me is that I don't have a man in my bed.

'Here.' Catherine hands me a tissue and squeezes my hand. It only makes me cry more. I don't even deserve to be happy anymore. Not after what I've done. I'm not worthy.

'Sweetie, come on, stop crying,' Scarlett says, looking like she has no idea how to make the flow stop. Well, to be fair, I've no idea either.

'What do they know anyway? They've never had to find love, they don't understand what it means to be single in your late thirties for a woman. This is just mansplaining 2.0. Don't listen to them.'

The canon drones on, '... and as you've chosen to focus only on yourselves, you have more disposable income, which brings me to my next...'

Ah yes, the old you're-single-therefore-you're-selfish line. The tears continue to pour down my cheeks, as if I were a plaster icon of the Virgin at a fake miracle site. I'm a fountain of grief, rage and helplessness, I don't grant miracles, only death and sorrow. *I'll never find anyone to love me. I'm utterly and completely unlovable.* Something must surely be broken in me and men are able to detect my flaw. That's why everyone else is married and I'm not.

'... there are forms here,' the priest points to the pile of forms, 'where you'll be able to donate. Also, consider that as you won't have children you could bequeath your money to the Church when you die.'

Oh wow. Wow.

'Ok ladies, that's it. Let's get out of here.' Scarlett's up.

She walks right past the forms, not even dignifying the priests with a glance and she's out. Catherine and I scramble to follow her, grabbing our coats and bags and apologising profusely as we leave.

Outside, Scarlett's already hailing a cab and she blows us a few air kisses as she hops in and rushes away to meet with François.

WE WALK the few blocks to Catherine's place in the silent night. Her small Pimlico flat is under the eaves of an art deco building, in the former servants quarters. Inside every surface is grey. Dove grey wall, slate grey bedspread, Gainsboro grey carpet. It's like *Fifty Shades of Grey* but with a lot less spanking— there's probably self-flagellation though.

'You ok?' Catherine asks as we head to her minuscule kitchen to make tea. 'What's going on with you tonight?'

That's a very good question isn't it? I open my mouth thinking I'll say *Nothing, I'm fine* or that I'll complain about my love life, as usual but the words that spill out surprise even me.

'I don't know if I still believe, Catherine. I always had faith in the original message of Christ, the message of tolerance and acceptance, forgiveness and love but tonight, I felt unheard, diminished. I'm not sure if I still belong. The path I'm taking in real life… it just doesn't match with the Church's teachings anymore.'

'I… I don't know Lily, faith is such a personal thing, sometimes I've struggled with it, too.'

'You?' I say, surprised.

'Yes, of course, everyone does. But right now, it's helping me, you know, with… everything. It helps to have a clear set of instructions and beliefs to hold on to when your life crumbles into pieces. My faith is the bedrock holding it all together, you know?'

My life's crumbling too, so how come I can't grab onto my faith as she does? I'm drowning and reaching for a lifesaver, only to find it's a ~~bed~~rock and I'm sinking.

Catherine continues, 'I don't mind if priests sometimes remind us that we're supposed to lead a more fruitful life within the bonds of marriage, there's nothing wrong with love. I wish I'd been able to have that…' her voice wobbles and she stops.

'Oh Gosh, I'm so sorry, Catherine. Here I am blathering about my crisis of faith when I should be asking you how you are,' I say, blowing my nose as the tears finally subside.

'You don't have to worry about me, I'll be ok,' she says.

Every time she speaks to me I wonder if there's another meaning behind her words. What does she mean? I did have to worry but I no longer do, now that Brett's gone? Does she know what I did? Does she hate me?

'Are you sure? Br… He was… I'm so sorry this happened to you,' I manage.

'I… I'm going through with it.' She looks down, her fingers gripped tight around the kettle handle.

'With what?' I wipe away black mascara tears and look at her blankly, as I get another sheet of kitchen roll.

She pours us two cups and then turns around, staring ahead as the water changes colour in her tightly gripped mug. A few moments later she murmurs 'I'm... what's the word? Enrolling, I suppose, to be a nun that is. I have the appointment.'

'Oh Catherine. You can't give up and run away.'

'I'm not giving up. I'm embracing my destiny.'

I snort.

Catherine continues, undeterred, 'Plus, I can't dawdle. It's not as easy as you think to become a nun; you have to be healthy and have a bachelor's degree and be debt-free and –'

'You're shitting me, they have *conditions*? The nerve on these p—'

'There's also an age limit. I must become an aspirant before age forty.' Catherine's getting flustered, trying to explain her choice with an urgency in her voice that wasn't there before. 'You don't understand, I'm running out of time.'

'No way. What do they need blooming young nuns for? Aesthetics?' I frown.

'There's a whole process too. I've been talking with my vocation director for months now. I just....' Lowering her face, she rubs her bruised forehead and nascent tears tremble on her lash line. 'So, in a way, we'll both race against the clock to get to the finish line before forty...' she half-sobs, half-laughs.

Sighing, I lean back against the counter next to Catherine, offering her a sheet of kitchen towel. We both stare at her Swiss Cuckoo clock. It's nine o'clock. The bird comes out, reminding us that time is passing with a shrill warble while the shepherd romances the milkmaid and goats frolic in their miniature wonderland meadow.

'This is so out of place in your flat, I've love that clock,' I say, a propos of nothing. It always gave me hope that Catherine wasn't quite as mousy grey as she aspired to be.

She blows her nose wetly. 'I know what I'm doing. This is my choice.'

'I didn't think you really meant to go through with it.'

'I've never...' she swallows and then folds her bony arms. 'I've never really felt like one of you. You and Scarlett, the lifelong friends, peas in a pod, the inseparables. Even Emma's been a part of the gang for twenty years. I've always been the fifth wheel. You won't even notice I'm gone.'

'That's ridiculous. Of course, you're one of us. Plus you never felt like that before. What's changed?' *I know what's changed and it's my fault.*

'I just...' her lips are chapped and she's worrying the dry skin with her teeth. 'I just think I need to get closer to God. That's all.'

'Catherine, I know Brett was... he wasn't right for you but please don't throw your life away because of what happened to him.' I stop, hesitate. She offers me a pack of chocolate digestives. I take one.

'Was he...? What happened to...?' I slow down, not sure how to ask if Brett used to hit her, if she's glad he's dead, if she hates me for killing him. I can't ask any of it. She misunderstands what I'm saying.

'Yes, Brett's body was repatriated to Australia, I'm leaving next week.'

'You're going back home for his funeral?' I say, feeling like the floor is giving way under my feet. Would she go back if he'd been abusive to her?

'Yes, of course, he was my fiancé, I loved him, he didn't

deserve to die like that. All alone on a dirty bathroom floor.' She stifles a sob.

Oh God, what have I done?

'I'm going to Brett's funeral and then I'm checking myself in as an aspirant as soon as I come back.'

I struggle to find the words for a few moments. But what can I say really? Nothing. Nothing at all.

'What order?'

'Carmelites, Notting Hill.'

'I hate to break it to you, but I don't think that particular Hill will be alive with the sound of music. Except perhaps at Carnival.'

She bursts out laughing but it ends in a sob.

Unsure what to do, I just rest my hand on her back.

'I feel so guilty...' she says to her stockinged feet. I can feel her vertebrae and her ribs protruding under my palm. They're shaking. 'It was my fault,' she whispers 'if I hadn't been in hospital, he wouldn't have gotten so distracted at the coffee shop.'

Oh Jesus, Mary, Joseph, I killed an innocent man.

'But sweetie, it wasn't your fault, it really wasn't. I... please just trust me, you did nothing wrong.'

'Sometimes I wished... I prayed for...' Her eyes are huge and dark in her pale face. 'I'm a terrible person and I deserve to atone for his death.'

I take both her hands in mine and turn to face her, whispering 'Catherine, listen to me. Please don't throw your life away. I don't want you to go to a glorified prison and let yourself wither and die there for no good reason. You had nothing to do with what happened to Brett. Nothing at all, you hear me? If anyone deserves to atone for his death it's...' I hesitate, '...well, it's certainly not you.' I finish lamely.

'What do you mean?' She searches my face, frowning.

Catherine's eyes bore into my soul and I suddenly feel like a monster. It's unbearable. I mutter an excuse and back out of her suffocating grey kitchen, her suffocating grey flat, her suffocating grey life.

With a pang of fear and shame, I realise that I never want Catherine to find out about my nocturnal habits. If she did find out I'd lose her. Just imagining the look on her face of disappointment, disgust and loathing...

I couldn't bear to lose Scarlett. Oh my God and what would Emma think? She'd never let me see her children again. Imagining how they'd feel about me, how they'd despise me makes the world spin. Without my friends' love and support, I'd be alone. Truly alone in a way I've never been before.

They must never find out.

As I run home along the river, blood pounding against my temples, the horror of what I've done really hits home.

I hurt my friend and stole away her chance at happiness and love.

I was so sure.

Now the love of her life is dead and I can never take back what I did.

Death has no return policy.

20

GIRLY SWOTS LOVE LISTS

After the rooftop, I'd convinced myself that it was all an unfortunate coincidence, that Cameron's accident would have happened whether I'd been there or not. But now I wonder. Was it really an accident? Was it?

Now with Brett's ~~mur~~ his unfortunate allergic reaction, I suppose I must face the facts... it's a trend, erm...a hobby? An extracurricular activity.

Whatever. But I'm terrible at this. I'm clumsy and ridiculous. I'm laughably incompetent.

In a way, this isn't about me at all, it's much bigger. The fact of the matter is that there is work to do. Someone needs to avenge women and end the cycle of injustice and violence, the endless exploitation and abuse.

Maybe I'm just the wrong person in the wrong place but I still need to step up and try to do the task that fate has offered me, to the best of my ability. Who else is going to do it? I can be that person. I *want* to be that person.

It scares me that I want to, but *I do*. So what if I'm not the perfect person for the job. I have talents. What can I call upon, what are my skills? I'm not just a miasma of emotions, I'm also a mind and a good one at that. Oh I know what will help... of course!

I should consider it like a job: an Avenging Angel position has just opened and I've accepted the Universe's offer, the salary is crap but the sense of purpose makes up for it. So, let's see... if this were a real job, what would I do? I would organise myself.

So, out comes my Excel spread sheet, but this time, instead of logging dates, men's profiles and assigning them a potential dreaminess rating, I open a new workbook and start a blank table. What can I say, girly swots love lists.

Let's see.

List of people I'd like to should kill:

- Movie directors who pitch young heroines against older middle-aged women who have their shit together. Like we're enemies instead of sisters.

- Photoshoppers who create unrealistic... Mmmh. I know a perfectly nice man in his sixties who does that for a living. I don't want to kill him. His dog is lovely.

- Magazine editors who hire the photoshoppers.

- Novelists who glamorise sado-masochistic practices. Scratch that one out. I don't kill women. Maybe actual sadists? Urgh, no, I don't want to traipse through that dark, dark corner of the web.

- Clothes designers who stop at size eight because they don't want to see their clothes looking "ugly" on "fat" women. Twats.

- Fashion show organisers who glamourise anorexia.

- Politicians who campaign on pro-life programmes to sucker people into neo-liberalism programmes that only benefit the richest strata of society (they're mostly outside of the UK though, mmmh).

- Men who direct, act in and watch perverted porn involving very young girls being abused (it's not like there are credits at the end of porn movies, so how am I supposed to find them exactly?).

- Polygamists (am not planning a trip to Utah anytime soon, so that one might have to wait).

- ~~Men who earn more than women for doing the same job, just because there's a penis dangling between their legs~~. Nah. Too complicated. I'd have to kill all the men.

- Paedophile priests (how to get a list though?)

- Rapists (look into sex offender registries?)

- Wife beaters (one down, thousands to go, I suppose).

I tap my fingers against my lips. I need something actually feasible. Maybe I should just concentrate on increasing my skillset for now. I get my To Do list out and realise, to my horror, that I haven't updated it in quite a while.

	To Do List last year		To Do List today
1	Watch the de-cluttering show and get some life-changing magic! (lol)	1	Watch How To Get Away With Murder (for research)
2	Update my OKCupid profile with a poetic description of my last holiday.	2	Update my council registration and make sure I'm registered to vote.
3	Buy matching earrings for my pink quartz ring (pink quartz is good for love!).	3	Buy a balaclava, mace and knuckle brass? (lol)
4	Watch latest YouTube makeup videos of LollipopSugar, SparkleGlitter and UnicornRainbowGirrrl.	4	Watch the bloke who teaches self-defence on YouTube and try the moves next time.
5	Try Shellac mani-pedi with Scarlett.	5	Try out a few knives and check which one has the best handle.
6	Get shorter skirts that don't look frumpy!	6	Get a couple of cheap black jeans and sweaters, that I can throw away or burn afterwards.
7	Book consult with the tarot card medium that Emma recommended and ask her when I'll meet The One.	7	Book consult with the 24h gym that Tamsin recommended to ask about core strength training.
8	Research Botox process and price options.	8	Research crime scene investigation process and success rate.
9	Figure out if I'm a Spring or Autumn and build my capsule wardrobe accordingly.	9	Figure out how to administer rat poison safely (well safely for me anyway).
10	Make sure I've paid my membership to the social club that's organising a Valentine speed-dating party next week.	10	Make sure I've got a good lawyer. Retain. Keep number on speed dial. What's speed dial anyway? Does that even exist anymore?
11	Read *The Rules*, *Get the Guy* and *Men are from Mars & Women are from Venus*.	11	Read *The End Of Men*, *Rage Becomes Her* and *Why Women Get Blamed For Everything*.
12	Buy the Scholl gel padding thingie to help with wearing heels.	12	Buy good running shoes for quick and quiet escapes.

Ok, that's good.

But what about love? Having a purpose is all fine and dandy but it won't keep me warm at night. Maybe I can continue dating?

Oh I know! I can use the dating campaign for both purposes! If I find The One, then great. I mean, why not? I'm not a quitter. I said I'd go on forty dates and find love and I will.

But if the dates are awful, like proper awful, I can kill off a few of the blokes and make the world a safer place for the next woman.

There. All sorted.

Am a master multi-tasker.

21

MOMMIE DEAREST

I don't want to sound shallow or anything but Spencer's fifteen years older than me so I'm not too sure. His Guardian Soulmates profile is nice though, he's very charming and he's clearly loaded given he mentioned in passing that he owns a townhouse in the heart of Mayfair plus a country house somewhere in Somerset. I've never been on a date with a man who had his act together to that degree. Maybe it would make for a nice change of pace?

I send him a message and his response is instantaneous. Prowling the net for a Saturday night date apparently.

'Really, you changed your mind? You'll go on a date with me?'

Erm... come on Lily, take the plunge. Let's see how it goes if you give yourself a proper chance of success with someone serious.

'Sure.'

'Fantastic, tonight, then,' he texts, 'Savoy at seven.'

Well that makes a nice change from kissing in the Tube and shish kebabs under the freezing rain. 'See you there,' I write, surprised to feel hope.

DATE 30

So at seven, I'm in the lobby of the Savoy, wearing my best stewardess costume: navy blue dress, kitten heels, straightened hair, tasteful makeup. Feeling like I'm going to a job interview, I ask for Spencer but the concierge shows me to a waiting area, he's not here yet.

Fifteen minutes pass, then a text. Finally, a full thirty minutes later, a man who looks a lot older than his pictures arrives with a savagely elegant woman in her late seventies.

'Lily, so happy you could make it. May I introduce my mother,' he drawls.

Sorry what?

'Oh hello Ma'am. I'm Lily.' Ma'am? *Oh Gawd, Lily why not curtsy while you're at it?*

'I know, dear.' She gives me a once over. My hair instantly starts frizzing under her stare, my thighs become humongous and my dress realises that it's woefully inadequate, somewhere between too middle-class and trying-too-hard-nouveau-riche.

'Shall we?' He smiles, looking pleased as lines appear in his sunken cheeks.

'Is your mother joining us for dinner?' I ask lightly.

'Yes, I hope you don't mind.'

'When Spencer mentioned that he was meeting with you, I just had to come and see the girl who has captured his heart.'

Mmh. We've barely exchanged a handful of text messages over the last week.

'You look quite pretty for your age, what have you done? Botox?

'No it's not Botox,' I smile sweetly.

Everybody's been remarking on how good I look lately. Maybe it's all the murders. I can't really sleep anymore and I've lost my appetite. But in a way, I also feel like I'm in touch with something primordial, a source of power, which I never had access to before, a sort of febrile electric energy. I feel more alert, I don't know... like I'm "on" where before I was just sleepwalking through my life. Everything looks brighter, more real, less futile. Whatever it is, it's doing wonders for my complexion apparently.

I SMILE to myself as she continues to grill me.

The room is dark and the staff clearly is on a first name basis with these two. The waiter, throws a curious glance at me then brings a very expensive bottle, showing it like a Wheel of Fortune prize before opening and pouring it with a few quick practised gestures. Nobody asks or cares about what I want to eat or drink, it's all ordered for me, down to the level of cooking of the steak.

Then they both turn to me. Good cop, bad cop.

'So Lily, tell us all about you. Where do you see yourself in five years?'

Anywhere but here?

We continue in that vein for four hours and finally, it's time to end the interrogation. Exhausted, my cheeks hurting from all the smiling, I say my goodbyes, hoping to make a clean exit but Spencer insists on driving me home.

Repeat after me, Lily, *he's a catch*. Scarlett's super excited about this date and I pinkie swore to report in with all the details the minute I step back home. So, I must stick with the script and allow him to be gentlemanly. Mommie dearest disappears upstairs no doubt to frown upon the fact that the Savoy's standards have gone down in the last twenty years and ask to see management about the room she was given, while Spencer and I hop in the Jag.

The ride is awkward; after all the food, I look like an overstuffed sausage and I'm feeling inadequate with my fat calves encased in Primark tights and my absence of ankles that ends in M&S shoes. Going for a Princess Di side legs look, I try to make myself small but now that we're in such close proximity in the tiny coupé, I feel enormous next to his slight build.

Midway through the ride I realise that it's a bad idea to let him drive me back because, (a) I don't know him from Eve and he could be a serial killer who will soon have my address and (b) he'll find out that I live on a construction site and think less of me.

Actually, upon reflection, (a) would be ironic, don't you think? A little too ironic as Alanis would say and (b) it turns out I don't give a monkey's. Also (c) nothing I can do about either of these now anyway.

I guide him through the maze around Battersea Power Station, navigating the danger signs, the waste authority building, the cranes and the stacks of building materials until we're finally in front of my building and he parks.

'You're such a Viking,' he says.

'I'm sorry?'

'Oh it's just a personality type,' he waves my questions away.

Ah, so I was right, tonight *was* an assessment.

We stay in the car for another minute in silence. I don't know what to do. He's not saying goodbye, he's not getting out of the car to open my door, he's not kissing me goodnight either. I'd better get out then.

'Well thank you for a lovely evening,' I lie.

'Good night, Lily.'

I extricate myself from his super low car and after he's gone, I stay there for a while, at the foot of my building, taking in the mess of it, the eviscerated pavement, the muddy patches, the sacks of plaster and the random detritus of the workmen's day: beer cans, polystyrene wrappings. I can't quite pinpoint why but it bothers me that the building still isn't finished, a year after it was supposed to be. That the neighbourhood was supposed to gentrify and never did, not quite. That the Tube line that was supposed to make this purchase a smart investment never quite materialised. Why does nothing ever work for me?

Do I even want Spencer or do I think I want him because society says I should? Because, having failed to achieve anything worthwhile with my life, the next best thing would be to marry someone who did achieve something with theirs?

Somehow, after a youth spent dreaming of accomplishments and professional success, my middle age has devolved into thinking that my self worth and happiness are tied to whether I marry or not. How did it come to that? That's not how I used to define a life well lived. And yet for all that crystal clear realisation, I don't think I can take another failure in my love life when everything else is imploding around me.

Feeling tears prickle, I look up to prevent them from rolling down on my cheeks and for some reason, my gaze is attracted to the only window still lit. My building's flats all have floor to ceiling windows to maximise the river view. Stacked shiny glass boxes in mountains made of steel.

The light in that one flat is dark red and dim but I can clearly see a naked woman who's leaning against the window, her forearms pressed against the glass as she sways, her breasts heavy. In the night's complete silence, her mouth opens in soundless pleasure as the man, hidden in darkness, takes her from behind. Her breasts are still jiggling with abandon when I retreat into the emptiness of the gloomy building.

22

OOPS, I DID IT AGAIN

Clearly Spencer's mother didn't like me. It's less clear whether Spencer did or not. Maybe I got a second date *because* she didn't like me. Fucked up Mamma's boy.

One thing is sure, tonight I'm invited to the poshest party I've ever been to. As I get ready, I listen to the BBC presenter talking about a royal who slipped and caused yet another embarrassing scandal by being friends with a millionaire who pimped impressionable young women to the rich and powerful. I shake my head *Is nothing sacred anymore?* I apply the bright red lipstick I bought for the occasion, watching closely for little wrinkles of disappointment and bitterness around my mouth. None yet. *You can't even count on the royal family to behave with some decency and decorum let alone moral probity?*

Anyway, looks like Lord Epsom's going to get away scot-free; he's paid for the best lawyers, his politician friends on both sides of the Pond have pulled a few strings and there will be a settlement. A couple of years of disgrace for the royal offspring, followed by a discrete comeback.

The main politician implicated in the scandal will joke with journalists who will call him a harmless ladies man, a bit of a rascal and a scoundrel. Cue envious smiles and backstage questions about how tender the young meat was. *Nothing at all you can do about it, Lily.*

Frowning, I slip the carton invitation in my clutch, checking my reflection in the mirror: nice left overs, I suppose, for a thirty-nine year old and change. I'm wearing a lacy number with a décolleté so deep you can practically see my belly button. The view's not so bad, I suppose. Good diversion. If Spencer focuses long enough on the milky globes bulging languidly through the black lace, maybe he won't notice my bum.

Well, it's as good as it's gonna get. Like my Grandma used to say, *There's better but it's more expensive.*

∽

DATE 31

THE CAB DROPS me off on Pall Mall, at a private club only a smidge less venerable than the best one there. I try to look nonplussed, but probably fail as I take in the gilding, the marble, the giant flower arrangements and the general sense of having passed into a secluded, by invitation-only parallel world. Champagne glass in hand, I look for Spencer; he's not here but I recognise quite a few people. In fact, I'm star struck, I've never been to a gathering like this one, every face here looks vaguely familiar; rich industrialists, famous singers, powerful politicians, legendary movie producers, actors I used to fawn upon as a teenager, footballers married to notorious reality-TV stars. The people I don't recognise look like they all have country houses on large estates and pied-a-terres in the Caymans. Spencer must be quite a bit richer than I thought.

'Ah there you are, Lily.'

Speaking of the devil, Spencer looks taller somehow, without his formidable mother by his side.

'Thank you so much for inviting me! I've never been to this club before,' or any other private club really. But he doesn't need to know that.

'Not at all, delighted you could make it,' he drawls, air kissing me.

I never got the appeal of private clubs until now. I suppose you get to hang out with people who are your equals or better, in a place away from prying eyes, so you can have confidential conversations, close deals and pretend for a while that the rest of the mundane, grubby world doesn't exist. And it doesn't hurt that once you're all acquainted, you probably all help each other, out there, IRL.

'It's all so impressive.' I gush, pointing to the room, the guests, the canapés, the vast amounts of money flowing around this room. I don't know what he sees in me, if I'm honest. He could go for a prettier, younger woman. He's powerful and rich enough, I suppose.

But he's solicitous, holding my elbow as we navigate around the guests. He introduces me as his "friend". No last names. We talk about the weather, the food, the latest entertainment news. Everything is so pleasant here. So civilised. I hold on to the same glass of champagne, feeling it get warm as I pretend to sip it. Meanwhile, Spencer's glass gets refilled quite liberally by passing waiters.

'Mummy didn't think you were suitable,' he whispers

drunkenly in my ear, exaggerating her drawl, "Quite ordinary, my boy. You can do better."'

'Oh.' My face falls.

'Oh gosh, terribly sorry, I should explain… that's a good thing.' He gulps down his Scotch and flags down another. I catch a glimpse of his signet ring. 'And anyway, *I* like you.' His fingers trail along my naked back. 'I like you a lot, Lily.'

I release a breath I didn't realise I was holding and the temptation to join his world overwhelms me, with surprising intensity. The comfort and luxury of it is so close at hand…

I could perhaps date Spencer, become a trophy wife, and have money beyond my ability to spend it. I suppose I could pursue any passion that tickled my fancy, I could quit my job, I'd live in a townhouse and do tea with the other desperate housewives, Mayfair edition. For a vertiginous minute, I imagine it all, a completely different life. Free from hustle, free from financial worry. A life where I would no longer have to make every decision and fight all the time, I could just let myself be carried along.

A young woman passes by with a tray of canapés and that jolts me out of my ~~Victorian wet dream~~ shameful moment of weakness. The women here are all young. Non-famous, non-powerful, non-legendary. I scan the room and notice the cheap Topshop dresses and glossy clip-on fake hair, the overenthusiastic fake tans, the young smiles and shy banter.

And that's when I see him. Lord Epsom. Smiling, joking with one of the guests, his handsome face for all the world like a charming fifty-something benevolent uncle. He's got his arm wrapped around a politician's shoulders and they both laugh as they check the dance floor. A few girls are there, teetering on platform sandals. It can't really be called dancing, not really, it's more like shuffling and trying not to fall.

Suddenly I see them all. I *really* see them: the paunchy Tory who's famous for cheating on his wife and paying off his mistresses with fake government jobs, the famous movie producer with a pockmarked skin and a few dozen Baftas who's been accused of handing out roles in exchange for sexual favours, the footballer famous for fondling female fans and reporters while wearing little more than a towel in the locker rooms. The TV presenter who paid his way out of a rape accusation, the has-been actor who got his wife to take down the photos of her bruised and bloody face from the internet by paying her a few millions in alimony.

How could I not see the rot before?

'Sorry Spencer. I need to go powder my nose.'

Felling lightheaded, I disentangle myself and totter away to the loos, trying to get my bearings as my heels sink into the deep carpet and my head swirls from the giant bouquets' smell.

Downstairs, I get lost and pad down a corridor lined with the portraits of all the men who have headed this club since the eighteenth century. Men with monocles and men with horn-rimmed glasses, men with pocket watches and men with Rolexes. Men, men, men.

At last I find ~~the oasis~~, the loos. What was this? This horrible greed-induced wobble? Of course I can't be a trophy wife. I'm strong, I'm smart, I'm capable. I'll succeed and make my own way in the world.

Shaking my head, I give myself a stern talking-to as I wash my hands and that's when I hear them.

Men's voices and bursts of laughter, muffled and raucous. On an impulse, I grab a glass and looking around to make sure I'm alone, I lean the glass against the wall and glue my ear to the other end. The voices come in then, as loudly and as clearly as if I were in the same room as them. Spencer's taking some flack.

'Who's the old bird, Spence? Did you bring her as a joke? She's twice the age of the others.'

He laughs. 'I don't mind the wrinkles on her face as long as her arse is tappable.'

'Holy shit, did you see that rump? I bet it's nice and deep. You've got to get in there.'

'Speleological expedition tonight!' One of them guffaws.

'Hey, leave the man alone. I get it. I also have a soft spot for chubby MILFs. They're so fucking... grateful.'

'The plebs will give you anything once they get a glimpse of what it's like on the inside.'

'Just make sure it's anal, not matrimonial,' another one says.

They all laugh.

'Fuck no. She's in her thirties,' Spencer laughs. 'And get this...' he draws the moment for effect, 'she's a career woman,' he sounds like he's crying with laughter. 'Probably makes 70K a year working in a dismal open-plan office in the wharf or something.'

They all chortle.

'Right.' I let my hand drop to my side and the glass bumps gently against my enormous thigh.

'Right,' I whisper to myself.

I reapply the red lipstick (too ordinary?), adjust the LBD (too middle-class?), throw one last glance at my face (too fat?), noticing crow's feet (too old?) but I lift my chin up and rejoin the thinning crowd. It's getting late.

Spencer's disappeared. Probably went to smoke cigars with his buddies in an upstairs salon or something. Lord Epsom and a few others are herding the waitresses under the pretext of giving them a tour of the club. I join the group as inconspicuously as I can and keeping my head down, I follow them, mingling with the young women.

We go upstairs. Here, the venerable oil portraits of men with sideburns, the velvet-covered walls and the gilded mirrors speak of an age when women would not have been allowed to set foot here. We're shown into private rooms where double entendres start to be whispered. We admire the painted ceiling and decorum frays at the edges as giggles start to fuse. We view the beautiful library full of first editions as powerful hands start caressing youthful bums. We're shown through to racketball courts and an underground swimming pool and finally, our guide unlocks the door to a spa area and we all congregate in the dim space, on the edges of a dark blue pool. All along, the tour was designed to corral us here. Various pills, patches and powders are already on display on the bar, offered as casually as M&Ms next to an array of bottles and finger foods.

In the close quarters and the hazy light, the party gets rowdier as the alcohol and the drugs lubricate the posh networking event into something else entirely. Honeyed tongues are thrust into startled young mouths, ties and suit jackets are removed as they all mingle and slither around the hot pool, half hidden by the wisps of warm fog and the dim lighting.

I fend off a couple of advances and just sit in a corner, holding a stale glass of champagne, observing Epsom and the two young waitresses he's set his sights on. He's got them down to their underwear by now and snorting something on the table.

I'm so absorbed by his manipulative game that I hardly notice that the rest of them have all disappeared, each one with a young thing in their clutches, into small shower stalls, saunas and changing rooms.

The last man to leave the main room has his arm wrapped about a slender woman already but as they make their way towards a massage cabin, he stops to propose a threesome.

When I turn him down, noticing that I'm staring at Epsom, his smile turns sour. 'Waiting for leftovers, grandma?'

His companion giggles, clearly high on something.

'Sorry, maybe another time,' I look away as he stares at my breasts.

'That guy only likes fresh meat. You're wasting your time.'

I smile. Come on. Leave.

Finally, we're alone. Lord Epsom jokes with the two remaining girls, pinching there, flattering here, as he guides them seamlessly to the hot steaming pool. Dazzled by the power, money and fame of the evening, the two young women only need the barest of coaxing to remove the last of their lingerie. Epsom sets his empty glass by the pool and undresses too, sliding into the pool between them.

Cigar between his fingers, he grabs one of the girls, pulling her face so his lips crash onto hers as his other hand snakes between her legs. She wriggles a bit but complies.

I'm completely still in a dark corner of the room, feeling like a voyeur. The other girl stares at me, evaluating my chances and realising that I'm no competition at all, she plunges her hand in the water, reaching for his dick. He groans and throws his head back. A furious blush burns its way onto my cheeks and the room feels a lot warmer all of a sudden, all clammy, moist and suffocating. Right, I need to focus.

While the two girls distract him, I pad to the side of the pool, take Epsom's glass to the bar and refill his Scotch and then, glancing over my shoulder, I grab the mirror and let the cocaine rails fall into the sex trafficker's glass. There's another drug there, something clear in a little bottle. I'm not sure what it is. I hesitate for a second and then grab the silicone cap and let a dozen drops trickle in his drink for good measure. A good swirl with a plastic stirrer and voila: karma cocktail. Not wanting to seem out of place, I strip down to my knickers and before I have a chance to feel self-conscious, I join them in the warm water just as it starts to bubble.

After that, all that's left to do is wait. Epsom drains his glass during a lull in the preliminaries. The threesome makes quite a lot of noise but soon he starts to slow down and finally he nods off, head back on the ledge.

Looking at each other, the two girls giggle and get out of the water. I'm the only one who notices his pinpoint pupils, his bluish lips and the fact that he didn't fall asleep so much as pass out.

The young woman who gave him a hand job throws me a puzzled look as she dresses up. 'There's no point in waiting, he's looks like he's out for the night.'

The other one is already at the door. 'Come on Amy, we gotta go back and finish our shift in the kitchen or they won't pay us.'

'I'll be right behind you. You go ahead,' I say.

At last I'm alone in the tub with Epsom but one of the pigs could make it back from the adjacent rooms at any minute. Heart racing, I glance around the dark place one last time and gently pull the predator into the bubbling hot water. Nothing much happens, he snorts as the water laps his face but he doesn't regain consciousness. There's a thrashing movement as I hold his head below the frothing surface. A bigger bubble. Then nothing.

Whimpering every time the floating body touches me, I struggle to wade away from him, feeling preposterous as my naked breasts bob on the sloshing water. I need to get out of here now. The smell of chlorine which hadn't even registered before is now so overpowering that I can't breathe. I scramble out of the tub and dress quickly, my heart bouncing inside my chest like a pinball.

I need to escape this tomb. I'm freaking out. But first, I wipe his glass with the hem of my out-of-fashion dress. Just as I bend to put the tumbler back on the ledge and grab my clutch and shoes, a movement catches my eye: there's a cleaning lady in the shadows. She's about sixty and petite, she looks Latin American.

Her face is the picture of astonishment as she realises that there's a man floating face down in the water. Still bent down, fingers around the straps of my shoes, dripping all over, I'm frozen in place. But as I watch her, feeling nauseous with fear, her features change to understanding and then… a very small smile stretches across her lips. It's gone in the blink of an eye and so is she.

I grab my glass of lukewarm champagne and hurry to the door. There's one more thing to do: I wipe the door handles on both sides and slink out. As I dart along the basement hallway, my bare feet sinking in the deep carpet, hyperventilating, I sway and hold on to the wall, close to fainting. Oh my God, what have I done? Lord almighty. That was murder. Not self-defense. Not a failure to assist a person in danger. This was outright murder. Oh my God.

Feeling the rise of vomit in my throat, I rush through the back corridors and make it back to the loos just in time. Half-sobbing, half-hurling, I hug the antique porcelain toilet bowl as I wait for my stomach to stop lurching. Wiping my mouth on the triple layered loo roll, I try to get up but my knees give out and I crumple on the floor. My cheek hits the floor's cold tiles and for a long time, all I can do is weep in silence.

My mind can't comprehend what I've just done. Like a toddler trying to fit an enormous cube through the round opening of his toy and getting more and more frustrated, my brain tries to match my actions to my personality and the more it fails, the more cracks appear. I'm breaking from the inside out. The person I'm becoming no longer makes sense. Adrift, I finally collect myself up to my knees, flush and then stand on shaky legs. I need to get back to the party as soon as possible. I need an alibi.

I splash my face with cold water and finally start to feel like myself again. But when I glance in the mirror, my stomach sinks; I'm a mess. There's nothing I can do to fix my face now. My nose is red from crying, my wet hair is plastered to my face and already curling, there are mascara streaks that nothing can fix at this stage and my dress is wet. I can't pretend I'm ok and continue my date with Spencer. Fuckety fuck, fuck, fuck, I needed Spencer to vouch that I was by his side all evening, I didn't think this through.

Sod it, I'm going home. Grabbing my clutch, I wrap my trench around me tightly and try my best to hide my wet hair under my scarf. Head down, I escape the private club and emerge into the blissful autumnal cold and rain.

'Lily?'

I hail a cab, ignoring the voice behind me.

'Lily, wait!'

It's dark outside. I turn around and spot Spencer coming down the stairs after me, like prince charming running after Cinderella. Well, that's if Prince Charming was hoping for a bit of anal before the clock struck Midnight. Somehow they always left that part out.

Before he can come too close and see the tears and the mascara on my cheeks, I yell back over my shoulder, 'I'm feeling sick, I drank too much and threw up. Sorry Spencer. Going home. See you soon!'

I hop in my pumpkin carriage, hoping very much to never see that bastard ever again.

23

STARK, BUCK, AU NATUREL

I can't sleep anymore. I guess it's true, what they say: a clear conscience is the softest pillow. Every morning since the first... one, my eyes open at four o'clock and I spend hours fighting to go back to sleep, tangled in humid bed sheets.

Epsom sent me over the edge: I can't pretend that this last one was an "accident". It was premeditated. I waited in a dark corner like a spider and when I saw a way to end him, I seized it.

I'm not even sure I can pretend that any of the others were accidents anymore either, TBH.

I'm stuck; my mind skids on the same images over and over again like a broken record: the outrage and surprise like indictments engraved on their features: *how dare you do this to us?*

My arms can't relax, as they lock at the elbow again and again, shaking from the underwater tremors of his gurgling death.

My stomach knots, clenching, again and again as I realise that the wrong latte is in my hands.

My feet are rooted to the spot, as my fingers try again and again, to catch him in the air before he tumbles over the railing.

The moon's grey light projects geometric shadows through the parted curtains. They dance on my walls while guilt's broken record skips endlessly in my exhausted mind.

In hindsight, maybe it would have been better to find a way to expose Epsom; what's the point of killing just one man when the issue is the whole bloody system?

But isn't the world a better place now that he's no longer in it? Aren't the girls safer now that they've escaped his clutches?

Maybe they'll just fall into the next predator's hands. Maybe his second in command will just take over the sex trafficking ring. I don't know anymore if I did any good or added to the amount of evil in this world.

And yet through the fog of remorse and self-flagellation, a thought flashes faster than I can stop it: *I would do it again*. And now I can't help but play with it like my tongue sometimes plays with a wound on the inside of my cheek, the pain sharp and yet irresistible: *I would do it all over again*. All three of them. Good riddance. Yes, the world's better off without these scumbags.

Oh my God, it's true then.

I really am a murderer.

My eyes burn and my forehead is damp. There's no point; I could stay in bed and try to catch the swaying tail of the night mare but I'd fail and the chase would leave me drained. The bluish numbers pulse hypnotically on my screen: five am. Another two hours of tossing and turning lie ahead of me. It's time to try something different.

Leaving my guilt and shame curled up in the still-warm imprint of my shape, I kneel in front of my wardrobe and root around for sneakers. There they are, at the back, dusty and outmoded. It turns out I don't own any sports gear, so I make do with pyjama bottoms and a fleece top. But who cares? No one sees me as I emerge into the vastness and solitude of the night.

I don't know what's come over me. I haven't done anything remotely resembling exercise in years, but somehow the tingle in my breastbone, the burn in my cheeks, the rush of blood through my legs feel right, they feel real.

Murderer, murderer, murderer, the night whispers, wrapping herself around my body like a seductive snake and making me trip.

Murderer, murderer, murderer, the leaves rustle in the trees, as tears run against my cold cheeks and the path becomes blurry.

But as I run, my soul stirs and finally comes out of its deadlock. Each stumbling, inelegant step brings me forward into the world of the living. I escape the smoky tendrils of my ghosts' claws and sprint the last twenty metres back to my front door.

Breathing hurts.

Everything hurts.

But as dawn dilutes the night all around me, I feel alive, I'm no longer looping.

EXHAUSTED AND SWEATY, I fumble with the keys, my steps echoing in the bare lobby where electric cables hang from the ceiling and a recently painted wall struggles to dry. Repressing a shiver, I hug myself and sigh, it was a mistake to move in before they finished the building. This construction is taking so long and sometimes it feels like it will never become the place I thought it could be. A bit like me, I suppose. I thought I'd be more polished and put-together by now.

I'm waiting in the cold lobby, rubbing my arms for warmth when the lift doors open and out comes a woman who walks right past me, absorbed in her own thoughts and very intent on leaving. The only problem is: she's completely naked from head to toe.

Slender with long carefully blow-dried locks and a pretty face, she's completely hairless everywhere else on her light brown body.

'Miss,' I call, hurrying in her wake, as she heads straight for the street, a confused look on her face. 'You don't want to go out there like that. It's cold outside,' *and you'll get assaulted or arrested*, I add silently.

She dodges me and keeps heading for the door, intent on escape. *From what?* I wonder, as I block the door. Careful not to touch her, I extend my arms and gently coax her back into the lift then to my flat where I give her a few haphazardly chosen pieces of lounge wear in the hopes that she'll figure out that she should put them on.

Closing the door of my bedroom to give her some privacy, I call the porter and a few minutes later, he's here with his junior colleague. Of course, the young woman chooses that moment to emerge from my bedroom still stark naked, holding my knickers between two fingers, a scowl on her face. She doesn't need words to make it clear that she thinks they're ginormous and she can't possibly stoop to wear them.

The junior porter's eyes are roaming all over her naked body as he sniggers like a little boy, half-hidden behind his colleague. The more senior one looks like he's swallowed a lemon rind as he gives her a once-over.

'Do you think you could watch the CCTV and figure out where she might have left her clothes?' I turn around and gently lead my guest by the shoulders back to the bedroom. 'Come on, sweetie, let's go see what else I've got that would fit you.'

The answer's not much because she's really fit and I'm really not. But finally, she's dressed and while we wait for the porter to come back, we share a surreal moment, sat side by side, eating toast with jam in silence, both sensing a strange sisterhood and yet also both lost in our own thoughts and our own separate miseries.

She was probably drugged and still can't form words but the food is helping and little by little, something stirs in her eyes, as her consciousness rises to the surface like a drowned body bobbing towards the surface.

When she finally speaks, her voice is hoarse. 'What I don't understand is' she mutters, as if more to herself than to me, 'what am I doing here?'

You and me both, sister.

Well, figuratively for me, literally for her, I suppose.

'Hi, I'm Lily.' I hold my hand out. She looks at it and frowns and then slowly, remembers what she's supposed to do and places her warm, soft hand in mine.

'Nicoletta,' she says.

The porter comes back and as we finish our breakfast, he looms over us, interrogating her.

'Are you a prostitute? What's the meaning of this? Why were you naked in the hallways?' he asks without an ounce of kindness.

'Hey, now wait a second...' I interject.

'Why is he here?' she pleads with me, fear etched on her features as she clings to my hand.

'Do you want us to call the police?' he threatens, 'answer me!'

'This is a trap,' she squeaks, trying to get up and leave.

'No one is calling the police.' I glower. For God's sake, give a mediocre man an inch of power and he'll take a mile. Men always struggle with accurate measurements. 'What did you find out?'

Apparently, the CCTV revealed that she started the previous evening fully clothed and in the company of a building resident called Paul. It's a bit suspicious that the porter located the Paul in question as quickly as he did. Not his first time then. There's no choice, if she wants her clothes back, we need to go meet this bloke.

Is she really a prostitute? Does that change anything? She's clearly in need of help. Even if doing drugs was her own idea, how did she end up outside? Did he kick her out?

She slows down and grips my forearm as we near his door. Not wanting to force this, I stop while the porter keeps going and knocks on Paul's door.

'Is there anyone I can call for you? Where are your parents?' I ask the young woman.

She looks at me, a pout on her face. Is it disbelief or bitterness, I wonder? What's so hard to fathom: that I genuinely want to help her or that I could be so naïve as to think her parents would? I don't know, I can't read her expression.

Paul emerges in a robe, his naked hairy paunch bursting out over an ill-fitting polyester tracksuit bottom with white side stripes. Greasy dyed hair grazes his shoulders as he shakes his head during his intense whispered conversation with the porter.

I see a flash of coloured bank notes passing hands. Not

his first time, definitely. Is he a John? A womaniser? A drug dealer?

'Do you want me to get your stuff for you?' I ask Nicoletta, unsure about what I should do next. Should I protect her from him? Should I make sure the porter leaves so she doesn't get arrested?

But Nicoletta's clearly back now and there's a smart mind behind the eyes that were vacant just an hour ago. She squeezes my hand and pushes past Paul and into the flat, a mix of determination and anger on her face. Neither of them spares us a glance as the door closes behind them and the muffled sound of raised voices reaches us.

The porter shrugs and starts off towards the lift saying 'Let's go, we've done everything we could.'

Did we though?

IF I HURRY, I could still make it to work on time. War paint on, hair in a messy bun with a pencil stuck in it for (I-haven't-got-my-life-under-control-by-any-stretch-of-the-imagination) effect, I rush out the door. A coffee mug pinned between my chin and my chest, I'm juggling my computer bag and locking my front door when the sound of a throat being cleared startles me.

I turn around with a smile, expecting Nicoletta to have come back to drop off the borrowed clothes but instead the annoying detective Whatshisface is standing behind me, an amused expression on his face, not moving a muscle to help me. Of course, that'd be beneath him.

'Oh it's you again,' I say, lightly, as my heart dances a panicked little jig against my ribs. 'What now?'

'Funnily enough, I was thinking the same thing.' He holds the coffee mug for me.

He's very close. So close that I'm afraid he'll somehow hear my very guilty thoughts spill out of my ears or something. I can't help but notice that he smells clean and wholesome. My sweaty palms struggle to turn the keys but at last, the lock clicks in place and I'm able to turn back towards ~~the rugby player sized hunk~~ I mean the pain in my neck that is DS Tom Mulligan.

'So to what do I owe this unexpected pleasure, Detective?'

'Tom.'

'Detective Tom.'

He smiles and lowers his eyes as we start walking towards the lift. 'Actually, I just came to check that you were ok. We had a call this morning about a disturbance in your building and I recognised the address on the dispatch.'

If he were anyone else, I'd call bullshit. Oh unless the porter called the police after all. I should have thought to get Nicoletta's phone number. I hope she's not in trouble.

'How kind.' It's entirely possible that my voice is dripping with sarcasm at this point. 'But as you can see, I'm just fine and fully clothed. I'm not the woman you thought I was.'

'Yes, that's very clear to me now.' A corner of his mouth lifts sideways.

'Is that a smile?' *Ugh. Stop. Flirting. With. Him. Lily. You. Bloody. Dolt.* 'I thought this was a business call.'

'It is actually,' he roots through his leather jacket and extracts his small black notebook as we wait for the service lift, the scenic one is still MIA. 'It appears you went to quite the upscale private club last night, in the company of one... Spencer... Clifford, is that right?' He looks up from his notes.

Oh God, what if the old cleaning lady denounced me? They must have found his body by now, watched the

CCTV by now, interviewed the guests and figured out what I did. Struggling to control my (unfortunately very expressive) face, I remind myself that I'm supposed to only have been on a mildly disastrous date last night. Nothing more.

'How could you possibly know about my date?'

'Handsome, powerful, very rich,' he muses, 'aren't there other qualities you look for in a man? Integrity, intelligence, kindness perhaps?'

Anger and shame battle it out on my blushing cheeks 'Why does my love life interest you so much, Detective?'

'Tom, please call me Tom.' We step into the small lift and while he leans in to press the ground floor button, I detail his stubbly jaw and the gorgeousness of his lips. So inconvenient that my arch-nemesis is so bloody sexy.

'You did tell me to get someone to corroborate my whereabouts every time I sneeze or get a cup of coffee. Don't you remember?'

'Ah. Yes. Quite.' He lowers his head and flips through the pages 'But it appears that you did not go home together. In fact, I understand that you were quite upset when you left the club.'

'Upset? No, I'm just not used to drinking. I was sick and thought it wouldn't be a good time to kiss my date, perfumed with Eau-de-Vomit.'

My words have the desired effect and he backs off.

'Why do you care about me throwing up in very fancy loos anyway?'

He goes quiet and just stares at my face for a while as the lift goes down. There's so much electricity in the small space that it starts to zigzag like lightning in my gut. Supercharged butterflies. I don't know if it's fear or a crush but oh my God, I'm about to melt. Just as he starts to answer, a neighbour gets in so we all ride in silence until the doors pings open on the ground floor.

The young man gets off and runs to catch his bus while the detective and I remain in front of my building, in something like companionable silence as we watch the rising sun cast its timid light over the river. The water is still and as glossy as a mirror this morning. The reflection of the boats' white underbellies shivers in tender ripples on the water's shiny surface. Swans bob gently around, playing with the reflected clouds. It looks like it's going to be a beautiful day.

'Lily,' he doesn't look at me, he just stares at two swans swimming silently past us. 'May I call you Lily?' He throws a sideways glance at me and I nod. 'You can trust me, you know.'

Can I?

'I'm going to be honest with you. I hope you had nothing to do with the last three deaths.'

'Three?' I'm not supposed to know about Epsom. It's not been announced by the media yet, I checked as I was getting ready.

He holds a hand up. *No need for the method acting quite yet*, it says.

'Because if you did,' he pauses, 'if you did, I'd have to arrest you for triple homicide, you see. Hypothetically.'

I stare straight ahead as the sky ignites in shades of orange and pink and the swans glide on, unaware that my life could collapse in the next few minutes.

'So, I'd highly recommend that you stay home for a while. Perhaps avoid dates? Stay away from situations that could be misconstrued.'

I nod.

But he's not quite done yet. 'Throughout our conversation, I was reminded of something Lao Tzu said: if you don't change direction you may end up where you're heading.' He pauses and looks in my eyes. 'Do you understand, Lily?"

I nod, feeling my throat constrict. He knows. He can't prove it, but he knows.

'Good.' He flips his notebook closed. 'Good. Then I don't need to ask you any more questions about last night. Let's just hope you won't be in the wrong place at the wrong time anymore in future.'

'I won't, Detective.'

'Tom,' he says.

He has such nice green eyes. He pushes his hands in his pockets and marches off.

The swans elegant silhouettes fade into the distance, reflected in troubled white shadows below.

24

THE BIG ONE

'Happy birthday to you, happy birthday to you, happy birthday dear Lily, happy birthday to you!'

Scarlett, Emma and, Tamsin are all gathered around a small table at the crowded bar singing tipsily while Catherine sets a crisp on fire. That's it: I'm forty. Game over. Or perhaps not?

I didn't make it to forty dates in the end. Only twenty-six. I'm not sure it matters, after all.

I blow the little flame out and shut my eyes to make a wish. And for the first time in twenty years, I don't actually wish for a soul mate, or The One or love or even a shag. Surprised, I pause for a second and wonder. What do I really want? I draw a blank.

'Cheers!'

'To old friends!'

'Hey, I'm not that old.'

'You're ancient,' Tamsin says with the utmost seriousness.

The youngster in our midst. Her hair is aqua this month

and she's wearing dungarees with a striped red t-shirt and thick-frame eyeglasses. She looks like Waldo. We all clink glasses and I realise she's right, I'm starting the downhill half of my lives. *Cheerful thought that, Lily, Jeez.*

Casting around for an easy topic, I ask them if they've seen the latest Netflix series, which features a six foot five blond hunk who spends most of his on-screen time naked.

'OMG yes,' Scarlett enthuses, 'my nipples were hard the whole time.'

We all burst out laughing except Catherine who looks scandalised. None of us has mentioned Brett again since she came back from his funeral in Australia and she seems to be recovering well. She's also going to turn forty in a couple of months, so she must be rushing against the clock to ~~commit herself~~ enrol at the nunnery.

'I haven't seen it yet, is it a good series?' Tamsin asks.

'Sweetie, he's naked. The. Whole. Time,' Scarlett says, speaking exaggeratedly slowly. She turns to me 'What's the actor's name again?'

'I can't remember, it rhymes with cinnamon,' I say.

'Oh yes, he's got delicious buns,' Emma sniggers.

'Cinabuns,' Tamsin chortles and we all burst out laughing again.

'Really? We're going to talk about naked men again?' Catherine says throwing her hands up with annoyance, 'It's like you're all actually trying to fail the Bechdel test, for Pete's sake.'

'Oh, oh, I've got a topic!' Emma says raising her hand like an overeager first-row pupil, 'I've signed a petition to end the pink tax, I'll send it to you, so you can sign it too. I always buy the men's deodorants now, they're so much cheaper,' Emma says.

She's recovering well from the initial shock of starting

divorce proceedings, she seems to be at any rate. Scarlett tells me that Emma's called her a couple of times, in tears. I wonder why she didn't call me. Maybe it's still that residual suspicion that I was the Other Woman. I don't know.

'Don't men's deodorants smell funky?' I ask.

Emma shrugs 'it's a question of principle. Why should I pay more for the same product?'

'So you can smell of rose instead of musk?' Scarlett chuckles. But the tide of outrage will not be stemmed.

'I use an organic one,' Catherine says. She always smells of sweat. I'd put it down to her ~~death~~ nun-wish but now the mystery's solved: it's her granola deodorant. I feel a pang of remorse for my uncharitable thoughts; Catherine's got other things on her mind and it's my fault. We haven't talked one-on-one since that night, in her kitchen. I'm afraid to spill my guts. She's been cold towards me, like she suspects something. Or maybe I'm imagining things.

'Is it aluminium free?' Emma asks.

'Seriously?' Scarlett stares at all of us. 'I suppose I'm the only one who wants to smell good here.'

'Can you believe that last summer I ran a 5K against breast cancer and the sponsor was a brand of beauty products who gave out aluminium deodorants at the finish line?' Tamsin rolls her eyes.

'Thanks for running for a cancer charity, here's breast cancer in a convenient roll-on form. Cheers!' Catherine chuckles.

'Incredible,' I mutter.

Scarlett finishes her glass of Spanish wine and pours them some more while I stick with my Diet Coke. She's looking a tad too fabulous today. Her tanned skin is turning orange, I'd swear her boobs are higher and fuller than they were twenty years ago and she's graduated to fake lashes and extensions sometime since I last saw her. Why is she trying so hard? She's got the rich boyfriend already, does she still need to look like a live Barbie doll? Suddenly it occurs to me that it's not just a matter of getting the guy. She's going to spend the rest of her life trying to *keep* him. I'm exhausted just thinking about it.

'Alright, I've got one for you' Scarlett says, 'Apparently, they add chlorine in tampons to make them whiter because any colour on tampons makes men queasy.' We all snigger as she continues, 'but the chlorine in that location,' she makes jazz hands around her middle 'is super toxic.'

'That's just typical!' Catherine's teeth are purple. She gestures to the waiter for more wine 'you can just picture the male product manager, sitting in a meeting room with the male marketing manager and the male ad creative: *Mmmh a mini penis shaped object that women insert in their vagina... Let's make it as white as possible. Purity and the absence of reddish colours. That's the ticket. What's that? It could kill women if we make the tampons too white? Oh well, needs must.*'

'Because we're worth it.' Tamsin laughs, throwing her hair back. Her aqua locks swing back around her face like underwater algae around a drowned corpse. Epsom's hair moved like that, as I held him down. Suppressing a shiver, I try to let myself be carried by the evening's boisterous mood and fail.

'Exactly,' Emma says. 'Have you seen the documentary about how Victorians used to put lethal chemicals in their foundations to make themselves look paler? I was busy feeling superior and thinking about how absurd it was to kill yourself, so you can make a prettier corpse but then I saw this article that came out last week: it turns out the FDA found mercury in skin creams and lead in one hundred percent of the lipsticks they tested.'

'That's nuts,' Scarlett says, looking through her makeup pouch, 'I need to check the ingredients in my stash when I get home.'

'There was also that poor woman who died... did you see?' Catherine adds, 'Her family successfully sued the brand of talcum powder that gave her ovarian cancer. How is any of this possible? How can this not be regulated?' she wonders aloud.

Emma jumps in, 'It's almost as if they didn't care because the vast majority of people who use these products are women. And most legislators are men. There might be a correlation there.'

Sarcasm? Emma? That's new.

'Also, nail varnish: highly toxic, and there's formaldehyde in hair straighteners and apparently hair dye... cancer.' Catherine no longer dyes her hair, since... since the incident with Brett. The grey strands shine like silver in the dim bar lighting.

'Is that why you no longer dye yours?' I ask. She looks more peaceful than I've ever known her, more self-assured.

'Well, yes, and no. The fumes are so toxic that I've decided I can't in good conscience jeopardise hairdressers' health just so I can look artificially younger.'

Admiration and shame simultaneously sting, as I exchange a glance with Scarlett. I'd never give up on hair dye to save some strangers' lives. What does that make me? Selfish and shallow, I suppose.

'Aaaaah our favourite little nun is back! Preach sister, preach!' Scarlett laughs.

∼

That's it. I'm forty now, I muse as I walk back to my flat, my keys between the fingers of my closed fist like Wolverine's claws, keeping my head down as I cross paths with inebriated revellers and hoodie-wearing youths.

I skirt the gravel mounds and the muddy holes full of pipes, thinking of the nine dates I'm still supposed to go on. I missed my milestone. Oh well, I did get thirty-one dates in before the cut-off. But somehow the urgency and the importance of finding The One have faded.

There are a few birthday cards in my mailbox and I seem to have a parcel but as usual the porter is nowhere to be found. I swear this position is staffed by the Invisible Man. I knock a few times and call the phone number on the door but there's no answer.

It's finally happened, the dreaded deadline yet somehow it doesn't feel quite as depressing as I'd anticipated. I wonder why forty no longer feels like The End, as I brush my teeth and get ready for bed in my silent flat. I suppose when I had accomplished absolutely nothing with my life, the forty years of void felt like absurd waste. Time was flowing backwards then, the years slipping away ineluctably like the seconds of countdown to the big four-oh. A countdown to my obsolescence, my unmarriageability, my menopause. I felt powerless. I felt useless. I felt superfluous.

But now something different is happening. Time has started to flow in the correct direction again, towards an unknown future, towards a destiny that I want to fulfil.

The purpose is still death…

…but this time, not mine.

Yes, forty is starting to feel like a new beginning.

25

INTERLUDE: PAROLE, PAROLE, PAROLE

Words matter. They matter a lot. Misogyny permeates all of society, even the way we speak:

- A working man is probably a plumber who votes for Labour. A working girl? She's a whore.
- A Professional. If he's a man, he's a lawyer, he's diligent, he's good at his job. If a woman's a professional, she's a whore.
- A courtier probably hangs out at Buckingham palace, drafting up press statements about the latest royal baby. A courtesan? She's a whore.
- A master is a man in a position of authority who employs servants. A mistress? She's a whore.
- Mister is a form of address to denote respect when speaking to a man. A Madam? She's a whore.
- A Top Dog is a boss, a cool guy. A bitch? She's an (unpleasant) whore.

Spinster:
/ˈspɪnstə/

NOUN; synonym: **old maid**

1. A woman who is not married, especially a woman who is no longer young and seems unlikely ever to marry. *Gee, thanks.* It's a derogatory term— *Barely nowadays, my loved ones use it interchangeably with "single"*— referring or alluding to a stereotype of an older woman who is unmarried, childless, prissy, and repressed.
2. Historically, denoted a woman who spun wool for a living and was therefore financially independent. *Really? I suppose society's forgotten that tiny important detail. Being a spinster was good. It meant you were self-sufficient and didn't need a man to survive. Wow.*

EXCUSE ME, whot? Apparently there's a girl on Twitter who says when you turn twenty-eight, you're no longer a Spinster, you're a Thornback. I love it. Now that I'm forty I want to be known as a Manticore.

What's that you say?

No, it's not a dragon. It's a mythical creature with the body of a lioness, the head of a woman, and the sting of a scorpion.

And if you mess with me, I'll add snakes in my hair and turn you to stone. For good measure.

There.

. . .

I KEEP SCROLLING down the Wikipedia article. Ooh a list. I love a list.

Notable women who never married:

- Louisa May Alcott, writer
- Jane Austen, writer
- Clara Barton, founder of the American Red Cross
- Emily Brontë, writer
- Lucy Burns, American suffragist
- Coco Chanel, fashion designer
- Elizabeth I, Queen of England
- Kylie Minogue, singer-songwriter
- Florence Nightingale, nurse

Well, that's encouraging. Maybe I could do something significant and end up on this list.

- Lily Blackwell, ~~serial killer~~ I mean female vigilante.

It has a ring to it.
Ha ha. Get it? A ring. Just not the diamond kind.
I should get business cards done. How GenX of me. No, I should get merch done. Hot pink t-shirts with a slogan or something, sell them on Instagram. Who you gonna call? Ball Busters!

26

LOCKED IN

He's trying really hard to get it in. He's thrusting it, a concentrated frown on his face.

'Oh for fuck's sake,' he mutters.

It doesn't fit. He shifts his position and tries harder, elbows out, completely ignoring me.

Finally he gives up with a sigh and lets the lock bump against my chest as his eyes roam the room, his tiny key clutched between his sweaty fingers.

'So...' I squint to see his name badge, '... Matt,' I yell over the pub's hubbub, 'Is this your first lock & key event?'

He barely spares me a glance and he's off.

We're supposed to use the pretext of the game to start a conversation and flirt. But the men think it's a competition about who will crack a lock open first and win... win what? Nothing.

'Men.' I roll my eyes and glance at Tamsin. She's surrounded by a swarm of blokes and she's laughing throatily, her freshly dyed green hair like a beacon that screams *I've got issues. I'm drunk and silly. Come hither.*

Most of the men look like business analysts, IT developers and junior associates. She's probably the most exotic thing they'll come across this month. Perhaps this year. Maybe she makes them feel like some of her quirkiness will rub off on them, in a good way; they'll be nearly cool. Nearly.

Tamsin kindly invited me to come to a singles event with her. Every day at the office, for the last few months, I've updated her on the progress of my campaign. She shows me her Tinder catch-of-the-day, gives me the thumbs up when she sees me coming out of the loos, my outfit changed from day to night, my makeup reapplied, the flats turned to heels. It's brought us closer, this common debacle of online dating. Ever since the boardroom melodrama, her attitude towards me has changed. I'm no longer just her boss, maybe more like an older sister. Our growing friendship feels like a safe oasis in the desert of our men-dominated workplace. So I didn't have the heart to tell her that I'm not really keen to go on the last eight dates of my campaign. I've made my peace with being alone. Really.

Reflecting on my last date, I realise that Spencer never called me back. Oh well. This evening, absurd as it is, has already been more fun in ten minutes than the eight hours I spent with that fop. Good riddance.

I join a group of four girls who are playing beer pong against the boys. We miss wildly, not even hitting the table. We pretend to have fun. Pick up the filthy ping-pong ball from the floor, plop it in beer, drink the germs, the hair, the dirt, with a smile. Ha ha ha, we have such poor eye-hand coordination. We're so drunk. Please flirt with us. But the men's glances glide over us, finding nothing to snag on, and move on to the next group of does to hunt down (maybe that dating guru was onto something after all).

I go to the loo. Often. It's a place to escape the crowd

(and the absurdity). Apply makeup, listen in on conversations, rinse hands. Repeat.

I'm not even sure what I'm doing here, I've missed my deadline. Maybe instead of continuing with the dates, I should give up and just *kill* forty men. Lol. Now that seems more achievable than trying to find a good one.

Shaking off my sombre mood, I scan the room for a man I'd consider dating and that's when my eyes fall on him. My heart stops. I turn around and pretend I haven't seen him, but it's too late. Oh gawd. My boss is here. Ethan Viles himself. Shit, shit, shit.

How awkward can this evening get?

I'm putting my glass of water down and surveying the exits when a hand alights on my lower back. Biting the inside of my cheek, I turn slowly hoping it won't be him. But it is. Of course it is.

His blue eyes focus on my previously unrevealed curves, my short skirt, the bare-back top that reveals and suggests too much, the ridiculous amount of makeup on my face.

'Wow, grasshopper, you scrub up well.'

He leans in for a kiss on my cheek and his hand remains on my waist. Then he's reaching for my cleavage. What the...? Ah, yes of course. He plucks the lock from its lanyard. Blushing a furious shade of red, I don't have time to protest and what would I say anyway? *Oh Lord. Please let it not—*

The lock clicks open.

Of course it does.

'Aha! We're a match!' he says smugly.

I already knew that, since the first day I set eyes on him. I smile, uncomfortably aware that he's my direct line manager and that my livelihood depends on his whim.

He grins back wolfishly and, relishing my embarrassment, loops both his hands around me and lifts the laniard up and off my neck.

'I've cracked her wide open!' he shouts, more loudly than necessary, holding the open lock in the air above us. The crowd of drinkers snigger and catcalls fuse. Tamsin is nowhere to be seen. She's probably picked up a guy and they've gone to McDonald's to sponge off the alcohol or maybe they've adjourned to a nearby nightclub. Who knows?

One of the organisers dashes over with a bottle of champagne, tittering about love at first sight and idiocies of that calibre. She insists on taking our picture, chatting enthusiastically while Ethan accepts the prize with his usual smoothness and gives her one of his dazzling smiles. She glances at me and having assessed me as non-competition, she beams up at him but for some reason, Ethan's found a mouse he'd rather play with and tonight it's Yours Truly.

He can't actually be interested in me in that way. He's powerful, he's whip smart, he's upper class. He could have any of the young women here, there's not a snowball's chance in hell he'd want me. His employee, pushing forty, out of shape and 'difficult'.

'Come on, let's go drink this bad boy.'

'I don't really drink...'

'Tonight you do.'

∞

DATE 32

I FOLLOW him upstairs and he finds a spot outside on the terrace where we settle into wicker armchairs, overlooking the city. Here, the bustle of the party is only a background hum.

My God. I'm really here with *him*. His familiar face is painfully beautiful to look at; his full lips beckon and his eyes have their usual intensity, but today we're not poring over some report that he's unhappy with, today, his eyes are trained on me. Electricity zings through my abdomen as I lower my eyes. He pops the bottle open, I flinch and he laughs. It's a rich, deep sound.

He takes a swig from the bottle and leans back against the armchair.

'Come on, loosen up a little grasshopper.' He offers me the champagne, 'we're off the clock.'

A part of me knows this is a very very bad idea. But that part is drowned out by a flood of bubbles and the buzz of bottled happiness, as I take a gulp of alcohol for the first time in years. I want him so much. I want him to think I can loosen up. The moment will curdle if I stay sober.

This delicious loss of control feels like a liberation too, an end to years of watchfulness and restraint. Maybe I can trust myself. I've been afraid for too long that if I let go of my fears, if I loosen up even an inch, I'll suffer a terrible wound again, as deep and as life-altering as the one Cameron inflicted on me. *Yes, maybe it's time to let go. And I want Ethan so, so much.*

A few swigs later, I'm honest-to-God giggling. At age thirty-nine. *Have I no shame?*

There's something like fondness and surprise on his features. 'You should let your guard down more often'. His deep bass tones send tremors through me, like music through a speaker.

'You mean I should be less professional and let you walk all over me?'

'Well, you *are* difficult,' he says.

'Determined,' I counter.

'Hysterical and shrill,' he says.

'Assertive and forceful.' I jut my chin forward.

'A bitch.'

I frown and stand up. My knees wobble a bit, unaccustomed to the rush of dizziness.

He stands up as well, a lot steadier than me. 'Oh don't be like that. It was a joke, where's your sense of humour?'

I hesitate, eyeing the door.

He pushes my curls back and lets his hand trail down my neck. Goose bumps pop along the path of his fingers but I shake myself and take a step away. *Bad idea, Lily. Bad idea.* I start to walk away but what he says next stops me in my tracks.

'You must know how I feel about you…'

That makes me waver. I look at the door. Appropriately enough, it's marked emergency exit. I can't do this. I mustn't. *Dating the boss, seriously Lily.*

'…how I've felt about you since I clapped eyes on you, at the interview, all these years ago.'

I thought I'd imagined it all. The sparks flying so hard that they seemed to bounce off the walls of his office. I reach the door and put a hand around the knob. The metal door knob unfortunately. *You're worse than me, get your mind out of the gutter.*

He's very close behind me now. I should just open the door and leave but instead I rest my forehead against the wood, my hand still on the handle. He liked me back. All these years, I harboured a massive crush for him and the whole time, *he liked me back*. How much time did we waste?

He swigs more champagne from the bottle and his fingers trace a path along my spine all the way down to the small of my back as he leans against the door, trapping me. He's so close, I can feel his hardness nested against my bum, his warm body against my naked shoulder-blades, his breath ruffling the curls on my neck. I shiver.

'You think I haven't seen how you look at me? You think I don't know?' he says.

'I have no idea what you're talking about,' I lie.

As I turn around to face him, he pushes me against the door and I tilt up towards his gorgeous face, but the kiss doesn't come.

'You think I don't feel your eyes on me when we work late?' he whispers, his voice hoarse, 'you think I don't want to fuck you right on that conference table, every single time?'

His fingers snake up my skirt as I mellow with desire.

'Ethan, we shouldn't.'

'You think I don't smell it on you now, how much you want me?'

His fingers breach into me, slipping in easily.

'I've wanted to do this since I set eyes on you,' his voice is raw, as his fingers ram into my cunt 'all these years, every time you refused to do as I told you, every time you stood up to me, every time you said no.'

He leans over me, his fingers bent deep inside. His hungry eyes search my face for the rise of desire. It climbs and climbs, like an overwhelming surge until my breath snags and my dam breaks.

He grunts with surprise as he finally realises the power he holds over me. The power he always held in his clamped wet fist but never released. Until now.

I melt into his embrace but he pushes me back against

the door and watches me, an air of proprietary satisfaction etched on his features.

'You're mine now.' He bites my lips avidly, his stubble deliciously rough against the tender skin.

And though my soul bucks against it, I realise, he's right: I am.

I am.

27

THE MAKEOVER II (THE SEQUEL)

Scarlett is wincing as she dangles a pair of my panties on the end of a pencil.

Sunlight streams through the window behind her and an ambulance wails past my bedroom window as dust motes waltz gently to the floor in a glittery dance.

I pluck absentmindedly at a hair on my calf, trying and failing to look glamorous in lounge bottoms, a pencil planted in my messy hair bun, as I sit cross-legged on my bed.

She's invaded my lingerie drawer and is now waging war against a pocket of guerrilla resistance in there; the white cotton knickers with the pink hearts all over.

'What in the name of God is *that*?'

'My most comfortable pair?'

'Comfort.' She rolls her eyes. 'It's gotta go Lily.' She drops them in the bin, as if they were radioactive.

'You don't understand, I have... hip issues.'

Her bum is perfectly shaped, toned and reasonably sized with just a tiny amount of bounce.

I hope she won't find my Harry Potter boxer shorts.

She takes a deep breath, like I'm a disappointing pupil who's being headstrong. 'So when you're getting ready to...' she makes wavy motions with her hands in front of her lady parts, 'you know?'

I know.

The hair on my calf is in good company. I try to pluck it with my fingers. He just gets curlier and resists me. Tonight's the night with Ethan. Or could be. I hope. Or not. Argh.

Somewhere along the way of this dating campaign, I suppose I gave up on finding The One. After all, there was very little chance that the man of my dreams might have been one of the blokes who trawled the net at two am looking for pussy.

But Ethan.

Ethan's my Achilles' heel, isn't he?

Maybe he's my chance to get off this blood-soaked merry-go-round before I lose control. Maybe if Ethan is The One and if it works – *oh wow the mere thought of it makes my heart pound faster* – maybe if it works, I can lead a normal life, forget about the murders and hang up my Avenging Angel gloves.

When he kissed me, it was as if a window had opened and I snuck through it, back to my old self, away from the path to madness. Maybe if I throw myself body and soul into this eleventh hour relationship, I can still be saved.

There's an undercurrent of despair and febrile urgency powering me, like a buzzing electrical current when I'm with him. I can feel myself grinning too much, agreeing too much, wanting him too much but I can't stop anymore than I can stop breathing. Ethan is my last chance to erase the horrors of this year, succeed in my dating campaign and put my life back on track.

When I went on a forty-date walkabout in the desert of

the modern dating scene, I didn't expect the demons to be so overpowering and so real. I thought the sum total of my temptations would involve saying no to drugs and turning down a bit of kinky sex. Not fighting for my eternal soul and forsaking murder as a way of life. *Gosh. You live and learn I suppose.*

I scrunch my eyelids and visualise myself going towards morality, goodness and light. I can do this, I can leave my Dark-Lily-shadow behind and take control of my life again. Love will save me. *Get thee behind me Satan* and all that.

'Lily, are you listening to me?' Scarlett's hands have come to rest on her hips.

'Erm, yes, yes of course.' I've absolutely no idea what she's been saying for the last ten minutes.

'So when it's nearly time. You lay him on the bed.' she pushes me back until I'm lying down so I get the picture.

'Uh huh.' I nod, fighting to remain serious.

'Then, once he's on his back and looking up, you strip to your underwear, but –and this is very important, Lily— you keep your shoes on.'

She probably doesn't mean my furry hot pink trainers.

'You do have sexy heels, don't you?'

'Erm…' I wonder where I put them. It's been a decade since I last wore them. I'm usually a Sketchers-on-the-Tube and kitten-heels-from-the-work-locker sort of girl.

She sighs theatrically.

'When I first, you know…' jazz-hands motions around her hooh-hah again, '… did it with François, I had on my green strappy Jimmy Choos and I'd matched them with green eyeliner. I wore the black lace.' – whirling motions around the breasts—'and nothing else, except a bit of Chanel number 5.'

I nod, feeling a fit of the giggles coming close to the surface, as I push myself up on my elbows.

'Then I went...' she strikes a pose, her thin shapely leg thrust forward Angelina-style, chin up, duck face on.

She waits for applause or something.

'Wow?' I venture.

'François never stood a chance.'

'Uh-Huh.'

'You have to do the same or Ethan could slip through your fingers. You won't get another chance like that, you know. He's the right sort and the best one you've come across in... well ever sweetie.' She taps her watch, 'Tic Toc, tic toc.'

Somehow I don't think her method will work for me. 'Sure. I'll try,' I say, sitting up on the bed.

She grabs both my hands in hers, looking earnestly into my eyes. 'The most important thing to remember is: whatever you do, Lily, just don't be yourself.'

I chuckle, thinking that she's joking.

'It's not funny. Just promise me.'

Ah blimey it's not a joke, it's an intervention.

'Which part of me do you object to?' I say, 'the bossiness, the wit, the sharp tongue, the lack of simpering or the complete cluelessness about how to get and keep a guy who's worth it?'

'All of the above,' she sits next to me on the bed. 'Just laugh at his anecdotes even if they're lame. Be pleasant, smile prettily. Shave your goddamn legs and don't treat him like competition, you don't need to prove that you're smarter than him.'

'Hey, I was planning to shave!' to be fair, I wasn't going to do any of the other things. But she's right: needs must.

I stand up, raise my right hand and swear solemnly that

I'll giggle, flick my hair and compliment him: the gorgeous, smart, educated type of man everyone thought I'd be married to by now.

Scarlett and I end up at a department store where I try on scratchy, black lace bras with devil-wiring that digs into my boobs from the sides every time I ~~try~~ fail to take a breath.

Scarlett opens the curtain wide and regards me critically.

'Hey! What?... Hey!' I cross my legs and hunch but Scarlett is having none of it.

The saleswoman is now smitten with her of course.

Scarlett squashes a roll of fat that's bulging out of the too-tight, itchy Brazilian. 'No, you see, Vera, that's not the right look, the pants need to be a size up.'

Vera makes a face. 'That's the biggest one we have, dear.'

'Oh well, we'll have to put her on a diet then. We'll take it.'

'Erm...' Yeah no. Clothes are supposed to adapt to our bodies. Clothes are supposed to be props to make us look good. We're not supposed to adapt our bodies to squeeze into the clothes. That's absurd.

I get back into my three-for-a-tenner panties with relief and consider the ~~torture implement~~ bra that's hanging on a miniature unrecyclable hanger in front of me. Well, if that's what it takes to get Ethan, I suppose it's worth the small discomfort.

Shrugging, I get out and join the Scarlett-Vera unit at the till where I proceed to have a heart attack when the amount is proffered. I pay, knowing full well I'll wear this three times in my life.

Actually, it ended up being twice. You'll see.

DATE 34

ANYWAY, so that Saturday, I don my ~~scratchy~~ lacy bra and knickers, a dress in which my curves are at their best and a brand new pair of heels. Feeling ridiculous, I hop on the Tube and go meet Mr MacDreamy.

Something weird happens on the way. I'm usually completely invisible, as in: people bump into me and fail to apologise, men ignore me, nose in their phone, harassed commuters shove me aside so they can get to the train door faster. But tonight, unfathomably, I get smiles, a seat is offered to me, a bloke effaces himself, so I can get off the train first. I don't know what's more depressing: that they don't usually do these things out of common courtesy or that they do it now only because of how I look. Ignoring it all, like a good Londoner, I stare somewhere between their breast pockets and their shoulders, as I smile blurrily. I can't run in these shoes and I've left my pepper spray and my knife at home because they didn't fit in the clutch. So no need to encourage unwanted attention tonight.

Anyhoo, long story short, I finally arrive at the Shard and after being searched and X-rayed and queued, the lift doors open and London unfurls at my feet, as the sun sets in an explosion of oranges and purples.

'Ah, there you are grasshopper,' I tear myself away from the view just in time to catch the small change on his face when he sees me. Before I can be sure that I really saw desire there, Ethan's features smooth again as he pecks me on the cheek. I've had a crush on him for so long that the scent of CK Eternity has become for me synonym with him and my unrequited love. I breathe in deeply as his stubble scratches my cheeks and he squeezes my hand tight. Maybe soon, the scent could mean something different. Something better. Is there such a thing as the fragrance of requited love?

'Come on, they're waiting,' his fingers let go of mine and he walks away.

The evening goes by quickly. Our business guests are all men and tonight, for some reason, they listen to me. They usually don't. Not that we're really touching on the merger at this stage, it would be in poor taste, but it's a nice change not to have to fight for the floor.

At last, dinner's over, the guests won over and packed off into a cab. Ethan wraps his hand around my waist proprietarily and hails a cab. He gives his address to the driver without asking me if I want to go – arrogant bastard – all the while kissing my neck with a low growl. The alcohol is going to my head again I only had one glass but it doesn't take much. I should learn about wine vintages, it seems to matter to him. Maybe I can adapt, grow a taste for it?

Finally we're there and it's a penthouse in Shoreditch. *Well of course it would be, wouldn't it?* He's so cocky and flash.

He starts to undress me in the lift and we spill into his flat, kissing urgently, pulling belts, removing scarves, breathing hard. His shoes drop on the shiny black floor, my bag is discarded on the marble-top designer table, we fall on the dark grey leather sofa and I then remember the bra.

'Wait, wait, wait.' I peel myself off him.

'What?' his voice is rough and deep with lust.

Tottering on my too-high heels, fighting the tipsiness, I stand above him, as he reclines on the sofa. I fight with my dress, trying to open it at the back with less-than-sexy jagged movements. He tries to get up to help, but I push him back and finally yank the dress off me. *Oh dear, this is a terrible angle, he's staring right up at my double chin from below.*

Unfortunately there is also an undershirt to contend with and tights. How am I going to remove the tights and yet keep the shoes on? The shoes are killing me and I'm acutely aware of the plaster + blister on my heel. I'm sure Scarlett wouldn't approve of plasters. She'd also be adamant that I should keep the shoes on. *Shit, I forgot to match my eyeliner with the... what was it again?* I remove the t-shirt and one of my boobs has sort of popped out of the bra, so I stuff it back in, oscillating dangerously.

'Woah there, grasshopper,' he chortles, 'you ok?'

'Yes, yes, absolutely.' I can't see how to remove the bloody tights sexily, so I stand there, attempting a duck face, hand on my waist, with a come hither look.

'You done?'

'Erm, yes.'

He comes up, in what I hope will be an enamoured embrace but instead he pulls me towards him and I lose my footing on the too-high heels.

'And that's terribly scratchy,' he unclasps my bra and throws it away.

As he takes me on the sofa, curtains wide open, like a cheap peep show for all the world to see, my eyes fall on the discarded black lacy bra and I think... the thought escapes me as I need to focus on being perfect. Sucking in my stomach, reacting just a tiny bit too much when he does something that works, pointing my toes in an elegant way. I need him to like me. I need this to work.

Somehow I'm now on top and fervently hoping that the light is dim enough to hide the cellulitis on my thighs as the rhythm reaches a frenetic tempo. I'm out of breath. *For God's sake Lily, you need to get yourself into shape*, I think fleetingly as I wonder whether to kiss him, but my breasts will look better if I stay upright. He's close. I don't dare stop and then with a rattle, he comes and I can finally relax.

I collapse (elegantly) on top of him and proceed to try and fit my boobs against his chest and my head in the crook of his arm. Am I sweaty? Do I smell ok? Well, there was no oral, so I'm probably alright.

Not long enough afterwards, he removes himself from my embrace, making me feel like I'm too much for his taste. Too affectionate. Too big. Too clingy.

He takes a while to come back, so my thoughts start to wander.

The sex wasn't fantastic, to be honest. It felt a bit like a teaspoon stirring a teacup. But what he lacks in girth he makes up for in gravitas and charm I suppose.

Perhaps I simply had too high expectations. The first time is never brilliant anyway. You need time to get to know someone, get to know their nooks and crannies, their secret language and their loveliness.

It's taking an awfully long time for him to come back.

I throw on some clothes and pad around his place trying a few doors as I look for him. Finally, I find him, fast asleep in his bed.

I suppose that's my cue to leave.

Just as I'm tiptoeing out of his bedroom, my phone starts to ring.

Ethan tosses in his sleep, while I struggle to pick up.

'Hello?' I whisper, throwing a glance over my shoulder. *He's still sleeping. Phew.*

'He proposed! He proposed!' Scarlett sounds genuinely delighted and ever so slightly drunk.

'Oh my God! Congratulations!' I resist the mean temptation to ask *Which one?* François, of course. The billionaire's son finally got it.

'Tell me everything,' I whisper, as I hop on one foot, trying to get my tights back on.

He took her to the Ritz, got down on one knee and apparently got so flustered that the little red velvet box escaped his grip and ended up knocking Scarlett in the face. She caught the box, accepted the proposal, (it goes without saying) and voila: she's now hitched the ride to the top she's always held out for. She sends me a pic of a diamond so big that I wouldn't bet on her chances of floating if she decided to go swimming. I gawk at it, as I wriggle into my dress and check one last time, on all fours, that I'm not forgetting anything embarrassing, like a used condom or something, under the designer sofa.

The wedding is being organised at the speed of light (before François has a chance to come to his senses), and I'm to be the maid of honour. Being her childhood BFF and all.

'Wow, Scarlett, I'm so happy for you.'

I am. *What? Don't be like that.*

Really I am.

Ok, fine, you're right, I'm also sick to my stomach with envy. But I don't tell her that of course.

As I pull Ethan's front door shut behind me, holding the phone pressed between my ear and my shoulder while she gushes delightedly, it occurs to me that tonight's the night Scarlett and I both got the man of our dreams. Maybe this is the beginning of something wonderful. Maybe life could finally be good? Yes, maybe it can!

28

IN WHICH OUR HEROINE FINDS HERSELF IN JEOPARDY AND CHOOSES DOOR NUMBER TWO

For the last three months, Ethan and I have been having "meetings" at every opportunity in the office. He usually finds an empty conference room, closes the door and corners me, his hands finding their way under my shirt as his hips grind me against the white board. His kisses probe deep and hard until we both come up for air. Then arrives the embarrassing moment to leave the room; I go to the loo, to reapply concealer on my chin while he waltzes back to his office, full of swagger and smiles. I don't really mind, I'm floating on a little pink cloud of happiness. I can't focus, I'm falling behind at work; all I can do is daydream.

On my way to work, I'm already getting butterflies and can't stop smiling, just at the thought that I'll see him again today.

As I near my office, I notice someone waving. How odd. It's eight-thirty am, everyone else on the street is marching down the pavement, head down, ready to bowl incoming traffic out of the way. What's that ditzy woman doing, facing the wave of oncoming commuters?

Oh. It's Catherine and she's waving at me.

'Gosh, Catherine, what are you doing here?'

She pecks me on the cheek and we form an eddy in the flow.

'I thought I'd surprise you. Coffee?'

What does it say about me that I have to think about it and weigh one of my best friends in the world against half an hour of additional preparation for my meeting? Ashamed of myself, I dismiss the thought and we head towards a nearby empty bar, which serves watery infusions and undrinkable coffees during the daytime.

Catherine's saying all the right things, talking about the weather and about how Emma's divorce is going (badly, she's getting fleeced in exchange for keeping the kids most of the time) but I can see that something's wrong: her normally pristine clothes are wrinkled, her shirt buttons are misaligned, her usually shiny hair is tousled and dull.

'So, Lily...' a small frantic laugh escapes her as she toys with her spoon and tea bag. 'A few months ago, you remember, in my kitchen... what did you mean when you said I shouldn't feel guilty about Brett?'

I take a shaky breath and think innocent thoughts. 'Just that Catherine. That you had no part in Brett's death and have nothing to atone for. I still think you shouldn't go through with all this joining-the-orders nonsense, it won't bring him back and—'

'It's just... you see, this detective came to see me. He said... he implied terrible things about you, Lily.' The string strangles the teabag around her spoon.

Oh shit. 'What do you mean?'

'He... gosh it sounds ridiculous, even saying it, now that I'm in front of you,' there's a bit of hysteria bubbling under her words.

'What did he say, Catherine?' Too sharp.

She looks up, startled, as her teabag ruptures and small specks of brown spread everywhere.

'He asked if I could think of any reason why you'd hurt Brett on my behalf.'

The sentence falls on the table between us with a little thunk and then it lies there, immobile, waiting for one of us to pick it up.

The silence stretches.

'And was there?' I ask, as my voice squeaks around the knot in my throat, 'Catherine, was there a reason why Brett might have needed to be kept away from you?'

She stares at me with wide eyes, her face pale.

'Lily, how could you?' she whispers.

I can't meet her eye. I can't look up. I sense her get up and leave and I stay there at the table, as the minutes spill out of my grip by the handful, impossible to count.

What was I thinking?

I failed to make a difference, I failed to impart justice.

Killing three random men didn't change society or the patriarchy one jot. It just made me a serial killer and a damned soul. I didn't even help Catherine, I broke her.

It was all hubris and now that policeman is closing in on me. Oh God.

This was the biggest mistake of my life and it can never be fixed. But perhaps there's still time to take the road to my salvation: Ethan. A normal life. No more murders.

Let the world right itself without my help.

Nobody ever asked me to take on the Avenging Angel mantle and I can stop, can't I?

Can't I?

I have to.

If I want Ethan, I *must stop*. He can never know about what I did.

It's all quite simple, really: behind door number one: blood, shame and eternal damnation. Behind door number two: love, marriage and a future.

I don't know why I ever thought this would be a difficult decision to make. I don't know why I'd ever hesitate.

The answer's obvious: I need to choose Ethan.

And apologise to Catherine.

And pray that DS Mulligan won't be able to prove anything.

And avoid any further trouble.

And shit! Get to my bloody meeting.

THE DAY GOES by like cold molasses, dragging itself miserably. The tower is plunged in fog and although some days, I can see the magic of being inside a cloud, so high up that we're touching the sky, today's not one of these days. The oppressive autumn mist envelops everything, trapping me in endless identical carpeted rooms. Even the recycled air that whirs round and round the building can't escape.

Ethan dragged me into his office at lunchtime, clearly intent on fondling my boobs or something but my heart was not in it. Now I feel his stare as I pretend to work, but I don't look up.

So of course, today's the day DS Mulligan chooses to make an appearance. The receptionist comes to get me and stage whispers about the handsome man in the lobby. Ethan looks up and his eyebrows arch quizzically but I ignore him and follow her, as if in a bad dream; wanting to stop but unable to.

She leads me to the meeting room where the Detective is

waiting. My heart accelerates even from a few feet away and it starts to pound so hard when I open the glass door, that surely he must hear it.

He takes up all the space in the small fishbowl room. His huge frame unfolds as he stands up, all six feet five of him. Delicious looking with his straight nose and his square jaw, his easy smile and lovely green eyes. But he looks grave.

'Lily.'

'Detective Mulligan.' I fight the urge to rise on my tiptoes and kiss his cheek.

He sits down and gestures towards a chair, like he owns the place.

'There's been a development.'

Oh no. From the corner of my eye, I see movement in the lobby but dismiss it, consumed by sudden dread as I sit down, feeling like I've been called to the Principal's office.

He figured it out. Catherine said as much. She thought his suspicions were believable enough to come all the way here, dishevelled and panicked. He must have been pretty convincing. I wonder if he'll drag me away in handcuffs. I wonder if my trial will be in the papers. What a stupid way to end my career and my life. I could have done so much more with it. Taken a higher road, effected real justice for women. It's too late now.

'Yes?'

'The medical examiners found bruises on Epsom's back... and there was evidence of peri-mortem intercourse. Clearly someone was with him in the tub. They're reopening the case.'

I nod, unable to say anything because of the lump in my throat.

'You see, Epsom was extremely high profile. He was

connected to a lot of very important people. Some of them want to know what happened to him.'

I nod, imagining what these very important politicians and industry magnates will do to me once I'm in prison. I won't last long. The colour drains from my face as I consider what to say and come up empty.

'The ME is now looking for a suspect... it's no longer considered to be an accidental overdose, so they'll start to actively analyse the samples they collected at the scene. Do you understand?'

I nod.

'They're tracking down the women who were seen with him in his last hours.'

'Oh?' I swallow hard, thinking of the two girls in the hot tub. The maid who saw me with his floating body.

Oh God, Oh God, Oh God. It's only a matter of days or even hours before they can place me in that pool with Epsom. Did I leave DNA behind? Fingerprints? Hair? Could they figure out I was there? I was half naked, my hands were all over him, dragging him, pushing him under. Will they find my fingerprints on him? My skin under his nails? Can they match the shape of my hands to his bruises? Years of CSI, NCIS, L&O SVU and other alphabet soup police shows swirl in my head as the room tilts off its axis and I grip the chair's arms to stay upright.

'Lily, talk to me. You can trust me.'

Tom leans towards me and the small room feels smaller and smaller, as he gets closer. I don't know how much longer I can keep up this charade. He knows. I know that he knows. It's over.

His hand alights on mine. Our faces are so close now. 'If you ever want to come to me for help or anything else...'

Should I just confess and be done with it? The uncertainty is starting to feel worse than a clean break would. For a moment, I look into Tom's eyes and see compassion there. Understanding.

'Oh Tom, I—'

The door bursts open and Ethan barges in, breaking the spell.

'What the bloody hell is going on here?'

Tom and I spring apart like guilty lovers and the words of my confession stay suspended on my tongue, bitter tasting and dangerous.

'Oh erm... Ethan. Tom came by to give me some news. He was just leaving.'

The detective tries to connect with me but I avert my eyes and with a regretful sigh, he gets up and stares down at Ethan.

Ethan holds his ground, making up for his shorter stature with the aura of wealth and power. The small room is buzzing with testosterone as the two men size each other up and then Tom turns to me with a smile.

'I see that reason won over imagination, Lily. I hope you got what you hoped for.'

What does he mean? Oh yes, Kant.

My heart does a silly little wobble as I understand his meaning. That my story with Ethan is only the illusion of happiness. He thinks I've settled.

Ethan loops his arm around my shoulders and frowns, as Tom excuses himself and leaves.

Oh God. That was close. What if the policeman had introduced himself and revealed that he was really here about a murder, or three? I'd have lost everything in one fell swoop: Ethan, my job, my freedom.

That's it: no more murders.

I can never come that close again.

The door closes and we're alone. Ethan turns on me and narrows his eyes. 'Is that why you've been so weird lately? Why this morning, in the conference room, you didn't want to…'

'I need to get back to work Ethan.'

He frowns.

This isn't how I usually talk to him.

I'm already padding towards the door, to escape the suffocating little room when Ethan takes a deep breath and grabs my wrist. 'I think we should go exclusive.'

My heart stops.

I turn slowly back towards him.

It's happening. It's really happening.

Finally.

So why doesn't it feel better?

He kisses me and wraps me in a big bear hug. Over his shoulder, I see Tamsin walk into the empty lobby. Her eyes go wide and her turquoise mermaid hair starts to flicks this way and that as she grins from ear-to-ear and gives me a double thumbs up.

29

"IT IS A TRUTH UNIVERSALLY ACKNOWLEDGED, THAT A SINGLE MAN IN POSSESSION OF A GOOD FORTUNE, MUST BE IN WANT OF A WIFE." (JANE AUSTEN)

I've been invited to be a maid of honour twice this year. We all know how my stepsister's wedding went. Fun times.

Weddings are such God-awful affairs. You're single, in your ~~late thirties~~ (argh) early forties, the only one left who's unmarried. They don't know what to do with you so they seat you with the priest, at the children's table or next to the completely unsuitable single guy who's (a) creepy, (b) in his seventies or (c) gay.

Anyway, all this celebration of love makes me either weepy, envious or angry. So, as a rule, I hate weddings. And the prospect of going to two of them in one year is, to say the least, daunting.

But it's Scarlett's wedding this time, I want to enjoy it and rejoice for her. I was open to just having anyone accompany me, so I wouldn't be the embarrassing ~~old~~ maid (of honour). I just needed a bloke, any bloke to make it look like I was a card-carrying member of the adult club. Somebody to elbow in the ribs, and say, 'Hey, look at that, Monte Carlo's Casino, pretty cool, no?' So I'd have gone with a clotheshorse, if I'm honest. But then Ethan happened. So, on the off chance, I asked him if he wanted to come over to South of France with me for the wedding and a weekend away. And lo and behold! He said yes!

∽

DATE 36?
(Can a whole mini-break abroad count as a date? Should I still be counting dates? Do months of booty-calls and sneaky office groping count as dates? I don't know, I don't care, I'm so happy I could sing with my arms outstretched like Maria at the top of her Austrian hill. But I won't. Because I'm in France. And I've got a sense of dignity. Fine. You're right, I don't and I just might.)

I WAIT for a while outside the Nice airport, under the curious gaze of the grizzled taxi usher, my roller suitcase at my feet. It's surprisingly warm for this late in the year and I'm glad I erred on the side of optimism with my hat (John Lewis £65), my lavender blue silk shift (L.K. Bennett £175), and my heels (Russell & Bromley £95). *I know what you're thinking. I'm trying too hard. But what do you propose? That I go to the wedding wearing jeans? So give a girl a break, will you?*

The eye-popping price tags are all in the name of catching a very handsome, smooth, sophisticated bachelor. *And you know why I need this*: it's either him or a life a bloodshed, gore and murder. *So be nice, ok?*

Ah speak of the devil. He skids in front of the airport terminal in a rented Jag convertible, looking so Ethan, with his megawatt smile, his cute cockiness, his stubbly kisses. We roar away and spend the next hour winding up panoramic roads towards the top of the ~~French Riviera mountains~~ world.

I've pulled all the stops for this trip, so we're in the gorgeous wedding hotel with sweeping views of the Menton bay surrounded by the Mediterranean's dark blue waters. The marble-floored lobby echoes under our steps as a grand piano accompanies our check-in and we start to whisper without really meaning to. The quiet sheen of luxury descends on us like morning dew, depositing its sparkle on everything and everyone around us.

An exciting trip ensues on the French Cote d'Azur. The convertible roars as we swerve around the island's scenic roads, soaking in the sea views, windswept and elated. We walk hand-in-hand, looking like a king and queen, attracting glances. A friendly waiter jokes about how he'd love to flirt with me but is too afraid to try. Ethan kisses me in sun-drenched village squares, we eat croissants, buy trinkets at the antique markets and marvel at the views. We rent a boat to explore deserted wild creeks and caress each other under the blue water.

THE HAPPY PARENTHESIS ends on the morning of the wedding. Ethan dons his tux and then proceeds to wait for me as I spend a good hour in the bathroom fighting to sleek down my frizzy hair, plastering on makeup, praying for my London manicure not to chip. Finally we're ready: it's show time.

We make our way to the honey-coloured village square, meeting other guests on the way towards the small village church. We're all in our finest outfits, waving as tourists point and smile, there are a few paparazzi too. The son of one of France's biggest fortunes is getting married, after all.

Look at the gorgeous bridal party, the beautiful wedding, the glamorous dresses! It's all so lovely and boisterous.

The church is full of musty missals and overenthusiastic choir singers, wandering toddlers and stray petals. Emma's happy tears dilute the hymn lyrics on the cream paper programme, so we end up singing from mine, heads together. The smell of centuries of incense has accreted in the air and absorbed into the golden stone, lending the weight of history to the occasion.

In short, the ceremony is lovely.

Scarlett finally gets her man.

Amen.

∽

THE AFTERNOON PASSES by in a whirl and soon, night falls fragrant and joyful. Ethan's at the bar, drinking with the men, looking smug and gorgeous while he mingles with France's business aristocracy.

Without him, I'd be the object of pity today. The unmarried one, the childless one. More importantly, without him, I'd still be murdering men in back alleys, coming home soaked in their blood, wrangling with my conscience. Ethan saved me in more ways than one. He can never know who I really am and what I've done.

A slender man with salt and pepper hair approaches Ethan's group by the bar and for a moment, I think it's Lord Epsom and my heart stops. The sex trafficker's charming demeanour and his easy smile transform into a grinning death mask as he turns to stare right at me. Cold sweat pearls all over my body. But it's only Scarlett's uncle; a perfectly inoffensive family man. I shudder and push Epsom's ghost away.

This part of my life is over. And if I try very hard, I can almost pretend it never happened. I'm just a normal Maid of Honour, at her childhood friend's wedding. I'm with the man of my dreams and life is good.

'It's time. It's time!' someone shouts.

The single women are all assembled. There's a gaggle of us. Most of them are twenty years younger than me though. They add the nannies, a few flower girls, random passers-by, it's mayhem and oh so French.

Scarlett positions herself and throws us a backward glance. Her dress is so tight, she might have been sown into it but she manages to take a few teetering steps and throw the bouquet over her shoulder.

It lands squarely in my arms. I wish I were too cool to care but out of nowhere tears of joy and relief start streaming down my face. *I could be next.* I could have my own sun-drenched wedding, all my friends around me, Ethan pledging to love me forever. This could be me next year. Admittedly not in that tight a dress. But still.

The girls are on me like a swarm of bees, squeaking with glee and I catch a glance of the men clapping Ethan on the shoulder with commiseration. His mouth curls in a half smile as he strolls over to me 'Happy, Grasshopper?'

I dab the corner of my eyes and nod, not trusting my voice as he bends to kiss my lips, slowly, tenderly.

An old lady comes to say in French that we're a handsome couple. 'Merci,' he grins. My heart swells. My handsome man. The One.

'Thank you.' I whisper as we gather on the church steps for the group photo.

'You'll pay me later.' He pinches my bum as our glamorous party faces the camera.

'Stop it,' I wriggle out of reach. 'Behave, Mister.'

Everybody yells 'Cheese!'
For once I'm not on the outside looking in.
I'm in.
I belong.
I fit.

~

'Where is that bloody idiot?' Scarlett's nostrils are flaring. Never a good sign.

François has disappeared. My friend ropes me into the search and finally we find him, Ethan and the rest of the groom's friends in a back alley watching a street fight. There's shouting, sweat, testosterone. It's all very Mediterranean.

'What are you doing?' Scarlett hisses, 'all our guests are waiting for you. You're supposed to give a speech about how lucky you are to have married me and instead you're here watching thugs fight in the street?'

Scarlett's husband is very drunk. Lurching, he extricates a piece of paper from his inside pocket, unfolds it laboriously and reads the beginning of his speech.

'If I were a dog, and you were a flower, I'd lift up my leg to pay you homage my dear, and give you a shower.' The best man bursts into laughter.

Scarlett's voice is measured but full of menace. 'What does that even mean, François?'

The fighters reach a frenzied climax and fall into the surrounding crowd. The groom is jostled by protesting spectators but he manages to stay on his feet.

'He's just saying he's glad you're his,' the best man slurs, throwing his arm around the groom's neck and breathing alcoholic fumes in our faces. 'He's marking his territory, that's all.'

My friend's gaze falls on the young man who's snickering now, as they both sway drunkenly. If looks could turn men to stone, there'd be snakes hissing and roiling in her hair right now. With an effort, she dismisses the handsome fop and her eyes go back to her husband's. 'Come, let's go back inside.'

'Putain, j'ai épousé une Anglaise. Elles ont aucun humour. Merde. C'est trop tard maintenant,' François laughs feebly, as his best man commiserates with him. Then he frowns and turns back to his new wife, concentrating 'Don't you like your poem, my love?'

The crowd is chanting *fight, fight, fight*, which seems oddly appropriate for the sideshow I'm witnessing.

'François. Fucking. Get. Yourself. Together.' Scarlett hisses.

Ethan comes to the newlyweds' rescue, sounding more coherent than the others, a cigar between his fingers. 'An unfortunate metaphor, to be sure. Don't worry ladies, I'll get them back inside.'

Scarlett hesitates for a moment and then turns on her heel and marches off. I shrug at Ethan and hurry back after her. She's silent on the short way back and then very quietly, a few words escape her lips, tinged with sorrow, 'he regrets marrying me.'

'What? No of course not,' I say, not daring to look at her face.

'He could have done better. Found a fabulous French woman who was from his world. Who am I? A two-bit London girl, a piece of trash from the dodgy suburbs. What is he doing with me? I'm going to wake up one day and realise it was all a dream.'

'He's head over heels for you, Scarlett. Everyone knows it. He couldn't help himself, he had to marry you eventually.'

'Exactly! He did it against his better judgment. Because, you know, we're so good in bed together. But what happens when I lose my looks and the sex isn't mind-blowing anymore? How long before he realises I'm not good enough for him?'

'Hey! Nobody speaks of my best friend like that. You hear?' I loop my arm into hers. 'Look Scarlett, I didn't want to say anything but he's not the sharpest tool in he shed, now, is he, your François? He's bloody lucky to have found a woman like you.'

'You think?' her eyes seem brighter than usual. Maybe tears. But no, not Scarlett.

'I'm sure. And who knows? You might end up helping him out, you know, with the family business. You've got the brains for it, the ambition, the confidence.'

She wipes something under her eye.

'Yes, he's very lucky indeed,' I say, ' and don't you ever doubt that, you hear?'

She nods.

A SPEECH from the groom is quite out of the question by now. But they manage to get their first dance done. It's an awkward Tango, which neither of them dances with enough confidence to pull off. The belaboured moves and the look on their focused, grumpy faces is all a bit cringe. Like actors playing a part. The part of the perfect gorgeous bride, the part of the heir to the luxury retail empire, the idyllic stage sets, the award-winning costumes. It should all spell dream-wedding but it's just trying a tad too hard. Any moment now, it feels like someone will yell "Cut!" and we'll all revert to our normal selves and go home.

A string of forgettable speeches ensues, fits of laughter and heckling. Ethan's gorgeous, he's charming, he's mine. Catherine tipsily calls him my 'beefcake' and all the bridesmaids giggle. The mother of the bride exclaims, 'Oh the boy can dance!' and I think *she's right*, as the room swirls around us and I surrender to Ethan's embrace.

Life feels light and sparkly again. I remember the sound of my own laughter, I remember the feel of my own body tuned into another human being's body. My blood runs faster, my heart starts to beat again, cracking its hard, dusty shell and pumping joy and pleasure and love into my whole being.

30
IT'S ALL GOING SOUTH AND A BIT PEAR-SHAPED

DATE 38

Ethan's at my place for the night, hurray! It never usually happens, we always go back to his penthouse in Shoreditch. It's just bigger and more practical, as he has all his stuff handy and can easily get ready in the morning.

It's alright, I don't mind, I've organised myself and I usually bring a change of clothes and my make-up kit to the office every day, just in case he invites me over. Which he does, once or twice a week. He jokes that I'm his Uber-sex. You know, as in "Uber-eats: We deliver!" Ha ha. The other day, when he asked me to come over at ten pm, he'd even left word with the concierge to allow me upstairs, *which kind of amounted to officialising things between us, don't you think?* Yes, it's only a matter of time before he gives me his keys.

So tonight is special. He's come all the way South of the river just for me! I've cooked a meal, got all the good china, the silver and the crystal out, the works. I even lit a few candles, feeling ridiculously cliché, but candlelight is marvellous to camouflage wrinkles and create an intimate mood, so hey ho.

But my plan must have worked too well because with the combination of food coma, dim lighting and Netflix, Ethan's fallen asleep on the sofa.

The movie's finished and I'm washing the dishes, debating what to do, I could wake him up and coax him to bed but then he might decide to go home, so I just let him sleep.

Dressed in nothing but a silk babydoll nightie, I brush my teeth, hesitate and then decide to leave my makeup on. As I slip into my bed, I realise that I mustn't fall asleep. I can't risk him finding me mouth open, drooling in my slumber, my enormous pear-shaped behind protruding from the too-short negligée.

Lying on my bed, I can't help it... and like every night, my mind starts to play its movie on the blank canvas of the ceiling.

For two years I have kept The-Forbidden-Place under lock and key, carefully bolting down the door. But my heart has been starved for so long that now it's ripped the door off its hinges and burst into the The-Place-I-Dare-Not-Go-To, careening like an out of control monster as it devours its sights and delights.

And what sights they are! As I lie on my bed in the darkness, eyes wide open, the film of my future life with Ethan is projected in glorious Technicolor across the ceiling: the glamorous evenings in trendy bars with all his friends, the anniversary weekends in New York, the diamond ring on my finger, the Soho House membership, the stylish in-laws, Ethan and me on a sofa in his penthouse apartment, reading books. His smile, his smell, the feel of his skin against mine. For the rest of my life.

I try to rein it in, I try to reason that it's too early, I try to chide myself for breaking my own rules but it's too late. The door to The-Forbidden-Place is hanging off its hinges and the monster is loose. The night's stillness envelops me, like the silent beat before someone says something they'll never be able to take back. My life feels like it's poised on the brink of possibility. Tantalising, mesmerising, impossible, just within reach yet also unlikely. *The absence of loneliness*. The thought is nearly too enormous for my heart to hold.

What if I screw it up? What if I say or do the wrong thing and my dream life slips through my fingers like smoke. What if he finds out about what I've done? How broken I truly am? Eyes burning with unspent sleep, I rest my hands on my stomach, feeling it lurch and the room with it. I'm so taut with hope that it feels like seasickness. I need to believe that it's possible. Because, after all, it is. We're dating. *If you can call it that.* We're together. *Sort of.*

Pinned on the mattress by the weight of my expectations, I imagine my life finally sorted. I wonder if my hair will behave in that dream future, I wonder if my thighs will magically rid themselves of cellulite and whether I'll finally morph into the adult I thought I would become by age forty instead of this eternally unfinished creature I seem to be.

I tell my impostor syndrome to shove it where the sun don't shine and instead I get drunk on the sweet nectar of happiness, pure, unadulterated joy and love.

I'm not actually happy yet.

Yet it feels so good even to just imagine it that tears start sliding down my face, carving two silent grooves to my ears and into my hair.

Don't be ridiculous, Lily.

Happiness like that only happens to other people.

. . .

I'M fast asleep when something wakes me up. Something inside me, moving. I jerk awake in the pitch black, fighting with the tendrils of nightmare and the dead weight suffocating me.

Ethan, it's just Ethan.

I push him away and his fingers plop out of me with a small suction sound.

'Hey, what are you doing? I was asleep,' I mumble, struggling to wake up.

'What does it matter? You're mine and if you'd been awake you would have said yes anyway.' His voice is low, raspy.

I wouldn't have refused him, so I suppose... it's ok? An unidentified disquiet squirms in my gut. 'That's not...' I struggle to express my unease through the fog of sleep. *This isn't right.*

In the darkness, he looks alien to me, his mask of charm is gone and the face behind it makes me uncomfortable. He parts my thighs and tries to penetrate me but I'm dry and something about this feels wrong. Rather than put in the groundwork, he spits on me. The gob of whitish drool dangles from his mouth and falls on me as I squirm to get away.

'Ew.' I laugh awkwardly.

He tries to push his penis in but it folds on itself, as if shying away from the entrance. I lay a tentative hand on the slobber-covered slug and find it flaccid and cold. Maybe I'm overreacting, maybe he doesn't need my consent every time if we're in a relationship. *So why does it feel wrong?*

Well I'm awake now and my frantic need for this relationship to work is awake once again too. I rub my sleep-filled eyes (ah shit, mascara) and try to focus on Ethan 'Maybe if you...'

'Don't.' He flops on his back, dejected.

'But do you want me to...' I say, trying to coax his shrivelled little appendage.

'I said no, goddammit.'

Snuggling up to him, I try to find the right words, 'It's OK, it happens.'

'No. It doesn't happen to me. Ever.'

It's not the first time it's happened actually and worrisome thoughts have been crossing my mind these last few weeks like clouds across a windy sky. How much would I be willing to give up in order to keep Ethan? What if the sex never really fulfils me? Would pleasure be something worth foregoing for the sake of love and a stable relationship? *Yes, definitely.* Could I give up pleasure for the sake of renouncing Dark Lily and her path towards murder and madness? *Probably.* For the rest of my life? *Maybe. I don't know.*

'You just had to laugh at me, didn't you?' he says.

'Sorry?' I ask, drawing a complete blank, 'When?'

He doesn't answer. He just turns away and ignores me.

'But Ethan, really, it's ok...'

'Shut up.'

Oh.

It's all my fault. Why did I have to laugh when he spit on me? I thought it was disgusting and demeaning, but maybe it's normal nowadays? What would I know? I haven't had a proper boyfriend in donkeys. Now I've gone and offended him. What if he dumps me?

Oh God.

What if I go back to being alone? I can't do it anymore. Not after tasting what life could be like. Worried and embarrassed, I get out of bed to wash off the spit and he follows me there.

'Hey don't come in!'

He sniggers. 'Oh give me a break, you pretend to be so clean and proper but you're disgusting.'

I freeze.

He gestures at my pubes.

'How can you let yourself go like this?'

'What do you mean? I've never done anything down there. I haven't let myself go.'

'Would you let me?' He rummages through his overnight toiletry bag.

When he turns back, he isn't looking at my face, he's looking down, past my nakedness, at the offending patch of curly brown hair. A shiver runs visibly through him, as he holds his razor up.

I can't give him up just yet, my first chance at love and happiness in a long time, so I say 'sure?'

He sits me down on the closed toilet lid, lathers shaving foam on me, sliding his fingers in crevices and generally making an effort to make this seem sexy. But it isn't sexy, I cringe as he scrapes the dangerous instrument close to my very sensitive parts, my toes curling on the cold white tiles. He wears a look of deep concentration on his face, crouching in front of me, his tongue sticking out, as he focuses on corners and hard to reach spots.

Why does he need me to match his expectation of beauty even in that innermost way? By the time he's wiped the soap off me, his member is hard and full for the first time in a long while and he throws me on the bed and takes me roughly, without an ounce of gentleness or affection. He slides in, gliding unimpeded through to the core of me.

I feel naked. I am naked. But I also *feel* naked.

Later that night, as he sleeps, I creep back to the bathroom and stare at the unrecognisable pink bulge between my legs. Absurdly, I felt like Samson after Delilah's betrayal, robbed of power. Reduced to a little girl.

In a vague, diffuse way, I sense that I'm losing Ethan but I don't know why.

The future he promised is also slipping through my fingers, I can feel it.

It's all going pear shaped.

31

THE LIFE CHANGING MAGIC OF TIDYING UP

A small dildo is hopping all over the table on small legs, a wind-up key swivelling at its back.

'Look what I got!' my colleague squeals as he unwraps a green rubber mankini while my neighbour squeezes two breast-shaped stress balls. One of the nipples is bulging out of his fist (*ouch*).

The pink wind-up toy falls off the table as Tamsin giggles. Her hair is (appropriately enough) pine green and she's wearing antlers and a super garish Christmas jumper with strategically placed blinking lights. She's a tad drunk and regularly collapses into a heap of laughter. She's not far from dancing on the table. She did last year and everyone's been daring her to do it again. One or two more mulled wines and she'll be up there, shaking her booty I think.

I wish I knew how to let go like she does, how to be happy and free again. She seems lit up from the inside, as she makes everyone around the table chuckle at her jokes, toast with cheap prosecco and sing modified lyrics of carols *While shepherds wash their socks by night....*

God, I hate Christmas.

Novelty secret Santa presents. Arguments with the parents. Phony good sentiment and repulsive overeating.

At least this year, Ethan will make every miserable minute more bearable. Yes, even the office Christmas party. Last year one of the VPs kissed a secretary in a nook they thought was private and turned out wasn't. I wonder if they'd have been fired if they hadn't both been women. I guess we'll never know.

Ethan's starting his second bottle of red by now and he eyes me across the table in a way that suggests he might want to test the unspoken edict against office trysts. No matter what, we're not having sex in a bathroom stall. Again.

I have standards. Plus we might get caught.

I wouldn't want to ruin everything now that it's going so well. I mean, I think it's going well. I text him a lot more than he does but I suppose that's to be expected, I'm such a romantic and he's a man, so of course he's more reserved.

It's going well. Definitely. I think.

It's just... I suppose I want more. It feels like we're regularly hooking up and that it could go on like this for months, even years. But something's missing, I can't quite put my finger on it, we're not actually together-together. It's small things. Like I don't dare let my guard down around him. Like he doesn't text to check that I got home safely. Like I'm still obsessing over his messages like I need to divine their true meaning. Like his eyes still roam when a pretty girl walks by. Like he hasn't introduced me to any of his friends. Like he hasn't told anyone we're together.

Three months is a long time to feel suspended by a thread and I'm slightly frantic now. I want peace of ~~mind~~ heart. I want commitment and tonight, I will get clarity. I need to. I can't take this uncertainty much longer.

The dinner finishes on a gloopy note with barely edible

Christmas pudding and congealed custard. Our group adjourns to the basement where booths plunged in darkness surround a small dance floor. Our colleagues flock to the bar to order the courage to dance and in the commotion, I corner Ethan in a booth at the back of the room.

∽

~~DATE 39~~ (?) *yes, definitely should count as DATE 39*

Lubricated by the alcohol, our easy banter starts, the ice melts, we laugh, he looks pleased to see me, I drink in his smile. *No, no, no, Lily you can't just let yourself be carried away by how easy it is to be with this man. You have to ask why it's so hard to see him, why he's never available. You have to ask the questions that itch at your soul when he's not in front of you, smiling his gorgeous smile.*

'Ethan, I wanted to have a chat with you.'

He freezes. Jeez, I didn't even say 'we need to talk'. Mental eye roll. Men. Scared bunnies in headlights. The lot of them.

I've been working on this conversation in my head for the better part of a week. It went from recrimination to confrontation to pleading to this:

'You said you liked me.'

He shrugs.

'And we're exclusive, right?'

'More or less.' In my imagined conversations I got a categorical "Yes" at that point. My brain skids to a halt with the sound of a vinyl record being scratched. Wait. That's the basis. If he doesn't ~~love~~ "like" me and he sees other women, then what's the point of any of this? *I should stop. I should stop.* I'll wish I had stopped, later but no, I forge on.

'Ok. Mmh. Well,' I falter, 'I really like our dates. I like the way we easily chat and how we are when we're together. I like the way you kiss me and... everything.'

I meant to say this as a way to connect with him but now it feels like I'm up on a stage, in front of an unforgiving audience and I'm losing my train of thought. *Keep it together Lily. If you can kill a man (or three), surely you can find the courage to be just a girl, standing in front of* ~~a boy~~ *her boss, asking him to love her....* But I digress.

'What I *don't* like, Ethan, is the in-between-dates. The lack of communication, the lack of depth in our conversation, the low frequency of our dates.'

'I'm very busy.' He crosses his arms.

'You know, life is short....' *Oh dear Lord, this isn't going terribly well, is it?* 'Why not just dive into this relationship like we mean it? Let's make a go of it, what do you think?'

He looks aghast.

'I don't want you to build any expectations, Lily.'

What does that even mean?

He continues, playing with the glass of scotch in his hands. 'The only reason I'm dating you is *because* of who you are; you're older, you're my colleague, you... you're not part of our social class. You could never be a serious prospect. I don't want a relationship. That's the whole point of dating *you*.'

'But I don't understand, why would you come to France with me then? You knew. You must have known how much it meant to me. The bouquet... the...'

He shrugs, 'it was an all expenses paid mini-break. You

paid for the hotel and the plane and you rented the tux, I didn't even have to carry it, you brought it there and back. Why wouldn't I go?'

Oh.

Oh Lily, what an idiot you are.

I avoid his eyes and swallow the ball of grief that has lodged in my throat. It's so large that no words can squeeze around it.

'So…'

'I guess you're just not The One,' I say more to myself than to him.

He physically throws himself back in the booth at that.

'And what a lucky guy he'll be,' he says with something like pity in his eyes.

Ah condescension.

Anger flares up and I welcome it. *Hello old friend, how I missed you.* I embrace the rage and discard the hurt. There's time enough for pain later. *I. Must. Not. Cry.*

'So anyway,' he rallies with a winning grin, 'your place or mine?'

Un-fucking-believable.

Out of nowhere, a small Japanese voice chimes in a corner of my brain saying "Does this spark joy? If not, discard it."

'Mmh. No. Thanks. I'm good,' I whisper.

'You're sure?'

'Yes. Good night Ethan.'

I walk away across the dance floor, dodging my drunk colleagues as his gaze burns my back. I thrust my chin up, hugging myself and hold on to the tears until I'm safely out of view.

. . .

HOME.

I close the door and crumple on the floor, in the dark, empty flat. My legs just fold and a flood of tears pours out. I mourn for all the times I tried and failed. All the dream relationships that never became real. All the kisses and blowjobs and compromises I regret giving away. All the love I need and never obtain. All the love I give and never get back.

I walked away from this one at least. I could have stayed for years, losing more and more confidence as he valued me less and less. I could have wasted all my energy trying to convince him to love me. At least, I got out early. *That's something, isn't it?* A sob shakes my whole body as I realise how truly and utterly alone I am. Again. *Lily, you're so stupid. Why did you think this time would be any different? Why did you think anyone could ever love you?*

That's when the decluttering starts in earnest. I yank my dress off, violently getting rid of this hopeful attempt to seem attractive. Suddenly I can't stand the sight of it anymore. Grabbing a rubbish bag I throw out my hopes, my dreams and the stupid garter belt I'd gotten as a surprise for him tonight. I tear to shreds a note he once wrote me and the soft, pathetic, tender bits inside of me. I shed my naiveté, my trust and a bottle of wine I'd bought for his next visit.

That bottle of wine, that's perhaps what hurts the most; I changed so much to be with Ethan that I lost sight of who I am. This whole affair was like an intoxication, I lost control. He was what I *wanted* but he wasn't what I *needed*. What I needed was to stay true to myself, to stay true to my path. I'm such a fool. How could I allow myself to be so altered by the mere possibility of love? I should have known, from that first sip of champagne, that he was wrong for me. Someone who cared about me wouldn't have pushed me to drink.

Wearing only a robe, mascara tears running down my cheeks, I drag the bulging plastic bag to the chute and wait to hear the satisfying thunk as it hits the bottom of the shaft, imagining the bottle shattering in a thousand shards of pain and spilling its purple blood everywhere.

32

INTERLUDE: SILVER SCREEN (MAGIC) BRAINWASHING

I'm so angry. I'M ANGRY ALL THE TIME NOW. *Yes, full caps. What do you want from me?* I'm angry. I can't even watch TV anymore and don't get me started on the classics.

<u>The Sound of Music:</u> Taciturn, authoritarian man well into his fifties seduces his virgin babysitter and convinces her to provide childcare for his seven children for free for the rest of her life. *But hey the songs are fun and catchy!*

<u>There's something about Mary:</u> Ah yes, the girl has not one but three stalkers and she chooses one of them? That's so fucked up. *But ha ha, hair gel scene. Hilarious.*

<u>Pretty Woman</u>: Way to whitewash prostitution Hollywood. The guy pays women for sex...*but he's rich and handsome, so I guess that's ok?*

. . .

<u>Love Actually</u>: Rick (of *Walking Dead* fame) is a stalker. No, the "say it's Carol singers" scene is *not* unrequited love, it's bloody stalking.

Mr Darcy takes advantage of his maid. What's that you say? They don't even speak the same language? Optional. As long as she's cute in her undies and doesn't stand up to him too much, he can make it work. She'll be a welcome respite from the snark of Elizabeth Bennett.

Professor Snape abuses his managerial authority with his employee who is portrayed as a temptress. Clearly, she alone, bears the responsibility for his adultery, *see a pattern here?*

Oh and Hugh, the prime minister underdog wins the pissing contest against the American alpha male over who will get to shag the tea lady. *How cute.* Except none of it is cute, it's a blooming ode to patriarchy and it inexplicably gets resurrected every Christmas.

CAN THE DYSTOPIAN, abusive, toxic merry-go-round stop now? Please?

33

HO, HO, HOES

I arrive at my parents for Christmas a few days early, exhausted from work and from the break-up. I was supposed to appear at the same time as Vivian and Jonathan on Saturday morning but I needed a rest from my dumpster fire of a life, so I came early, hoping for some TLC.

I haven't taken a proper break from work in years but what are they going to do? Fire me? The whole department rests on me. I'm allowed a few days off for reason of murder, heartbreak and self-pity, aren't I?

I stand on the threshold with my suitcase as Mum looks around me, behind me.

'Hi Mum.'

She gives me perfunctory air kiss. 'You didn't keep up with your diet?'

I shake my head no and shuffle on the doormat, waiting for her to invite me in, to hug me, to ask me if I'm ok.

'I sent you the Daily Mail article on endomorphs, didn't you read it? You just cannot afford to slack, Lily, with your heritage.' Her eyes land on my hips as her mouth thins into a line.

Mum wishes she'd never met my Dad, the Cypriot, the summer fling, the regrettable eighties dalliance, the alimony-dodger, the author of my frizzy hair, my brown eyes, my wide hips. It was before she knew better, before she moved to Essex and started voting Tory. Stephen's so much easier to explain to the neighbours.

I push past her and carry my suitcase up to my room. Well, I say *"my room"*... as soon as I left, Mum and Stephen redecorated it hotel-style. My stuff got tossed out, handkerchief-sized towels appeared in the bathroom, the kind you use once and leave in a basket, miniature shampoo bottles and body lotions materialised in the M&S marble tray and all photos of me vanished from the area. I think I might still be in one or two snapshots downstairs, in family groups. Well at least mine's still a bedroom, Vivian's bedroom is now Stephen's office with no bed in it at all. Not that Vivian will stay at home this Christmas, Jonathan and her have booked an exclusive B&B nearby, for privacy and because, you know, they're adults.

I roll my suitcase to the room-formerly-known-as-mine and hang my clothes as Mum sits on the bed and starts her litany, you look exhausted and why do you look so bloated and is there a reason why you've arrived early and don't you know, the neighbour's son was recently promoted at a very-famous-and-prestigious law firm and I never saw why I had to pay for your studies to become a lawyer if it was all going to be for nought and you ended up working in a bank and I can't understand what you do anyway. And why are you always wearing black it's not as slimming as you think and it makes you look frumpy. Where's the lovely Ethan, I'm so fond of him and it's the first time I'm really keen on anyone you've ever dated and—

'He's not coming, Mum.' I interject before she starts to hyperventilate.

'What do you mean?' she looked stricken.

'We broke up.'

'What did you *do*?' she says horrified.

Thanks for the vote of confidence there, Mum.

'Commitment issues,' I say vaguely, hoping she'll leave it at that.

She shrugs, 'Oh duckling, shouldn't you know this by now? No man ever wants to commit. You need to call him, tell him how you feel about him.'

I never know if she gives me bad advice on purpose.

~~Ok, Boomer,~~ I mean 'Yeah, I don't think that would work, Mum.'

'But don't you understand that he's your last chance? He's the best you'll ever do, at your age. How could you fail again?' There's a wailing note in her voice, as she shakes her head, staring at me. 'You must get him back before it's too late.'

'I don't want him back,' I say, fighting tears as I sit on the bed, hoping for a hug.

Stephen pokes his head in. He has a nose for misery and gossip. He loves it most of all when they combine for his entertainment.

'Ethan dumped Lily,' Mum says with raised eyebrows.

'Actually it was me who...'

'Did she go all intellectual on him? Try to lord it over him and show off how smart she thinks she is?' Stephen asks, with distinct glee. 'She's so bossy and opinionated. It puts men off.' He puts away my empty suitcase as Mum closes the wardrobe. They're both standing over me now, as I crumple on myself, sitting on the edge of the bed.

'Well, maybe if she lost weight, someone would want her,' Mum adds.

He nods, 'True, she's also too prudish, with all the no-drinking, the no-smoking, I bet you she's frigid. Men aren't very complicated. There's got to be something wrong with her.'

I'm right here FFS.

They continue their debate as they leave me there.

I wonder if there is really something wrong with me. *Yes. Probably.* Did I ever really love any of the men I was with? Or did I love the idea of them, the idea of being normal? Perhaps I just wanted a man so I wouldn't be left behind as my friends launched into the next screen (marriage) and the next level (children) while I remained perpetually at the entry level of the video game of life? Did I genuinely want to marry or did I just want my family's acceptance and recognition?

There is something broken and wrong in me, I just know it. My Mum and Stephen are right: I'm a bloody psychopath and a serial killer. And the humongous bum doesn't help either. I'm clearly going to be alone for the rest of my life. I don't deserve love. I'm disgusting.

EXHAUSTED AND DEPRESSED, I spend the next day in bed, in my favourite flannel pyjamas, watching Netflix and going downstairs only for meals. Stephen's passive aggressive remarks don't even get a rouse out of me, I'm so accustomed to them. 'Um, something stinks, open a window, darling,' as I come in the room. Implying I haven't showered. I did. I just got back into loungewear after the shower. 'What's wrong with youngsters nowadays, always tired. When I was young, I was dynamic, always ready to take on life. Nowadays...' I don't hear the end as I turn around and retreat to my room. 'It must be nice doing nothing while your Mum slaves away in the kitchen,' muttered as Mum puts a lunch of fish fingers and frozen chips on the table. I usually put the table on and do the dishes, but I'm not active enough it seems.

I'M STEELING myself to go downstairs this morning when I hear a commotion.

'Quick! It's them! Get the door Stephen!'

I'm thinking that I should shower, dress and put some makeup on before I go say hi when Mum materialises by my bedside. Puzzled, I look up at her, rubbing my eyes. She's stuffing all my belongings in my suitcase.

'Ah, [ugly] duckling, you're awake. Your sister's here. You need to move downstairs.'

'Mmmh, what?' I mumble, fighting to wake up properly.

'Vivian and her husband need your room. I've put you in the downstairs bedroom.'

There is no downstairs bedroom. There's a laundry room cum basement.

'But... what?'

'There was a mix up with their B&B. Come on, stop being so lazy and selfish. Get out of bed.' She pulls the duvet off and starts to change the sheets as I get out of bed and trudge downstairs in my pyjamas.

So of course, as I reach the last step, I find myself face-to-face with Jonathan who's more handsome than ever.

'Hey Lil.' His eyes roam over the car crash of a look, my hair, without the benefit of product has sprouted a nuclear mushroom of curls and I haven't got a gram of makeup on my face, my t-shirt's decidedly dorky, sporting a "Nevertheless she persisted" banner over a WWII feminist flexing her biceps and I'm dragging my suitcase while carrying my toiletries under my chin. 'Do you want some help?' he asks as he kisses my cheek.

Words jam in my throat as his warm, solid presence envelops me. His arm wraps around my shoulders for a side hug, fleeting yet so precious.

'I'm ok,' I say, meaning, *I can take care of myself*.

But I'm not ok. Not by any stretch of the imagination.

'Jonathan, come tell Dad about your new car!'

His eyes stray towards the sound of Vivian's voice. 'Duty calls,' he says with a small smile.

I watch his back as he sways out of view, gorgeous and tantalisingly out of reach.

In the laundry room, behind the bicycles and the stacked suitcases, next to the humming wine fridge, Mum's set up a camp bed. I let my stuff fall out of my arms and slump down on it. It commiserates with me with a forlorn creak.

~

A WHILE LATER, showered and semi-presentable, I'm unwrapping the nativity scene as perfectly-put-together Viv tells them about her cracking career success at the middling marketing firm where she's a glorified sales person.

They ooh and aah.

The nativity scene has moulded since last year. We've displayed it every year since I was born. But this year, the plaster figures are covered in furry green mould and the hand-painted featured have melted under the fungal assault. Frantic, I unwrap one figure after another, speeding up as I try to find one salvageable figurine but my heart breaks with each grisly discovery. Fingers shaking, I unwrap the last one and with a small whimper of relief, find the Virgin Mary intact, her delicate face still smiling her enigmatic smile.

'Throw these old things out' Mum says with a grimace.

I do, but I pocket the little Mary.

THE REST of the family arrives. This year, my uncle and his wife have come back from their retirement in Marbella to spend the holidays with their kids and one or two brand new grandkids. Stephen's brother and his prolific wife are also here. The house is full of screaming children, meddling cooks, men drinking beer in the backyard and teenagers slouching in corners, transfixed by their phones.

My Brexit-voting uncle who didn't understand that it might affect his ability to stay in Spain asks about my career. So I tell him, the team of employees, the C-level reporting, the responsibilities, the prestigious company, the elegant flat with the river view. There's no two ways about it, I'm bragging and it's unseemly. But in truth I'm reminding myself as much as him about the fact that I'm a smart, resourceful adult, forty years of age. I tend to forget that when I'm here.

When I'm done, he throws himself back against the sofa and says 'and with all that you've not been capable of finding a man?'

I could literally have said anything about my accomplishments and it would have had no value whatsoever. In fact, by extension, what he means is that *I* have no value because there is no man in my bed at night.

CHRISTMAS DINNER IS a grand affair this year, there's twenty of us around the table, we're all dressed up, the turkey's enormous, the trimmings are overcooked, the paper hats are ridiculous, the crackers are full of plastic junk that will end up in the stomach of my sushi next month. The carols have been playing on a loop since yesterday and I'm just about ready to shoot Rudolph between the eyes. There's a mountain of presents under the tree and I can already predict that we'll neither like nor need any of it.

Mum wants everything to be Disney-ified so there's a list of taboo topics as long as my arm, ranging from immigration to the legitimacy of strikes, gay rights and the outlandish feminists who ruined it for all women. Stephen, who enjoys nothing more than seeing us all at each others' throats, makes sure to hit every theme on the list and stokes the flames of discord until Mum threatens to walk out.

Casting for a happy topic to get all our minds off politics, Mum throws a meaningful glance at perfectly-put-together Viv. With her natural elegance, her blond hair and her barely audible voice, she's been an island of grace and femininity during dinner. She didn't do anything of course. I'm the one getting up and down every five minutes to serve the sprouts, fetch the mustard and can you bring more wine, duckling and uncle Dan dropped his fork, so could you please, since you're already up.

Throughout the whole sweaty, screaming, mediocre affair, Vivian has remained immobile, gliding like a swan above all of it, her hand pressed against her stomach. And now, finally sat down, as I catch the glance between Mum and my perfect sister, the hand takes on meaning. I know what she's about to announce. The floor has disappeared from under my feet and I'm falling, falling. Encased in foggy shock, I see Vivian blush and rise, Jonathan by her side, the family raises their glasses of prosecco, their faces full of grins and teeth.

34

THE NIGHT IS DARKEST BEFORE THE DAWN

Later that night, I lay on the camp bed, feeling barely tethered to life, as I linger in the basement like the ghost memory of my family, deep in the bowels of the house. Relegated to this last resting place before I disappear at the next car boot sale.

The faces of my victims flash before my eyes, decayed and grim. *Murderer, murderer*, they whisper, as shadows move in the basement corner, behind a trunk of memories, coated with dust. *Murderer, murderer*, they accuse, as something scurries between shelves of jam and plant pots.

A creak and a shuffle, a whisper.

Sleepless and uneasy, I dash upstairs to escape. The whole house is asleep, it must be two am. Darting quietly in the dark corridor, I make my way to the kitchen to look for a midnight snack, but as I approach, I sense a movement and my guilty soul conjures up spectres in the lurking shadows. Fear plants its claws in my gut as the shape of a man materialises in the gloom. But it's not a spirit, or maybe just The Ghost of Relationships Past: it's Jonathan, wearing only tartan pyjama bottoms and a six-pack.

He hasn't seen me, he's rummaging in a drawer, looking for something. As quietly as I can, I retreat before I have time to think. Why didn't I walk in? Now it's too late, I'm hiding in the living room's shadows like a stalker. This is ridiculous.

It would be so easy to kill him.

The thought comes unbidden, jarring. A leaf or two from the garden's pink laurel in his morning smoothie. A few drops of oil on the floor, an unfortunate fall and a caved skull. An inadvertent mix-up of Jonathan's vitamins with Stephen's cardiac medication and his cheating heart would stop forever. Anything could happen really.

Dark Lily, tall and featureless as Death herself, rises and grows, stretching her arms wide open behind me. She embraces me, slowly, slowly, her liquid obscurity engulfing me as she grins. I let her whisper her awful tales in my ear as I glare at him. He's fumbling with an armful of Tupperware, oblivious to the threat, his back still turned.

It's such a thin line between vigilante and serial killer, isn't it?

Between righteous kill and satisfying revenge.

Such a thin line between Right and Wrong.

Would it feel good I wonder, to feel his neck snap in my hands? This man who made me feel for the last two years like a pale copy of the person I once was? Would it feel good to stare into his eyes as the life leaked out of them and he realised...

'Did you find any sweetheart?'

Oh.

Vivian's in a long lacy nightdress, her blond hair cascading down her back in honey-coloured waves.

At the sight of her, the shadow of madness and death

retreats reluctantly. I shudder with terror at how close I just came to tipping over into the abyss.

In the beam of golden light amid my ocean of tar, Vivian pads lightly onto centre stage, over to Jonathan and he smiles tenderly, as she nestles into his arms.

'I can't find any, my heart,' he says, 'but I'll go out and get you some if you're craving it...' his hand falls gently to her belly 'if *she's* craving it.'

A girl! Unexpectedly, something warm and hopeful lights up inside me.

Jonathan smiles at his wife with a tenderness I don't recognise on his familiar face. That smile is for her and her alone.

'Oh Jonathan,' Vivian smiles up at him.

There is so much love in that one word. So much softness and unspoken years of trust and history woven together like threads, binding them together. I've never seen them like that, unguarded, natural. They're so... right for each other.

'Ah! Look!' he reaches past her and retrieves something with a rustle, 'I found some!' He brandishes a Cadbury Fruit & Nut bar with a triumphant smile and she chuckles.

'My hero.'

I slink away in the shadows and go back to bed, unsettled. I wasn't meant to witness this and yet, in a way, it saved me.

∽

THE NEXT MORNING, it's Christmas and as always, we go to Mass. The choir sings out of tune, the incense thickens the air and the back-of-the-cupboard-missals are exhumed to cater to the once-a-year crowd, the priest gets carried away, heartened by the full church and delivers a much too long homily.

I'm not sure how, but Vivian and I are side-by-side at the end of a crowded pew, and the rest of the family is scattered in other rows, Stephen and Jonathan over there. Mum, her brother and our cousins on the other side of the alley.

… glo-ooooo-ooooo-ooooo-ria in Excelsis De-e-ooooooo.'

We're sitting down when Vivian whispers in my ear.

'I'm so sorry.'

I face forward, not daring to look at her face.

'Lily, can you ever forgive me?'

If I look at her, I will cry. How long have I waited for these words? And now that I've heard them, I realise that I *can* forgive her. I didn't think I ever could but when all is said and done, Vivian is my flesh and blood. She's as much a part of me as the beauty spot on my cheek, my fondness for biscuits or the memories of my childhood. She holds a piece of my heart inside her heart. My sister.

And she saved me last night. With a shudder, I remember the embrace of darkness and how it nearly engulfed me, as the choir's voices swell in the morning's innocence and purity. There's something about Vivian that keeps me tethered, something that reminds me that there's good still is in this world.

'I worry all the time, Lily. I worry that I stole away your happiness and you'll never find someone else.' Tears are trembling on her blond lashes, as she rummages in her clutch for a tissue.

Did I really want Jonathan or did I want to be cherished, seen, and cared for? Would I even know what to do with it now, if love came at last? Would I want the stifling bonds of marriage, motherhood and a symbiotic co-dependency?

Somewhere along the line, something changed. I've changed. Even Ethan was in a way, my perfect match. Not willing to commit. Independent. Driven. Hard. I'm like that now too. And wishing for the softness I witnessed yesterday in the kitchen is a delusion. Clearly my destiny lies elsewhere now and there is no point in wishing for a life that I no longer really want.

And just like that, I realise: it's time to move on.

'Vivian, no. Thank you, thank you for saying this. But I'm OK. I'm not sure a man could complete me at this point anyway. That's not how I'll find my happiness. And it's clear to me now that the two of you are soulmates...'

Once upon a time, I would have done anything, anything at all to get my soulmate. Can I honestly say, here, before God, that I wouldn't have done the same as her, if I thought it would bring me love for the rest of my life? I know the answer. I would have done everything she did and worse. I'm not even sure I would have felt as guilty as she does now.

It's Christmas after all... I should say it.

'... I forgive you,' I whisper. It costs me to say the words but once they're out, the day lifts up and the world feels brighter and lighter.

Her shoulders tremble, as she cries in her tissue. I hesitate for a beat then try a tentative pat on her back and suddenly we're hugging, crying and laughing all at the same time, as the chorus swells into happy Hallelujahs.

Kids in nativity costumes wander down the aisle, wearing tea towels headdresses and tinfoil halos, looking lost. Vivian and I hold hands, silently as I remember all the times we clutched to each other as children. The times we wore angel wings and sang Away in a Manger. The times I helped her with her homework and the times she consoled me when the bullies teased me about my weight in gym class.

This year, little Mary is on her own, filing at the head of the procession. There was a blunder, a train strike, Joseph didn't make it. Mary doesn't look phased though, she marches down the aisle like a boss, holding the plastic baby Jesus like a rugby ball, meeting everyone's eye with a grin and just a little bit of swagger. She's five and she's my new hero.

Watching her, it occurs to me that I walked alone this year too. Maybe that's the take-away, I ponder as I watch the little Mary march chin up down the aisle. Her face is cute as a button but she's resolute and doesn't seem to give a flying fig about Joseph failing to materialise by her side.

Yes, maybe that's it, the meaning of it all: that you can walk alone and yet face life head on. That crossing through the desert for forty dates will test you in ways you could not have imagined but that it will also make you stronger and that when you come out the other end, you're forged from sturdier stuff and made anew. *Yeah. A bit grand. But fuck it, I'll take that.*

Back at the house, I pack my things and steal the little Virgin Mary statue.

'Where are you going?' Mum screeches. 'I need help in the kitchen!'

'Sorry Mum, emergency at work. I need to go.'

'On Christmas day?'

I hug Viv, kiss her belly and promise to call her soon. For years I thought that perhaps I was Cinderella and she was the undeserving stepsister who wanted to steal my happy ending. But now I wonder. Maybe I'm exactly where I'm supposed to be and in a way, it's thanks to her.

Life is not a fairy tale and I have but one sister. Men will come and go but Viv is mine forever and I'm hers too, we pinkie swore it long ago: us against the rest of the world. Maybe she'll need my love and my help some day. Maybe I can be a fairy Godmother to her child. They're single and older, aren't they? Godmothers. They grant wishes.

I can grant dark wishes.

The darkest kind there is.

I wave at everyone and escape back to London.

35

DISCARDED

On Boxing Day, I open my eyes and there is a new hope in my soul. Something like self-acceptance perhaps. I am who I am and it's ok.

As usual it's 4:00am but I know from experience that there's no point in trying to fall back to sleep, no rest for the wicked and all that so I get up and get ready for my morning run. I grab my phone hoping to see a text from Vivian or Scarlett. Instead there's a voicemail from Mum.

I listen to it vaguely, getting the gist of it as I prepare a smoothie. 'A monster of selfishness and arrogance... ruined Christmas for everyone... You're well and truly your father's daughter... Stephen finds it very difficult to have you around when you're depressed. It's better for everyone if you only come for the day from now on.'

That feels like a sucker punch to the stomach, TBH.

Refusing to let it ruin my newfound sense of acceptance and calm, I get dressed and go for my usual run.

. . .

THE CRISP AIR slaps against my face, still full of night, as I jog in the pitch-black pre-dawn, relishing the burn in my lungs.

The rhythmic thump of my feet against the deserted Thames path is like a metronome: one-two, breathe. One-two, remember who you are. One-two, you are loved (not by your Mum, but others... Viv?). One-two, you're not a monster (well maybe a little?). One-two, you'll be ok (will I?). One-two, you're not a serial killer, you're a vigilante, *but I nearly killed Jonathan for no reason, I felt the darkness circle in and God help me, I wanted to kill him. I wanted to. I'm becoming a monster and I can't stop myself. I took three lives already.*

My feet are uncooperative today, as if self-pity were a physical thing I could actually stumble over. I nearly trip and have to stop, out of breath, clutching the railing and staring at the Thames' muddy banks. A few drops of sorrow splatter against the banister with small metallic thunks.

The Thames is at its lowest and ugliest; a narrow grey spill surrounded by wide stretches of taupe mud. Panting, I wipe away my tears and stretch against the railing, eyes on the riverbank, not really seeing it. Something's in there. Probably a car tyre or a piece of detritus.

I have to stop. I can't kill anymore. I suck my breath in, clutching the rail. *This vigilante stint wasn't my life's purpose, it was just a moment of madness and it has to stop.*

That's not a car tyre. Maybe a bag of sand? I frown, cursing my middle-aged eyesight. What the...

Oh my God. It's a person.

Dawn's tentative glow is slowly illuminating the scene and I'm starting to see details. A protruding arm. Muddy, matted hair.

Heart racing, I scan the river path for a ladder and find one a few metres away. The steel bars are like ice against my palms as I rush down, not daring to look below me.

Finally, the rungs run out, so I jump down, wincing as my running shoes sink deep in the cold loamy mud. The bank is littered with random refuse, a wheelbarrow, a buoy, a few bottles. I trudge along, my feet fighting to break free of the cloying sludge with every step, as I navigate among the glass shards, the rusty shrapnel, the unidentified objects crunching under my weight.

All the while, my gaze stays fastened to the shape just a few steps ahead. The closer I get, the faster I go. It's a woman and she's completely naked. I need to get to her. She needs help. *I saw her breathe. Didn't her chest rise?* I can't see her face.

Finally, I reach her and kneel in the filth. As my fingers alight on her neck to look for a pulse, I see the bruises, dark against her skin. But there's no time to wonder what could make such marks, I turn her to start CPR and that's when I recognise her face. It's Nicoletta.

'No, no, no, no,' I push the muddy hair off her face and placing my clasped hands between her breasts, start the compressions. How many was it again? Five, I think. Is that right? I start the movements but I can't help but notice the cold skin under my palms, the vacant eyes staring at the gulls screaming overhead.

The river's pungent, damp smell permeates everything but with it something else. A wrong and nauseating odour.

I push away the thought and, five compressions done, I hesitate. Her body has sunk into the soft mud and her body and face are now framed by a soft grey shroud. My lips don't want to touch her cold lips.

She's dead, Lily.
She's dead.

Suddenly, the touch of her cold, clammy skin is more than I can bear and bile comes up. I scramble away from her and retch on all fours, tears blurring the world into an endless expanse of mud and rubbish.

My hands sink in the mud. The old lady Thames licks my fingers like a bitch sensing my distress. She laps Nicoletta's hair, cleaning the mud off our fallen sister in gentle little ripples.

I catch Dark Lily's reflection in the approaching water. She cannot comprehend why I look so defeated. The power is within my reach. I only need grab it.

My fists close around the gravel and a scream bursts out as rage overflows like an oil spill. And as the murky sun rises over the two of us, one felled and one still alive, kneeling there in the mud, I birth a harder, darker me.

No more pain.
No more vulnerability.
No more.

WIPING tears shakily off my face, I wipe my mucky fingers against my leggings and dial 999.

A disembodied voice asks me 'Emergency. Which service?'

Words tumble out of my mouth, meaningless, disjointed. '...dead ...come... help... hurry... you need to get here before the tide...'

The rest of the morning is a blur. Vanfuls of cops arrive at the scene, some wearing white paper overalls, some wearing uniforms. Blue lights flash and perimeters are set. Someone helps me back up the ladder. I'm sat down in the back of a van and a thermos cap full of sweet tea is pushed into my hands. I have to fight down a fit of hysterical laughter. Tea. Of course. Tea will make it all ok.

The Thames wants to take Nicoletta away and hide her

in the depths of her inner folds, but she can't have her. The body's lifted up and taken away.

'Miss Blackwell.'

The sound of my name feels far away, like I'm wrapped in cotton wool. There's someone standing next to me. I'm not sure whom.

'I came as soon as I heard. I thought...'

I drift away as the words flow over me like watery music, not making much sense. I've never been so cold.

'Lily, can you hear me?'

Oh. It's the irritating detective. I'd forgotten all about him. It's been months. He looks... I don't know. Anxious?

'You're here,' I say. There's a sort of nervous electricity coursing through me but I feel hollow and drained.

'Right,' he says, his face closed and doubtful.

He disappears and I watch the gulls and ducks bobbing on the dull grey waves for a while. The river seems to be yearning for the ocean, as she dances turbulently towards her beckoning freedom.

'Here,' his arms are around my shoulders before I realise what's happening. I think he's leaning in to slap handcuffs on my wrists but it's only an emergency blanket. He smells of soap and something else, something pleasant. I want to let go and rest my forehead on his shoulder but I'm just exhausted and ridiculous.

'Thank you,' I say through chattering teeth.

He straightens up and, frowning, pries the cold tea from my fingers and guides my hands, so I end up clasping the crinkly foil under my chin.

'Can you tell me what happened Miss Blackwell?' He flips his notebook open and pats his pockets for a pen.

'Nicoletta's dead...'

'How did you know the victim? His face is grave. 'What happened between the two of you? Why did you kill her?'

'You think *I* did it?' I say slowly, frowning to capture my thoughts through the fog of the adrenaline crash.

'Well, it wouldn't be the first time. People like you can't help themselves.'

'People like me?' I'm struggling to link my thoughts to my mouth.

'Psychopaths, serial killers...'

'What?' for some reason, this hurts, coming from him.

'Do you deny that you killed this one?'

'I didn't hurt Nicoletta, I wouldn't,' I stammer, gathering my thoughts, 'she's...' I struggle to express what's so obvious to me. I'd never hurt Nicoletta because she's... 'she's a victim.'

'Yes, clearly. Your latest victim.'

No. He doesn't understand. It seems very important to make him understand the difference between Nicoletta and the other three. *Why can't I pull myself together?*

'We'll find what we need to prove that you did it, this time.'

A policewoman who has been hovering nearby and interviewing the porter, approaches us and whispers something in his ear. They argue for a moment, beyond my hearing, then she leaves with a worried glance at the two of us as the detective turns his attention back to me.

'It was that woman...' he says, putting two and two together. 'I remember, I was here a few months back, on the day you met her. I'm told you lured her to your flat until the porter found her belongings and got her out.'

'No it wasn't like that...' I clamp my jaws shut to stop them chattering.

'What happened that day? What did she say that triggered you? Why did you kill her?'

'No, I.., why would you... She was running away from *him*...' the thought rips through my mind, as I suck my breath in. Why didn't I realise this sooner? Even while she was high as a kite, her subconscious alerted her to a danger. Why else would she run away from him as naked as the day she was born? How could I have not seen this before? She was *afraid*.

'The porter will know his name,' I manage, slowly.

'On the day you found her naked, roaming your building, why didn't you call the police?'

Absorbed in the maelstrom of guilt and regret, I have trouble focusing on his questions. 'You'd have arrested her... I wanted to protect her,' I say vaguely.

He points to the body bag resting on the gurney near the ambulance. 'Yes, because not calling the police worked out really well for her didn't it?'

He's right, it's all my fault. Nicoletta would be alive if I had called the police that day, why did I worry about getting her arrested? That seems absurd now. I should have protected her better. I should have asked her to stay over for a few weeks, helped her get her life back on track. Now it's too late.

A stab of anger finally pierces through the fog and my mind starts to clear. 'I didn't... You really don't get it, do you? You're part of the problem. The police, the prosecution service, the judges, the whole system is rotten. All skewed in favour of men. Why would I trust that any of you would have protected a prostitute? How dare you suggest that I had anything to do with her death?'

'You can get off your soapbox now, it's not a pretty look,' he says coldly.

'Oh yes, because my ultimate ambition in life is to be pretty for you.'

'I'm not here to talk about politics and I don't give a toss that you're pretty,' he says, as anger takes hold of him, 'but I can tell you with complete certainty, Miss Blackwell is that I *will* get to the bottom of this murdering spree.'

Oh blimey. Me and my big mouth. He was just baiting me and I fell right for it, of course. I'm so utterly bad at this murder-thing. I'm perpetually in over my head.

'So I'll ask again. What happened here and how did the victim die?'

'I don't know, I only found her body.'

'How convenient.'

'For the last time, I didn't kill Nicoletta!' I wanted it to sound forceful but there's a sob in there somewhere.

He just stares at my face for a long moment, eyes narrowed while I shiver under his glare and tighten the metallic blanket around my shoulders.

'I think my client's had quite enough for today,' a familiar voice pipes up.

I turn towards the sound and see Catherine approaching in full lawyer mode, marching towards us with a decided air on her face, her heels clicking against the pavement.

Detective Irritating looks from her to me and back.

'*She's* your lawyer?'

'Erm... yes?' I have no clue what's happening actually.

He shakes his head and steps away to argue with my friend for a few minutes out of earshot, then in short order, I'm released and Catherine and I are on our way up to my flat.

The Thames' swampy smell accompanies us in the small lift and I blink at the violent lighting. 'You're here.'

'Wow, sharp deduction skills. Are you always that bright

or are you making an exception for me today?' She pats my wet pockets and finds the key.

I'm quiet for a while, my brain struggling to catch up. My teeth are chattering. '... and you're my lawyer?' I say, blankly as she opens my front door.

She frowns, 'They didn't mention injuries. Did you hit your head Lily?'

My brain is still full of shock and tears. She must see it on my face because her expression softens and she says 'I was listed as your ICE and when the police called, I figured... given what you'd said to me the other day in Canary Wharf... I thought you might need a lawyer's help.'

She said lawyer. Not friend. My heart shrinks a bit. 'I didn't kill Nicoletta.' *Why does everybody think I killed her?* 'I liked her. I tried to help her.'

The flat is just the same as it was two hours ago. Its normality feels wrong, I can't let myself be swept back into the meaningless meetings, the meaningless dates, the meaningless family events. The meaningless meaninglessness of it all is more than I can bear.

'What happened, Lily?'

'I was out for a jog. Then I saw her...' the sob escapes now as I remember Nicoletta's body thrown there like a piece of trash, her limbs at odd angles, her muddy hair plastered to her blank face. 'I tried to help. I tried CPR,' I shudder at the memory of her clammy skin and how I nearly felt the cold kiss of her lips.

'Oh.' Catherine's face is turned away as she removes her coat and busies herself with finding something in her bag.

I take a few steps into my flat, staring at the furniture, the objects, the paintings without seeing them. It's the sight of the sofa where we shared a mute breakfast which finally snaps me out of my daze. It rips something in my chest and that's when I break down into wracking sobs.

'I should have saved her. I should have done more,' I stammer, through my tears, 'I was always so obsessed with retribution that I forgot to think about how I could help the victims. I forgot to save them. I forgot to save *her*. It's all my fault,' tears burn a path on my cheeks as I repeat in a loop, unable to stop 'it's my fault, it's all my fault.'

Catherine guides me gently to the bathroom and when I slide along the wall down to the cold floor, she waits in silence for the worst to pass, her warm hand resting between my shoulder blades as grief pours out of me.

'Breathe. Breathe,' she says, her voice soft.

I try to empty myself of the sorrow, but when I'm done with the tears, the bitter dregs of rage and powerlessness still swirl at the bottom of my soul.

'Earlier, I meant... why are you still a lawyer? Why aren't you a nun?'

'Oh that,' her head dips as she sits down on the side of my bathtub and focuses on running me a bath. After a few minutes of silence, she searches for something on her phone and hands it to me.

As she plays with the foam, I try to focus on the screen, exhausted, as the headlines collide against the inside of my skull like pinballs.

Pope forced to close several convents following scandal of clerical abuse.

Nuns kept as sex slaves.

One nun was raped thirteen times by a bishop.

The pontiff admits that the Church has a problem.

Roots of the issue originate in society "seeing women as second class."

No shit, Sherlock.

OH.

'Oh, I'm so sorry, sweetie, your dream... your future...' I glance at Catherine. She's drying her hand methodically on the towel.

'I couldn't join an organisation that... I found that I couldn't... Well, it is what it is.' She removes my muddy jacket, gently, carefully, avoiding my eyes. 'I can't run away, there's nowhere to run to anymore. Not even there...'

'Catherine, I'm so deeply sorry. I'm the one who ruined everything. I killed Brett. He was the love of your life and I... I'm a monster.'

My hair is coated with mud, my hands are smeared in caked brown muck. I've trailed filth all over the pristine white tile floor. I'm disgusting.

She says nothing.

The water is the only sound in the small bathroom as I sit there, crumpled and shivering in my undies, covered in sludge.

'No Lily. He was the monster,' she says it so quietly that I wonder if I heard her right. 'I moved from Australia to London to escape him.' She's perched on the side of the bathtub like she might take flight at any moment, her delicate limbs frozen in a protective self-hug. 'He'd have killed me eventually.' She looks down at last and our eyes meet.

'You saved my life, Lily.'

Tears are running down my face but I'm too tired to wipe them off.

'Do you know who murdered her? The girl in the Thames,' Catherine asks.

I nod.

'We're going to have to do something about that then, aren't we?'

36

NEW YEAR, NEW ME

I've always hated New Year. It's the one time in the year when all the couples would rather be coupled up and all your friends are off to far-flung beaches, living their best lives on Insta. I've spent the last few with Emma and her kids, with my parents, with random colleagues, so needless to say, the last few New Year parties have been complete and utter shit.

The fireworks are about to start and we're all gathered in our coats, shivering on the rooftop terrace of my building. Vivian's bump is showing in earnest now. Jonathan is on a business trip to Dubai, so she's come over tonight. I can't remember the last time we spent New Year's together. Probably when we were both still teenagers, wearing braces and sitting cross-legged in front of the TV, watching longingly at all the people who seemed to be having the time of their lives in Trafalgar Square.

'It's nearly midnight!' someone shouts on the pitch-black rooftop overlooking the river's silvery ribbon weaving through the city. There's a tremor of anticipation in the small assembled crowd of my neighbours.

Cameron met his fate on a rooftop just like this one, I think with a shiver. But tonight is not the night for ghosts.

'Ten, nine, eight,' the crowd chants.

'Ready?' I smile at Vivian, looping my arm in hers, reflecting on how unlikely this reunion would have been even a year ago. It was hard to forgive her and it will be long, but I know I'll get there in the end. She matters more to me than any man. She's my blood and she carries our lineage. Yes, we'll be alright. Because I'll make it so.

'Seven, six, five!' we all shout, grinning and hugging each other.

Emma really deserves a break from it all tonight. Money's tight, I gather, because of the solicitor's fees. She's applied for a second job as a salesgirl for Debenhams. She's not sure she'll get it. Too old, too fat probably.

Charles is doing well, on the other hand. He's shacked up with the woman he was cheating with all these years. She's in her mid-twenties apparently. He's arguing that Emma earned less and that as a result, she was little more than a parasite, leaching money off him. He's gunning for alimony and full custody of the rug-rats. Alimony. For him. And the scumbag of the year award goes to...

'Three, two one, happy New Year!'

The sky erupts in reds and golds, scattering its sparkling shower over the London sky. The night is lit up above us while Emma, Vivian and I embrace and then wish a happy New Year to my neighbours.

A while later, we all congregate by the lift to go back down to my flat, smiling and chatting. I suppose more people have moved into the building than I realised, there must be at least thirty of us.

Finally, we get in to the last lift and just as the door closes, an obese man wedges his arm between the doors and waddles into view. The woman on his arm is so much like Nicoletta that I stare at her for a few heartbeats too long. But neither of them notices me.

He's repugnant, in his food-stained tracksuit that hangs loosely under his paunch. I lower my eyes and cringe at the plastic swimming pool sliders slung over white socks. His pudgy fingers roam all over her tight purple lycra dress while she giggles. I wonder what Nicoletta was wearing the night he killed her. She was naked both times I met her, once warm and once cold.

Emma and Vivian are oblivious, chatting happily among themselves about the view and how lovely my building is but I can't help staring at him. Even in his drunk state, he senses my glare and looks directly at me but fails to recognise who I am. He snorts, mistaking my interest. I wonder if he even thinks of Nicoletta sometimes. What are the police doing? Why isn't he in custody? This woman could be next.

'So Big Boy, you ready?' she giggles, draped around his arm like a liana.

'Yes, always, you know me. Got the little blue pills, you won't be coming for nothing,' he sways on his feet and catches himself on her with a wet chuckle, 'get it? You won't be coming.'

She teeters on vertiginous heels and her jaw tightens, as she bears the brunt of his weight. We exchange a glance. Her eyes are too old for her pretty face. Nicoletta's eyes were the same, before. After, they were just glassy, staring at the sky, as she sunk in the mud.

The girl frowns. I've stared at her too long, lost in nightmares and grief.

With a visible effort, she dismisses me and shifts the expression on her features, giggling, 'I know, you always prepared, Big Boy, with toys and things. We gonna have fun!'

Their floor. They exit awkwardly, tangled in each other. Their laughter recedes as the doors close. There on the linoleum floor, there's a credit card. The lift is already in motion so I bend down, picking up the card in my gloved fingers. It's his.

Emma and Vivian continue chatting happily as the lift continues its downward journey and I pocket the credit card.

Wellwhatdoyouknow, New Year's eve turned out ok this year, I muse as I wave goodbye to Emma and Vivian. They promise to text me when they get home and I close my door with a smile.

Yawning, my arms still full of hugs and my heart warm with belonging, I do the dishes and straighten everything up. I wasn't alone for once, grasping at last minute ~~straws~~ plans. I was part of something genuine and wholesome and that makes me happy.

I'm unzipping my sparkly dress when a knock interrupts my thoughts.

'Did you forget something—' I say, opening the door.

'Hello Lily,' his voice has always made my insides melt.

For a moment, I don't say anything, afraid to dispel the illusion. He can't be here. But his hand reaches for my cheek, then caresses the side of my neck and I shiver, my whole body suddenly taut with desire.

He's really here.

Ethan.

He came back.

Looking roguish and irresistible with his charming smile and his slightly ruffled blond hair.

DATE 40

He doesn't waste much time with words. In a blink, his mouth is on mine and we're kissing like our kisses are water after days in the desert. The scent of him ensnares me, heady and overpowering as he drops his jacket to the floor and closes his arms around me.

He came back to me.

I knew it.

I knew he loved me after all.

'Happy New Year,' he rumbles, his voice hoarse, as his warmth and stiffness swell against me. We bump into things, as he presses me against the door, then the wall, directing me, in slow, groping stops and starts towards the bedroom.

Out of breath, I disentangle myself just enough to devour him with my eyes.

'You came back,' I smile.

'Mmmh?'

'I knew you cared,' I grin, as my heart pounds so hard that I can feel its beat in my belly.

He smiles. But it's not a self-assured smile. Pushing him lightly back, I look up at his beloved face.

'Let's go to bed. I missed the taste of your cunt, I want to be inside you... Come on Lily, don't make me beg,' his hand is climbing up the inside of my thighs. I start to pulse with desire, imagining, remembering...

He kisses my cleavage hungrily but I push him back, gasping for breath, my palm gently but firmly in the middle of his chest. 'You... you came for sex.'

It's his turn to be surprised, 'yes, what else?' His mouth

crashes into mine as his caresses get rougher against my nipples. I feel myself go wet. Our kiss deepens and my knees weaken.

'Wait...'

Wait.

'Ethan. Stop.'

'Come on, I couldn't find anyone else tonight and I don't want to spend the night alone.'

Mmmh.

'I... no...'

This isn't right. I thought he came back, to give me what I wanted. A life of love and commitment, as a grand romantic gesture on New Year's eve, the moment for new beginnings. They say that the way you spend this night is a portent of how you'll spend your whole year.

'This is just another booty call, isn't it?' I say, frowning.

He sighs with frustration.

'Look, I came all the way here, from Shoreditch. Are we going to shag or not?'

Another me, a gentler, needier me would have said yes. A million times yes. But I'm not this person anymore.

I shove him away, flustered, breathless.

'I think you'd better go Ethan,' I whisper as I readjust my clothes.

'What the fuck do you mean? You're going to leave me like this, with blue balls? You're going to send me back with my dick in my hands?'

I shrug and step around him, opening my door.

His face darkens when he realises I'm not going to change my mind. 'Well, happy fucking New Year to you then!' he spits as he leaves.

And as I watch him walk away in a huff, I feel unexpected... relief.

37

HE SHOULD HAVE TAKEN THE RED PILL

The entrance lobby is deserted. The workers have put the marble down this week and somehow it seems even emptier and more absurdly grandiose than it was before. I'm sitting on the last step of the fire stairwell. I've wedged a piece of cardboard to maintain the door ajar, just enough for me to observe without being seen. I've been motionless in the dim staircase for so long that my bum is frozen.

For the fifteenth time at least, I go over my plan, examining each facet for a flaw. Halfway through my whispered litany, the door of the porter's office opens. The young man yawns and picks his nose then he disappears from view to do his rounds. His steps echo in the silence and soon, I'm plunged in silence and darkness once again.

Two am.

Slowly, slowly, I push the door open and risk a glance. No one.

Skirting the wall, I pad to the office door and push it open. *I could still back out at this stage.* I could always pretend

I just knocked on the door and peaked in to see if the porter was in. *I haven't done anything wrong. Yet.*

The spare keys are all aligned and neatly labelled. There, Flat 603. Glancing behind me, I grab the key off the hook and slink back out and into the stairwell. So far, so good. I knew that the night porter never locked the office because I took advantage of this once already to get the parcel... I adjust the satchel across my shoulder to reassure myself. Yes, I've got everything.

On the sixth floor, the new dark blue carpet has gone down already. It's nice. They haven't reached my floor yet. Heart pounding in the darkness, I hurry to the flat and fumbling with my gloved hands, manage to insert the key in the lock. My palms tingle and the only sound is the beating of my panicked heart. *I could still back out at this stage. I haven't done anything wrong. Yet.*

Jesus. I'm really doing this. I shouldn't blaspheme but actually I'm sure Jesus would approve. Justice for a prostitute. How biblical.

Step one: break in - done.

The smell hits me first: feet and souring food. Holding my breath, I close the door behind me, taking care not to lock it. Maybe I can see well enough like this, I already know how the flat is configured, as it should have the same floor plan as mine. I take a few steps in the pitch black and bump into an unexpected obstacle. A squeak of fright slips out as the thing vacillates at my eye level and then stabilise.

Panting, I search the satchel and retrieve a small torch. It's a tiny thing and it was such a pretty rose gold colour that I thought, *why not, it's only a pound*, now I'm glad I brought it. The light is so bright after hours of darkness that I'm blinded for a moment.

Cold sweat breaks on my forehead. Surely anyone

passing by on the Thames Path will see me through the huge windows? Or he'll wake up because of the racket I'm making and the sudden ray of brightness? I stay perfectly still and listen, holding my breath. But nothing happens.

The beam of light reveals piles of magazines rising like stalagmites towards the ceiling. Wondering fleetingly how a man of his girth can squeeze through the mountains of hoarded rubbish, I pad to the master bedroom and freeze on the threshold.

Am I really doing this? His huge form is lying on the bed, the comforter rising up and down as he snores. There's a smell of fart and a lack of oxygen in there. I could turn around and pretend like none of this ever happened. I could return the key to its hook before the night porter finishes his patrol and just go back to bed. I could throw out the small pump spray in my bag, the porter would never know that I'd stolen the package when it arrived. The sleeping man would probably never notice that I'd stolen his credit card to buy something so cheap. £5.89+ delivery. Which reminds me. I extract the credit card and wiping it one last time against my sleeve, I drop it on the sleeping man's desk.

I could still back out at this stage. I haven't done anything wrong. Yet.

I can't tear my eyes from him as he snorts and shifts under the covers. My heart does a panicked little jig in my chest as I contemplate the enormity of what I'm about to do.

Right. Can't dawdle. I glance at my watch. Only forty-one minutes left before the porter goes back to his lodge. I need answers and I mean to get them. I pad to the bathroom and for a terrified minute, I can't find what I'm looking for until finally, I see them. The little blue diamond-shaped pills. I got lucky, there's only one left.

Clutching the blister pack, I hurry back to the bed.

There's a grease stain on his yellowish pillowcase and his boxer shorts are sprawled out on the carpet. I step gingerly around the stained undies, noticing a snickers bar wrapping, a half empty bottle of scotch and a few open condom packs on the nightstand.

Step two: nylon zip ties. Extra Strong £2.49 for a bag of a hundred. I only need two. I get them out of the satchel and hesitate.

I hover for a while, uncertain about whether to proceed and my foot gets tangled in the underwear. I stumble and he stirs. *Come on Lily, come on.* He's so big. I don't think I can do it. He could overpower me in an instant.

I could still back out at this stage. I haven't done anything wrong. Yet.

Thankfully the bed isn't one of these padded types. It's a basic wooden Ikea model with bars. I'm pretty sure he's bought it on purpose for the kind of game we're about to play. Well, without the happy ending.

I've dithered too long, he's waking up, his large form wobbling like whale blubber as his breath splutters. *Oh Jesus, Mary, Joseph. Here we go.*

Gently, gently, I take his hand and hold it against one of the headboard's poles and as his lids flutter, I loop the nylon strip around his wrist and pull. He gasps, sleep evaporating from his eyes and replaced by confusion, shock and then anger.

He's starting to fight me, one arm pinned awkwardly against the headboard. I can't reach his other wrist, it's too far, I'm going to lose control of the situation. *Shit, shit, shit.* Leaning over him in a quick lunge, I slam his forearm against the bedhead. He's strong and nearly breaks free but I'm faster and more awake and in an instant it's done. I tighten the nylon strip and jump backwards, out of reach of his kicks.

'What the hell?' he shouts, as I pop the pill out of the blister pack. 'Who the fuck are you? What are you doing in my flat? Let me go.'

'Just go with it Big Boy.' I stand next to his bed, the blue pill between two gloved fingers in one hand and the whisky bottle's neck in the other and smile enticingly.

His face is the picture of confusion as I push the pill in his mouth and pour a large glug of the amber liquid in his mouth.

Ok, step three: getting him to believe in the subterfuge - done.

It was crucial that he swallow that. If I can fool him about who I am and convince him to talk to me, that is. *I could still back out at this stage. I haven't done anything wrong. Yet.*

With a big shaky breath, I put the bottle back on the nightstand and steel myself for the next part of the plan. Standing like Scarlett showed me, one foot forward à-la-Angelina, chest fully deployed, bum sticking out, I slap on a come-hither look on my face and imagine strip tease music in my head. Swaying to the silent tempo of *You Can Keep Your Head On,* I start removing my top, enough that he can see my (black, lacy, scratchy) bra (*yep, that one*).

'I didn't order any BDSM role play tonight.' With his hands up, he looks absurdly like a bank client during a hold-up.

I stop and roll my Sandy-from-Grease top (*thank you Emma*) back down on my stomach. 'Oh. I thought you were my next John tonight. You want me to leave?'

You sound way too nice, you nearly apologised, FFS. Damned Lily, focus: you're a dominatrix, you need him to confess to what he did to Nicoletta. It's the only reason you're even going through this charade. *Come on, you can do this.*

'No.' He takes a breath, his eyes on my exposed midriff. 'No, stay, show me more.'

'Now, now, Big Boy. I'm the one in charge here.' I try to laugh but my throat is too tight. When I was planning this, it looked more likely that he'd talk to another prostitute, in the throes of passion. Maybe he'd brag about it, to scare me? Maybe he'd hesitate during the encounter, in fear of killing someone again? I was so sure he would confess to someone he didn't suspect, someone who could never report him. Now I'm not so sure he'll talk. Why would he? This plan isn't as good as I thought it was in broad daylight, within the safety of my own flat.

'So, you like your women rough, Big Boy?'

'No, actually...' he frowns. 'I'm usually the one...'

I ignore him as search his bedroom. 'Toys?' I ask. He points to his wardrobe with his chin and I walk over, my stilettos wobbly on the stained carpet, dodging socks and crisp wrappers strewn about his room to go kneel by a large chest at the bottom of his closet.

Step four: Search for evidence - initiated.

As I root around in the box, conscious of my bum, in full display, I'm suddenly certain he won't talk and it's all starting to look like a terrible idea.

I could still back out at this stage. I haven't done anything wrong. Yet. He'd never know who I was and probably wouldn't remember my face.

Come on, it's gotta work. I don't want to think about the alternative. It's my best chance to get some answers; I want to be able to direct the police to the right suspect, conveniently trussed to his bed, delivered by anonymous phone call, courtesy of your helpful (non-murderous) neighbourhood vigilante.

With a grimace, I push aside an assortment of sticky penis rings, an odd looking pump, a whip, looking for things he could have choked Nicoletta with. 'Anything for choking?'

He narrows his eyes, 'Hey, do I know you?'

'You'd remember me if you'd had me before, believe me.' I smile as sexily as I can but he doesn't seem convinced. 'So, how do you like it, Big Boy?' I ask, over my shoulder.

'Release me and I'll show you,' his voice deepens as his stare details my curves with a malevolent smile. The atmosphere tips over for a moment and I shudder, intensely aware of how he'd like to hurt me and how vulnerable I really am. I haven't brought any weapon. He's twice my size and on his own turf. It's night and no one would hear me scream. No one knows I'm even here. I could disappear without a trace. Wow. This was such a bad idea. I need to regain control, like now.

'Silence,' I snap, continuing my search in his wardrobe, more to hide the fear on my face than anything else at this point. If I could find a trace of Nicoletta's passage, maybe her clothes or her bag, that would prove that he did it, wouldn't it? Then the police would have no choice but to investigate him.

'This isn't working, release me.' He jerks his wrists and violently shakes the bedposts. 'I don't know why the agency sent you but they got their wires crossed. I like to be the dominant one.'

'I bet you do,' I give up on the search and lower my head, hands on both sides of the trunk, defeated. *I could still back out at this stage.* It would be hard, I'd have to avoid him in the lift and he'd think I'm a prostitute and spread the word in the building. *But I haven't done anything wrong. Yet.*

And just when I'm about to give up, that's when I see it. There. At the bottom of the box of horrors. It looks like a dog collar, with a metal ring. Exactly the kind that could have left the mark I saw on Nicoletta's neck. With a tremor of hope, I stand up and turn around with the black leather strap in my hand and notice a small mound stirring under the duvet. *Ew*. The pill is working.

Approaching the bed, dreading the next step, I take a deep breath and tip my hand, showing him the dog collar. 'Is that what happened with Nicoletta?

Step five: encourage self-incrimination - now in motion.

'Who?' his jowly face is completely blank.

'Nicoletta,' I repeat, frowning. 'Did you play a game with her? A game where you... dominated her? Did you go too far and hurt her?'

'I've no idea what you're talking about.' His eyes narrow. 'Wait a minute, who the fuck are you? You're not a professional.'

Well that's not very nice, I'm always professional.

'Why do you like pain?' Standing at his bedside, holding the large leather strap, I look into his face, trying to discern whether there is evil there. 'Why does that arouse you? I don't understand it. Can't you just love a woman as your equal and try to make her come instead of strangling her to get your pecker up?'

His eyes shift to the nightstand. His phone. The game is up then.

I'm too far in; I might as well confront him now. *Bugger, this is escalating way too quickly. Still, I haven't done anything wrong. Yet. I could still back out at this stage.*

Fingers shaking, I fumble with my satchel and extract a

very small red bottle. Getting uncomfortably close to his ugly, hostile face and his fetid breath, I lean over his bed and hold the small bottle up, nozzle towards his mouth.

'What's this?' he's still oscillating between lust and anger.

'Something that will make you sick. Answer me or I'll spray it on you and you'll end up spending a very uncomfortable night in hospital. Do you understand?'

Step six: (urgh, I was hoping it wouldn't come to this) threaten him to obtain confession – activated, I repeat, activated.

'HELP!' His scream takes me by surprise.

He struggles against the ties, his huge body slamming against the headboard which in turn clatters against the wall. Fuckety, fuck, fuck, fuck.

Fighting fear and disgust, I jump on the bed and straddle him as he bucks and grunts. One gloved hand on his mouth, the other clutching the small spray bottle in front of his face, I tighten my hold on him with my thighs. An unwelcome thought flutters in my mind *what an odd parody of sex we're miming*, as he turns apoplectic purple. *Argh, I'd better not asphyxiate him*. I need him to confess and go to prison.

'Look I don't want to hurt you, I just need answers.' My hand shakes as I hold the tiny spray angled towards him. This isn't working. I'm losing control of the situation. 'Stop fighting. I just want answers. Did you do it?'

I tentatively release his mouth and he stops bucking under me as air returns to his lungs. He pants, glaring at me

'Do what, you crazy bitch?'

I thought I could just pretend to... I thought he'd brag about it to a working girl... I don't know what I thought anymore. This was such a stupid plan.

'Did you kill Nicoletta?'

He jerks his wrist roughly against the restraint, startling me and when he sees me flinch, he laughs unpleasantly. 'You're completely out of your depth, aren't you?'

'The girl in the river, did you kill her?'

'Fuck off, you feminazi,' he snarls. My face is much too close to his greasy shoulder-length hair, his alcoholic halitosis, his smelly polyester t-shirt. He's straining against the flimsy nylon bonds, grunting with effort as his face reddens and a vein starts to bulge in his forehead. *Bloody hell, he's not going to stay tied for very long if he keeps this up.* Below me, somewhere, his little wiener is stirring in spite of everything.

I could still back out at this stage. I haven't done anything wrong. Yet. Well... I have: theft, breaking and entering, assault...but none of it irreversible.

What on earth did I think I'd accomplish? He's a slob. He pays women for sex. But that doesn't mean he should die. I could threaten to reveal his disgusting little habit to his employer and we could go our separate ways. He wouldn't dare say anything to anyone about my nighttime visit. Would he?

'I just thought... Never mind. She didn't deserve this.'

My shoulders sag and the hand that holds the tiny red bottle lands softly on his paunch and that's when he yanks his wrist hard and the tie snaps. Before I have time to react, his pudgy fingers have wrapped around my throat. I try to scramble off him, but he's got me and he knows it. His expression morphs from confused pleading to sadistic pleasure.

'Why the fuck do you care about what happened to that little cunt?' he snarls, crushing my throat while his penis hardens against my cunt. I try to fight him, claw at his fingers, desperate to get away but his fingers are like steel around my neck.

'The girls I pay, they're cheap whores, a dime a dozen, disposable. There's a thousand more wherever the fuck she came from.'

No... air. Can't breathe...

'No one cares what happened to her. She was trash and now you're going to know what it feels like to —'

My vision is starting to swim so I can't be sure if I aimed correctly. He gasps so I press my finger blindly on the spray nozzle again and again and again until he lets go. Air burns its way through my throat and at last, my lungs fill with air again.

I slide off him and collapse, hitting the floor with a thud, choking and coughing. Crawling away frantically, I retreat until I reach a wall. The whisky bottle's fallen to the ground in the tussle and it rolls towards me in the darkness, so I grab it by the neck and hold it tight against my chest, like a club. Huddled on the floor, in the corner of his bedroom, I wait there, for the huge mass of him to get up and come for me.

A minute passes. The deep rasps of my own breath subside enough for me to focus on other sounds.

There's a weird noise.

Heart pounding madly in my chest, I get up leaning against the wall with one gloved hand for support. Holding the bottle high above me, I pad towards the bed expecting him to jump out of the shadows and overpower me at any moment.

He's slid down onto the floor but his handcuffed hand is still holding him tied to the bed. There's something wrong with his fingers, they're curled and his elbow is at an odd angle.

As I approach cautiously, his head rolls back and hits the headboard several times. *Oh my God, he's having a seizure!*

My first instinct is to rush to help him, I drop the Scotch bottle and lunge forward but his legs start to convulse with frantic motions and the duvet slides off as he arches backward. He's only wearing a t-shirt and nothing underneath. His shrivelled little penis is flopping back and forth amid a coarse bed of black, wiry pubic hair. His spasms are spectacular, his huge body heaves, his eyes have rolled inside his sockets and he's hitting his head against the board as he bucks and tosses.

Oh God, oh God, oh God, what have I done?

I could still back out at this stage. I could always call an ambulance and save his life. *I haven't done anything wrong. Yet.*

Ok, Lily, time to get a fucking grip.

He's only making small grunting noises by the time I find his phone among the debris of his overturned nightstand. Bugger, it's fingerprint locked and I didn't bring mine. Fighting to grab his free hand, I try to activate the bloody phone but he's convulsing.

I finally manage to get the call through to the emergency services but instead of speaking, I throw the phone next to him on the bed and then wipe the small red bottle and throw it next to him as well. Then, pulling my gloves on tight, trying hard to control the panic that's mounting inside me, I stare at the scene, trying to think. How would it look if I'd really been a prostitute who ran away? Bottle of whisky on the floor. Empty Viagra blister and opened condom packs. No underwear. Clearly in the midst of a sex game gone wrong.

Throwing a backward glance at him, I escape the dark, stuffy room as his grunts become whines. I rush back to the entrance, leave the door ajar and run down the staircase two by two.

When I reach the bottom of the stairwell, I scarcely throw a glance to make sure the porter's office is still plunged in darkness before I sprint across the lobby. There's no time left, I'm three minutes late. Can it only have been forty-one minutes? How? I hang the keys back on the hook then dash back up the stairs to my floor, fling myself inside my flat and close my front door, slamming my shoulders back against it as I catch my breath. My knees are shaking and I'm dizzy.

'It's going to be ok, it's going to be ok. Everything's going to be ok. Breathe, Lily, breathe,' I say in a loop.

I can no longer back out at this stage. What I have done is so wrong. There is no going back. The deed is done.

I feel so soiled. I'm a proper murderer now. Not a happenstance, seize the opportunity, kill by accident vigilante. I'm a bona fide serial killer. *Oh God, what have I done?* This was premeditated murder.

No, no, no... that's not what happened. I just wanted to get a confession, to find some evidence. Maybe accelerate the police's progress. I never thought it would come to... Or did I? Am I going to lie to myself and pretend that it wasn't a deliberate plan? I bought a nitrolingual spray days in advance. I knew it would interact with the erection enhancing pills to make his blood pressure drop. But I never thought... I assumed he'd feel a bit dizzy, enough to make him panic and tell me the truth.

But in retrospect, it was obvious that in an obese man the chemical cocktail would precipitate a heart attack, I did my due diligence, I read the articles. *I knew. I knew.* Did I want him to die? Was it a revenge killing? *Oh God.*

I wish he'd confessed to murdering Nicoletta but I'm

sure it was him even if he didn't say so. It must have been him, right? He practically admitted that she was disposable and that he'd taken out the trash.

His last stare is seared into my retinas, as I yank my gloves off with shaking hands and hug myself.

He looked terrified but also... outraged.

38

ANGEL AND THE BEAST

The church is deserted. Under my knees, the embroidered kneeler feels knobbly. I wonder how many women have knelt here over the centuries to look up at an idol and pray. Maybe even before Jesus came with his Roman swords and his male hierarchy, maybe even then, some woman traipsed through the marshes on a wet February evening like this one, in the dark, soggy twilight of what would become Chelsea. Maybe she brought a hare to sacrifice on some mossy altar. Maybe she said a prayer to Andred the goddess of slaughter and carnage or to Frigga, the goddess of death and sex. Maybe the woman hesitated before the blade struck the hare's neck. Maybe she looked into her goddess's eyes, wondering, like me... wondering. No she wouldn't have hesitated. Slaughter, sex and death sound just right.

I sigh and play with the candle's flame. When did we lose the right to pray for death, to pray for blood and mayhem? When did we lose the right to anger, to righteous vengeance? My Cypriot ancestors prayed to Artemis, the eternally single goddess of the hunt, they called for Athena's protection, the goddess of war, who was famous for her ferocity in battle but who only fought for just causes, and they feared Nemesis the goddess of retribution for their evil deeds.

Why did we trade these fearsome goddesses for the simpering one I'm looking at now? In this sad day and age, women are only acceptable if they're virgins: demure and compliant or mothers: nurturing and sweet. I suppose Mary won the patriarchy jackpot, didn't she? She's both.

Pity that for her trouble, she had to be raped by a god, had to nearly be stoned to death and had to give birth in squalor under life-threatening circumstances. But I suppose it all worked out in the end because now millions worship her and try to emulate her example: obey, submit, be silent. Turn the other cheek and all that crap. The meek shall inherit the Earth. *Erm... not in my experience.*

She's clutching a lily, the symbol of purity I suppose. Aren't lilies also a symbol for death? Her plaster hands are broken and the steel rebar is just visible under the soft flesh-like fingers. She's like that too, isn't she, Mary: the soft wrapping around our millenary oppression. You can't do much when you have broken hands and no voice.

Shakespeare did it too, to his Lavinia, her rapists cut off her tongue and her hands so she wouldn't be able to denounce them. The patriarchy still does it to us all the time, doesn't it? Yes, you can be a celebrated actress who's won awards but you can also expect to have sex with producers whether you want to or not, earn a fraction of your male co-stars' salaries and be quiet about the whole system or pay the consequences and sink into oblivion.

Yes, you can marry a prince, but you'll have to give up your job and you won't be able to speak up anymore, about any topic of importance, but on the plus side, the media will treat you like a walking mannequin.

Yes, you can participate in this presidential election, but don't be too vocal or you won't be electable, they don't really want you to do anything or change anything. Don't be difficult, sit down, be quiet.

Nevertheless, we persist.

Mary's face is abstract and blank. She stares in the distance, looking ethereal. Jesus though has a rather insistent glare for a toddler. He doesn't look at all pleased with me. The flame stings my finger, yanking me out of my reverie.

A long time ago, an eternity ago —what was it, seven months ago now— I could still pray. I used to come here and put my coins in the ~~merchants of the temple~~ collection box and I'd light a candle and kneel and pray. What did I pray for? I hardly remember. A husband, I think. A family. Love. Acceptance. Belonging. I prayed to be normal. I prayed to be ordinary. I prayed for a future that She never deemed me worthy of.

I used to adore Mary, she was the reason I loved being Catholic. The only religion of the Book in which you can pray to a woman. I thought *It's the closest thing to a feminist religion!* But looking at her now, I find her distant. I don't recognise myself in her embrace anymore.

I rub absentmindedly at my forehead and my fingers come back sooty. I was just looking for an escape from the constant ballet of police officers in my building, the CSI units in white coveralls everywhere in the hallways and the constant patrols and police cars downstairs. The stress was unbearable so I thought some fresh air would do me good. My feet brought me to church of their own accord. I suppose a part of me must have remembered that it was Ash Wednesday.

Unfortunately, far from offering a respite from constant scrutiny, the gloomy church service made me feel worse. Guilt is such a cruel companion, it pulses in my bloodstream like a heartbeat, constantly reminding me that I'm a monster.

The priest seemed to know that I was beyond redemption as he drew the sign of the cross on my forehead earlier this evening. 'Remember that you are dust and to dust you shall return.' *Oh I know about death, Father.* I know that it's not peaceful. I know that it's not dignified. I know that before the dust settles, there is blood and shit and sweat involved.

My soul shivers and all around me the dead shiver too. I'm surrounded by them, they beckon from their marble plaques, they writhe under my feet, trapped under the floor. The gruesomely massacred saints stare at me from their alcoves whispering about death too as the smell of incense lingers in the air. I wish they'd already covered them all in Lent shrouds. I wish they'd all stop glaring at me. *Murderer, murderer.*

'I know, shut the fuck up,' I whisper, a tad too sharply perhaps. After all, they're right.

Something stirs in the shadows.

'Who's there?' I squeak.

Absurdly, I think maybe an angel has come to strike me down for daring to tread on hallowed ground. My heart starts to beat like a death knell in my chest and the hairs on my forearms rise. Still kneeling, head turned away from the effigy, I scan the darkness behind me, as fear prickles the back of my neck.

There's a creaking noise and I get to my feet, rummaging for the mace spray in my handbag.

'I know you're there. Show yourself,' I say to the darkness.

Steps resonate on the stone floor as a man comes into view. *Not an angel of death then.* Close. It's the detective and he's just as gorgeous as I remembered. Very inconvenient.

'Miss Blackwell.' He inclines his head.

'DS Mulligan,' I nod, as we size each other up.

'What are you doing here?' I ask.

'Irish,' he shrugs.

I notice the ashen cross on his forehead.

'I've never seen you in my parish before. Are you following me?'

'Just checking up on you. You were in here for a long time, so I wanted to make sure you...' He stops mid-sentence, scanning my face. Perhaps he sees something there because he tips slightly forward, as if he were going to walk over but then he rocks back on his heels, still a few paces away.

The time for pretence has passed and Lent is as good a period as any to come clean, I suppose. 'Checking to see that I'm not killing a priest or something?' I say, unable to prevent a note of bitterness in my voice.

He does that sexy thing where his jaw squares and he rakes his hand through his hair, looking sorry. *God, I wish he weren't so damn charming. It's so much harder to hate him.*

'Well, did you?' he asks with a little smile.

'Did I what?'

'Kill a priest... or something.'

'Not that I recall but if I had you could be sure he'd have deserved it.'

His eyes trace the tombstone beneath both our feet as he

says 'We are neither angels nor beasts and unhappily whoever wants to act the angel acts the beast.'

'I'm sorry?' I ask, frowning.

'Something Blaise Pascal once said, about people who try to be righteous and fail.'

'You're so smug and condescending. You think you know it all, don't you? What's right, what's wrong, who's guilty and who's innocent. Well, I'm discovering that things aren't as clear cut as I once thought, detective.'

'You're trying to be an avenging angel, I get it Lily, I really do. But in the process you're becoming a monster.'

I glance around the church, checking for his colleagues, half expecting them to jump out of the shadows to arrest me.

He starts to unbutton his shirt.

It's such an incongruous thing to do, in the middle of a church, that I stumble on my words, forgetting what I was going to retort, unable to detach my gaze from him. He pauses when he reaches his belt and parts his shirt, just enough to show a toned body, a reasonable amount of short hair and a chest completely free of listening devices. No one's listening to us.

I nod and he does the buttons up again.

'I worry about you Lily.'

'I don't know why. I'm doing fine,' I lie, touching the scarf around my neck without meaning to. That's where my neighbour strangled me. The bruising makes my voice hoarse and the skin is bruised and tender but I can't stop touching it all the time.

'Killing someone, it's...it's not something I'd wish on my worst enemy, let alone...'

'What would you know about it? I bet you never killed anyone—' the look on his face tells me I'm wrong.

'I did.'

An odd urge to get closer to him submerges me. My whole body yearns to take him in my arms, to comfort him and wipe away the sadness from his face.

'The killing Lily...it eats away at your soul.' He tilts forward again and this time takes a step towards me as his hand alights on my arm. 'You have to stop.'

I bite my lower lip wondering whether to trust him. *I can't risk telling him, can I? It's got to be a trap.*

'I have no idea what you're talking about, I've never killed anyone.' Dark Lily stirs, so near the surface. She's in control of everything I do these days, it scares me. 'But since you want to talk about ethics, then answer me this, detective: why is it that men always want us to turn the other cheek? Why should women always concede, let it go, surrender? Do you think predators will ever stop hurting women? Why would it not be morally right to remove them from the world once and for all? To protect their victims.'

His hand releases my arm and falls to his side and the dark church feels colder all of a sudden.

'There are other ways, Lily. You can't appoint yourself to be judge, jury and executioner. Society would collapse if we all did this. You have to believe in the social contract, give up on the right to exact revenge yourself and trust in the State to protect you. It's the moral, civilised thing to do.'

I snort, 'you speak to me of philosophy and grand ideas but the reality is that we're dying in our own homes, we're raped on our own streets, we're overlooked in our workplaces. Where is the safety the State supposedly gives us in exchange for relinquishing our right to defend ourselves? And meanwhile, what do you want us to do? Go shop, get into makeup, discuss the latest romcom? Is that what being civilised looks like? Well I don't want it, thank you very much. The social contract is broken, detective. The State looks the other way while we're being slaughtered. By men. Every day. Where is your justice?'

'Don't you think I want to kill them as well, all the scumbags?' he blurts out, his face red. 'My Mum was a battered woman for God's sake! But we can't just execute them. I became a cop so that I could stop men like that. I became part of the system to accomplish the same thing as you, Lily: removing predators from our streets. Can't you see? Law and order depends on us refraining from killing each other. Our civilisation, our whole system depends on it.'

'Well sod the system! What's the system ever done for women? I say we take back our freedom, overturn the patriarchy and kill our oppressors. Let's finally see what women can accomplish when they take power.'

'By force, through chaos and murder?' he shakes his head. 'You're not starting a revolution Lily, you're just murdering people. It's not romantic or noble. It's sordid and mediocre.'

That stings.

'Well, the victims would disagree with you there, det—'

He laughs, 'You're not doing it for the victims. You're doing it for yourself. You're not some sort of saviour, you're just selfish and short-sighted.'

'How dare you? I'm not...' I try to protest but he's planted the seed of doubt in me. Did I really care about anyone other than myself? The hubris, the megalomania of my actions in the recent months is suddenly evident.

'You don't even know if they're guilty.' He says. 'We weren't looking into your neighbour for the prostitute's murder. We think she was killed by her pimp.'

It feels like a punch in the stomach.

No.

No, no, no.
I killed the wrong man.

He looks at me with pity. 'You're killing innocent people, Lily. They don't deserve to die. This country abolished the death penalty for a reason, what makes you think you can singlehandedly reinstate it?'

The guilt submerges me. *It can't be, it's all a trick.* He's trying to get me to admit to the murder so he can arrest me. It's a trap. It has to be. In an instant, the guilt becomes anger and I lash out, tears brimming on the edge of my lashes. 'How dare you tell me what I can and cannot do? How dare you judge me? I have no lessons to receive from a murderer in uniform.'

He looks like I physically slapped him in the face. Guilt seeps through the anger but I can't stop myself. I can't stop her... Dark Lily.

'You must stop,' he pleads, 'I can't let you continue—'

'Let me? *Let* me?' I snort, 'this is not something you can allow me to do, you can't bestow your permission on me. Why don't you do your bloody job and arrest all of them for a change? If you like your precious system so much, then show me that it works. Arrest the next one...' I stop myself just as I'm about to say *before I take care of it myself.* I came too bloody close to confessing to multiple homicide.

He glances at my lips and then looks away, sadness etched over his features.

Signing himself with a quick genuflection, he turns around and leaves me there, like there is nothing left to say.

The church's shadows swallow him. I hear the enormous front door creak open and a metallic clunk as it closes and then nothing.

I stay behind, alone in the darkness under Jesus's insistent glare.

INTERLUDE: THERE WAS JUST THIS ONE TIME WHEN

Like something moving at the corner of my vision, I was aware of it but I didn't register it. Even though I was a victim myself, I didn't even realise it.

In my own eyes, I was a successful career woman, self-sufficient and strong even if in a dark recess of my mind, there were a few stories that started with '*I've never had any problem but there was just this one time when...*' We all have those, don't we?

"*I've never had any problem but there was just this one time when*" I was in middle grade and my class went to the mess hall, each day, two blocks away from school. We held each other's hands as we walked two by two, wondering what was on the menu today. One day, we passed by a parked car and the man inside was masturbating. He had clearly waited to climax while we passed by, with our school uniforms, our braces and our pigtails. We squeaked and scattered like a flock of scared birds.

. . .

"I've never had any problem but there was just this one time when" I was going to university for an important presentation, dressed in a business suit, the kind we wore in the nineties: absurdly boxy jacket, skirt below the knee. The Tube was so crowded that there was a man squashed against me, who rubbed himself against my bum until he came. I was still a teenager, I froze and rather than say something, I escaped when I reached my stop. I didn't even turn around. I spent the next thirty minutes in the loo, cleaning my skirt and went on to take my final.

"I've never had any problem but there was just this one time when" I was in my early twenties and interviewed for an entry-level position at the firm I wanted to work for more than anything else in the world. It was an offsite weekend for all the candidates. One of the senior consultants offered to help me prep for the next day of interviews. I was so desperate to do well that when he proposed to drive me to a nearby bar instead of preparing in the hotel reception area, I didn't dare insist on staying. I got into his car and he drove me to his bachelor pad as I became more and more apprehensive. He tried to have sex with me, I refused and finally managed to get back to my hotel, safe but shaken. I failed the interviews the next day.

"I've never had any problem but there was just this one time when" I went to a hotel on a work trip and, exhausted after a long day, I said the number of my room too loudly to the receptionist. One of the hotel guests heard me, followed me and banged down my door to try and have his way with me. I was stuck in an unfamiliar room, in an unfamiliar city but

thankfully, the hotel staff helped me. I couldn't sleep a wink that night and I never say my room number aloud anymore.

"I'VE NEVER HAD any problem but there was just this one time when" I was about to present in front of the (all male) management team and my then-manager approached me from behind, put his hands on my waist and inhaled my hair. His face was so close that I felt his moist breath on my earlobe. I was in my early thirties, he was in his fifties. He was my manager. What was I going to do? I gave the presentation to the ten men in the room who all pretended they hadn't seen anything. I also pretended that nothing weird has happened. We all pretended.

I never got promoted

You have one of these stories too, don't you?

40

FIND YOUR OWN LOOS TO CRY IN, THIS ONE'S TAKEN

Ethan laughs. A big throaty, heartfelt laugh that makes me flinch. Touching the scarf around my throat to make sure it's hiding the yellowing bruises, I let my gaze roam like a moth in search of his flame. He's clapping Darren on the back as they exit his office. My eyes fall on my keyboard again.

'You could have told me you were leaving,' one of my young associates says as he drops a piece of paper on my desk.

'Sorry?' I tear my gaze away from Ethan and focus on my young team member.

'You promised you'd take me with you if you changed banks.' He frowns, taking in my puzzled face, his anger wavering.

'Wait, what?' I pick up the printed page and see my job description, my title, my grade. 'What is this?'

'Well,' he looks at his nails, 'don't hate me. I was looking for a new position...'

I let it slide. I can't say that work has been much fun lately.

'... and I came across this on the job boards. What's going on?'

They're replacing me, that's what's bloody going on.

'Have you told anyone else about this?' I ask.

He shakes his head.

'Keep it that way, ok?'

He nods sheepishly and goes back to his desk to shop for running shoes or whatever the hell he does all day.

I re-read the job spec, trying to find a clue; perhaps the description was posted when I was hired or it's for another department? But no, the opening was posted a few days ago. Start date is in a couple of weeks.

I look around the open plan office but I can't make sense of any of it anymore. What am I doing here? Why do I try again and again to prove myself to men, to pry power from their closed fists? I'm wasting my time. They will never relinquish it. And I've other more important things to think about than this bloody job and Ethan's approval and Darren's absurd little turf war.

Grabbing the printout, I march to Ethan's office. He's on the phone, feet on his desk. When I slam the paper on his desk, the sudden slap of my hand on the wood startles him. He turns around, glances at the piece of paper and blanching, says 'I'm gonna have to call you back, mate.' He hangs up.

'You bastard.'

'Lily...' He takes his feet off the desk and throws a glance behind me at the open door.

'You fucking bastard,' I say, seething.

'Surely you can see that it's not possible for you to continue working here. Your work has been going downhill for a long time.'

'How dare you? My work is irreproachable.'

'You're not like you used to be anymore. You've lost your spark.'

'Don't you dare make this about the quality of my work. You know very well why the spark is gone and it has nothing to do with my ability to do the job.'

'It's not personal, it's just business. I need the best people in my team and you're just not cutting it.'

I can't even find the words.

With a smirk, he adjusts his jacket and cufflinks. 'We're very happy for you to stay to support Darren. You'll have to take a pay cut of course and a back seat on the project. But given your lack of managerial qualities, I think you'll be happier following his lead.'

'Darren?' I'm shaking with rage but I manage to keep my voice down in lower octaves with a considerable effort. 'You gave my job to that little weasel?'

'Well, he always makes excellent points during meetings.'

'He's just regurgitating what I just said but when it comes out of his mouth, magically everyone can hear it.'

'Please don't get hysterical on me. It is what it is.'

'Like hell it is, Ethan. I'm done with you and with this bloody bank.'

He didn't expect that, his project is screwed if I leave now. His eyes narrow and his hands find each other on his desk, forming a steeple.

'I think you'll find that your contract requires you to give us a six-month notice.'

'And I think you'll find that I'll sue your arse for wrongful termination if you don't pay me my bonus, a fucking enormous severance payment and give me a glowing reference, Ethan. Oh and I'm leaving today, I'll be serving my six-month notice period from home with full pay, thank you for reminding me.'

He looks like I've sprouted antennas. To be fair, I have no idea where all this assertiveness has come from. For once my face doesn't betray me and I hold on to my anger to camouflage the bluff. He starts to protest but then realisation of the sticky situation he's put himself in flickers across his face and finally his lips settle into a thin line. The wrinkles around his eyes are no longer charming, he just looks older today, smaller.

'Is that really how you want to play it, Lily? I thought what we had was special.'

I snort. 'You can expect to hear from my lawyer then.' I stand up and start to leave. I'm walking across the threshold of his office when he says, 'No. Lily, wait. There's no need to go to these lengths. I'll see what I can—'

I don't turn around. 'I want the paperwork in my inbox by COB today Ethan, or I'll have a very interesting conversation with HR.'

'I'll get it done.'

I walk out, straight ahead, shoulders back and chin up but inside, I'm reeling. I can't believe I pulled this off. A few months ago, I would have cried with frustrated impotence, possibly in front of Ethan. I would have pleaded and clung to the job, moped around and worked for Darren for months, perhaps even years.

Back at my desk, I'm startled by an unexpected thought: perhaps it's not hubris but powerlessness that made me resort to violence. If I'd had the confidence to say no to Cameron when I was young… if I'd tried to convince Brett to go back to Australia more forcefully, none of this would have happened. Did I kill them simply because I couldn't find another way to assert myself? Just because in this society ruled by men, there was no possibility of justice for Nicoletta or recourse for Epsom's victims?

Aghast, I consider the possibility that my violence is only a by-product of female powerlessness and I feel worse. Much worse. I'm not taking matters into my own hands, I'm just reacting to an outside stimulus, like a predictable cog in an unjust system. The last resort of the weak is violence, isn't it? I couldn't find a way to outwit these men or bend them to my will, so I killed them. It's not powerful at all, it's pathetic.

So why don't I feel pathetic? I feel stronger and more powerful than ever.

Hands shaking, I walk to the loo, indignation throbbing in my temples. I need to hold on for a few more hours, I can't just pack my things and leave. A shaking breath escapes my lips as soon as the door of the ladies' closes behind me. Holy crap, did I really just stand up to Ethan and flush my career down the drain? *What did I do?*

I splash some cold water on my face and stare at Dark Lily in the mirror, appalled and elated in equal measures. Drops of water are sliding down the woman's cheeks. She stares back at me, but doesn't make any move to dry it off. There's no yield in her eyes anymore and rage pools around her like tar. She scares me.

I don't know what she wants.

No. I do.

More blood. More death. She wants to kill Ethan off... for good measure. The perspective sits there, tantalising and terrifying. It would be so easy to tip into darkness altogether. Righteousness is such a relative and tenuous concept. Dark Lily *wants* to kill him.

I shake myself out of this trance and pat my face dry, wondering how it will all end. Not well, I suspect. My life has imploded. I no longer have a boyfriend, I'm not even close to finding love and now I've lost my job and threatened to sue my employer. And my supposed mission to right the wrongs of men? A senseless blood bath. It's too late for my soul but maybe I should at least give myself up to the police and end this killing spree. *Oh dear, things are not going to plan, are they? Understatement of the year.*

The sound of quiet sobs drags me from my sombre thoughts and back into the gloomy bathroom. Someone is crying in the last stall. Knocking gently on the door, I ask if they need help.

'I'm fine,' a pitiful voice replies.

A few moments later, Tamsin comes out, eyes swollen, looking shrunken and not her usual bubbly self. My heart quivers like someone's reached into my chest and squeezed. I never realised how protective I felt of the kid.

'What's wrong? Is anyone here giving you grief?' I ask, handing her a handful of tissues. She blows her nose wetly and shakes her head.

'Love trouble?' I venture.

She shakes her head and silent tears roll down her blotchy cheeks.

I fall silent then and just wait for her to tell me, as she grabs more tissues.

'It's just... I ... my friend and I went to a bar this weekend and we both had only one drink but... but I blacked out and she's been hospitalised.'

'Oh no! What happened to her?'

'I keep trying to remember what happened. We were just chatting together, it was just a relaxed catch-up, the drinks tasted normal but... but someone must have slipped us a roofie because when I try to remember the night, it just stops half way through that gin and tonic. I remember that my friend was joking and I was laughing and there was a group of blokes, not far but we weren't talking to them or anything. I remember thinking that it all felt normal and safe and then I remember nothing.'

A sob shakes out of her.

'My friend's been raped, she knows because her flatmate took her to hospital right away. But I can't... I can't remember what happened to me. I don't know how I got home... When I woke up the next morning, I still had my clothes on but they were put on wrong. My blouse was on inside out,' she rubs her forehead back and forth, back and forth until it's red. 'And my tights and my underwear were missing.'

'Oh sweetie...'

She shakes her head and keeps going, staring at her shoes, 'Yesterday morning, I was shaking and I had palpitations. I thought I was dying, I couldn't get my hands to move and I thought...' she shudders and a sob bursts out of her. 'I thought... if I stopped concentrating on breathing, I'd just stop and I'd die. I didn't know what to do or who to call.'

'Did you call the police?'

Her shoulders sag. 'The police can't help because I only contacted them the next day, when my friend's parents called me to tell me what had happened to her. I'd already showered.'

She's not even crying anymore but it's as if the colour and life are draining out of her with every word. I don't know what to say, so I just hug her and we stay like that for a long time.

I'm struggling to reconcile this with the work setting, the normality of the workplace loos. What are the chances? What are the chances that I'd stumble upon so many abused and violated women this year? Is it destiny or was it there all along, endemic and just beneath the surface of everyday life? Did I ignore it all the other years, happy to keep my blinkers on, so I could lead a normal, successful life? How many signs did I miss? But I see the signs now. I see it all so clearly at last.

After a long while, I whisper 'Tamsin, if you want to find out what happened to you and... do something about it... I can help.'

'How?'

'Leave it to me.'

41

VOULEZ-VOUS TUER AVEC MOI CE SOIR?

'So, where were you last Saturday?'

'There.' Tamsin points to a dim corner of the rowdy bar. The Bunga Bunga's decoration is a garish mix of harlequin wallpaper, mounted boar heads and exuberant Italian ceiling frescoes. On stage, a woman wearing a frothy tutu and penis antennas is screeching the lyrics of "Lady Marmalade" as her friends, wearing pink glittery sashes sing along, cackling and making suggestive hip motions.

Tamsin and I push through the crowd, trying and failing to hear each other, as we elbow socialites in various states of drunkenness out of the way. The young royals used to come here to slum it on the wrong side of the river, a few years back, when they were still sowing their wild oats. Now it's just a tawdry bar on the verge of seediness and neither of the princes charming is eligible anymore.

'Here?'

Tamsin nods, biting her nails. She's wearing no jewellery and not a trace of makeup. There are dark rings under her eyes. She's very pale and her short bob is a subdued shade of brown today. Her hair looks wrong and forlorn in its natural shade.

She's darting panicked glances towards the door, as if thinking of bolting. I try to distract her but can't really think of anything light and fun to talk about.

'You ok?' I ask, idiotically.

She shrugs.

Behind the stoic mask, there's a gaping hole of terror and helplessness. I don't really know what to say, so I just squeeze her shoulder.

'I've been hibernating. I crawled into bed after you sent me home on Monday and I've only come out again today.'

There's a hint of reproach there.

She's right of course. Does she really have to be here tonight? What can we possibly accomplish? Identifying a couple of blokes who were there on the same night as Tamsin doesn't prove that they did anything wrong.

This is a bad idea. Detective Mulligan would most definitely not approve of this stupid plan. Plus it's probably not what she needs to heal, but I couldn't think of any other way to identify her rapists. I'm not sure what exactly I'm going to do once we find them. Maybe take their photo and pass it on to Tamsin's friend, the one who did a rape kit, in case she presses charges, so the police can look into them? I don't know.

Tamsin's holding her drink, knuckles white around the glass but not a drop has touched her lips. We've closely scrutinised the barman since we arrived but he seems above board. Well, as far as we can tell. Still, I haven't touched my Diet Coke either.

All around us the meat market is in full swing. Women display as much skin as possible in super tight skirts as they teeter on the edge of unreasonable heels. All I can think is that these are shoes specifically designed to immobilise women and make it hard for them to run. Now why would society think that's sexy? Systemic stuff just leaps at me all the time now. And I don't like what I see.

Shaking my head, I try to get in the spirit of things. I'm underdressed in my skin-tight black trousers, long sleeved black top and flat black trainers but given what I've come here to do, the outfit is just right.

Tamsin's voice pulls me out of my reverie.

'I don't want to be here Lily. This is stupid. I told you already, the police can't do anything. What would I tell them? That I drank but I wasn't drunk? That I was awake but can't remember any of it? Let's just go. Please.' Tears hesitate on the edge of her lash line and one of them spills over. It's quickly whisked away.

She's right. This is not well thought-out. We start to head for the exit but just at that moment, Tamsin grabs my wrist in her cold fingers.

'These guys. It was them.'

I follow her gaze to a group of three men who just arrived in the bar. I don't know exactly what I expected them to look like. Evil. Brutish perhaps. But they just look like normal, run of the mill employees who got out of the office and are getting ready for a Friday night out. They're tall, handsome but not too handsome. One has a goatee, a tame haircut and a charismatic look about him. One's pudgy with a wide face and a potbelly, he's making a girl laugh. The third one has a nice smile, he looks younger than the others, shy and baby-faced with blond curls.

From where we are, I can hear them clearly, their voices happy as they banter and flirt and charm.

'Yeah, we're the Jackals,' the charismatic one says, 'because my name's Jack, get it?'

She giggles and nods.

'We all got this in Ibiza last year,' the pretty blond guy says, showing the girl a tattoo on his shoulder. It looks like red claw scratches against his flesh. She seems to like the young one, she touches his tattooed skin and smiles up at him.

'We do everything together,' the fat one says, as he sneaks a glance down her décolleté and smirks at his mates.

The girl's very young and she looks quite tipsy. I scan the room for her friends but can't see any.

The youngest Jackal comes back with drinks and hands them all around. He gives her one as well. *Bugger, I should have watched what he did at the bar. I was too focused on her.* She looks little more than a teenager.

'They didn't get me a drink,' Tamsin whispers. 'I had my own and I watched over it. I'm not stupid.'

We've all heard the advice about not going out alone and guarding your glass. Such simple seeming advice that between the lines says: *Don't be an idiot. Smart women avoid getting themselves into those situations in the first place.* It's a slippery slope from that frame of mind to victim blaming. And from there, we're just a hop and a skip away from *Lock yourselves at home, dress modestly and don't invite rape with your behaviour, clothes or alcohol consumption.*

'You're not stupid, Tamsin. Sometimes predators put the drugs in your drink from behind, even as you're holding it.'

Tamsin's face is stricken.

'What's wrong?'

'I thought I'd been careless. I didn't go to the police because I didn't want to be blamed.'

I let my hand alight gently on her shoulder. She flinches and then leans into it.

'It wasn't your fault, sweetie. You were here with a friend.

You bought your own drink and guarded your glass. You didn't do anything reckless. And even if you had it still wouldn't be your fault,' I say, staring at the pack of Jackals who are laughing and closing in around the young girl like she's prey.

What an ugly world we live in; replete with lip service to feminism and female princesses and queens in our cartoons, female superheroes in our comic books, female generals, presidents and soldiers in our TV programmes. But when the lights go dark on the silver screens, in the shadows of the real world, the age-old loathing of women still lurks, as strong and as foul as ever. As powerful as the hatred that gets women beaten to death in Asia for 'dishonouring' their families, as violent as the contempt that subdues women in the Middle East, as horrid as the exploitation that gives young virgins HIV in Africa. Men are just better at hiding it in this part of the world, that's all.

The girl can't be more than seventeen years old. She's positively beaming with radiant happiness now, laughing at all their jokes and playfully tussling with the predators as they exchange looks and elbow each other in the ribs, joking.

Then, just as fast as she soared, the girl abruptly crashes, she stops talking and just stands there, a vacant look on her face.

'What's happening to her?' Tamsin asks, eyes wide.

This must be awful for my friend, like a mirror where she can see what happened to her, played out like a dream. My skin crawls at the thought of my mind turning off and my body becoming a puppet, I can't even imagine how awful it would be to be trapped inside myself, screaming, as someone used me like a disposable toy. But Tamsin doesn't have to imagine it. It's already happened to her and she can only witness it, powerless once again. I shouldn't have brought her here.

The chubby Jackal bursts with laughter. Alarmed, I look up and see him whisper something in his plaything's ear. The teenager lifts her foot and stands like that, her foot up, eyes empty, waiting.

The leader says something harsh and checks the dim room for witnesses but nobody's noticed his mate's antics except us. The young girl has clearly been roofied, although it's probably a misnomer. Roofie was a pun about Rohypnol, the original sedative used by rapists & co. Nowadays, they're more likely to have dosed her with GHB, the liquid ecstasy. Extreme suggestibility. Passivity. Compliance. Amnesia. It fits the bill to a T. It was one thing to read about it but it's quite another to witness this. It's chilling to the bone.

They start moving towards the back of the bar, corralling her in practiced fluid motions. She's still standing and walking but as they near the exit she bumps into a wall.

'They're leaving. What do we do?' Tamsin's small fingers have tightened around my wrist, cold as ice.

'Stay here, ok? Call the police.' I sling my satchel across my shoulders and follow them through the throng, pushing people out of my way.

I've packed a few essentials but I didn't expect three of them. Tamsin never said... *Bugger. I should turn back.* My only weapon is a small kitchen knife.

They've reached the back of the bar and the tall buff man who seems to be the leader of the pack stops and scans the room. As his gaze sweeps over the crowd, I turn quickly away, pretending to chat with a nearby group.

A few heartbeats later, biting the inside of my cheek, I turn around, trying to appear inconspicuous. *They're no longer there.* Pins and needles tingle in my palms. *How can this be? I only looked away for ten seconds.*

Standing on tiptoes, I look this way and that above the heads of the Friday night mob, but I can't spot the group. Tamsin has disappeared too. Hopefully she's calling the cops. Panicking, I fend my way towards the back of the room as quickly as I can. Time seems to pass in slow motion and it's like my feet are stuck in nightmarish molasses.

Pushing the tipsy hen party out of my way, I finally reach the back of the bar. A black-painted corridor leads to a staircase that goes to the basement. Hoping it's the right decision, I clatter down the stairs and run to the loos. They're full of gossiping, lipstick-applying women. *I should be one of them* I think with a pang, *I should have nothing bigger to worry about than whether I'll find a date tonight.* Backing away, I let the door close on the bright happy scene and turn towards the men's room. *I don't know that I really want to push that door open. How do I find myself carrying all this weight, all this responsibility? I don't want—*

As I rummaged in the satchel, my fingers made contact with the edge of my small knife. The knick jolts me out of my thoughts. *There's no time for whining and daydreaming, Lily for God's sake.* I barge in and ignoring the lone guy's protests, push my way past the urinals and open every stall. Each door clatters open as I run to the next one and the next and the next. Nothing.

Fuckety, fuck, fuck, fuck. How long has it been? It'll be too late by the time I reach her.

Back in the basement corridor, I carefully open the third door and, gripping the absurd little paring knife, I pad inside the musty space but it's only storage. *Oh God, I've lost her.* Perhaps I should retrace their steps from the point where I lost eye contact? I don't know what else to do, how could they all have vanished into thin air like that?

Cursing my incompetence, I rush back up the stairs and the deafening music hits me like a wall. The garish décor and the crowd spin around me, the boar heads on the walls seem to grin malevolently and everyone in the room appears to grimace and sneer at me. I'm just about to dive back into the crowd, when I notice it.

A door.

Painted black against the black wall. That's why I didn't see it before.

I push it open and find myself standing on a fire escape staircase, overlooking a back alley. My eyes take a minute to accustom to the gloom so I hold very still, letting the door clang shut behind me. The sound of bad karaoke dies and all that's left is the low throbbing of too much bass.

Broken chairs and beer kegs obstruct the way but I manage to squeeze past and clatter down the steel steps. A few rubbish bins overflowing with bottles emit a sour smell and something scurries out of view as I reach the bottom of the graffitied staircase and stand under the London night sky, getting my bearings. I'm at the back of the bar and there's no one in sight in the deserted alley. A sign spells "The Back Passage" in neon bulb and as I step in a rain puddle, the pink words tremble and dissolve under my trainer.

I stop again, listening with tense foreboding.

It's so faint I nearly miss it.

The glacial wind carries the sound of laughter and something else. A sort of keening. It sends a shiver through me.

I run, as fast as I can towards the weak sound. The cold

air slaps my face and my trainers splat in puddles. *Faster. Come on, you ridiculous unfit middle-aged spinster. Faster.*

I skid to a halt when I reach a construction site nearby. There's no one around, it's night, it's cold, it's raining, the streetlights are broken. No one would willingly linger here.

The sound is coming from behind the makeshift gate. Holding the metal chain to prevent it from clinking, I push the wooden panels open and squeeze through. *What am I doing? What would Tom think?* I should wait for the police to arrive but it will be too late for the girl by the time they get here.

The air smells of wet saw dust and cement as I pad towards the sounds, skirting the rough concrete wall and sidestepping machinery and piles of grey cement blocks.

'Come on, Matt, come on, destroy that cunt,' a deep voice is saying.

I creep around the corner and risk a glance. The girl's eyes are open but she's not there. Her naked body is rocking as if she were drowning in a tide, the waves rolling her body back and forth as she floats in limbo. But it's not waves that are moving her. The fat one's cock is ramming inside her, as his paunch presses into her belly. He's making throaty noises and his eyes are closed, in the rapture of orgasm. The leader's standing above them, masturbating as he growls encouragement.

The girl's face looks so young, all expression wiped off her features. Except her eyes are open. Except her tears are reflecting the moon's dim light. Except there's a thin, low wail coming out of her lips.

Something cold plants its claws in my gut as I back away from the wall's edge and flatten my shoulders against it.

I can't take them on. Who am I kidding? I'm not exactly talented for this new hobby of mine. I'm a clumsy fool and I nearly got killed by the last man I confronted. I'm hardly equipped to stop these criminals. Three of them. I have zero self-defence skills, no muscle tone and I'm way out of my depth here. Where are the police goddammit. I glance at the exit, biting my lip.

And yet...

I can't just leave that girl to her fate.

Taking a long breath, I close my eyes and make the sign of the cross.

'Andred, Nemesis, Mary, guide my hand,' I whisper as my fingers close around the yellow handle of the tiny paring knife.

I lunge, screaming like a banshee and push the tub of lard off her, slashing at him wildly. I miss and he scrambles away, his naked bum white and hairy.

'Get away! Get away! Get off her you fucker,' I scream, trying to get the girl up, as I stand over her, knife pointing towards the two of them.

The two men are caught by surprise. The one who was masturbating is looking down as he tries to button himself up and the chubby one has retreated to the back of the half-built room, a startled look on his face. He's naked from the waist down and his erect penis looks incongruously small against his heft.

This is my only chance. I need to get her up and back away as quickly as possible. The girl is still making that awful sound and her eyes are completely blank.

'Come on, sweetie, come on. Get up.' I plead, pulling her up by the hand but she slumps to the ground, boneless and heavy.

I can sense them regrouping now, I look up, gripping the small knife and lunge at them, they jump back. For now. I thought they were drunk but maybe only the fat one is. The leader's stone cold sober and he's glaring at me with a calculating look on his face as they start closing in again. *Not good. Not good at all.*

'We have to go, now,' I urge the girl. I break eye contact with them and try to hoist her by the arm, in a desperate bid to save her.

But just as I bend over to help her, blinding pain explodes in my left kidney.

I fall to the ground heavily.

While I'm down, the man who surprised me from behind comes round. It's the young one. *How could I be so stupid? I knew there were three of them.* He's holding a crowbar in one hand and his phone in the other, filming me.

'Did you see that guys?' he screeches, too hyper - probably cocaine or speed.

Struggling to get back on my feet, I'm on all fours, when he kicks me in the stomach, flipping me over. I crash on my side, a few steps away and my breath stops. Cheek against the rough concrete, I gasp like a fish, my mouth open, wheezing but no air enters my lungs.

Panicking, I writhe on the filthy ground, choking but he's already pulling back his boot for another kick. Barely able to move, in foetal position, I hold the back of my neck as he kicks me again. And again. I crumple around the pain, forming a protective ball as I continue rasping for air. His kicks land on my forearms, my shins, my head. The pain looks like fireworks behind my eyelids but all I can think of is air until at last, something unclenches and oxygen flows back in. I gulp it down, still holding my neck, as I wait for the next kick but it doesn't come.

'Well boys, it looks like it's two for the price of one tonight.'

I let go of my neck and open my eyes, breathing

raggedly. The Jackals' leader smiles down as he crouches to have a look at my face, clearly enjoying my fear and powerlessness. The paring knife must have flown out of my hand. I can see it on the dusty ground but it's too far to reach. Gulping down the dusty air, I can only lie on the floor, winded and bruised as pain and fear awaken properly in my gut.

'Yeah but that one is past her sell-by date,' the fat one says, as he approaches, his private parts glistening as they swing from side to side.

'Hey Grandma, too many cobwebs in there, you want a good chimney sweeping?' the young one says, as he gets closer for a zoom-in.

Gasping for breath, I can't even push the young one away as he gropes my breasts and dry humps me, filming himself. I try to slap him but miss wildly and he dances away, sniggering. I need to get up *now*. They're circling, like a real pack of Jackals that's sensing a wounded prey.

'Don't knock the MILFs till you tried them, kid. They're desperate and they'd do anything for a little pick-me up.'

I'm getting up as best as I can when the fat guy yanks my hair back and licks my face. 'Would you do anything for a good fuck, you old cow?'

His erection's coming back now that I'm not longer a threat but rather an amusement. He lets go of me and fondles himself for the camera, while the other two laugh.

This isn't good at all. God knows what they'll do with us now. They won't want to leave a conscious witness alive who could recognise them. What have I done? Instead of saving the poor girl, I'm probably going to cause her death. And mine. My ribs aching with every movement, I crawl closer to the teenager's inert form and try to wake her up but she's completely unresponsive. Shielding her with my body, I look around for a weapon or a way out of this. Nothing.

'Help!' I scream at the top of my lungs. 'Somebody help!'

The young one pins my face down against the ground, grabs his mate's boxer shorts off the floor and stuffs them in my mouth. Gagging, I try to fight him off but he's too strong, his weight holding me down.

The fat one is getting himself ready again and the young Jackal is staring at his screen, parting his fingers to zoom on his friend's erection. The leader is looking around to check if someone heard me. They're distracted. The small kitchen knife is right there, a few inches from my hand.

I stretch desperately towards the small kitchen implement but just as my fingers close on the yellow hilt, the leader steps lightly on my wrist, immobilising me. He crouches and uncurls my fingers one by one until he's holding the preposterous yellow paring knife.

'You call that a knife? That's not a knife,' He chuckles and throws it a few metres away. Hope drains out of me as I watch it skitter out of reach.

'*That*'s a knife' his hand comes out of his jacket holding a military grade serrated blade at least twelve inches long. His face breaks into a smile as he watches my expression. He grabs a handful of my hair, lifting my head off the ground. Panic surges as I picture him slitting my throat open. He flicks the blade a couple of time to see me flinch. The others hoot and cheer him. He smiles for his friends.

While he's looking elsewhere, I squirm to break free. My fingers claw at the rough cement floor, as I try to wriggle out. It's just a desperate attempt but maybe... maybe I can...

There's a blinding flash of pain as the Jackals' leader straightens up and stands on my wrist, crushing it.

. . .

I MUST HAVE FAINTED.

Darkness dissolves into blurry mayhem. A sound like a siren blares in my ears. I blink. My brain tries to catch up with what my eyes see but it fails.

On the floor, inches from my face is another face. Dark blood is slowly trickling down the young Jackal's temple. It takes me a while to come to, as I stare at the blood, viscous and slow, snaking its way onto his cheek, his nose and then dripping onto the dusty floor. Dust motes float between us as I blink slowly and emerge back into consciousness. His phone is a few inches away, shattered. The construction site's orange night-lights glint and play with the screen's shards.

Still groggy, I pat my face and remove the disgusting gag then gulp air in long desperate mouthfuls. Cradling my wrist, I scramble into a sitting position. Every part of my body is bruised, cramped or broken. The young girl's inert form is lying next to me, motionless but I can see her breath coming out in small white puffs in the cold air.

Someone is shouting.

I think the screams woke me up.

The sound is strident and desperate.

'Lily! Lily! Wake up for fuck's sake!' the voice screams.

With a grunt, I pull myself up on my elbow and the scene starts to swirl, revolving like a merry-go-round in full Technicolor.

It takes me a couple more blinks to finally understand what's going on.

Tamsin is backed into a corner and both of the remaining predators are closing in on her. There's nowhere for her to escape, they've cornered her.

Tamsin's gaze is fastened on them, as she holds a small brick in her hand, screaming 'Back off! I'll use it. Back the fuck off,' but she's the one backing off and as I finally manage to get on my hand and knees, she hits the wall with her back and stops, her hand shaking around the useless weapon. Even if she manages to hit one Jackal, the other will get her.

The huge serrated blade gleams darkly in the leader's hand, as he prowls closer, taunting her with a swipe. She flinches back and they both laugh. Her chin is dimpled and her eyes are shiny.

The Jackals haven't seen me get up, I'm behind them. My little yellow kitchen knife is nowhere to be seen. Where is my satchel? I look for it, frantically, holding back screams of pain every time my wrist moves.

'Hey man, does she look familiar?' the pudgy one says.

There. My satchel.

'Yeah. Now that you mention it.'

Cringing with agony, I crawl over to the bag and push aside the snapped shoulder strap, searching the satchel's contents with desperate shaky gestures.

'We did her last weekend.'

There.

'Yeah, you're right!' the leader chuckles. 'It took me a minute. She looks different.'

My old pepper spray can. It's been at the bottom of all my handbags for years. Wondering fleetingly whether it will even work, I get it out and take a second to grip it correctly. *With my luck, I'll probably spray myself.*

'You liked it, love? Came back for seconds?' the fat one laughs.

I hear Tamsin whimper.

Straightening up, I hold my broken wrist against my chest as the construction site starts to spins around me but I have to get up, *I have to.*

'Yeah, turns out she wasn't a natural bluehead,' they guffaw.

'You fucking bastards! I'll kill you!' Tamsin's voice is soaked with tears as she cries and lunges at the fat one, the brick held high in her small hands.

He dodges her easily and lands a punch in her stomach. That stops her in her tracks and the brick thumps to the ground. While she's bending over, fighting for breath, he grabs a handful of her hair, yanking her head back and the leader approaches her exposed throat, knife ready.

Darting behind them, I'm nearly within range when I step on some debris and the noise betrays me. The leader turns around, swiping his blade at my stomach, just as I start to spray him. His blade snags on my top and rips it but miraculously, he doesn't gut me. Unfortunately he was so fast that his stabbing arm knocked the spray out of my fist. It doesn't help that I was aiming with my left hand either so the spurt goes wide.

Still, some of it must have made contact because he starts to bellow, scrunching his eyes closed and rubbing them frantically with his sleeve. I skip away from the huge knife which he's stabbing around him blindly and look worriedly over to Tamsin.

'Are you ok man?' The fat guy's concentration breaks and Tamsin uses his distraction to escape his grasp. She runs towards the back of the construction site. I can't understand what she's doing until I see the glint of something yellow near a cement bag. I'm about to go help her when the huge man in front of me, pounces, his blade just missing my face.

'Fucking bitch, this is all your fault. Sticking your nose where it doesn't belong,' he bellows, squinting through tears of pain, as he lunges again.

I jump back and with a low rumbling growl, he charges

as I stumble on something behind me and nearly fall. He's the strongest one, the leader, we don't stand a chance against him. I need to attract him away from the girls. With an anxious glance at Tamsin's moving shadow, I spin around and start to run.

It works. He follows me.

42

FASTER PUSSYCAT, KILL! KILL!

The pavement unfurls under my feet, as I run, my legs taking over of their own accord. The night air feels like fire in my lungs and the back of my neck tingles. Any moment now I'll feel his fingers close around my ponytail. I can't let him catch me. If he does, he'll kill me and then he'll go back for Tamsin and the girl.

Maybe I should stop, climb the few steps to the left of me and knock on the front door of this house. Or this one? Their windows are dark, would they wake up on time? Would they think I'm only a drunk playing a joke and not even bother to turn on their light? And even if they did believe me, would they put their families at risk to help a stranger?

There's a church across the street, maybe if I scream someone will come help? But the leader of the Jackals is so close behind, so close that I don't even dare to turn around in case it makes me lose a few precious seconds. The Prince Albert is plunged in darkness and there are no pub-goers anywhere in sight. Last Call has come and gone long ago.

There's no one left to help me, he's going to catch-up,

tackle me and in a hand-to-hand fight, I won't stand a chance. He'll gut me like a fish right there in the middle of the street. Whimpering with fear, I look for a way to get off the street. If I can't fight him, I need to hide.

There! Battersea Park!

If I can sprint fast enough, I can hide there.

Panic rises, mixed with the burn of adrenaline as my feet accelerate. My wrist is throbbing and the pain is unbearable. I stumble. My heart misses a beat as I right myself and run faster than I've ever run. When I get to the gate, I don't even think about it, I step on an electric counter near the barrier, grab the top of the poles and using the momentum, climb over the high bars.

In my desperation, I manage to scrape my thigh on the sharp points of the fence. A bloody gash rips open, as I land awkwardly on the other side, gasping in agony. I clamp my good palm against my mouth to stifle a scream.

I need to be quiet now. I will myself to shut up and limp away. Cradling my useless hand, I run towards the large open football fields. *That won't do. I'm exposed.*

Above the sound of blood rushing through my ears, I can make out the sound of metal against metal, a heavy thump and released lung air. *Jesus, Mary, Joseph, he's just jumped the barrier. He's much closer than I thought.*

My injured leg dragging, I sprint across the deserted field, trying to think. Most of the park is open fields of grass. But there are buildings, loos, sheds and a handful of places to lie low. I know this park like the back of my hand. If I put just enough distance between the Jackal and me, I could lose him then circle back to go help Tamsin and the girl.

I turn right towards the botanic garden and then veer left at the duck pond as I keep running. But it's a mistake. The frightened birds quack in alarm and the sound of heavy footfall and panting swerve towards me. I thought I could hide by the water's edge under the low hanging trees. But that's idiotic, he's heard the ducks, he'll find me and then I'll be pinned between him and the water.

Fuckety, fuck, fuck, fuck, I'm so rubbish at this.

Taking a spur of the moment decision, I jump over the low fence, past Henry Moore's statue and into the underbrush. The dry leaves rustle with an impossibly loud noise. I need to stop but my feet aren't under my control anymore, they're terrified. They don't want to stop running, ever. They don't want to stay still.

Stop, Lily, stop. Stop.

There's an enormous tree whose branches nearly reach the ground and a group of bushes and evergreens here. Fighting against my instinct to run, I force myself to crouch and hold very still. My breath sounds like a steam engine and I'm sure the Jackal must be able to see me, hiding so close to the statue. So close to the ducks that made a racket a short while ago. He'll figure out where I am.

I'm going to die tonight. Stupidly. Because I thought I could be some sort of female vigilante. I'm a complete idiot. The hubris is breath taking. It wasn't my problem to solve. I had no skills whatsoever to do this. What on earth possessed me to get involved? I'm a bloody bank employee.

His boots appear on the path, down by the pond as he treads very slowly, deliberately. I can only see up to his knees.

'Come out, come out wherever you are.' He's out of breath but his voice is full of glee.

I go rigid with fear.

He heard me, he knows exactly where I am. I'm done.

'I know you're here. There's no point in hiding.'

The tip of his knife gleams in the moonlight as he walks

calmly along the path. Cringing at the thought of the pain he'll inflict with the blade, I hunch protectively around my middle, cradling my pulsating wrist. The move makes a leaf rustle.

His black boots stop and turn. Towards me. *Oh God.* Can he see the white plume of my panicked breath? Am I pale against the black background of the night? I thought the large solid stone of the Three Graces would hide me but it's too obvious a hiding place.

'Come out and play, love. We have time, the night's still young.' I can only see up to his waist now. He's playfully passing the knife from one hand to the other, humming to himself.

'You know what I'm going to do to you first? I'm going to stick this knife in you, nice and deep and then I'll start cutting off pieces of you until you beg me to kill you.'

The wrought iron gate creaks as he opens the fence and starts to climb the small knoll straight towards my hiding spot. I mouth the silent words of all the prayers I know as terror engulfs my paralyzed limbs.

'And, when I'm done with the cutting, I'm going to fuck you and I'm going to enjoy it. And then I'll go back to my friend and we'll take care of your girls, so you'll know that you didn't make any difference. In fact, their death will be your fault, you stupid cunt.'

Fear is gripping my chest so hard that I whimper, my good hand clasped against my mouth. I have nothing with me. Nothing. The pepper spray slipped through my fingers when he swung at me. The yellow knife is hopefully gripped in Tamsin's fist by now. I let my hand drop slowly to the ground and grope for a rock but find only leaves and mulch.

He's stopped. His feet are angled away from me, so he

must not know exactly where I am yet. I hold my breath and now I hear it too. A crackling in the dry leaves, several metres away from my position.

A flurry of ducks quacking tears the silence of the night-soaked park.

His boots turn and sprint towards the sound. He jumps over the fence and he's gone. I stay completely still, listening to the sound of his boots recede, as my ragged breaths threaten to become sobs. *I need to get away from here.* He's going to figure out that it wasn't me and come back to this spot.

But what if I move too soon and he's nearby just waiting for me to make a sound? I don't know what to do. My wrist is throbbing, it's so excruciatingly painful that I can't even cradle it now. I hear rustling behind me and freeze. *Oh God, he's circled back and he's about to overpower me from behind. It's over.* I can nearly feel the bite of his knife against my skin as my breath catches.

My heart's pounding like a battering ram against my ribs. Still crouching, I turn to face him but there's no one there. *Wait.* The crackling noise continues, the same exact sound as before. About a metre away from me, there's a patch of night darker than the obscurity all around it. Something scurries and I stifle a scream when the thing jumps into my arms and curls into the crook of my elbow. As soon as it's there, the creature starts to purr. She's only skin and bones. A small cat, black as night.

I just stare at her, at a loss for words. That kitten just saved my life. She's the one who attracted the Jackal away just moments before he would have found me. What was she doing there? Trying to catch a duck?

I don't dare move for fear of scaring her off but my wrist is so swollen and bruised that the smallest movement makes me want to weep. In the half-light, I can see that my wrist is changing colour and the shape is wrong somehow. Just looking at it, I feel nauseous and dizzy. I need to move before I faint. The last thing I need is for my would-be murderer to find me conveniently unconscious so he can finish the job.

Knees nearly buckling, still hidden in the trees, I move away from the statues and the pond,. There's a small cricket ground on the other side of the grove. Holding the cat against my shoulder, my injured arm held protectively against my chest, I dart, bent in two, hoping the high hedge of the cricket pitch will hide me until I reach the open area near the bandstand. Everything is dark, the air is cold and humid, it smells of mulch. It's so quiet and deserted. Somewhere far away, dogs bark.

I can't hear any movement as I crouch by a tree, hiding in the shadows. The pavilion silhouette is stark against the greyish sky, the branches swaying slowly as if they were dancing to the rhythm of a ghost band. The park is so silent at this time of night. It's so ominous. Gone are the babbling toddlers, the picnic-thieving dogs, the joggers and the slaloming rollerbladers. If I make an attempt to cross here, I'll be visible and audible, I'll be the only thing moving in the vicinity. It's a very exposed crossroad with multiple angles from which my pursuer could spot me. But in the end, the pain in my wrist propels me forward. I can't stay on my feet much longer.

The fountains are dark and silent. A swampy smell wafts in my direction as I creep next to the staircase's edge, hiding behind a metal bench. Nothing and no one that I can see. The city's sounds are so tantalisingly close. I can hear cars rushing past, a honk, a bicycle's rattle. If I get near enough, maybe someone will stop to help me.

Trepidation makes my skin crawl. If I stay here by the pools, he might jump me and I'd have nowhere to run to, I've put myself in a corner. But if I try to escape through the Thames path gate on my left, I'll be completely exposed. If he's anywhere near the Pagoda, he'll spot me. And if he spots me, I'm dead.

I can barely stand at this stage, each time my wrist throbs, the pain shooting to my shoulder practically makes me pass out. My only hope is to escape the park and get help. With a bit of luck, he's looking for me on the other side of the park by now.

The exit's so close.

I adjust my grip on the small kitten and feel her claws dig into my shoulder.

Taking a deep breath, I make up my mind and start to run.

Last stretch. Come on, Lily.

I dart past the pagoda, under the golden Buddha's impassive eyes and swerve left, onto the river path, cringing in the sudden glare of the bridge's lights. I'm in full view but I'm only a couple of minutes from the exit. I'm in so much pain that I moan every time my feet hit the asphalt.

Only twenty metres to the metal gate. That's when I hear the sound of heavy footfall behind me.

Oh God.

Heart pounding, I reach deep for one last spurt of energy and find nothing. I can't make it. Tears of agony are running along my cheeks and I'm biting my lips to stay as silent as possible. The kitten's meowing piteously as I jostle her along.

The gate is ten metres away now but the Jackal is so close that I hear him panting behind me.

God, oh God.

The Albert Bridge twinkles like fairy lights, so beautiful as it gracefully rises towards the black sky. I don't know why I'm still running, I won't be able to jump the gate anyway.

I'm going to die here.

My friend the Thames rushes past, dressed up in gold and copper, as the bridge plays with her reflection.

My hair on the back of my neck rises as I imagine his hands grabbing me from behind and the blade carving into my flesh. I wonder if he'll throw my body in the water's waiting embrace once he's done. I hope the kitten escapes him, she doesn't deserve any of this.

Only five metres left.

I stumble and nearly fall, righting myself with a painful stretch of my right arm when a deep voice yells 'Stop!'

I can't stop.

I don't want the kitten to die. I don't want to die.

The Jackal's going to tackle me to the ground. Any second now, my chin will feel the bite of the asphalt and the gravel.

I'm nearly at the gate, only a few steps.

I can't see anything through the tears.

The only thought is escape.

Run. Escape.

'I said stop right where you are! Police!'

The footsteps behind me are silent. The world spins and I clutch the gate's bars to stay upright.

Wait. The sound of steps behind me died down.

Slowly, slowly, as if I was going to turn into a pillar of salt, I turn around, expecting the Jackal to be there, poised to strike and end it.

Behind me there's only night. The vast black sky and spectral shape of the trees. The nearby rush of the golden river, the graceful soar of Albert bridge's spires. He's gone. How? I should have died tonight.

'Hands above your head, right now!'

I turn back around, wiping my eyes on my grimy sleeve, dazed.

Someone slams into me and throws me to the ground, straddling me. I yelp with pain, then the man who's bellowing orders shines a torch in my face and the grip around my shoulders slackens.

'Lily?'

I hold the kitten close, staring up blankly at the man.

'What are you doing here?'

Oh it's Tom, the policeman who wants to arrest me. Well, he's going to get his wish now.

'Two bodies were found murdered and mutilated not two blocks from here. Tell me you didn't...'

His hands are tightening around my shoulders again. It hurts.

'Answer me.' He shakes me.

The girls. Oh my God, the girls are dead. Sobs I'd been holding in start to pour out of me, shaking my whole body as I lay helpless on the cold wet ground.

'Right.' There's something grim in his voice.

He lets go of me and gets up then whisks a pair of handcuffs out with a practiced gesture but when he touches my wrist I scream with agony.

Taking a step back, he shines his light below my face. My wrist is double its usual size and turning purplish blue. The kitten is mewling now. I can't form words. My teeth are chattering and my mind is completely blank.

'Is that a cat? What the...'

From the racket of gear and clicking metal, I'm guessing the cavalry has arrived. 'Detective, do you have the suspect in custody?' Beams of light criss-cross the darkness all around us. Then he surprises me. He pulls me gently up to a sitting position and loops his arm around my shoulder as he shouts 'Over here. Potential victim. Call an ambulance and search the park!'

'I'm so sorry.'

He frowns. 'Is that a confession?'

'It's all my fault,' my brain is so foggy. *I should have been there for Tamsin and the girl but I ran like a coward.* 'I did this. It was me.' *I left them to die.* 'They're dead because of me.'

That's my last thought before darkness closes in.

43

DARK KNIGHT OF THE SOUL

They let me keep the kitten. I'm pretty sure that's not standard procedure. She's on my lap now, as I wait.

The interrogation room has no windows and they took away my watch, so time has become a theoretical construct measured only by the increasing burn in my eyes, as the hospital hours melted into one another, as I was processed at the police station, as I wait and wait here, alone.

I raise my right hand to rub my eyelids but it's heavy. *Ah yes, the cast*, I think as a lightning strike of pain zings through my arm and bursts into my brain. *Left hand then*.

My mind is still foggy from the adrenaline withdrawal and the pain-killers. The only thought that's clear, pulsing in my brain as if it had been branded into the soft grey matter, is the fact that I killed Tamsin and the girl.

I should have waited for the police. The girl would have been violated but she'd have lived, Tamsin wouldn't have needed to come after me and they'd both still be alive. They're dead because of my ego.

I thought I could take on injustice, I thought I could take men on and win.

I was wrong.

I'm just as pathetic as I ever was but now I took two innocent girls down with me. Two victims of an unspeakable crime who would have been better off if they had sought protection from anyone else. Literally anyone other than me would have done a better job.

All I had to do was call 999 and trust that they'd come. Tom was right. They'd be alive if I'd listened to him.

The minutes trickle by like hours on the uncomfortable chair, under the glare of twitchy neon bulbs. Their stark light bathes the room, bouncing off the sickly green walls, highlighting the finger smudges on the two-way mirror. I shift in my chair.

The kitten's paw clutches my cast, holding it close to her small nose as she sleeps. The linoleum floor makes squeaking sounds of protest under my soles every time I twitch on the hard-backed chair.

I stare at my reflection and wince. I'm wearing clothes I don't recognise, my own are with forensics probably. My face is filthy and my hair is in a messy bun. It's not easy to make a ponytail with one hand.

At least, I'm alive. That's something.

I need to get my story straight but what's the point? I don't see how I can get out of this one. Perhaps it would have been better to die last night. Better than the indignity of a trial and life in prison. Better than carrying the terrible guilt that I'm responsible for the girls' deaths, for the rest of my life.

At last, the door opens. I expect to see Tom, but another man comes in...

Oh God, oh God.

I freeze, completely unable to move a muscle as panic grips my entire body, liquefying my insides. There's nowhere to go. He's come to finish me off and I cannot escape. How did he get in?

It's the leader of the Jackals.

And I'm trapped here. With *him*.

I'm turning towards the door, ready to scream for help, when Tom comes in too and they both sit down in front of me, their faces closed.

There's a jarring beep as the tape starts recording and when I flinch, the Jackal's mouth curls into an imperceptible smile. They state their names but I can't hear anything, as I drown in a glacial wave of fear.

'Tom? Why is he... What's happening? Please help me...' but his eyes are lowered. His jaw squared.

'So, miss...' the Jackal looks at his file, 'Blackwell... it's not looking very good, is it? Two dead bodies, blood everywhere...'

Tamsin and that poor girl.

'Tom, please just tell me what happened to them, nobody will tell me anything and—'

'You will address my colleague as DS Mulligan,' the Jackal says. 'You left your handbag at the scene, your phone. The fingerprint and fibre analyses were very clear, they revealed that...'

I can't hear the rest over the surge of panic.

'But I... no... he's the one who...' I search Tom's face to appeal to him but he's looking at a file.

'What was that?' the Jackal asks pleasantly.

I clamp my mouth shut. He continues, as if Tom weren't in the room with us. *This is a nightmare. I'm going to wake up, now. I want to wake up. Now.*

The pepper spray you used to disable your victims had

your fingerprints all over it...' The Jackal stares at me, a smile playing on his lips, daring me to say something. But I can't. Who would believe me?

His smile widens, 'Mmmh, mace is a section five weapon. We could have arrested you just for carrying one.'

'Figures,' I say, finding untapped deposits of snark in my depleted mind. 'A self-defence weapon used mostly by women against predators. Of course they'd make it a criminal offence to carry one.'

'My colleagues are searching your flat as we speak and I'm already told that they found a knife identical to the one used to kill your victims last night,' Tom says, looking down at his file.

I think of the ridiculous yellow handle kitchen knife set that had cut nothing more threatening than carrots until yesterday. Now, one of them lies in a lab, covered in bloody fingerprints. Tamsin probably died at the other end of that small blade. I stifle a sob.

The Jackal turns to Tom and says in a conversational tone, 'I thought I'd seen it all in this knife crime epidemic but this has really taken things to a whole new level.' His right eye is red. I wonder how long it took for him to rinse it, then get changed and come in to work, like it's a normal day, like he's a normal policeman.

He's prattling on, looking very pleased with himself. 'It appears you've been leaving a string of deaths in your path in the last few months. I'm pretty sure the press will love you when they learn about it. I might even suggest a nickname.' He taps a pen against his lips, 'I like the Grim Spinster, what do you think Tom?' He chuckles. Tom doesn't say anything, he just stares at me, a look of profound disappointment on his face.

I wonder how many years the Jackal has been raping

young women and then coming into the station to pose as a good guy. I wonder if any of his victims ever came to the police to report it and turned around when they realised he'd be the one investigating it. I wonder if Tom, *my Tom* is in on it. They must be protecting each other, like men always do.

'You bastard,' I whisper to the Jackal. Tears burn as I fight to rein them in.

'Abuse of our officers won't be tolerated,' Tom says, poker-faced.

'Two dead...' the Jackal whistles, looking at a file, 'a fucking blood bath too.'

My stomach rises. *Mary mother of God, pray for them at the hour of their deaths.* The girl was unconscious, Tamsin was no match for the two predators. *How could I have run? Oh God. It's all my fault.*

'They're dead because of me.' I try to reach for Tom's hand but he flinches back. I retract mine and hunch over as the tears slide silently down my cheeks, stinging on each cut and scratch.

'Good, a confession, we're getting there.' The Jackal says, checking that the recording's capturing everything. 'So, one man's head bashed in, another's gutted like a fish. Both mutilated,' his voice is grim.

What on earth is he talking about? Are they just randomly pinning murders on me now? The convenient serial killer. I frown and risk a glance at the Jackal's face and see pure hatred there. The intensity of his stare is enough to make me recoil.

He scatters a dozen photos on the table. They slide along the brushed steel surface, fanning out like a nightmarish kaleidoscope. The metal table is cold under my forearm but that's not the reason why my hair stands on end. The two

Jackals are spread out on the glossy paper, splayed with the abandon only death can confer. Blood everywhere. Bowels spreading on pavement, close-up of a caved-in skull. My gorge rises.

'Answer the question, Miss Blackwell,' Tom's voice is stony. He looks so troubled. He must think I've done this. That I'm a monster. That I'm a bloodthirsty psychopath.

'Answer the fucking question!' the Jackal bangs his fist on the table, startling me out of these depressing thoughts.

What question? Were they talking to me? I can't think, all I can do is stare at the carnage.

What happened? When I left, the young man who had pinned me under his knee was unconscious. Tamsin must have hit him on the back of the head with the brick to get him off me. She saved my life, of that I'm certain.

The fat one had cornered her when I started running. I thought if I ran, the leader would follow me and she'd be more evenly matched. I thought perhaps she could escape and call for help. It looks like she did a lot more than that. Stab wounds. Severed genitals. I have to look away.

'...fucking psycho. You're a danger to society and you're going to spend the rest of your life in prison.' The Jackal's been shouting at me for a while I think. Tom throws him a sideway glance.

'I want to call my solicitor.'

'It's not possible right now.' Tom lifts the folder and reveals my phone. It's weird to see it in a plastic pouch like it's evidence. It's pink and innocuous looking. The screen has a long diagonal crack. I'd forgotten all about it, they must have found it in my satchel, at the crime scene. He presses on the voicemail button and Mum's voice fills the small interrogation room.

'Lily, how could you do this to me! The police at our

home, in full view of the entire neighbourhood. What will people say? Have you any idea what this is doing to me? I can feel it already, my blood pressure's rising. You'll be the death of me, Lily, the death of me! And all this only two days before we're leaving on our cruise with the Morgans. You're always hogging all the attention, aren't you? Making sure none of us can have a normal life and enjoy ourselves. Even at your own sister's wedding it's always about you, you, you! Well, I've had it. I wash my hands of you, Lily. I won't have it said that I raised a serial killer!'

Tom presses the off button and the room goes quiet but Mum's words still resonate as if they were bouncing off the walls in a frantic game of psychological squash.

A single tear rolls down my cheek and splats on the kitten's black fur. She licks it off and then rearranges herself on my lap.

A young policewoman comes in, pads over to the Jackal and whispers something in his ear, placing a folder in his hands. Tom throws a glance with the Jackal who's absorbed in the file, then says 'Tell me what happened Lily. It's the only way to get leniency at this stage. You only have this one opportunity to tell me the truth before someone comes forward to accuse you. There will be witnesses. The crime lab is accumulating evidence as we speak. You're going away for life unless you cooperate. I can help you Lily, but only if you explain to me why you did it.'

Over the last few months, he's become for me the epitome of integrity and kindness. Something in me desperately wants to live up to his standards and prove that I'm worthy. I... I once thought he'd come to respect me. Maybe even that he might like me. Now I just want him not to hate me and despise me.

I open my mouth to defend myself, to say that I only

wanted to defend the girl yesterday night, that I'll confess to anything as long as it all stops. I'm so tired. I just want it to all end. But just in that moment, I see the Jackal's smirk and instead I say 'Solicitor,' and clamp my mouth shut.

The next few hours are horrible. They yell at me, show me photos the bodies of my other victims, horribly disfigured, bloody, resting on morgue slabs, black thread protruding from their puckered Y scars. They tell me that the press will never stop hounding me, that I'll lose my job. They take the kitten away. Time loses all meaning and my mind shuts down. I've been awake for how long? It seems like days. The Jackal make oblique remarks to make me understand that he'll kill me if I don't confess. That he wants me to pay for his mates' deaths.

The only way I'll be safe from him is in jail. Prison would protect me from him. He couldn't get to me there. Maybe I should just sign the paper they're pushing in front of me. Just have done with it. Sleep. Stop all that yelling.

THE PEN IS in my hand. I'm not sure when I picked it up.

The door opens and it takes me a moment to recognise her.

Catherine.

Catherine's here.

She bats the pen away and comes to stand next to me, her arm around my shoulder and I lean in, exhausted.

'Are you ok, sweetie?' Catherine says under her breath.

I don't know. I honestly don't.

'Release my client immediately.'

'What the fuck do you think you're doing? This is an interrogation,' The Jackal's on his feet, shouting at her but she's not budging, looking up at him defiantly from her five-foot frame.

'The hell it is. My client is a victim, a witness at best and you're treating her like bloody Jack the Ripper.'

I don't know where new assertive Catherine has come from, but I like her. I like her a lot.

'That's because she is!' Tom gets up as well, to face Catherine, 'Have you looked at the murder scene? She knows what she did was wrong; she's about to sign a confession, admitting to the two murders and you know better than most what she's capable of.'

'Back off DS Mulligan. Lily had nothing to do with these deaths. Have you seen the state of her?' She gestures to the bruises on my cheek.

'That's besides the fucking point. She might have gotten these after she murdered them,' the Jackal splutters.

'Oh really? I'll add abuse of authority and police brutality to the count then,' Catherine replies.

'Hey, I didn't do that to her,' the Jackal protests, jabbing his finger in Catherine's face. Although he did. While I was curled on the floor in foetal position and he was kicking me.

'Release her. Now.' She's slams a folder on the table. 'You've known about this development all along. I'm told my client asked for my presence several hours ago.'

'What development?' I ask, struggling to follow.

'The men who were killed. There wasn't a single drop of their blood on your clothes. You had a broken wrist. You couldn't have done any of it. They know it, I know it. It's over. You're coming home with me.'

'Now wait a second, we know she was there,' the Jackal says.

Tom throws him a glance, frowning.

'The real perpetrator's hair and DNA was found at the

scene. It's not a match for my client's. You really want to push this, be my guest. I'll eviscerate you in court.' Catherine's seems to have grown by several inches and she's radiating anger and power. 'No? That's right, I didn't think so. Your case doesn't have any legs and this is intimidation pure and simple.'

The Jackal's face is scaring me. I don't want him to stare at Catherine that way. She doesn't know, she thinks she's just fending off a policeman. She needs to stop.

'She left her bloodied knife and pepper spray behind at the scene. We know that both belonged to her and were used on the victims. She knows more than she's letting on...' Tom says, his face calm but grave.

'What sensible woman doesn't bring the means to defend herself when she goes out on a Friday night in London? That's circumstantial at best.'

'Her fingerprints were on it,' the Jackal says.

'Yes, which proves exactly one thing: my client tried to save a poor girl from being raped, got some mace into the attacker's eyes and had to run for her life.'

'Two men are dead.'

'Yes, quite. And it's your job to find out who killed these scumbags.'

A flood of relief submerges me, I try to get up but my knees aren't responding, and my wrist throbs painfully. Catherine notices me struggling and helps me up.

'The girl, is she ok?' I whisper.

She pinches my arm, so I shut up.

Detective Mulligan excuses himself saying he'll go prepare the paperwork for my release.

When he's gone, the Jackal turns back to us. 'So you're the famous Catherine,' he appraises her like she's steak and he's hungry.

I tense up and try to stand between them with moderate success.

'Pretty,' he says with a sneer, detailing my friend frail silhouette, his head cocked to the side. 'We'll see each other again soon,' he says.

Although which one of us he means, I'm not sure.

Catherine's looks alarmed as she pulls me back. 'Come on Lily, we're leaving.'

We walk out of the claustrophobic, windowless room and into a hallway milling with people going about their daily business. It seems incredible that I managed to get out of this one. I want to run out of the station but we walk, Catherine fussing a bit. I suppose I must look quite battered.

We're nearly out, when DS Mulligan stops me by the reception desk. He's holding a plastic carrier cage.

'I was just doing my job,' he whispers as he hands me a form to sign.

'Don't. Just don't,' I shake my head, fingers trembling around the pen as I sign my name through the blur of unspilled tears.

I'm willing myself to say nothing, to just grab the kitten and leave but I can help blurting it out. 'I thought you were better than most men. Honest, trustworthy. But you're just like all the rest of them, aren't you?'

'I have a duty to perform, I'm sworn to …'

'Don't you care that your colleague's a monster? You always protect each other at all costs, don't you? No matter what they do, no matter who you have to sacrifice.' I wipe the tears away angrily with the back of my hand.

Frowning, he hands me the carrier and his fingers brush against mine, sending a shock wave to my heart. I don't want to feel that way about him. He made me think he cared about me but this whole time, he was working alongside a rapist. Did he follow me all this time, gathering evidence against me while he also covered for his colleague to make sure he walked free? I know I'm not perfect but how dare he act like a saint the other day in church? Sod the social contract. It's rotten to the core and I refuse to be its sacrificial victim anymore.

I look him straight in the eye. 'How can you look at yourself in the mirror knowing that you're on *his* side, helping to put us, the victims behind bars? Shame on you Tom Mulligan.'

'Come on Lily, let's go.' Catherine pulls me gently by the arm and as she tugs me away, Tom's fingers finally lets go of the carrier's handle and our hands slip apart with an electric caress.

Outside the world is a mind boggling sunshiny day full of normal people going about their tasks, children with backpacks walking back from school, joggers in bright colours, shoppers with full bags.

'Come on. Let's get you home.' Catherine steers me through the crowded street.

'Where is T...'

'Not here.' We're attracting stares. 'She escaped, the girl's in hospital, they're both going to be ok.'

I go with her after that, following her in a daze as we get into a cab.

I can't believe that I'm free.
I can't believe that I'm still alive.

~

HOME. Finally it's over. Catherine and Tamsin are getting each other up to speed as I come out of the shower, struggling to towel dry my hair because of the cast. I'm feeling marginally better but my place is a mess, the police searched it pretty thoroughly. I don't know why they thought they'd find evidence of me being a murderer in my Great British Bake-off recipe book but there you have it. I pick up a few bits and bobs off the rug and put them back on the shelves as I listen.

'You're sure?' Catherine's saying. She's pacing back and forth, still in her dark charcoal suit and white silk blouse. As soon as we came back from the police station, we called Tamsin to make sure we all stuck to one story.

The kid's shaken up. She's biting her nails and her usually open face is drawn and pale. She's huddled on my sofa, in dungarees and a striped t-shirt, channelling distressed Waldo today. Someone made tea. There are three steaming cups and some scones on the table, untouched, looking incongruously normal in the surrounding chaos.

'Look, I can't be sure that no one saw me, but I was careful. I kept my head down on my way home. It was dark and I was wearing black. I barely crossed paths with anyone.' Tamsin tugs on a strand of her unremarkable brown hair, 'I'm pretty sure they won't figure out it was me.'

'Thank God your hair was brown,' I say. 'You didn't stand out as much as you usually would have.'

'The most important thing here is to avoid any connection being made between you and Lily.'

Tamsin's face blanches. 'You're going to throw me under the bus to save her, aren't you?'

'What? No!' I say, as I sweep up the broken pieces of my favourite cup and saucer, the Buckingham palace one with the pinks and golds. 'No one's throwing anyone under any bus.'

Catherine's eyes narrow. 'Look, all I'm saying is that we don't want to graduate to a conspiracy to commit murder'

'We arrived separately and we left separately.' I say, thinking back on this fortunate coincidence. If no one identifies Tamsin, then it will be impossible to find out that she's my colleague. 'I don't think we talked for more than a few minutes inside the bar.'

'And there weren't any cameras, I checked,' Tamsin says. When Catherine raises an eyebrow, she adds 'because I thought maybe there might be footage of my... of the night they attacked me.'

'Ok, good. We don't want the police to think that any of it was premeditated.'

'It wasn't, why won't you believe me?' Tamsin's getting worked up.

'Have you seen the state of the victims?' Catherine pushes.

'They weren't victims!' Tamsin's voice is filling up with tears. 'I'm the victim! The girl is the victim. Not these fuckers.'

Catherine throws me a glance then turns to Tamsin and says carefully, 'But you went looking for them, you confronted them. You could have called the cops.'

'I did! They still hadn't arrived by the time the fat one tried to bloody kill me.'

'Ok, everybody calm down,' I say as I try to separate the kitten from fluffy clumps of eviscerated cushions.

'You called the cops?' Catherine interrupts.

'Yes of course, Lily asked me to. I couldn't get reception, so I got out of the bar and waited out front for them to arrive. While I was waiting, I heard Lily scream. So I ran towards the sound.'

'That must have been when the leader broke my wrist.' I cradle the cast and give up on the mess, sitting down on the sofa next to Tamsin. The kitten pads over, jumps in my lap and starts to purr contentedly.

'You'd fainted. They were talking about killing you and the girl. I had to do *something*.' She takes a tearful breath. 'I just grabbed the first object I could find and came at the young one, screaming like a banshee.' She gives a small sobbing chuckle. 'I wasn't exactly stealthy but he had his back to me and just as he started turning...' she falters. 'brick, skull. Game over.' She shrugs and falls silent, folding into a small ball of misery.

'Thank you.' I slide my good hand along the sofa until it's close to hers and squeeze her fingers.

She nods, knees folded tightly against her chest, not looking up.

'Ok, so up to now, I can argue self-defence if it comes to that. But what about after?'

'After what?'

'After Lily woke up?'

I glance at Tamsin and seeing her distress, take over for a while. 'I woke up and saw that the young Jackal was out of commission, so I focused on the other two; they were closing in on Tamsin. The big one had a knife. The fat one had already punched Tamsin in the stomach. They'd cornered her,' I recall, shuddering. 'My wrist was broken and they'd beaten me up, so I wasn't going to be much help. But I remembered the pepper spray, so I tried to incapacitate the bigger one.'

'They were taunting me.' Tamsin sniffles. 'They said... they said...'

She must hate me for running. I scampered and left her to her fate. *I'm such a coward.* At the time I thought I was drawing the most dangerous man away from the girls but now I'm not so sure. Did I run to save myself? I was afraid. I was hurt. It's no excuse. I should have stayed and fought with Tamsin.

'What happened after I...' I hesitate, '... after I left?'

'He came for me, the fat bloke.' She shudders, 'but he was half naked and not as quick as I was.' Her voice is hoarse and sort of blank, shell-shocked. 'I... it wasn't... I didn't mean to...' she falters and falls silent.

'Tamsin, I saw the photos, it was a fucking massacre,' Catherine says, sounding stern. I frown and point to the armchair with my chin. She gets it and sits down.

As Tamsin looks down at her knees, her hair swings forward like curtains on both sides of her face. 'I made it to the knife first and when I turned, he was on top of me, he was so big, he overwhelmed me, I fell backwards,' her breath snags 'but I didn't let go of the knife and he fell on top of me,' her voice is barely a whisper. Tears streak down her face. 'I... I couldn't get him off me, I had to... I had to...' you don't understand. You weren't there.'

He was stabbed multiple times in the gut.

My hand hesitates but I fold it back into my lap. The silence in the room is vibrating with tension.

The strawberry jam drips sluggishly down the side of the scone and my stomach lurches as an image of the carnage in the back alley flashes before my eyes. Severed genitals. Dark red puddles. Carved flesh.

'We're not... we won't denounce you, Tamsin. We just needed to understand,' Catherine says gently.

Tamsin wipes the tears angrily from her face. 'The girl is alive, Lily's alive, I'm alive. What else is there to understand?'

What happened to the girl after you... afterwards?' I ask, 'they wouldn't tell me during the interrogation.'

'She didn't come to,' Tamsin says, 'After... after I'd

removed the danger, I waited until I heard the ambulances sirens, then I ran.'

Catherine nods, 'The paramedics found her. She was hospitalised. She can't remember any of it. The drugs...'

Tamsin bites her lip. 'I should have stayed with her.'

'You did and she's alive thanks to you,' I say.

'And the Jackals' foreheads?' Catherine asks, looking dubious. They both had X carved on their foreheads.

She shrugs, 'It felt right.'

Now I understand why the cops released me. If it had been me, I'd have been covered in blood. I didn't have anything except my own blood on my clothes. They had no evidence that I killed either of the men. Because I didn't.

'Why Tamsin?' I whisper aghast, 'Why?'

'You know why,' she hisses. 'He joked about me. He said he'd do it again. I just... I wanted them to pay and then I wanted the world to know what they were. These... these pieces of scum,' she stops, her gaze fastened to mine, burning with rage.

Unable to bear her gaze, I turn to Catherine. 'It's all my fault. I shouldn't have taken her there in the first place, it was too soon after her trauma, I triggered this. I will bear the responsibility if anyone is arrested. You know why, Catherine. And that's non-negotiable.'

Catherine nods.

I turn back to Tamsin 'I'm so sorry. We should just have called the police as soon as we recognised them and we should have waited. Nothing will happen to you, I promise.'

Tamsin frowns 'Why? Why would you protect me? You don't owe me anything.'

'You saved my life, if you hadn't intervened when you did, they'd have killed the girl and me both. Of course I owe you. I owe you everything.'

'What about the third one? The one who chased you in the park, what do we do about him?'

I hesitate. Proving that he was involved in any of the rapes will be impossible. He didn't have time to rape the girl last night, so his DNA won't be at the scene and plus he's a cop. Put it all together and I bet that'll amount to a get-out-of-jail-free card. If we back him into a corner, he'll make a deal for the improvable rapes and denounce Tamsin and me for the very provable murders. We'll both spend the rest of our lives in prison while he'll be free to continue attacking young girls. Not an option.

'I... he...' I stammer.

They both stare at me, puzzled.

'What is it? Catherine asks.

I hesitate. While telling the police is out of the question, I wonder if there's any point in telling my friends that I know who the leader of the Jackals is. I can't think of any upside. I'm too hot to touch right now, but sooner or later he'll come back to finish the job and at that point, if I can convince him that neither Catherine nor Tamsin knows who he is, then maybe, just maybe, he'll just kill me and leave them alone. They won't know his name, so he'll have no reason to kill them. Catherine thinks he's just a cop and Tamsin only knows his face, not his name or where to find him. If they never compare notes, he should be unidentifiable. I'll be the only one at risk. I'll die but they'll be safe. Right?

But wait. *He* knows Catherine's name now and he could recognise Tamsin on sight. Say he puts Catherine under surveillance and Tamsin visits her... He'll know where to find them. He'll see them as loose ends to be eliminated. I must tell them who he is otherwise, he could take them by surprise, posing as a cop, getting their guard down, until it's too late and then all three of us will be dead.

'Girls, I have bad news,' I say, holding the mug tightly in my good hand.

'What now?' Tamsin sighs

So I tell them.

There's a long silence afterwards, as we all process exactly how vulnerable we are. He has the whole system at his disposal. What can any of us do against a cop? He has the means to track us, kill us and get away with it.

It's a sobering thought.

We spend another hour devising useless plans and trying to find a way out of this. In vain.

The only thing we can do for now is align our stories so we work out all the angles until exhaustion takes over and finally there's nothing left to say.

44

INTERLUDE: LAW AND ORDER?

Until 2016 in Malta, a kidnapper could technically avoid punishment if they convinced the victim to marry them. "If the offender, after abducting a person, shall marry such person, he shall not be liable to prosecution." (Global citizen 28 Nov 2016)

"2017: the Russian parliament votes overwhelmingly in favour of an amendment that decriminalises domestic abuse. [...] According to estimates from the Interior Ministry, a woman dies every 40 minutes at the hands of an intimate partner in Russia." (Weforum, 8 May 2017)

"April 2017: Maryland fails to pass a law that would have protected rape victims who decided to keep their babies. Along with Alabama, Mississippi, Minnesota, North Dakota, Wyoming and New Mexico, the state has no laws blocking rapists from claiming parental rights." (Weforum, 8 May 2017)

Forty Dates and Forty Nights

. . .

"CASE of alleged rape by New York officers calls police loophole into question.

[The law in thirty-five states and in] New York may allow officers to escape [rape] charges by claiming sex was consensual. The case underscores a chronic problem that was documented in an Associated Press investigation in 2015 that found about 1,000 officers across the country had lost their badges in a six-year period for rape, sodomy and other sexual assault. That total didn't even include New York or California because those states didn't track the number of officers fired for such offenses." (The Guardian 19 Feb 2018)

"1999 RULING by the Italian Supreme court in which "a rape conviction was overturned because the justices felt that since the victim was wearing tight jeans she must have helped her rapist remove her jeans, thereby implying consent. "That reasoning, which infuriated most Italians, did not surprise Simonetta Sotjiu. She's one of 10 female judges who serve on the Supreme Court, which is dominated by its 410 male judges. "The law is solidly in the hands of men," she told the newspaper." (The New York Times 16 Feb 1999)

"TURKEY'S 'MARRY YOUR RAPIST' law has taken women's rights right back to the 1950s. To say this is alarming is an understatement. With the president conveying this message, it will only be a matter of time before society buys into the idea that women's rights don't matter." (The Independent, 23 January 2020)

. . .

"A word of advice from a cop to a group of female students in Toronto: "You know, I think we're beating around the bush here. I've been told I'm not supposed to say this — however, women should avoid dressing like sluts in order not to be victimised."" (Mic.com 27 April 2016)

"Brett Kavanaugh sworn in as US Senate approves Supreme Court nomination despite sexual misconduct allegations" (ABC News 7 October 2018)

"The president stands accused of rape, again. Among the most gloomy things about [the] accusation is how unsurprising it is." (The Economist, 29 June 2019).

Twenty-four women have come forward (to date) to accuse the "Grab them by the pussy" president and nothing has come of it.

Q purrs in my lap contentedly as I read on, my laptop overheating on my knees. Story after story unfolds on the screen and a pattern emerges. It wasn't just something that "happened" to me. It wasn't just that Catherine was unlucky and got an abusive fiancé. Nicoletta didn't "ask for it" when she was murdered. The young women that Lord Epsom pimped to the rich and famous were not just in the wrong place at the wrong time.

There's a pattern. There's a system.

I'm crushed by these stories because they show that the oppression has been going on for ~~years,~~ ~~decades,~~ well might as well make that *centuries*, in plain view, it's so deeply pervasive and ingrained that we don't even see it anymore.

Detective Mulligan's words swirl in my head, Angels and Beasts, innocence and guilt, judge and executioner. I see his point about the social contract, I really do. The problem is that I no longer believe in a system that systematically oppresses women. I no longer believe that by giving up our freedom to defend ourselves, we will in exchange receive protection from the state. I no longer believe that the law will protect women. I no longer believe that, in the cases where the law is just, it will be applied. I no longer believe that lawyers, judges and Supreme Courts will protect us. I no longer believe that presidents and parliaments will make laws that have women's best interest at heart.

And here's the rub: we're forty-nine percent of the world's population.

I wonder what would happen if we rose up. I don't mean demonstrating with clever placards while wearing pink crochet hats. I don't mean marching in a dignified manner while brandishing thongs and covering our naked chests in marker pen while teenage boys ogle and snigger. I don't mean doing sit-ins in the Senate and chanting pretty songs about female strength.

I mean WHAT IF WE ROSE UP?

45

THE NIGHT OF THE JACKAL

'How are you holding up?' Vivian asks as I hold the phone between my shoulder and my cheek. I didn't realise how much I'd missed her these past few years. It feels wonderful to be close again.

'I'm alright. My face is starting to heal. Wrist still hurts like a mother though.'

She chuckles, 'you'd know all about that, wouldn't you?'

'Ha ha, very funny, she's your mother too, you know.'

'She's not as bad as you think she is, Lily. She loves you.'

'Uh-huh.'

'Hey, listen, I'm in town tonight. I had to stay at the office late for meetings... I'm trying to wrap things up before I go on mat leave,' she says as I make my way to the parking entrance. They're pouring cement or putting in marble steps or whatever so the main entrance is inaccessible for a few days, there's a side entrance through the parking lot. It's annoying.

Phone communications usually cut off mid way through the underground parking, but on the off chance that the line will hold, I hold the phone against my ear as I rummage for the electronic fob.

'... so can I come over?' She asks.

The garage door opens with a rattle and I sneak inside, feeling quite exposed in the darkening twilight. The neon lights flicker on hesitantly but at least they're working today, the other night I had to make my way in complete darkness because the optical sensors were malfunctioning. I mentioned the fault to the porter who mentioned it to the builder who may or may not fix it in the next two months or six.

'There's something I want to ask you, it's about the baby. Are you free for dinner? I can be to your neighbourhood in–'

'Hold that thought sweetie, I'm in the garage and I need to get to the lift.'

Where are my bloody keys? As I hasten towards the lift, the hair on my neck stands on end and my palms start to sweat. I slip the phone in my pocket, hoping the communication will not cut off. With the cast, I can't manoeuvre the keys, phone, a handbag and a grocery bag full of cat food. I hurry along the deserted parking lot, wishing that my shoes didn't make such a loud racket. I'm closing my good hand on the keys and reaching the door to the lifts area when my instinct screams to stop.

I stop in my tracks and stay very still.

He's here. I'm sure of it.

I knew he'd come. In a way, I wanted it.

We have unfinished business.

He picked a spot where there's no light yet, just a couple of wires protruding from the naked cement. There are no cameras yet either. That's where I'd have waited too, in the dark recess by the lifts. There's barely a handful of residents in my tower and the likelihood of being disturbed is low.

'You've come,' I say to the shadows.

Nothing moves. The patch of darkness to my right is unnaturally silent and still. I strain to listen but there's only the flicker of the neon bulb overhead and the drip of this afternoon's rain in the garage's bowels.

My right hand is slick with sweat inside the cast and my heart is beating unevenly. Am I imagining things?

I take another step, yes, it's just shadows playing with my imagination. *What an idiot you are, Lily, speaking to the empty air.*

But my feet are reluctant to move and the prickling in my palms intensifies.

It's nothing Lily, don't be ridiculous, just get in the lift as quickly as possible and lock yourself in your flat for the night.

I take another step.

The darkness stirs and he comes out. Slowly.

He smiles.

Fear stirs in my chest but I hold still.

'I thought you'd come sooner.' I try to sound confident but my throat has closed and it's barely a squeak.

'I needed to make sure we wouldn't be interrupted.'

In other words, he waited until Catherine finally went home after weeks of sleeping in my guest bedroom. He waited until the patrol car in front of my flat stopped monitoring my comings and goings. He waited until I was all alone and at his mercy.

'One of my neighbours is bound to come any minute.'

'What makes you think anyone would help a murderer? I'll just flash my badge and they'll leave.'

'You know that I didn't kill your friends,' I back away, anxiously looking for an exit.

He smoothes his goatee down, detailing me as he takes another step forward, and I take another step backward. 'You don't look like much, you know. Old, fat, plain. To be honest, I completely underestimated you when we first met. You can be sure I'm not going to make *that* mistake again.'

'I have no idea what you're talking about.'

I should have prepared better. I knew this moment was coming. Maybe a part of me wanted to believe it would all go away if I didn't think about it.

'It's a superb file DS Mulligan put together. The man's very thorough. He must have been following you for months. I must admit, it made for an interesting read. One suspicious heart attack in this very building,' He tut-tuts, amused, 'only a few weeks after you "found" a body in the Thames' he air quotes.

'No... that's not what happened—'

'Oh dear and *Lord* Epsom. An upstanding member of the community, mysteriously dies at an event you attended.'

He's huge. Six foot five at least. Buff. Trained to fight. I don't stand a chance. He chuckles, evidently taking pleasure in watching me panic.

'It was an overdose, an accidental drowning,' I take another step back and risk looking away: there's a fire axe in a glass case by the lift. But it's behind him and I could never reach it.

'Then there's the "accidental" death of your friend's fiancé.' He lingers for a moment, 'Catherine, the pretty one,' he smiles. 'I'll be paying her a visit too.'

'You fucking bastard. She's got nothing to do with this. Leave her alo—'

He whistles, 'Oh and a *judge*. You really *have* been busy, haven't you?'

Without breaking eye contact, I search my bag for something to use as a weapon. When the police let me go, I couldn't very well rock up to a shop and buy a replacement for my twenty-year-old pepper spray. Guns aren't exactly over the counter in this country either. It's really striking how little a woman can do to defend herself (especially when she's the subject of police surveillance and under suspicion of multiple homicides). I settle on holding my keys tightly in my fist. Maybe I can throw them in his face and run, or scratch his face if he overpowers me.

'So what's *your* number?' I throw a glance behind me, as I retreat slowly.

'What?'

'I'm sure a guy like you will remember his number,' I taunt, trying to distract him as I scan my surroundings for something to defend myself with. The parking lot isn't in use yet. It's basically just a storage room for all the construction material. There are buckets, bags of plaster, pieces of wrapping material, tarpaulins. There's nothing here that I could use to keep him at bay.

'Well thirty-five, if you must know. I didn't get to sample the goods the other night because of you, otherwise it would have been thirty-six.' His face sharpens as an evil hunger distorts his features. 'You owe me one,'

My breath catches. I thought he'd say two, three rapes. Oh God, thirty-five women.

'You're a monster,' I whisper.

'What is it to you anyway? You're about to die, don't you think you have more pressing concerns?'

This is it then, he didn't come to negotiate for my silence. He came to tie up a loose end. There's a staircase at the other end of the vast parking lot. Maybe if I run...

'You can't kill me, they'll be able to link my death to you.'

'Will they though? I've been monitoring you. I don't

think you told anyone that I was the leader of the Jackals. Not even your lawyer or she'd have thought of something clever,' he smiles, 'it's too late now.'

I slowly take another step backward, and he takes another one forward. It's like an absurd dance, the steps are slow and we're several metres apart but we move in tandem.

'I can't denounce you. I know what you did but you also know what I did. Why don't we call it a stalemate? We can just let each other be.'

'You know and I know that you could never let me have fun with another girl. I'd always be looking over my shoulder to see if you were there, trying to catch me in the act with a cop in tow. That won't do.'

'Why? You don't perform as well with an audience?'

He snorts, 'Sarcasm under pressure. Nice. You're a tough old bird aren't you?' He rubs his finger against his lips, with a disturbing smile, evaluating my curves. 'Actually if you must know we filmed it all and we posted it on the dark web. We made a small fortune selling it to... likeminded people.'

'You filmed it all?' I can't believe my ears. The arrogance of it is breath taking.

Something gleams in his hand as he swings his arm and the serrated knife appears. *Fuckety, fuck, fuck, fuck.* The time for stalling is over.

'Mmmh. Yeah. Me and the Jackals, we did twenty-nine together, we had a special bond.' His huge frame tilts abruptly forward, taunting me, willing me to run.

But I don't run.

Hi eyes narrow, as he assesses me.

The blade is glinting darkly in the basement's darkness.

So that's how I die? Cut into pieces?

'Everything was better with my mates. You robbed me of that. Well no, your little friend did, didn't she?'

Tamsin. That's why he hasn't killed me yet. He wants Tamsin.

'And you're going to tell me her name and where to find her, long before I'm done with you. You'll see.'

The light flickers with a buzz.

That's the sound I've been waiting for...

Just at that moment, the neon lights flicker again. I drop my bags and turn on my heel, making for the staircase at the other end of the parking lot, holding my cast against my chest. But as soon as we're plunged in darkness, I veer to the left towards a pile of construction materials.

His footsteps clatter right past me as he runs in a straight line towards the other exit. Cast flattened against my mouth to hold my breath in, I let my good hand trail along the rough cement wall as I pad among the tangled hosepipes, the discarded plastic buckets and the sand piles.

In the near total darkness it's impossible to see whether I'm about to step on something, so I slow down, ignoring my heart's panicked jolts. My ballet flats are silent as I advance step by step, testing the ground, afraid of a sudden pothole, an obstacle, a hidden nail. I can't hear him anymore.

All around me, the darkness is pulsing with threat, in time with my blood. I nearly scream when something grabs my wrist. But it's only a plastic wrapping, floating as my passage moves the air. Where is he?

'You just had to make it more exciting didn't you?'

His voice is so loud that I flinch with dread, re-evaluating where he might be. Somewhere ahead I think, but he's retracing his steps. *Oh God he's coming towards me.* I can't help it: the terror makes me take a step backward and I nearly bump into a tall container. I stop at the last minute but it's too late, my cast connects with the metal with a small thud.

'Ah there you are.' The excitement in his voice makes my bones go cold.

He's getting closer.

Heart hammering out of control, I crouch behind a pillar and pat the floor blindly, hoping to find a plank or a pipe but I only find foam padding and a handful of gravel. *Fuckety, fuck, fuck, fuck.*

'I'm really going to enjoy playing with you.'

Oh my God, he can't be more than two metres away. Just on the other side of the pillar.

A skittering metallic sound makes me flinch and he stops as well.

The silence stretches.

Then he chuckles and my heart sinks. I thought someone had come but he must just have kicked some debris down the asphalt.

A long rasp of metal against concrete. He's dragging his knife along the wall. Wait, the wall? There's only one that close.

He's... he's behind me.

The air moves behind me and a squeak bursts out of my mouth.

He grunts and he's so close that I feel the swing of his arms as he tries to grab me in the pitch black.

Run Lily, you fool!

I crash through the field of materials, holding my cast arm in front of my face, hoping that my instinct will guide me. Lungs on fire, I sprint towards the staircase, it should be in front of me and to the right.

There!

A pinpoint of green light blinks feebly in the complete darkness.

It's the emergency exit sign, I'm sure of it.

My soaked feet splash through the puddles as I run. Something primal in my brain can sense the bulk of him hurtling behind me. His strides are longer than mine. His breath is so loud. I don't dare to turn around.

I just run, my shins crashing against unknown objects as they painfully resist and then yield, my left arm bruised by unseen obstacles as they clatter to the ground and give away my position. I don't care, I just run.

Finally, I'm through the construction field and on the main path again. I'm nearly at the door when I stumble and fall head first, my chin hits the concrete floor and I see stars.

The door is right there, if I could just...

His boots are clattering behind me, echoing in the empty garage.

I don't want to die. Not here. Not like that.

I'm scrambling to get up when he digs his boot in the small of my back, pinning me down. My cheekbone knocks hard against the rough floor and gravel.

Desperate to wriggle out, I fight him with everything I've got. But he's too big, too heavy and his weight in the middle of my back is like an immoveable boulder. I only manage to scrape my belly and my elbows.

For a moment, he releases the pressure and I try to twist away but he grabs me by the hair and drags me, kicking and biting, down the ramp to the lower level. *Oh no. Nobody will hear me scream down there.* It's completely deserted, they've been pouring concrete here these past few days. There's nothing yet at that level, no lights, no cameras, no lifts. I fight harder, sensing that I'll never come back if I let him entomb me there. But he flings me like a marionette in the far corner of the lower level parking lot. I collapse in a heap, next to the liquid cement section that's drying quietly in the damp obscurity.

I try to get up but he's too quick and I find myself immobilised again, as he straddles me. He holds my face down with one hand as he slides the huge knife between my breasts, tearing the fabric of my shirt.

'I won't lie, not to you, Lily. This is gonna hurt.'

I reach up to scratch his eyes out but he easily deflects. I can't even reach his face. Growing desperate, I try to hit him in the crotch with the cast. He retaliates with a blow to my face. My eye socket explodes with pain as a bony, solid thunk reverberates inside my skull.

'So. We need to talk,' he says as he takes my cast in his hands.

The powerlessness and fear threaten to overwhelm me as he looms above crushing me under his weight. I try to pry his hands off but I'm as ineffectual as a child from this position on the floor.

'The one who killed my mates. Her name. Her address.'

The tears start of their own accord. I pull desperately to yank the cast out of his grip but I'm trapped. He's putting away his knife in its holder. For an absurd moment I think *this is good* but then his words kill any faint hope I might have had.

'I'm going to play with your fingers until you talk, ok?' The thing that scares me the most is how he says it. Like he's talking about foreplay. *I'm really going to die here. Tonight.*

'Then I'll play with the rest of you until you beg me to end it. So you might as well spare yourself the pain.'

Tears burn in my throat as I clamp my mouth shut and pat the floor blindly with my good hand for something to hit him with. Nothing.

'I was kind of hoping you wouldn't talk actually,' he smiles as he holds my broken wrist close to his chest, 'at first, anyway.' He slowly selects the pinkie protruding from the cast. 'The bitch who killed my friends. Who is she?'

I buck under him, pushing with my heels, writhing but he doesn't budge as he bends my finger backward until it snaps.

I didn't think I could make that sound. I didn't think it was possible to feel that much pain. It explodes like a firework inside my brain, unbearable pain that obliterates all thought.

I'm still whimpering when he takes the small digit in his mouth. For a panicked moment I think he's going to bite it off but he sucks on it, staring in my eyes. The feel of his warm tongue is excruciating against my broken bone but he seems to like the terror in my eyes because he hardens against my groin.

'Her name.' He grabs my ring finger with a smile.

I shake my head violently, eyes wide, pressing my lips together, not trusting myself to say anything.

Stay silent, Lily.

Tears are falling on the sides of my face. I can't give Tamsin up. It's my fault she was ever involved. It's all my fault and it's too late for me anyway. He's going to kill me whether I tell him or not.

He bends my finger backward and the scream starts, thin and high, as I squirm and lurch, trying to escape.

'Your friend, tell me where she is. Now.'

The tendons bend and I brace for the pain as the scream builds up in my lungs. There's a crack. My shriek of despair and agony echoes in the empty parking lot, reverberating in the darkness.

46

'I'VE GOT SOME UNFINISHED BUSINESS WITH HIM – I NEED HIM LIKE THE AXE NEEDS THE TURKEY.'
(THE LADY EVE)

'I'm right here you fucking arsehole,' the voice echoes in the dark parking lot.

Still holding my broken fingers, the Jackal looks up 'You?' he yells at the darkness beyond his shoulder. Then it all happens in a second: his eyes widen as a plank of wood connects with his jaw, there's a big thwack and he's projected sideways, off me.

Catherine comes into view holding a plank in her small hands. She's breathing hard, a concentrated look on her face. Tamsin, approaches him carefully from the other side, they both stand by me, as I try to get up and fail, holding my useless hand gingerly like a broken piece of china.

'Are you ok Lily?' Catherine whispers without turning around to look at me. All our eyes are on him.

A sound half grunt, half sob comes out of me. 'Ok,' I manage.

The Jackal was taken by surprise, but he recovers quickly, gathering himself off the floor. My friends take a step back as he unfurls to his full height, looming a good foot above the both of them. A nasty smile stretches on his face.

'Ah brilliant, all the women I was looking for.'

He pulls the huge serrated knife out from its sheath. But he doesn't lunge for Catherine or Tamsin. He's so quick, I don't even have time to see him coming.

'Come here you,' he grabs a handful of my hair and hauls me to my feet, pulling me against his chest.

I struggle against his arm, wild with fear until I feel a sharp prick against my throat. Taking shallow breaths, I try not to move or cry.

Catherine and Tamsin exchange a grim look. There's something warm oozing against my throat. I have a pretty good idea what it might be.

'Lily and I were just talking about you,' he says, angling us towards Tamsin, as he backs away, his arm like a vise against my clavicles. 'Really nice of you to join us. It will save me the trouble of hunting you down.'

'Let her go. It's over, we've called the police,' Catherine says, adjusting her hold on the plank.

He snorts, 'yeah right. So that's why you felt the need to come here yourselves and risk all your lives? Because the Met is what, five minutes behind you?' He backs away. 'You wouldn't want the little one there to get arrested for double homicide and this fat cow to be put away for what quadruple homicide.' He pauses. 'No... No, I think it's just us and I think you're both going to lay down your weapons or Lily here is going to come to a sticky end.'

He digs the blade against my skin and I can't help but cry as the huge knife bites into my flesh.

'Ok, fine,' Catherine places the wooden plank on the floor and gets back up slowly, holding his gaze.

'No, Catherine, what are you doing? He'll kill me anyway,' I say.

'Shut the fuck up,' he snarls in my ear.

'Get him so he doesn't hurt you and Tamsin. Don't worry about me.'

'Ah Tamsin is it, love? We called you Blue, that's the thing when you plough a girl on GHB, she doesn't really have the wits to tell you her name.'

Tamsin rushes at him, the brick held high, but he just moves at the last minute and lets the knife trail as she passes. Tamsin gasps and when she comes back into view, her t-shirt is ripped and there's a long gash along her rib cage.

I barely have time to struggle and the blade is back against my neck, at an angle this time, he's about to slit my throat open. I can feel it.

'Come on, drop it, Blue. I won't say it again.'

The brick clatters from Tamsin's hands as she clutches the wound on her stomach and blood seeps through her fingers. Shock paints itself on her features as she stumbles. Catherine rushes to support her and the Jackal stops backing away.

'Good girl,' he sniggers.

This is it. Now I die. He's got them both disarmed. He doesn't need me alive to give up Tamsin's name. I'm deadweight now.

His arm tenses as he raises the blade to slice my throat from side to side and I close my eyes, bracing for the sharp cut and the gush of blood.

Just at that moment, a scream pierces the darkness. His hand hesitates and then there's a deep thud. I feel the shudder of an impact. His arm goes limp across my chest. I spring free and turn back to face him.

He sways on his feet, a stunned look on his face.

And then he collapses.

As his body falls, Emma comes into view. Her hair is even wilder than usual and she's heaving as she stands above his prone body. There's a red fire axe planted in his back.

We all stare at her.

'Nobody hurts my friends, you bloody bastard,' she pants. She pokes him with her shoe but he's very dead.

Just at that moment, the emergency exit door slams open and bangs against the wall. Flinching, we all look up to see an enormously pregnant Vivian waddle into sight, followed closely by Scarlett who's wearing a ridiculous hot pink velvet tracksuit with Juicy written across her breasts.

'What did we miss?'

~

CATHERINE RUSHES to Tamsin's side. Bending over, hands on her knees, she's badly injured 'I'm ok, I'm ok,' she says in a loop, staring at the blood all over her hands, the red stain is growing on her ripped white t-shirt 'I'm ok, I'm ok, I'm ok.'

I look down at myself and realise my shirt is ripped open and there's blood on my bra. My limbs are covered in scrapes and cuts where the Jackal dragged me along the concrete floor. In fact, now that the adrenaline is crashing, the pain hits me all at once. My eye socket starts to throb, a bump on the back of my head starts shooting stars across my line of sight and the pain in my broken fingers is so excruciating that it takes all I have not to scream. The room starts to spin.

I should be dead by now. How?

'How did you all know that I was in trouble?' I ask, gingerly touching the cut on my neck.

Vivian's eyes are flitting back and forth between the body and me. 'I heard your conversation over the phone, he sounded weird, like a jilted lover or something, so I called Catherine to ask her what to do. She was closer than me, she said she'd come check on you... what... what happened?'

'He... I overheard him say he was going to kill all of you, didn't I? That's what he was saying? I saw the fire axe on the wall by the lift and I... I just... I didn't think this through.' Emma's voice is shrill with panic 'Oh Mary mother of God, I killed a man, I killed a man,' she says, frantically wiping her palms on her skirt.

Scarlett rubs Emma's back, 'it's ok sweetie, you did the right thing. It's ok, deep breaths, that's it.'

Catherine throws me a meaningful glance. 'I was the one who called everyone. I figured you could use all the help you could get.'

'We have to dial 999 right away.' Vivian says 'Who is he? One of the dates?'

'A cop,' Tamsin says, wincing.

'Was he here to arrest you because of what they said to Mum?' Vivian blanches, horrified. 'It's all true then? You're really a murderer? Oh no, oh no, no, no, no...' her small dainty voice is pitching into an anguished wail as her hands fly to her bump and she backs away from all of us, her lashes fluttering like she's going to faint.

'No sweetie, it's not like that. I'll explain. Just breathe ok?' I say trying to get close before she passes out and stains her Burberry trench in the pool of blood.

'He was a bloody cop?' Emma moans 'What did I do? Oh no, how could I be so stupid —'

'It wasn't stupid. He was a—' Catherine starts.

'A fucking predator!' Tamsin chimes in.

'We have to go, now,' I say, holding Vivian's elbow. 'She's about to pass out.'

Scarlett's strident whistle cuts through all the rambling conversations. We all turn to her as she removes her fingers from her lips. 'Can you all shut the fuck up? Lily, what the *hell* is going on?'

Catherine, Tamsin and I exchange a glance. Emma's stops wiping her hands obsessively and looks up at us, tears in her eyes. Vivian sits heavily on a stack of cement bags. We have very little time, so I speed through everything in under five minutes while Tamsin leans against the wall, arms crossed and Scarlett paces in front of us.

I see their faces work through the surprise and the shock as the story of the last year finally spills out of me in a rush of words. It feels good to finally tell them and oddly, liberating too.

'But they're saying in the papers that the bodies were horribly mutilated,' Scarlett says, her long colourful nails fly on the screen of her phone. 'Gruesome discovery in Battersea,' she reads out loud, her eyes wide. 'Blood and gore splattered all over the street. Maniac on the loose. That's you they're talking about right, Lily? You're the ripper?' She stares at me with disbelief. 'Grisly murders, barbaric mutilations...'

'Actually, no, that was me,' Tamsin says, as all eyes converge on her. She thrusts her chin up. 'I cut the fuckers' dicks off. They raped a girl. They also raped me.'

They all stare at her.

'Oh sweetheart,' Emma's face crumples with pity.

'Holy crap,' Scarlett whistles.

'The dead man there... he was one of these rapists?'

Vivian's voice is pitiful.

'Yes, he was.' The way forward is suddenly crystal-clear. 'Look, I started all this. It was my idea. In for a penny, you know... I'll just take responsibility for the three Jackals as well. Tamsin, Emma, you have nothing to fear, I'll say I killed him too. None of you were ever here, ok?'

They start to protest but I square my jaw and forge on. 'Look, thank you but this isn't a negotiation. None of you should suffer for my actions. It was *my* killing spree. *I*'m the serial killer. You all only got involved because of me.'

Tamsin starts to protest.

'No Tamsin, you have your whole life ahead of you and I'm going down anyway.'

Emma's crying and looking at her hands as if she were Lady McBeth, 'and you Emma, you're in the middle of a divorce. If you get arrested for killing this scumbag, you'll lose custody of your kids.'

Vivian is staring at me like she's never seen me before. 'And you sweetheart, you don't want to be in jail while someone else raises the baby. Enough now. We've been here too long already, someone's bound to come soon. You must all leave. I'm going upstairs to call the police.'

'No.' Catherine's voice is small but firm.

'What do you mean no? It's the only way to save you all.'

'No: you're not taking the fall for us. No: this isn't your fault.' She gestures at the Jackal's body. 'No: just no.' She crosses her arms, frowning.

'I know what to do,' Scarlett says getting up, dusting her Juicy velvet bum with a determined look on her face. 'Kid, go get a wheelbarrow and a large tarp.'

Tamsin hops on her feet and walks to the upper parking floor, holding her injured midriff.

'What are you doing? We can't move the body!' Emma

squeaks.

'And what do you propose? That we leave it here for the police to find? I'm not letting my best friend go to prison for the rest of her life for ridding the world of these degenerates.'

'No, Scarlett. Seriously...' I protest.

Scarlett's having none of it, 'Vivian, go back upstairs with your sister, give us a fifteen-minute head start and call the police.'

Scarlett's turns to me 'Fob key.' She snaps her French manicured fingers impatiently.

Rubber-legged, I fetch my discarded keys and drop them in Scarlett's open palm and go back to help Vivian to her feet.

Meanwhile, Tamsin's squeaked by with a wheelbarrow and she's already laid the tarp next to the body by the time Catherine comes to help her. Together they roll the Jackal onto the tarp.

'No,' Emma protests 'What are you...? Oh my God.'

Catherine's face goes pale as Tamsin does something I cannot see.

'Hey,' Scarlett calls over her shoulder at the girls, 'leave his phone, his shoes, his car keys and his knife out of the tarp. Don't touch anything with bare fingers, ok?'

Scarlett's not quite done yet. 'Emma, on your feet now. You did the world a favour. Get over yourself and go look for bleach.' I smile, throwing a glance at my BFF, she looks quite formidable and as impossible to stop as a tsunami. Emma must have reached the same conclusion because she gets up and goes in search of what Scarlett asked for.

When everything's in motion, Scarlett turns to Vivian and me, considers us for a moment, head cocked to the side. 'Ok, here's what we're going to do,' Scarlett says.

47
RUMOURS OF MY DEMISE HAVE BEEN GREATLY EXAGGERATED

My building's a circus. I'm sitting on a bunch of parcels, huddled in an unobtrusive corner of the porter's lodge, watching it unfold, bemused. I can't believe I'm not in cuffs.

After they found the porter knocked out, trussed and gagged in his bathroom, and saw the state of me the police started treating this as an attempted murder (Which in all fairness it was).

The unfortunate porter has been sent to the hospital with a suspected concussion. I wondered why the Jackal seemed so unconcerned about being interrupted. In a tower building of seventeen storeys where most residents lived in the upper floors, there was no chance anyone would hear me scream as he slaughtered me.

There are a whole lot of cops now, milling in the marble entrance, climbing up and down the staircase to the parking lot, hurrying about in white coveralls.

An EMT appears in front of me, looking concerned. She took one look at Vivian earlier and sent her right to hospital for observation. I'm glad that Vivian's safe and out of harm's way but I also feel a bit vulnerable, on my own.

'May I?'

Everything has slowed down. I have trouble focusing. I nod, so she pulls a chair next to me and starts examining my wounds.

A couple of uniformed cops are going over the camera footage of the entrances and the garage itself. I hold my breath, as I sneak a peek at the screen from afar, but it's all as Tamsin said it would be: she was right, there were no CCTV cameras yet on the lower parking lot level and as a result, the only footage available shows me on my own, running away from my attacker. The lights go dark but the camera picked up images of the Jackal dragging me by my hair, kicking and screaming, to the lower level. I watch it mesmerised; it's as if it happened to someone else.

I'm so cold.

I can't believe I'm alive.

I wince as the paramedic touches my broken fingers.

'Sorry, sweetheart,' she says and our eyes connect. 'I'm sorry this happened to you.'

I try to smile but my lip breaks open, and that's when I see him.

Detective Mulligan is here. He stops at the entrance and his eyes scan me from head to foot, a cold expression on his face. He beckons to the EMT and she stands up to go debrief him.

I can't hear what they're saying from here. He's frowning. She's adamant about something. He asks again. She glances at me and repeats it.

He's going to arrest me. He knows what I am. He knows what I did. Scarlett's plan is going to fail. Detective Mulligan is the only one who can see right through this charade.

He walks over and I steel myself for it. The detention, the handcuffs. The humiliation and the shame. But he veers towards the two officers who are reviewing the surveillance footage.

'Sir,' the younger one moves away from the screen with deference and Mulligan acknowledges it with a small nod.

They play the whole recording back for him as I watch his face. His jaw contracts, he frowns. 'Rewind that passage.' He watches the remainder without a word.

'Anything else on there?'

'No. The whole building is a bit of a shambles, Detective. New equipment not yet plugged correctly. We're trying to retrieve footage from the lower ground but it looks like the cameras aren't even installed there yet. It's pretty clear where this was going though.' The young policeman glances at me with a small wince. 'She was lucky to survive it.'

'Any idea why he didn't finish the job or where he went after that?'

The other patrol officer shakes his head, 'our working assumption is that the pregnant sister must have interrupted him and since he was... erm... recognisable... we think he decided not to risk being seen attempting to murder the victim. He clearly ran from the scene. We've put a ATL out on him, we think he could be... erm... equipped, sir.'

'Nice theory,' Mulligan says, his face like thunder. 'Now find me evidence.'

'Sir, is it really Jack?... I mean DI... I mean it looks a lot like Jack...' the young one stammers.

They both look at their shoes.

'Get the footage over to the lab. Let's run it through facial recognition. We need to be sure it was really him.'

'How about the victim, sir?' The young one shuffles.

'Get her statement,' and with that he turns and leaves without a glance, without a word.

I release a breath and feel my shoulders relax.

If he could arrest me, he would. He's probably thinking that he needs to find his friend so they can align their stories and then he'll come back to arrest me. Except his friend hasn't run away from the crime scene.

His friend is sleeping in a fresh slab of cement in my building's basement tonight.

48

THE MAKEOVER III (RELOADED) – SPECIAL EDITION WITH BONUS

The department store's tidal wave of sensations washes over me with its chattering women, inane elevator music and the soft embrace of familiarity. It's all very pink and warm and pleasantly scented.

The makeup counter assistant has jet-black hair and a lightning-shaped splatter of blue makeup all over her temple, eyebrow and forehead. I think she's meant to look fierce and heroic, the female aspiration of the moment. We're allowed to express our kickassitude through makeup, clothes and shopping, as long as the oppression machine continues to purr. But woe betide us if we actually try to express our revolt by turning against our rapists and abusers, then we're attention seekers. And if we demand equal pay and representation, then we're man-haters after a free pass.

Yes, they're happy for us to play dress up and pretend to be Katniss.

Mmh. I should learn to shoot a bow.

The black-haired girl pulls on the nose ring between her nostrils and considers me critically. She turns to Tamsin.

'I did what I could with what I had.' She glances at my cast and fusses with the marks and bruises on my face. I'm not sure I like how expert she is at hiding violence on the face of her clients. I mean I'm grateful but it's a pretty sad skill to have.

The two Gen Zers discuss me as if I wasn't there and they settle on a look. I suppose I should have gotten around to make-up much earlier in my life. But I never felt the need beyond a bit of mascara and some lip balm. I throw a glance at the result as they both wait for my reaction.

I look like a clown. Let me rephrase that. I look like the clown from IT.

'My skin's not too pale?'

'No it's perfect!' the girl's hands form a steeple under her chin as she stares at my face. She seems like a very sweet girl despite the war paint on her face.

'The bright red lipstick's not too much?'

'No, no, that's exactly the right shade for you. You look amazing! Very femme fatale.'

I look at the brightly-coloured, more defined woman looking back at me in the mirror and think *Dark Lily is gone*. I thought Ethan could save me from her and when he left me and I found Nicoletta in her shroud of mud, I thought she'd taken over. Maybe for a moment, she did. Dark Lily's cold embrace nearly drowned me but I held myself together. My soul, if dented is still intact. I was right, it was love that saved me in the end. Just not the love of a man.

Perhaps there's something to be said for enjoying the trapping of femininity while embracing our strength. Perhaps there's something to be gained by supporting each other to hide the bruises and using the tools in our arsenal to control the image we present to the world. Maybe there can be something joyful about enjoying sisterhood. I take another look in the mirror at their encouraging expressions and then at my own transformed face and decide, *actually, I look alright. This is ok.*

I thank the sweet mall warrior, and to my surprise she hugs me and slips a few free samples in my shopping bag, whispering something about things getting better soon.

Emma and Catherine are already on Peter Jones' top floor. The kid and I get our cakes and our pots of tea and we join our friends. Vivian waddles into the café shortly after. For a few minutes, there's a flurry of tray stacking, trips to get extra cutlery, a fuss about non-dairy milk and then finally, we all settle. Of course that's when Scarlett arrives, looking utterly fabulous. There's a long silence as we complete the ritual of afternoon tea. Then at last, we're done and we all look at each other.

'So...' Scarlett starts, 'the media has been having a field day.'

The last Jackal's car was found a few days ago near Wimbledon Common. There was a serrated knife with traces of my blood in the boot and his phone was abandoned in the glove box. His footprints in the mud were leading into the forest.

'Serial rapist on the loose, man hunt under way, the police looking for any information about his whereabouts,' Emma reads. I think she's going to say something guilty and remorseful but I'm surprised to see a small smile etch itself on her lips. 'They didn't find the body.'

'They weren't looking for one. His car was on CCTV, driving away.' Scarlett says.

'Women are coming forward by the dozen to identify the Jackals on the survivor forums.' Tamsin throws in, 'I'm trying to convince a few of them to go to the police.'

My gaze lingers on the green cupolas and the tiled roofs

outside the cafe's window. Spring has sprung and the street is full of trees swaying in the breeze, laden with pink blossoms. 'I can't believe they let me go,' I say, watching a bird fly off a branch in the tranquil street below.

'You were the victim, why wouldn't they let you go?'

Seeing my doubt, Catherine adds, 'I really don't see how they could have arrested you, given the state of your face, your broken fingers and Vivian's testimony. The knife they found in his car was covered in his fingerprints and you had the corresponding cuts on your lacerated throat to match. It's an open and shut case. It's obvious you came very close to being rape victim number thirty-six and murder victim number one.'

I touch the scabs on my neck and shiver.

'You don't think they'll figure out it was us?' Emma whispers, checking if anyone is looking at our group, but all around the tearoom, young women in cashmere jumpers chat to their friends, distracted mums run after toddlers, old ladies discuss the latest painting exhibit. All the normal things we should be doing. Instead we're talking about blood and mayhem.

'There's nothing to figure out, Lily. Just let it go,' Vivian says, her hand reaching for mine.

'What about the others?' I ask quietly.

Scarlett shrugs, 'Accidental fall from a roof, one less rapist. Good riddance.'

'Violent abuser dies from an allergic reaction,' Catherine grabs my shoulder and squeezes, smiling.

Emma continues 'Powerful sex trafficker dies of an overdose in a hot tub. One less predator to threaten my daughter's future.'

Somehow it's not the same as when I just thought about these deaths in the silence of my own head, at night.

Hearing the enormity of my body count, spelled out by my friend in broad daylight is crushing. 'How about my neighbour. I had the wrong guy.'

'Didn't you tell her?' Tamsin says, 'he *was* the murderer. You were right, Lily. The police would never have found the proof if they hadn't analysed his flat to investigate his death. The bruises on Nicoletta's neck were a perfect match to a collar they found in his flat. Apparently he was also a DNA match for skin they found under her nails.'

I nod, unconvinced. 'Won't the same happen with the Jackal then? The crime scene scientists will find the proof that we killed him. Isn't it always like that? A drop of blood, a thread, a microscopic speck of dirt and then you will all end up in prison because of me. I should surrender to the police before it happens.'

'They searched the leader's apartment and found evidence,' Emma says.

'He had videos of every rape,' Tamsin adds sombrely. She must wonder if hers is in the lot. It's only a matter of time before someone identifies her and puts her at the scene.

'The Jackals were part of a ring of perverts on the dark web. The police have told me unofficially that they're mounting a huge operation to catch this network,' Catherine says. 'They're close to apprehending these scumbags. The police have been looking for a way into that shadow site for years. They'd never have gotten one without the lead Jackal's computer. They're pretending to be him, on the run, and reeling his contacts in. They're pretty chuffed, to tell you the truth. A lot of arrests in the pipeline.'

'That's good, right?' Vivian asks. 'Hopefully they'll focus on finding these people instead of coming after us.'

I hope she's right.

Catherine interrupts that dark train of thought. 'My contacts at the Met tell me that the police have classified Tamsin and Lily as victims. They're no longer persons of interest in the Jackals case.'

Tamsin's face relaxes and I feel my gut unclench. All of this seems so surreal. Did we just get away with murder, like literally?

'So, what do we do now?' Vivian asks.

'Nothing,' I say. 'You've all done enough. Thank you all for your help but I can't let you get involved any further. It's my mess and I still say that if any of it comes back to haunt us, I'll take the fall gladly for any one of you.'

'Jesus Christ Lily, would you lighten up already?' Scarlett says

'Blasphemy,' Catherine whispers.

'So, what's your long term plan, Lily?' Emma says considering me pensively.

'What do you mean? My long-term plan is to find another boring bank job, forget this ever happened and pray every day that we all escaped unscathed. I'm shit at this, should never have started the whole malarkey in the first place.'

'You're pretty good at it, actually, you know.' Catherine looks at me, her eyes level and measuring, 'they all looked like accidental deaths. Until the Jackals' fuck up of epic proportions.'

'Oy,' Tamsin protests.

'Even so,' Catherine continues, 'you can't go on killing every monster out there. For one thing it's a lot of work, it will take too long to get rid of them one by one.'

'It's good cardio though,' Emma chips in 'I lost a pound with all that swinging and lifting and carrying.'

Unable to decide if that's a joke, I stare at her agog, as she drinks her tea.

Scarlett snorts. 'Yes, but it's bloody and disgusting. You'll ruin all your outfits, Lily.'

'And you'll get yourself killed. My baby needs a Godmother, so I'd rather you didn't get murdered please,' Vivian adds.

Tamsin frowns at them, 'Let me guess, you had one little brush with a dodgy situation and now you all want Lily to sit on her hands while predators just go on, killing, raping, sex trafficking?'

'Well, not exactly, what we're—' Emma starts.

Tamsin pleads with me 'We can't go back to the way things were before, Lily.'

Catherine shakes her head 'Tamsin's right, Lily, no one's saying you should go back to the bank, that's for sure. And clearly you can't keep killing random blokes either. You should just aim higher.'

Scarlett's already obviously understood where Catherine's going with this and her face breaks into a smile.

'Yes, she's right Lily. What are you?'

'What do you mean? A murderer, a serial killer, a vigilante...'

'No, you silly sausage, you're a lawyer.' Scarlett lets that sink in.

'The only problem with your strategy up to now is that you're not ambitious enough.' Catherine sips her tea, thinking aloud. 'We're not really fighting individual men here, we're fighting a system. A status quo which advantages predators over women. Which systematically ensures that our attackers go free.'

'So what are you saying?' I frown.

'They're saying that you should take down the patriarchy,' Tamsin snorts.

I look at all of them, eyes wide. 'You're nuts.'

'You've already started. You just haven't thought big enough yet,' Vivian says.

'What, you want me to kill them all?' I laugh.

'No, just use your actual skillset to give women a fighting chance,' Catherine says.

'If I remember correctly from university, you're an exceptionally talented lawyer,' Scarlett adds with a smile. She's known me since we were five, we were flatmates at Oxford. She was super jealous of my grades in university. Of course she remembers correctly.

Emma nods enthusiastically 'We were all floored when you decided to go into banking. We couldn't believe it. Top percentile of our year.'

'What are you all talking about? We can't stop now!' Tamsin half yells.

The yummy mummies turn to have a stare at her hot pink hair, her denim overalls and her angry face. Emma smiles at them and turns to Tamsin, eyebrows raised. The kid continues in a whisper.

'The police would have done nothing about my rape and they won't do anything about future ones either. Do you know how many reported rapes are actually prosecuted in this country?'

Scarlett shakes her head and her hoop earrings bounce on either side of her tanned face.

'One point seven percent. That's just another way of saying that ninety-eight percent of rapists walk away free. I'm done with it. I'm done with all of it.'

Tamsin's eyes are intense as she tilts forward in her seat, appealing to me. 'We've got to keep going, Lily. With your experience, we could make a difference. We could make them pay. Not like the girls are saying, not in court. We could make these bastards pay in real life, with a pound of flesh.'

I turn to my friends 'The kid's right you know, that's why I started rectifying the course of justice in the first place. The system always wins.'

'Not if we own the system. Not if we shape it. It's long past time women took charge,' Catherine says.

'No, Lily, don't listen to them,' Tamsin pleads. 'You're already making a difference. Men are afraid now. They know someone will come for them if they hurt us. We can't stop. We'll start a bloody movement. Take it online, get all the women to kill their rapists.'

I shake my head, torn. 'I don't think I want to kill anyone anymore, Tamsin.'

'You could leverage what happened to you to get women to come to you. We could open a law firm together,' Catherine says. 'Hire likeminded lawyers and take on only rape and battery cases. What do you say?'

'People always like a good underdog story,' Emma says.

'Underbitch,' Scarlett corrects with a grin. '"The woman who survived the band of Jackals takes on the predators, call for an appointment and start your lawsuit today!" it has a definite ring to it.'

Tamsin's not happy but I don't think I have another murder in me to be honest. I'm done. She must see it in my eyes because she gives a big theatrical sigh, shakes her pink head and starts to rummage in her backpack. A moment later, she pulls out a small cylinder and lays it in the middle of the table with a firm thunk. We all look at the tool curiously. It's somewhere between a chunky pen and a syringe.

'What is it?' Vivian asks.

'A portable tattoo device,' Scarlett says.

'You know, the symbol I carved on their foreheads...' Tamsin's words are followed by silence. Catherine looks a bit green around the gills. She's seen what the kid did to the leader of the Jackals before they sunk his body into the foundations of my building.

'The symbol... we should tattoo it on predators' foreheads,' Tamsin says.

'After they're dead?' Catherine swallows.

Tamsin shrugs, 'After, before, I'm not fussed.'

'That's a good idea actually,' Scarlett sips her Earl Grey, thinking. 'We don't have to kill them.'

'No, you don't understand, we have to kill them. I want to kill them—' Tamsin starts but Emma interrupts her.

'It's not about revenge. It's about protecting women,' Emma says. 'We just have to make sure the predators can't hurt our daughters.'

Vivian nods, rubbing her bump.

'Branding them could work,' I say, thinking out loud. 'A universally recognisable symbol that would warn women to stay away. Like a warning triangle with a cross in it? The universal symbol for danger.'

Tamsin seems unconvinced. 'You're lying to yourself Lily. You *did* kill them for revenge. I did too.'

'But you don't have to continue. Killing them won't quench your anger,' Catherine throws in.

'Actually it did.' Tamsin swipes the device off the table, returning it to her bag.

'OK, how about a compromise?' I say, looking at Tamsin's deceptively sweet face. 'Catherine, you and I will fight them by day in the courtrooms and Tamsin, I'll share what little I know, so you can fight them by night in the back alleys. But we don't kill them. We save the girls and tattoo the rapists. What do you think?'

Catherine smiles and nods.

'Deal?' I extend my hand.

Tamsin chews her lower lip for a while 'You'll show me everything you know?' she asks.

'Yep.'

Tamsin's thinks about it and then a grin breaks on her face and she shakes my hand. 'Deal.'

I look at all of them and I see something new in their eyes. Somehow this has brought us closer. This has rekindled hope.

I hold my tea up and we all clink our cups.

'Ok, so how are we going to do this?' I smile.

49

#NOTALLMEN?

After our tea, I walk Catherine back to her flat. As it's such a lovely spring day, we stroll along Sloane Street and chat, seeing the shops without seeing them. All around us, people are going about their weekend, looking happy, there's a sweet scent of flowers and a sense of possibility in the air.

'That detective, Flanagan, Sullivan?' Catherine snaps her fingers.

'Mulligan.' The name tastes bitter in my mouth, the Jackal's friend. I bet he'd have loved to arrest me the other night.

'Yes, Mulligan that's it. He's been passing me information about the investigation all week.'

My heart does a little backflip at that.

'I've read all the files...' she glances at me as we pass a few tourists coming out of a luxury shop their arms weighed with large orange bags. She continues, 'and in light of what's happened to you, he told me he won't be charging you with anything. Your previous... activities have all been dismissed. Case closed.'

'There's no way Detective Mulligan would have done this. He was awful to me during the interrogation. It lasted hours.' I shudder just to think about it again. 'Plus he made it very clear that he'd arrest me if he could. He knows what I did.'

She shrugs, 'It's his job. But I don't think he really wants to put you away. He broke the news to me himself, over the phone: there is no evidence at all that any of the previous deaths were murders. He'll make sure nothing sticks to you.'

'And the Jackals' deaths?'

'They have no clue who killed them. They think it might be a relative of one of the previous rape victims. She chuckles, 'they think it's a man.'

'And you're sure it's detective Mulligan who told you all this?'

'Uh-huh, you know, I heard rumours around the station about this guy Mulligan. Apparently, he had a juvenile record that needed to be reviewed before he was allowed to join the police.'

A juvenile record.

Out of the blue, the information falls into place in my mind like a Tetris piece. In the church that night, he mentioned that he killed a man. Then he said his mother was a battered woman. How could I not have seen it before? He killed his father to protect his mother.

He was my ally all along.

Not my enemy.

Catherine hasn't realised that I'm not listening. '...he's an odd duck that one, isn't he? He quoted some philosopher, said something, like "all people make mistakes, but the righteous try to repair the evil they've caused" or something like that. Very odd bloke.'

My stomach flutters, 'Yes that sounds like him.'

There's a tiny smile at the corner of her lips as she hugs me and says goodbye on Kensington High Street.

I stand still on the pavement, watching her leave, as my mind struggles to catch-up with all of it. I've escaped scot-free. The police are looking for a man in relation to the Jackals' murders. My friends have closed ranks around me despite what I've done. And Detective Mulligan... he...

Oh Gosh.

The police station where he works is just three blocks away. I glance at my watch, maybe he's still there?

'Sorry, sorry.' I say as I run past the startled pedestrians. 'Sorry.' Most laugh as I pass, my summery dress floating behind me as I swing this way and that, avoiding a pram, steering clear of a kid's ice cream.

He wiped my slate clean. Why would he do that?

I'm close to his station. In the last few metres, I nearly bowl into an old lady, glance back to apologise and slam right into someone.

'Lily?'

I look up and it's him. He's got a stubble and slightly tousled hair but he's wearing a fresh white shirt over dark jeans and the collar of his leather jacket is turned up. I disentangle myself from his arms, inhaling the warm, clean scent of him. He's looking at me with a weary expression on his face.

'Detective Mulligan.'

'Did something happen? Why are you here? Are you ok?'

'Oh... I... no, I'm fine. I just...' I stammer, as a blush creeps up my cheeks. 'I just came to ask why you let me go.'

'Keep your voice down.' He glances over his shoulder at the station and guides me away at a brisk pace. I feel ridiculous in my light dress, excessive makeup and girly ballet flats. He must think I'm so ditzy, having come here to his place of work, so soon after the end of the matter.

'I didn't kill any of the Jackals, I swear,' I say as he pulls me by the hand away from the station. 'I listened to what you said. I... you were right that night in the church. You were right about the anger; it was eating away at me.' We stop at the crossing. 'Thank you. For caring.' I start to turn away, intensely embarrassed.

'Wait,' his face looks conflicted. 'Come.' We cross the road into Holland Park and walk side by side for a while, in silence as we watch mini footballers play under their coach's encouragements, dog walkers chatting as they pet each other's dogs, squirrels risking a foot on solid ground among the blossoming daffodils.

'I'm sorry, I shouldn't have come.... I didn't intend to get you in trouble Sergeant Mulligan. I just wanted to say thank you. And sorry. I won't bother you anymore.'

'I'm the one who's sorry, Lily.'

'Why? You made it very clear what you thought of me, when you stalked me at the church,'

'It was a stakeout.'

'Stake, stalk, you say potato...' I wave his semantics away.

He doesn't smile. 'I was too harsh with you that night. You made me angry,' he says 'You mentioned my mother.'

I start to apologise again but he continues, 'What I did as a child... killing my father to save my mother's life, it was terrible. It broke me in ways I've never truly recovered from.' He throws a pebble in the small Japanese pond and we stop there for a while, watching the carps move under the water like watery ghosts. 'I think I was angry with you Lily, for making me relive it. For making me question everything. You forced me to think about whether I'd do it again...' He inclines his head to the side, watching me. 'And it threw me for a loop when I discovered I would. I would do it again Lily. More importantly, you made me think about why a ten-year old boy had to do it at all.'

My heart feels like an invisible hand is squeezing it as I watch his face, his lovely kind face and I can't help but put my hand on his arm.

'I'm so sorry.'

'Please stop apologising. None of this is really your fault,' he falters, 'I guess, what I'm trying to say is, I admire you in many ways.'

I snort as I push a bit of gravel in the pond with the tip of my shoe.

'I admire your passion. The fact you care about the victims enough to put yourself in harm's way to save them. The fact you do something about your anger, your sense of injustice.'

At a loss for words, I can't think of anything to answer.

'You're fearless, Lily. You never thought of the danger to yourself, you just dove right in and saved lives. You took a few too, but I think on balance, the world just might be a better place because you're in it.'

The small smile I've come to know so well twitches on the edge of his mouth.

'I wouldn't have had to do any of it if your famous social contract had kept its bargain with the female half of the population, you know.'

'I know. We failed you.'

I don't know if he means all women or just me.

'But you knew about the Jackal. You protected him.'

He looks down at the dark waters and the shadows moving beneath them.

'I didn't know. I swear. I should have spoken up over the years when he made crass jokes in the locker room, mocked our female colleagues but I thought, you know… I thought he was just a jerk. I never…'

Gently, gently, his hand moves up towards my face and when his fingers make contact with my skin, a shiver shimmies up my spine. He angles my chin up and details the marks on my face. I'm under no illusion that the makeup is hiding much of it. His jaw clenches.

'I'm so sorry. I should have protected you better.'

'I can protect myself,' I say, taking a step back. 'In any case, Detective Mulligan, I wanted to thank you, that's why I came over.' I hold my hand out.

He considers it for a moment and then takes my hand in his but he doesn't shake it. Instead, he pulls me gently towards him, until we're so close I can feel his breath against my lips. A delicate silence has wrapped itself around us like a cocoon.

'I'm going to be honest with you, Lily,' he whispers, 'I like you. I like you a lot. In fact I should have probably recused myself from this case from the beginning, but I didn't.'

'Oh.'

The sound of my surprise lingers for a while, as if the note were trapped in the folds of his collar.

'It's done now. You're free and you don't owe me anything. You can walk away.'

He lets go of my good hand and I stand in front of him, stunned.

'But…' I say, 'when would I see you again? I'd have to kill another predator just to get you to come round…'

'I'd be happy to come over and fix you dinner, if you wanted. Keep you off the streets and out of trouble. You know, as a preventative measure.'

Surprisingly, the thought is pleasant. Not entirely as

ludicrous as it sounds.

'I think I'd actually like that, Detective Mulligan.' I whisper. 'You never know what I might get up to if you don't keep an eye on me.'

'You're right, I should keep a close eye on you,' he says, his breath feather soft against my lips. 'And maybe at some point you could start calling me Tom?'

'OK... Detective Tom,' I whisper.

His lips brush against mine so softly at first that I think I must have imagined it. My heart is hammering as his hand moves carefully around my bruised parts and wraps itself gently around my waist.

He smells of soap and leather and something else too. A sort of kind sexiness that makes my head spin. He's holding my broken hand against his chest, protecting it and I'm engulfed in a sense of gratefulness and love.

And for the first time in years, as this man kisses me, I'm sure: I want him, I love him. I've known for a while now and it feels good to finally let the feeling engulf me like a river that's been dammed for too long.

He's holding me so close now that the warmth of his chest seeps through the flimsy fabric of the summery dress. His lips become hungry, searching. Electricity zigzags in my abdomen as his kiss deepens.

Suddenly the little pond is like a puddle of quicksilver playing with the sun. The sky is bluer than I remember, the koi fish are not ghostly at all, they're red and orange and the air hums with the fragrant scent of spring as petals fall in a shower, covering the grass with a carpet of pink.

So that's what love feels like.

Wait... maybe that's... DATE 1

50
EPILOGUE: ONCE UPON A TIME, OUR STORY BEGINS...

There's a boisterous laugh and I throw a glance through the French windows at the happy group inside. Tamsin's hair is bubble gum pink these days and she's dancing with zest, bouncing around the dance floor like a Duracell bunny. She's been doing good work in the shadows these past few months. Over the summer, she's recruited an underground network of women who help victims. I don't want to know too many details but I gather that there have been dozens of successful catch and release raids since the Spring. The women group together to capture the bastard and they let the survivor mark him. There have been so many that the press has been forced to take note. Once word spread, other groups started blossoming across the world. It's all very hush-hush and Tamsin won't tell me much, understandably. But I've surmised that things are going well, given how much happier she looks now that she has a purpose to pour her anger into.

Catherine and I have started taking on cases together. Ones that help victims. Ones also that have a chance of changing the law. We're taking on the system little by little.

Sometimes it's like we're digging a tunnel to freedom with a teaspoon but sometimes... sometimes it feels like progress. Real, tangible progress. Compared to the work I did at the bank, it feels like I've finally found my way. Oh and by the way, I know I shouldn't be too happy about this... you know, Christian charity and all that... but a few months after I left the Bank, Ethan was finally ousted by the sharks who wanted his job and the project got canned because of Brexit. Darren lost his political backing and was made redundant. I guess he'd still have a job if he hadn't stolen mine. Ha.

Anyway, it feels like a million years ago now. I don't know how I ever cared about that job and the small men that inhabited that world.

Catherine and I have gained a reputation of sorts and clients are starting to come. We should be fine. Next week we'll be finalising Emma's divorce for her. We took Charles to the cleaners and she'll keep the kids and she'll have enough alimony to raise them. It was the least we could do to thank her for saving all our lives. She's lost a lot of weight and she swears she didn't diet. I guess the stress is simply shedding off her. She's glowing today as she dances in the middle of the floor with an enthusiasm I haven't seen in her since our University days.

Scarlett's taken to her new position in life like a fish to water. She's swapped her LK Bennett for Chanel and Dior and she's quit her job to be full-time fabulous. I wouldn't be surprised if she takes over her in-laws' empire in a few years. We all know who's wearing the trousers in that relationship. François's at the bar while Scarlett's shaking it up on the dance floor and drawing fascinated glances from all the men in the room.

The Christening today was lovely and it took me completely by surprise when, as the water fell on my niece's wispy red hair, a tear rolled down my cheek. In that moment, holding the infant in my arms, I felt a fierce need to protect her and a surge of love unlike anything I've ever experienced. A small pint sized woman.

Oh I can't wait to teach you about life, little one. How fast you will grow into a proud, strong woman. I will show you all the wonders of the wide world. And the monsters I must teach you to protect yourself from them.

My kin. My blood. My Goddaughter.

My arms felt heavy with the weight of that responsibility while my heart soared with joy.

THE BAPTISM PARTY is a resounding success and Vivian is radiant with happiness as she holds my brand new niece in her arms... Jonathan's arm loops around her shoulders and Viv sort of melts into his embrace, in a gesture so natural, pure and loving that I feel the warmth of it, just looking at it from afar. Somehow, the anger and the envy are gone. I'm happy for her, she's worked hard for her fairy tale ending.

Grinning, I follow Vivian's gaze to see who she's smiling at with such delight. It's Tom, *my Tom*, he's bowing in front of Mum, offering her a dance.

And suddenly as I stand there in the gardens, outside the hotel reception room, looking at the people I love most on this earth, it occurs to me: I've never been happier in my life.

SMILING TO MYSELF, I head for the lighthouse, I heard it's remarkable and that the beach in that spot is beautiful, with its cliffs and its black rocks. I just needed some fresh air when I stepped out of the party but now I'd like to see it, so I walk across the golf course until I'm alone in the gathering dark, on the Scottish moors.

In a way, my forty dates and forty nights were a trial, I can see it now. I set out to battle demons, the real ones and the ones in my head and I came out of it cleansed, renewed and stronger. I've found the hard kernel of steel at the core of my being and I know now that it'll be there no matter what.

The golf course is full of dips and swells and I breathe in the salty air and the calm depth of the inky night.

Who could have guessed this fateful year would end like this? I could be dead. I should be in jail. Instead, I'm here, I'm happy, I'm in love.

I move towards the ocean's siren song, adjusting the shawl around my naked shoulders as a few golfers cross my path with a friendly wave. The dress is new, a sparkly affair, very glamorous. I feel better in my body. Being so close to death has made me realise that I'm lucky to have a body at all. And this round, feminine one will do. Also Tom is crazy about my curves, so I'm not complaining.

I used to fear the dark, like a rabbit who knows instinctively that the fox will clamp its jaws across my neck before the night is out, like a mouse who knows that the owl will pick the flesh from my bones before the sun rises again.

I used to be afraid but now, something has awakened in me. Something feral and ancient. My ears prick at the merest of sounds, my eyes have accustomed to the obscurity, my footing is sure as I prowl the night, feeling my newfound power pool inside of me.

I am one with the night now.

I fear not death for I am death.

As the party's sounds fade, my kin comes out. A fox sits noiselessly on a mound, observing me as the golden crescent hangs in the night sky like a beacon calling us forward, *Crawl out, creep out*, the moon murmurs as we pour out of the shadows and into the fields. Her creatures, the children of the night.

Soon, I reach the lighthouse. It's much bigger this close up. I go round and come to a standstill on the cliff's edge, taking in the vastness of the sea as the stars puncture the night sky with pinpricks of light.

'Hi there,' he says.

I can't see him very well as he staggers towards the edge to stand next to me. He's fat. Old.

'Hi,' I say quietly with a smile. I go back to watching the horizon.

He says his name in a loud American accent. I know him. His name is on the luxurious hotel's door.

He leers at my curves, on display in the sparkly dress and then holds his hand out for me to shake. His hand is very small, slightly moist and floppy.

'And what's your name?' he asks.

'Lilith,' I smile innocuously. I've decided to go by my real name lately. It feels right.

'Lilith,' he says. 'Wait, I'm a man of faith. I know that name...'

I throw a glance behind him. There's no one in sight. Just the night, dark and velvety all around us. The sea. The cliff. The sharp rocks beneath.

'You mean Lilith, like the rebel who wouldn't submit to Adam?' he sways and the smell of alcohol wafts over on his stale breath. 'Like the wanton demon of the night?' he laughs, assessing my breasts.

'Yes, exactly like that.'

ALSO BY O.M. FAURE

THE LILY BLACKWELL SERIES

Before the Fall

Forty Dates and Forty Nights

Before The Fall, the date-packed prequel is yours for FREE. Simply visit www.omfaure.com to claim your FREE NOVELLA today!

THE CASSANDRA PROGRAMME SERIES

The Disappearance

Chosen

Torn

United

ACKNOWLEDGMENTS

Thank you to my amazing agent, Tanera Simons, who really "got" Lily and helped me to bring out the best in her.

I'm eternally grateful as well to my writing group friends who painstakingly went through my extracts and at every session came back with such fantastic ideas on how to improve the story and characters: Graeme Maughan, Matt Jones, Stephen Hicks, Tara Biasi, Nacho Mbaeliachi, Amanda Gabrielle Jones, Clare Kane and Luke Tarrant.

I was really lucky to get a great structural edit note from Faber Academy and I'm grateful to Nicci Cloke and my reader Nicola Mostyn for giving me such enthusiastic encouragements.

Thank you to my beta-readers for the detailed feedback and enthusiastic late night feedback: Anton Laurens, Alan Kelly, Jessica Hutchinson, Dorothee Tonnerre, Juliette Miremont, Larae Mitchell, Elzabé De Villiers, T.A. Young, Jessica Gravelle, Sandra Kanck, Emma Pratt, Susanna Teixidor, Kenna Roberts and Georgina Landrey. You guys all rock!

ABOUT THE AUTHOR

O.M. Faure is a feminist, a Londoner, a Third Culture Kid, a budding activist and an enthusiastic singer. She's struggling to become vegetarian, worried about the direction the world is taking right now and she's happiest when baking for the people she loves.

O.M. has studied political sciences at Sciences Po in Paris and then obtained a Masters degree in International Affairs at The Fletcher School of Law and Diplomacy in Boston. She has worked at the United Nations in Geneva, lectured at the Hult Business School and worked for several London banks.

She lives in London with her family, her dog and her (black) cat.